SUMMER OF LOVE

ASHLEY QUINN

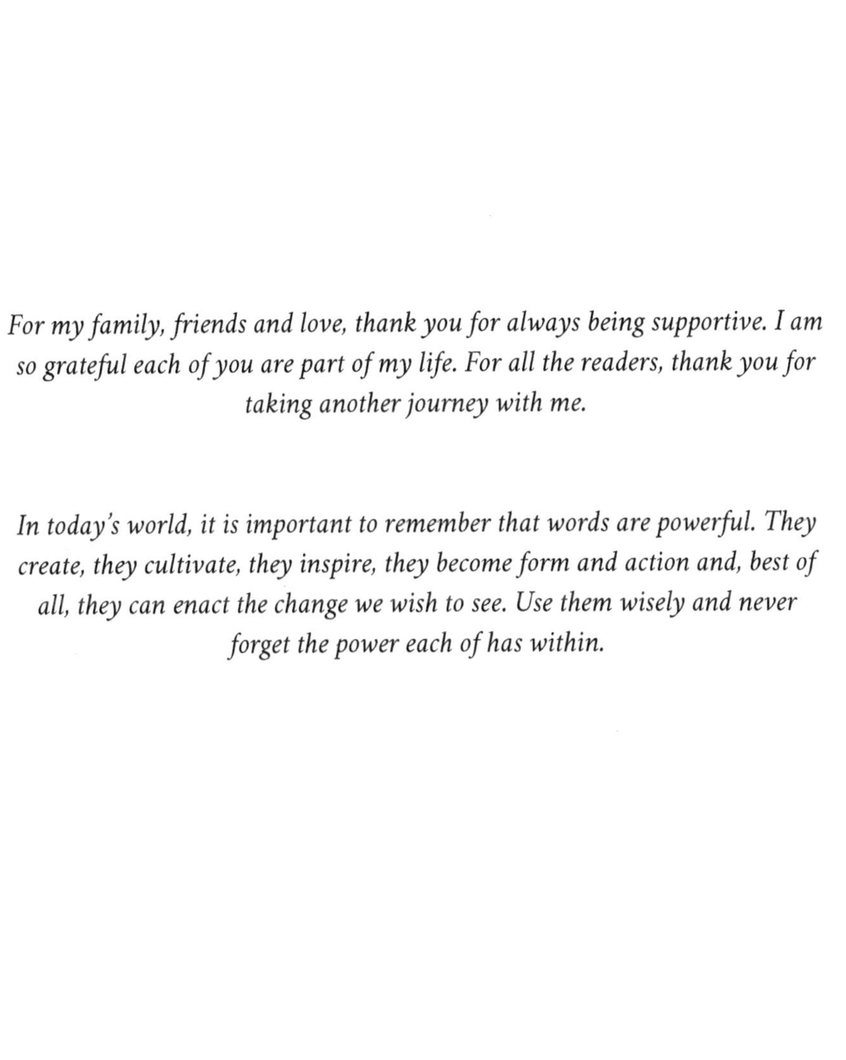

For my family, friends and love, thank you for always being supportive. I am so grateful each of you are part of my life. For all the readers, thank you for taking another journey with me.

In today's world, it is important to remember that words are powerful. They create, they cultivate, they inspire, they become form and action and, best of all, they can enact the change we wish to see. Use them wisely and never forget the power each of has within.

CHAPTER 1

Brooke Adriani couldn't help but stare. Her yoga teacher was *so* hot. The tiled room was darkened and the soft strains of an Ecuadorian bandolin strummed from a hidden speaker, but the atmosphere only served to heighten her senses. A small smile played across her lips as she scoped every detail of the clingy leopard-print yoga pants that curved over her teacher's very best parts.

Leopard print yoga pants Brooke thought ruefully. *Those should be downright illegal.*

She shifted her weight from one foot to the other as the downward dog pose sent a delicious stretch through her thighs and calves.

"Ahh, feel that healthy pull," her teacher sighed, a blissful grin across her face. "You just *know* when you reach that wonderful place, right? Where it just *feels* right. That's what yoga is all about."

She has got *to know what those pants do to people* Brooke thought darkly. The young teacher, known as Lydia to her students, spoke with a light Indian accent and looked to be no older than her mid 20's. She appeared not to have a care in the world as her head hung freely over her mat. Brooke glanced up as curls of long, impossibly silky black hair fell over Lydia's shoulders when she relaxed her neck. *She knows. She knows damn well how perky her ass looks and how toned her thighs are and how damn sexy that blissful little smile is when she gets into position.*

"Looking good, yogis," Lydia called approvingly as she straightened.

Brooke could feel her teacher's dark eyes dance over her for a lingering moment. Her heart rate accelerated as Lydia took a few slow, soft steps toward her mat.

Focus Brooke commanded herself. *Concentrate on the yoga. That's what calms and centers you, right?* She took a deep breath. *Yeah, right. How can* anyone *possibly concentrate on the yoga when they're staring at a beautiful woman in yoga print leopard pants...*

A calm hand on the small of her back caused Brooke to nearly jump out of her skin. Lydia's laugh was light and tinkling as she patted her gently.

"You must have been *really* focused!" She exclaimed. "I was just telling the class how phenomenal your transition into plank is, Brooke. This is beautiful."

Brooke felt her face instantly heat up as she raised her eyes to the rest of the group. Sure enough, the other ten or so yogis in Lydia's express lunchtime class were grinning back at her. She forced herself not to meet the eyes of her longtime best friend, Justin Cole. With a hard swallow, she realized that Lydia's hand was still firmly pressed to her lower back.

She's touching me. And she said I'm beautiful. Well, technically that my plank is beautiful, but I'll take it Brooke thought quickly. *Oh my God. Oh my God. She's* so *hot.*

Much to her disappointment, Lydia padded quietly back to the center of the haphazard circle and began leading the class in a second salutation.

"She has got to be the hottest woman in Key West. And I'm not even *attracted* to women." The whisper came from Brooke's immediate right. She grinned at Justin as they carefully stood into the warrior one pose.

"You're so right, Justin," Brooke agreed. "I can't even focus on the exercise. I'm too busy getting lost in that smile and staring at her, um, choice of yoga attire. Besides, you can't un-see those pants on a woman like that."

She glanced again at Lydia's lithe form at the other side of the room. A tight sports bra left her mid-section nearly completely exposed, giving Brooke a clear view of the large tribal tattoo that started somewhere beneath the waistband of her yoga pants and wound its way up her ribcage. The tiny diamond glinting in her belly button was also not lost in her observations.

Justin snorted. "You are *such* a lesbian, Adriani. Getting lost in her smile?"

Brooke laughed. "Guilty as charged. And come *on*, I know you like men and all but that smile? Totally contagious."

"I told you, grasshopper," Justin whispered conspiratorially. "Stay away from the contagious ones. And don't go turning all domestic-y, I-want-to-find-my-soulmate on me, okay? At least not for another ten years or so. We're thirty-three and we're in our prime. Not so young and dumb that we're making the same silly mistakes we did in our twenties and not so old that our ships have already sailed. This is the life."

Brooke turned and spread her arms as she flowed seamlessly into warrior two. "Don't get ahead of yourself, Justin," she finally replied. "I didn't say anything about that. I have yet to see that real love lasts. Besides my parents of course, but my father went through women like socks after my mom passed away. He has yet to find something enduring and it's been over twenty years. I don't want to waste time on meaningless relationships like he did. Or be like that next-door neighbor we had growing up; she threw a *frying* pan across the yard at her husband's head once. It wasn't pretty."

Justin shrugged one shoulder and opened his mouth. He abruptly closed it as the teacher clapped her hands gently from the center of the room.

"All right, ladies and gentlemen," she announced. "We've done an excellent job today." Her eyes fell on Brooke and her grin widened. "Everyone looked amazing. I've seen such a transformation in all of you since we started our lunch hour class. Before we head out, I'm going to show you all something new."

Brooke took a swig from her water bottle. As the icy water cooled her, she let her eyes dance over the waiting lips, delicate throat and slender fingers of her teacher as she lowered herself to her flowered mat.

God, she's sexy Brooke thought admirably. *I could do yoga all day if it meant being able to watch her. No wonder those women that do yoga all the time are always in such great shape. Maybe they're all in lust with their instructors too.*

"Now I don't expect any of you to do this right away," Lydia started seriously. "But you're welcome to try if you feel up to it. This is called bridge pose."

The teacher paused and laid flat on her back. "This is a fairly easy beginner's backbend and it's great for your legs and thighs." She bent her knees and lifted her hips, thrusting them into the air as she slowly edged her bare feet apart.

"Your feet should be about hip distance apart so that your legs are open and not locked together…" Lydia started.

Brooke's mouth dropped open as she tuned out the teacher's voice. With her shoulders and head still firmly on the mat, she was quite sure that bridge pose could also double as a variation of missionary pose…Er, position.

"…Really open up your chest, open that heart chakra…" Lydia continued happily as she turned her wrists and opened her palms to the ceiling.

"This isn't even fair," Brooke whispered to Justin.

He shook his head as a thin trail of sweat trickled down his forehead from his closely cropped blond hair. "You're telling me," he agreed. "Why doesn't Greg, our Saturday morning instructor, demonstrate poses like this?"

Lydia sprang up quickly and grinned around the circle. "Who wants to try? Don't worry, I don't expect you to do anything more than your body will allow." Her gaze fell on Brooke.

She swallowed hard. The teacher's eyes seemed to darken as she held her gaze for just a touch longer than what felt necessary.

Or maybe those damn yoga pants got into my head.

"Brooke? Would you like to try bridge pose? I can guide you through it," Lydia offered.

You could guide me through anything, so long as you wear those pants. Until I take them off, that is.

Brooke's mouth dropped open, surprised at her own lascivious thoughts. Sure, being one of the youngest and most successful real estate brokers in Florida's Lower Keys had made island life rather comfortable. Admittedly, her experience with women had grown exponentially since relocating to join her father in Key West about five years ago. *But when did I turn into a player?*

"N…No, thank you," Brooke stammered quickly. She smiled politely back at Lydia. "I'll…I'll fall, I think."

Lydia shook her head but grinned. "All right, no worries."

She turned and spoke to the rest of the class. "Okay, you're all free to go. Excellent job today, everyone." She clasped her hands at her heart and bowed her head. "Namaste."

A few students echoed her, but most of them began putting on shoes, reaching for purses and making a beeline for the door.

Justin slipped his feet into his flip-flops and stretched. He turned and held out his palm teasingly. "Coming, Princess?"

Brooke rolled her eyes, but accepted her friend's hand as she stood. "Princess, my ass," she retorted. "Let's not forget who had to kill that daddy long legs in your shower last week and who ran into the living room screaming as though there was a serial killer on the loose. You're lucky I came over early before the wine tasting!"

Justin's face colored slightly. "I had shampoo in my eyes. Plus, it looked like a brown recluse without my contacts in."

Brooke laughed. "Whatever you say," she teased. "Don't judge a feminine book by her cover. I may *look* like a girly girl, but when it comes to things like spiders in the shower? We know who the *real* brave one is."

They laughed as they walked toward the door of the studio. Bright sunlight filtered through tinted window panes as the heat of the day encompassed the small island.

"Oh, Brooke?" A familiar voice caught her as she pulled her phone from her purse to check her text messages.

Two from my managing broker. Probably wants to make sure everything is good to go for the Peterson closing this afternoon. After all, 1.3 million is the highest priced listing I've sold this year. So far.

Brooke smiled as she turned and quickly pocketed her phone. "Sorry, yes?"

Lydia's eyes were welcoming as she leaned casually against the wall. "Are you sure you don't want to try bridge pose?" She asked. "I mean, now that the rest of the class has cleared out. I didn't mean to put you on the spot earlier. I know it can be embarrassing to be asked to do something in front of a group. You have a natural gift for yoga, though, and I can see it growing each session. I'd love to teach you more. I think you'd really enjoy it."

Brooke stood for a long moment as she tried to discern the subtext behind her words. It wasn't until she felt Justin's foot in her calf that she blinked and grinned.

"Sure," she replied quickly. "I mean, now that everyone is gone. Less pressure. You'll still guide me through it?"

Lydia nodded and walked slowly to the center of the room. She glanced over her shoulder, a question in her eyes. "Come here, I'll show you. You'll like this one, I promise."

Brooke dropped her purse with a soft thud onto the floor. She glanced at Justin, who shot her a knowing grin.

"Go get her, Adriani," he whispered. "What did I tell you? We're in our prime."

He's so right. "Okay, sounds good," she replied a bit louder. "Dinner tonight then. I'll see you later."

"Later," Justin replied as he hurried out the door.

Brooke strode confidently to the mat that her teacher had motioned to. She flipped the blonde hair expertly layered just below her shoulders into a messy ponytail. "Flat on my back, right?"

There was a curtain of black and then Lydia's face appeared above hers. "Perfect," she replied in a low voice. "Let your body sink into the floor. Relax everything."

Brooke tried really hard to follow her instructions, but found that relaxation was far from her mind. "Okay and then, um, knees bent?"

"Just wait a minute," Lydia went on gently. "Let your body relax. Your spine should be in a straight line..." her voice trailed off as she ran her hands along either side of Brooke's body. Her fingertips lingered around her hips. "Good. This is excellent."

"Okay," Brooke closed her eyes. *Just do it. Relax. You can do this. Pretend the super-hot yoga instructor is* not *leaning over your completely prone body right now.*

"Your eyes are beautiful," Lydia went on. "I haven't been this close to you, so I never realized what a piercing shade of blue they are. A reflection of that gorgeous ocean just yards away."

"Thank you," Brooke murmured. "Now how many yoga classes do I have to take to get a stomach like yours?" She raised an eyebrow in question as she let her eyes slide down Lydia's tattoo, drinking in the rounded curves and sharp points of the ink's unique design.

"I teach belly-dance as well as yoga," Lydia replied with a smile. "I just finished my Master's in dance and movement therapy at the University of Miami last year."

Brooke met her eyes and smiled easily. "Sexy *and* smart."

The energy in the room was positively charged as their gazes held. The low sounds of South American music reverberated gently off the walls and the heady scent of patchouli wafted over their bodies. Thin incense sticks burned on a corner table, causing long curls of smoke to dance across the room.

Lydia took a deep, shaky breath. "For bridge pose, you want your knees about hip distance apart." She paused and shimmied carefully between Brooke's knees. "See, if someone about my size were to be between them, that's how far you'd want them spread. It should feel natural."

"It does," Brooke replied. *Oh my God, it does.*

"Beautiful," Lydia replied with a small smile. "If you lift your hips off the floor, how does that feel?"

"I..." Brooke carefully lifted her backside from where it rested against the mat. Lydia remained rooted between her knees. *There is nothing remotely platonic about this anymore.* "I feel good. This feels good."

"Excellent," the teacher's voice was barely audible. She leaned further over Brooke as their eyes met through a cloud of patchouli. "Turn your wrists so your palms are open. Open to the ceiling, open to the universe..."

Brooke didn't give her a chance to finish. She tangled her right hand in Lydia's thick hair and closed the short distance between their faces. Her hips hit the mat as the teacher quickly moved over her and fisted the hem of Brooke's top.

She bit her lip to hide the moan she knew was bubbling in her throat as Lydia's lips left her mouth and traveled lightly along her neck until they reached her earlobe.

Justin was right Brooke thought satisfactorily. *We're in our prime. I wouldn't trade my life for anything in the world.*

CHAPTER 2

Twenty-eight-year-old Amber Lucas reached her arms above her head and smiled at the lingering stretch in her biceps and shoulders. She wiggled further beneath the warm comforter as she heard Dr. Lena Mielkute's bedroom door open somewhere in the back of her mind.

"Good morning," Lena greeted her with a wicked grin. "Nice to see your smiling face so early in the day."

Amber forced herself to sit up as she met her eyes. "How could I have *not* slept well after that amazing night? Dinner in Highland Park and then joining a beautiful woman at her penthouse condo in the heart of Dallas." She blinked and then sighed. "I am *so* glad I don't have to be at the hospital until this afternoon."

Lena walked to her dresser and quietly opened a drawer. Amber watched the older woman appreciatively. She looked as though she had just stepped out of the shower. Her shapely legs were all muscle and the thick yellow towel barely covered enough of her to be considered decent. Her short brown hair stood up in tufts and her skin looked extra soft and touchable.

"You know, I seem to recall a certain someone talking about a possible breakfast date this morning," Lena replied with a wink.

Amber straightened expectantly. "I thought it would be nice," she admitted. "When we hang out, it always has to be so discreet. You know, I'm always having to come to your place and when we do go out, it's always way on the other side of McKinney Avenue. I understand that you've been in the process of splitting up with Sarah for, God I don't know, six months now, so we can't really announce that we're together..."

Lena took a deep breath. "Amber, you know we cannot be together, right? Right *now,* I mean. I just need some time. I still want to see you. I still love the way you look in my bed..." she paused as her eyes fell to the blanket covering her body. "I just...I cannot have any commitments right now."

Amber nodded as an unexpected lump rose in her throat. As a newborn photographer and graphic designer at Parkland Hospital, she didn't have much interaction with the physicians on staff. She remembered the day that she met Lena, one of Dallas's most acclaimed foot and ankle surgeons, as though it was yesterday.

I sat in the cafeteria reading my book. It was only my second day at work. Even in her scrubs and long white doctor's coat, her stethoscope slung loosely around the back of her neck, she carried herself with quiet authority.

It was why her patients seemed to love her, Amber reasoned, and why she was one of the most respected surgeons in the metroplex. It didn't, however, seem to translate as well into her interpersonal relationships.

"I understand," Amber finally replied. "But *you* chased *me,* Lena. If you were emotionally unavailable or still figuring things out with Sarah, then you shouldn't have...You shouldn't have let me believe we could be together."

Lena sat gently on the edge of the bed and clasped Amber's hands in her own. "I'm sorry, darling," she whispered. "You looked so beautiful and so sweet, like a perfect angel. And then I found out that you tasted as sweet as you looked and, well..." she took a deep breath. "Sue me. I got selfish and I wanted you. I *still* want you. I have two surgeries this afternoon. Spend tomorrow night?"

Amber raised an eyebrow and leaned further into Lena. *Only she can get away with saying stuff like that. Calling me a perfect angel? It has to be that damn Lithuanian accent; it makes her sound so...so sexy.* "You mean it?" She asked. "What about Sarah? She moved out for good?"

Lena clucked her tongue lightly. "She's spending a couple of weeks at her parents' house in Fort Worth. Maybe she is planning to move back in with them, I don't know. Say you'll stay tomorrow night. I do believe I have some making up to do, don't I?"

Amber smiled and let Lena envelop her into a tight hug. She rested her chin on her shoulder and breathed in deeply. "I don't want you to make things up to me. I don't want you to feel like you owe me. I just want you to desire something real with me as much as I want that with *you*. You can be so hot and cold, Lena. It scares me. I want to believe what you tell me, but..."

"Shh," Lena whispered. Her lips lingered along the shell of Amber's ear. "I know, darling. I'm sorry. You've been so patient with such a complicated situation. You have to understand that I'm a little older than you. At forty-five years old, I've been with Sarah nearly two-thirds of the time that you've been alive. We must break things off cleanly and then you and I can be together in the right way."

"Okay," Amber relented. "I'll stay over tomorrow night. Maybe we can, like, go on a date, you know? Go dancing at that new salsa club in Deep Ellum or something. All of my shifts at the hospital this week don't start until the afternoon."

Lena smiled and curled a long lock of Amber's light brown hair behind her ear. "Good. Very good. I've missed you in this bed. And waking up to those big hazel eyes in the morning. You know what?"

Amber grinned. "What, Dr. Mielkute?" She asked teasingly.

Lena pursed her lips. "All I want to do is make love to you..."

Amber laughed at her suggestive tone and the lyrics to her current favorite song. She had never been one for power ballads or 80's music, but the classic tune was one of Lena's favorites and gave Amber a soft spot for all things Heart.

"So how about breakfast?" Amber asked. Her stomach growled loudly and elicited a surprised chuckle from Lena. "I thought we could go somewhere casual. You know, find a cool diner and get coffee and pastries. People-watch out the café windows. Talk about art and family and…"

Lena shook her head slowly as a bemused smile played at her lips. "Amber, you're such a young romantic," she replied. "But here's *my* suggestion. We go to the café, pick up the coffee and pastries to go, bring it all back here and eat breakfast in bed. Eat some more, take our clothes off. Drink a little coffee, play beneath these covers. Until we must go our separate ways at the hospital, of course."

Amber knew that no one at the hospital was aware that they knew each other, let alone had been carrying on a six-month affair. She had grown accustomed to the gentle ache that flickered through her chest when Lena blatantly ignored her in the sterile hallways, but her flippant attitude was beginning to deepen the hurt Amber felt.

Lena stood and pulled a soft t-shirt over her head. "How can I stand to be in a café, where I can't have my hands all over you, while pretending to be smart? Talking about art and things, when all I can think about is my tongue on your skin."

"Fine," Amber muttered. She pulled back the covers and flipped her legs over the side of the bed. "Maybe some other time then."

Lena knelt gently in front of her and ran her hand over the soft underside of Amber's forearm. "I'm selfish, darling," she finished with a shrug. "I just want you all to myself."

Amber bit her lip and searched Lena's mischievous eyes for a moment. Something inside of her ached for…depth. "But Lena, I want to know you on a personal level too," she started. "I mean, don't get me wrong. The physical stuff is *great*. Beyond great, really. But I want to know *you*. I want to have never-ending conversations about everything and nothing…"

Lena rolled her eyes and stood resolutely. Amber had come to recognize this as her signaling the end of the conversation. "These things will happen in time," Lena replied frostily. "Right now, we're two good friends who happen to be *very* compatible in bed and we enjoy one another's…*company*. In three months? Who knows, I could want to marry you."

Amber shifted and looked down at her hands. "If you say so," she muttered. "I might not even be here in three months, you know. I submitted some photos to a tourism exhibition in Key West a while ago. They could call and invite me to be part of it any day. Besides, my mom retired out there a couple of years ago and she loves it."

Lena threw back her head and laughed, though Amber wasn't sure what was funny. "You'd break my heart if you left for even a day, beautiful girl," she replied as she casually dumped her wet towel in a wooden hamper. "But perhaps it's an adventure unfolding before your very eyes. You never know."

Amber glared at her defensively. "It would be too difficult to leave Dallas for more than a couple days," she replied crossly. "*If* my photos are accepted. It would be too much time to take off from my career at the hospital anyway..."

Lena laughed again. "Amber, darling, you do not have a career," she replied incredulously. "You are a newborn photographer at the hospital, no? It is not as though you are Ansel Adams."

Amber chewed the inside of her cheek as the sting of Lena's comment hit her full force. "I *know* I'm a newborn photographer *and* graphic designer, but it pays my bills. I still do the occasional wedding or corporate event, but getting those gigs can be very competitive..."

Lena patted her thigh. "I know, I know," she continued patronizingly. "I'm sorry, I did not mean to insult you. Bringing a child into the world is very important and I'm sure those parents are very appreciative of the pictures you take. See, we are talking and discussing things just as you like. Why don't you get dressed so we can run to the nearest café and get that strong, delicious coffee that you put into my head? And then we'll come back and I'll have just enough time to *really* make it up to you."

Amber felt torn between her feelings as she stared at Lena for a beat. *I ought to walk out of here right now with my dignity intact. Who does Lena think she is? Insulting what I do, treating me as though I'm a toy. Then again, maybe I'm being putting too much pressure on her. She wants to take things slow because the break-up with Sarah has been hard on her.*

"Coffee sounds great, but I should head out after," Amber finally replied.

Lena nodded. "I'm going to run downstairs and take Cayenne out to relieve herself. Get dressed and we'll head out after, yes?"

The older woman didn't wait for a reply before slipping out of the bedroom. Amber could hear her French bulldog whining in the living room.

She glared at her lap. "'Get dressed and we'll head out, yes?'" Amber whispered as she mimicked Lena's heavy accent.

She pulled on her jeans with a sigh. *Could my feelings for her be changing?* Amber wondered as she picked through her purse for her Chapstick. *She's so...judgmental. She keeps pushing me away. Everything that I thought I liked about her is disheartening. Everything that I thought was oh-so-cute and charming is irritating me worse than a day-old sunburn.*

The front door opened and Amber froze. "Honey, I'm home!" An unfamiliar female voice called as it echoed off the vaulted ceilings of the spacious penthouse. Cayenne began barking happily. Her deep bellows of appreciation for whoever had walked through the door bounced loudly down the hallway.

Shit.

"Ah...Ah, Sarah!" Lena called in surprise. Amber listened as she padded through the living room quickly. "My darling, what are you doing home already?"

Double shit. And why the hell did Lena just call her 'darling'?

CHAPTER 3

Amber listened closely as a closet door was opened. "I couldn't stay in Fort Worth any longer," Sarah admitted. "I know we've been having some problems lately, but I missed you so much. My parents were asking about you and why you weren't with me. It made me realize that we've been through too much to let this relationship go. Twenty years is a long time to love someone, but I have no doubt we can be happy together for the rest of our lives. I woke up early this morning and the first thing I did was hop in the Escalade so I could come home and surprise you."

Amber felt as though she had been punched in the stomach. The bitter taste of overwhelming guilt closed her throat as she desperately wished she didn't have to listen to their conversation.

"Oh, that...that's wonderful, darling," Lena replied, the shock evident in her voice. "I...I was just about to get some coffee and take Cayenne for a short walk. Would you like to come with me?" Her voice grew louder and more pointed.

"Baby, why are you screaming?" Sarah asked with a laugh. "Besides, you are not leaving this condo until I get my hands on you. I thought of all the beautiful things I wanted to do to you on my entire ride from Fort Worth. I want to *show* you how much I love you and how much I believe in us. Cayenne can certainly wait a little longer and *I'll* make you coffee when we're done. Although by then, it may be the afternoon so perhaps I'll make you lunch before your surgery."

Amber stared at her feet for a long moment and swallowed hard. *This can't be happening* she thought. A wild torrent of emotions, ranging from anger and jealousy to terror and confusion, coursed through her and they each fought for control. *I thought Sarah and Lena were finished. I thought they were barely talking, let alone sleeping together. Why would Lena tell me these things if they weren't true?*

"Oh, uh, darling," Lena tried to laugh off her advances. "I've thought of you too. More times than I care to count. But, you know, things have been very bad lately for us."

Amber quickly looked around the expansive master suite. *Escape route* she thought. *I need an escape route now.*

"Rough patches are normal in a long-term relationship," Sarah insisted. "And it's only been hard for a couple of months. I mean, call me crazy but I thought maybe you were having an affair or something. But I know you couldn't possibly. There's too much between us. The fire of our love will never flame out. Isn't that what you told me last week?"

Amber whirled around. "What. The. Fuck." She whispered. Her ears were ringing and she felt a rush of blood in her temples. "Lena told Sarah she still loves her...last week? They've only had problems for a couple of months?" Amber felt sick to her stomach as she recalled Lena lamenting the details of their break-up to her six months before.

How could I have been so stupid? She thought angrily. *Lena Mielkute is nothing more than a liar. A slimy, manipulative liar who thinks she can get away with anything because...because she's successful and handsomely beautiful and she...she makes up those stupid lines that sound like they're straight out of a cheesy romance novel! And they actually sound good because of that silly accent.*

"I need to get out of here," Amber muttered as she slowly turned once around the room. "The question is, how?"

Two large picture windows looked out over Oak Lawn Avenue,

eight stories above the tiny cars that sped by. The only door to the bedroom led into the hallway, which fed directly into the open living room and kitchen.

Panic slowly ebbed aside the anger that Amber felt as she realized there was no way to leave without being seen.

"Why don't I help you bring your bags from the car?" Lena tried. Amber recognized the slight desperation hinged in her tone. "Did you park at the lobby?"

Sarah laughed. "Yes, but you know Bart," she replied. "He's the best doorman in the city. He'll make sure I don't get towed. Or, worse yet, booted."

Lena laughed along with her. "Oh, I'm sure he has many things to do," she went on. "Let's move your car now and come back upstairs. I'm sure you don't want to leave your bags unattended in the Escalade."

There was a long moment of silence. "Are you trying to get me out of the condo?" Sarah asked accusatorily. "You're nervous and you're never this off-balance. Did I walk in on something that I shouldn't have?"

"No, darling, of course not!" Lena responded immediately. "See, this is why we have problems. You do not trust me. You think I'm doing things behind your back."

Anger bubbled in Amber's veins. *She's so full of shit* she thought. *I'll never forgive her for putting me in this position. I ought to walk out there right now and show Sarah just how much she shouldn't trust this woman.*

She curled her lip in steely resolve and stared at the door for a long moment before a single thought clicked. "Oh my *God*, my underwear," she whispered. Turning, her gaze swept the long planks of shining hardwood flooring. "What the hell did we do with my underwear last night? Come on Amber, *think*."

She absent-mindedly touched the waistband of her jeans and turned in a slow circle. Nothing in the room besides the unmade bed looked out of place. "Retrace your steps," Amber whispered to herself. "Okay, we got here." She closed her eyes and ignored the sharp stab of hurt that welled up inside her. "And Lena brought me right to the bedroom. There was a lot of kissing and then she took off my shirt. We stopped to compose ourselves and I washed my face and brushed my teeth. Then..."

Amber paused and sank onto a corner of the bed. "*Shit,* I need to get out of here," she muttered. "Focus. When we got back into bed, Lena threw my underwear over her shoulder. She tossed them and her tongue...Never mind." Her anger grew as she listened to Lena's desperate attempts to appease her partner just steps away. "But *where* did they go? If the dog took them, they could be anywhere. Damn it, *Cayenne.*"

An excited yelp from the living room caused Amber to freeze in place once again. *Oh no* she thought. *Dogs have, like, supersonic hearing, don't they? She couldn't possibly have heard me, right?*

Eager scratching at the bedroom door and a much louder yelp kicked Amber's heartbeat into high gear as she looked around the room wildly. The door to the walk-in closet was slightly ajar.

That's my only option Amber realized. With a start, she pushed open the closet door and forced her lean frame behind racks of clothing. A few evening gowns hung gently in the corner, their sequined fabric barely grazing the hardwood.

Lena doesn't wear dresses Amber thought as a lump rose in her throat. *And these are too expensive to wear only once or twice.* She fingered the tag of a dress and blinked away a tear. *Versace. My God, this is straight out of Vogue or something. These must belong to...*

"What is she barking at?" Sarah asked sharply. "Answer me, Lena!"

Her.

"I don't know," Lena replied weakly. "Perhaps she heard a noise."

"*What* noise?" Sarah shouted. "What does she hear in there? Or should I ask *who?*"

Why did I ever think I had a real chance with Lena? Amber wondered miserably. *She likes trophy wives who wear designer gowns and worship the ground she walks on. I will never be the woman who wears Versace and diamonds. I'm just...me.*

"I...I...Sarah, I'm sorry," Lena pleaded. "Please don't be upset."

"I'm getting to the bottom of this right now." Sarah's voice grew menacingly closer.

Amber flinched as the door swung open and bounced hard off the wall. She peeked from behind a gauzy maroon evening gown, where she could just make out two figures between the slats of the closet door.

Sarah turned slowly, her hands on her hips. Cayenne bounced eagerly into the room and stopped just short of the bed. She panted and looked around the room in confusion.

Lena entered slowly and looked as distraught as the dog. "Sarah, I…"

The other woman turned and jumped into Lena's arms. "Oh, sweetheart," she breathed. "I'm so sorry." She covered Lena's face with kisses. "I feel terrible. Things have been so tense with us lately and I really thought you were having an affair. All these insecurities finally got the best of me…" her voice trailed off as she met Lena's lips once more.

Amber looked away and blinked in the darkness of the closet. *Don't you dare cry* she told herself warningly. *Everything Lena said and did should have been a red flag. It's your own fault you let your guard down and ignored your gut.*

"Come here," Sarah gestured to the bed. "Let me make love to you. I've missed you so much."

Lena swallowed hard and glanced around the bedroom out of her peripheral. "Why don't we talk?" She pleaded. "You know, go to the café and get coffee and pastries. People-watch out the windows. Talk art and family and, you know, revisit with each other."

I hate her Amber realized. *How could I have been so gullible? I'm twenty-eight, I have no real career and I already gave her everything she wanted without question. And now? She's forced me into the closet. Literally.*

Sarah grinned and traced Lena's strong jaw with her thumb. "That's so sweet, baby," she replied. "That does sound nice. I'd like that."

Relief washed over Lena's face. "Yes?" She asked cheerfully. "Let's do that. Come, we'll move the SUV while we're downstairs."

Amber slumped against the closet wall as hurt and relief washed through her. She blinked as Lena was interrupted by a high-pitched whine from Cayenne.

"Cayenne, hush," Sarah scolded the bulldog gently.

The dog continued to whine and Amber's heart sank as she caught a glimpse of her pawing at something just beneath the bed. She cried louder each time she couldn't drag the object out.

"Oh no..." Amber whispered as a cold panic spread through her gut.

"Cayenne, no!" Lena turned in exasperation as the dog trotted back to them happily. A pair of strangely familiar white lace underwear hung from her jaw proudly.

"What the hell is that?" Sarah asked in confusion.

"My underwear," Lena replied quickly. She swiped the panties from Cayenne's mouth and balled them up in her fist before smiling brightly. "I was actually looking for these."

Sarah glanced from the underwear to Lena and back again, dubiousness written all over her face. "Lace? Those don't look like any that you own."

Lena sighed. "You cannot possibly..."

With a flash, Sarah grabbed the underwear from her hand. "*Mossimo*?" She asked incredulously. "Isn't that the generic clothing brand from Target?"

Lena colored slightly. "I...I don't know."

Sarah glared at her. "You *bought* them, how could you not know? In the twenty years that we've been together, I've never known you to purchase bargain-basement underwear like...like *Mossimo*." The brand fell from her lips like an unfashionable anvil.

Amber felt a rush of indignation. *I may not spend an entire paycheck on a wardrobe of lingerie, but they're clean. They're new...ish. They aren't* that *bad.*

Lena backed up slowly. "I suppose they...they could belong to a friend."

Sarah took a step forward, the panties still balled up in her hand like a prize. "What *friend* could you *possibly* have who would be leaving her underwear in *our* bedroom?"

"No, I mean, uh..." Lena swallowed. "I let a friend do laundry here. Perhaps she got mixed up. I'm sorry, you know my English is not the best..."

Sarah threw the wadded panties at Lena. "Oh, shut up!" She yelled. "You've been in this country since you were *fourteen*. Your English is fine!"

I need to get out of here Amber thought. As she contemplated how to exit the closet without a black eye from Lena's crazed lover, a familiar song began to play. It was tinny and muted, but it was her unmistakable ringtone.

All I want to do is make love to you
Oh, say you will, you want me too
All I want to do is make love to you
I got lovin' arms to hold onto...

Amber quickly tried to decline the call from her mother just as Sarah ripped the closet door open. Cayenne wiggled excitedly between neat rows of shoes to lick Amber's hand.

"Who the hell are you?" Sarah screeched. She turned to Lena. "Who is this? Why is she in our closet? What *is* this?"

Amber swallowed hard and looked between them. Lena stared stonily at the floor and refused to meet anyone's eyes.

"I'm sorry," Amber whispered. She lifted her chin. *You have nothing to be sorry for* she tried to console herself. *Except letting your feelings blind you to what this really was.* "I was born into a family where my father left my mother when I was thirteen. I would have never *knowingly* been the other woman." Amber stared hard at Lena.

"What is that supposed to mean?" Sarah asked angrily. "Lena?" She turned to her partner and was met with silence. "How long? When did this start? Wait..." Sarah paused and shook her head. "Why are you still in my home? Get out! Both of you! You are *not* welcome here. Get out or I'll call the police!"

Amber strained to maintain a single shred of dignity as she gently scooped her underwear from the floor and straightened her spine.

Without a word, she left the condo. Sarah was still screaming as Amber quietly shut the door behind her.

"You *bitch*!" Sarah screamed. "You dirty, rotten liar! Who was that? How can I ever trust you again? Where did you pick *that* one up from, Craigslist or something?"

The screaming echoed off the hallway walls even as the elevator dinged once with its arrival.

I can't believe this just happened Amber thought in disbelief. She bowed her head as she stepped into the regal glass and wood-paneled elevator. *I can't believe this.*

As she walked quickly through the lobby, the doorman smiled and nodded in greeting. His white-gloved hand reached out to gallantly open the door for her.

"Thank you," Amber muttered.

The doorman glanced at her hand and then quickly looked away. His grin faltered as he let the door swing shut behind her. Amber looked down and grimaced at the balled-up underwear still in her clenched fist. She sighed and shoved them into her purse before lifting her face to the hot late-morning sun.

Turning slightly, she shaded her eyes and glanced at the top of the glass skyscraper behind her. With a hard swallow, Amber resolutely turned back, squared her shoulders and faced a future without the idea of Dr. Lena Mielkute.

CHAPTER 4

Brooke slid into a tall leather chair behind the glossy wooden conference table at Key West's only title company. She smiled around the table at the attorneys present and then nodded in greeting to the broker for the house's buyers.

Summertime was her favorite part of the year in Key West, and not just because it was the high season for the real estate market. During the summer months, most of the snowbirds had already returned north and the island seemed quieter and more serene. Even still, Brooke never complained about the wealthy families and couples who traveled to Key West each year to escape winter.

It wasn't long ago that I *was one of those East Coast people heading down to Key West* Brooke thought with a wry smile. *The only difference was, I had no intention of just being a snowbird and sticking around only to avoid the cold. It was time to make a permanent change, leave the New York City rat race and enjoy life.*

In New York, Brooke had been a relatively successful real estate salesperson for a large Manhattan brokerage. She had specialized in first-time home buyers and her calendar was always filled with appointments to help busy city folks find the condominium or brownstone of their dreams.

Even still, business up there was nothing like it is here she mused. *Limited real estate and consistently high demand means home prices will always be well above the national average. I can broker a third of the transactions here than I did in New York and still walk away with higher take-home commissions.*

"Lovely to see you again, Ms. Adriani," Joy, an elderly assistant at the title company, greeted her as she placed a pitcher of ice water on a corner table. "Is this the fifth one this month?"

Brooke smiled politely as she slid a manila file from her laptop bag. "Likewise, Joy," she replied. "It's only the third sale this month. I was acting as the buyers' agent for the other two closings you're thinking of. No complaints here. In fact, I hope you'll see me a few more times before the summer is over. 'Tis the season, right?"

Joy nodded knowingly. "You're telling me," she went on. "We have been *inundated* with closings since the end of March. We expect it to be a good season, with no slowing down until September. I suppose now that the market has just about recovered, everyone wants this island lifestyle."

"I don't blame them one bit," Brooke replied. "I'm forever grateful to my dad for convincing me to join him here five years ago. I haven't looked back at New York City even once since."

"Yes, Key West is a wonderful place," Joy smiled kindly. "How was your lunchtime yoga? Do you still go mid-day twice a week?"

Brooke fought the blush that she suspected was creeping up her neck. "Oh, yeah, um, yes," she stammered and then quickly recovered. "Yes, I do. Over at Sun Studios in Mallory Square."

Joy looked impressed. "Well, that's terrific," she remarked. "I've heard yoga is fantastic for your body."

Brooke bit back a smirk. *You have no idea.* "I've noticed a difference," she replied carefully. "My best friend Justin and I also try to go on Saturday mornings. We motivate one another to stick with a regular schedule, of course."

Joy opened her mouth, but a bell above the entrance door jangled with an arrival. "Oh, I bet those are your sellers right now," she went on with a wink. "I'll go get them. Good luck this afternoon."

~

Exactly two hours and ten minutes later, Brooke sank happily into the driver's seat of her white Lexus. The soft buttery leather seats were moderately cool, thanks to a rare parking space she had nabbed in the shade. She pressed a button and waited as the roof slowly retracted, rendering the speedy sports car a convertible.

There's just something intoxicating about the scent of the ocean and the breeze in your hair Brooke decided as she pulled onto Flagler Avenue. With her brokerage's commission check nestled snugly in her laptop bag, she briefly wondered if there was enough time to stop at the office. She knew their controller would be cutting individual commission checks on Friday and the idea of right away depositing the largest check earned so far in her career was incredibly enticing.

Dad will be so proud Brooke thought with a smile. *I suppose I* am *quite a chip off the old block.*

As she slowed the Lexus at a red light, she smiled at the tiny hula girl statue bobbing on her dashboard. *My Key West good luck charm* she thought with satisfaction. *Always looking out for me.* Brooke hit the gas as the light changed at the same time that her phone sounded from somewhere deep in her bag. She quickly fished it out and grinned at the name displayed on its screen.

Speak of the devil. "Hi, Dad," Brooke pressed the phone to her ear and greeted 63-year old Dave Adriani. "How's it going?"

"Good, honey," Dave replied. "How you doin'? How was the closing?"

Brooke bit back a smile at her father's unmistakable Brooklyn accent. The heavy accent coupled with his strong, stocky build gave the impression to most that Dave was far gruffer and more intimidating than he actually was. To Brooke, he was the big teddy bear that had raised her on his own from the time she was ten years old and her mother lost her battle with cancer.

"It went perfect," she responded. "A small issue had come up with the current fence on the property versus the survey that was done, but nothing major. The sellers had obtained all the required permits before replacing the fence, so it'll be something the buyers will have to take up with the city if it becomes a problem later. Other than that, I'm relieved to say it was all smooth sailing."

"Congratulations," Dave replied proudly. "Say, why don't you stop by the house for dinner tonight? I know it's short notice, so I understand if you and Justin already have plans or somethin'. But," he paused as Brooke listened to him take a deep breath. "I...I do have someone I want you to meet."

Brooke stilled as she processed the implication of her father's words. *A woman* she realized. *A few months ago he said he met someone interesting at that Cuban café. They've been going out together pretty regularly, but I didn't know it was anything other than casual.*

"You...You want me to meet her?" Brooke clarified. "The woman from the café?"

"Sandra," Dave corrected her. "But yeah, the woman from the café. I got to tell you Brookie, this woman is something else. She's really changed my life for the better over these last few months."

The fact that her father, who had no less than eight back-to-back girlfriends throughout Brooke's teenaged years, was now gushing about Sandra was almost disconcerting enough for her to ignore that he'd used her childhood nickname.

"I mean, she makes me this amazing organic breakfast every morning," Dave went on. "I'm talkin' egg whites, turkey bacon, fruit salad, gluten-free pancakes because she says those are better for me and don't have certain ingredients that ain't good for you, the whole spread. And it's all organic, so there's no pesticides, all the meat was raised without those antibiotics and hormones..."

"Yes, Dad, I know what organic is," Brooke cut in tersely. She took a deep breath. "I'm happy for you. In fact, I don't think I've ever heard you this...*different* about a woman."

Dave laughed. "Because she *is* different, Brooke," he replied. "You know you just meet someone and something shifts? You, uh, you *know* they're different. You'd do anything for them because they bring so much joy into your life. You could, you know, *love* 'em."

Brooke's expertly tweezed eyebrows shot up at her father's

casual use of the "L" word. "Well, I'm going to have to meet this Sandra then," she replied. She bit her lip as she drove to the end of Duval Street and pulled into a parking space facing the ocean. "Unfortunately, I do have plans with Justin tonight. Maybe later this week?"

"All right, no worries," Dave responded. Brooke tried to ignore the guilt she felt at the slight disappointment in his voice. "I know it was a shot in the dark, since you two like to go out for your dinners and happy hours. How about I call you? Maybe this weekend?"

Brooke stared at her dashboard. "Perfect. I'll talk to you then, Dad."

As they hung up, she shut off the Lexus and tried to sift through a mix of feelings. After a long moment, she walked onto South Beach and shaded her eyes as she looked for Justin. She carefully leaned over and removed both low-heeled black pumps she had been wearing. She wasn't exactly dressed for a beer at the beach with her best friend, but she didn't mind. South Beach was one of her happy places; a peaceful stretch of prime, palm tree-dotted real estate favored by Key West's locals.

Brooke spotted Justin's blond head not much further away. He was slouched in a folding chair and a pair of stylish Ray-Bans covered his eyes. More exciting to Brooke, however, was the small cooler at his side. It was unzipped just enough that Brooke recognized the familiar blue and yellow bottle caps poking into the air, as if inviting her to take a load off, relax and let the stresses of the day slide away like water from a duck's back.

Corona she thought with satisfaction. *He knows me too well.*

Brooke smiled at the hand-painted, multi-colored wooden sign that welcomed her to the beach and proudly proclaimed that it was the southernmost beach in the continental United States. Just beneath a short list of beach rules, the tall sign concluded with a Tennessee Williams quote.

I work everywhere, but I work best here royal blue lettering said boldly against peeling white paint. Brooke shook her head as she trudged to the empty beach chair next to Justin. *Ain't that the truth.*

She plopped unceremoniously into the chair and gazed thoughtfully at the rolling ocean waves a few yards further. "I just had the strangest conversation with my dad," Brooke remarked.

Justin glanced up, a Corona bottle halfway to his lips, and raised an eyebrow in question.

"He's in love," she went on in confusion. "And he really wants me to meet his new girlfriend."

"Big Daddy Adriani?" Justin asked incredulously. "No way."

"Yes, way," Brooke confirmed with a nod. "Also, he hates when you call him that."

Justin looked momentarily wounded and then appeared to shake it off. "It could just be the excitement of a new relationship. You never know."

Brooke shook her head. "No, he's been in a *lot* of relationships since my mom passed away. I always got along fine with the women, but never bothered to get attached. Even when I was younger, I knew they wouldn't last. I knew he was trying in vain to replace something that he couldn't. And, sure enough, they would each be gone, usually within a few months. But I don't think I've ever heard him sound the way he did now about any of his exes."

Justin paused as Brooke ordered a freshly squeezed juice from the waitress. After she walked away, he spoke conspiratorially. "So, do you think you'll meet this one?"

"He wants me to," Brooke replied. "He actually invited me over tonight to meet her. It caught me off-guard. Besides, we had plans already."

Justin shot her a knowing look. "We always have plans. You know I'd understand if something came up."

"Well, maybe I need time to get used to the idea too," Brooke replied irritably. "Don't get me wrong, he deserves it. He deserves to find someone special more than anyone I know. He just sounded so different. He was talking about all the organic breakfasts that she cooks for him..."

Justin took a sip of his beer. "That must mean she's spending a lot of time over there."

They both paused and wrinkled their noses as the full implication of their frequent shared breakfasts dawned on them.

"Ew," Brooke muttered as she tried to push the thought from her head.

"I think it's sweet if he's in love," Justin declared. "He's all alone in that big house he built over on Big Pine Key. You should be happy that he's found someone to share his life with."

Brooke considered this as she watched the families that dotted the shallow surf. As she squinted into the evening sun, she could make out a few paddle-boarders further in the ocean. "You're right," she admitted. "I know you're right. Ready or not, I guess I'll have to meet Sandra soon. Just not...tonight."

"So what else was he saying about her?" Justin asked. "Besides the monstrously evil fact that she's brainwashing him with healthy organic food, of course."

Brooke rolled her eyes at him. "I never said she was evil or brainwashing him. I'm sure I'll be more comfortable once I see that he's not setting himself up for disappointment." She sighed. "I don't know. He was talking about how when someone is right for you, you just *know*. Something shifts inside you, because they bring all this happiness to your life and you know you could love them."

"Big Dad...I'm sorry, *your father* said all of that?" Justin spluttered in surprise. "The man who rarely says more than three words at a time in that thick New York accent?"

Brooke threw a hand up. "I know, right!" She exclaimed. "I've never felt anything like that. I mean, maybe I've never been in love. Is that what it feels like?"

Justin smiled and Brooke recognized the kindness in his green eyes. "We're in our prime, remember? There's plenty of time for us. Just focus on being happy for your dad. He deserves it. How about you try...cautiously optimistic for now?"

Brooke considered this for a moment and then nodded. "Cautiously optimistic. I think I like that."

"Good, now drink up," Justin finished with a wink. "You know there's no better way to end the day than a cold Corona with lime on South Beach."

Brooke shook her head ruefully as Justin handed her a beer from the cooler. "All those calories burned in yoga are going to come right back to me like some cosmic boomerang."

"Maybe not *all* the calories you burned..." Justin started with a snort.

They burst into laughter and Brooke settled back into her chair comfortably. As she cracked open the bottle with a light *pop,* she smiled at the bright orange sun. It had begun sinking into the wide horizon and a gentle breeze rustled nearby palm leaves.

Life is good she thought with a happy start. *I have everything I could've dreamed of and more.* She contemplatively sipped her beer as her dad's words rang at the back of her mind. *'You just meet someone and something shifts. You'd do anything for them because they bring so much joy into your life.'*

For a fleeting moment, Brooke was wistful. The excited shrieks of a toddler being playfully chased by her mother brought her from her thoughtful reverie and she quickly blinked and shrugged off the unfamiliar tugging sensation.

"Music?" Justin asked as he dug a small portable speaker from his beach bag.

"The louder, the better," Brooke declared.

CHAPTER 5

Amber tossed her keys onto what had become the "catch-all" table next to her apartment door. Her roommate Emily, a friend of a friend, hadn't been home in two days, but Amber knew she was staying with her boyfriend.

More and more often she thought as she walked into the kitchen. She opened the refrigerator door and peered blankly at the meager contents. *It's only a matter of time until he invites her to move in with him. And then I'll move to an even smaller apartment, because God knows I can't afford a two-bedroom by myself.*

Amber hated the bitterness that seemed to have tainted her outlook on everything over the last few days. *I should be happy for Emily. She deserves a good guy.* The hum of the old refrigerator seemed to sound in time with the low buzzing that had been gently pulsing through her temples since The Incident. It had been precisely four days and eight hours since she had narrowly escaped Lena's apartment, her pride nowhere to be found...Not that she was counting.

As Amber pulled sandwich bread, a nearly-empty jar of mayonnaise and leftover cold cuts from the refrigerator, she couldn't help but feel a small shiver of relief snake down her spine at not having seen Lena at the hospital since. She grabbed a knife from the dishwasher, quickly inspected it to ensure its cleanliness and then scraped it along the sides of the mayonnaise jar. The knife clinked loudly against the glass as she tried to scoop up enough of the condiment for at least one slice of bread.

I could just run over to the store and get another jar Amber thought, before deflating as she remembered it was only Thursday. *But I don't get paid until tomorrow morning. I had $20 and change left in checking...Oh, but then I had to get gas this morning and I bought a Gatorade too...* Amber pushed the empty jar down the counter in frustration and dropped her head in her hands.

"No wonder Lena was never serious about us," she muttered as she allowed herself to wallow in self-pity for a moment. "Look at the way she lives." Amber closed her eyes as she briefly recalled Sarah's designer dresses in their walk-in closet. Her throat unexpectedly closed at the memory. "I mean, *look* at me. This is pathetic." She opened her eyes and glared at the empty jar. "I can't even afford a goddamn jar of *mayo* until I get paid tomorrow. I spent my twenties chasing a passion for photography and where has it gotten me? Twenty-eight years old, still living paycheck-to-paycheck, no real savings and a maxed-out credit card."

Amber's frustration boiled over as hot tears welled up in her eyes. She swiped at them angrily, hating that Lena made her feel so insecure. She nibbled a piece of salami as a single thought exploded in her mind.

Honestly, I don't know if I would want me either.

The sudden ringing of her phone sounded loud and unwelcome in the dark, empty apartment. Amber swallowed her last bite of salami and nearly choked at the display on her phone. The name "Lena", followed by several multi-colored heart emojis, blinked expectantly back at her.

"Don't answer it," Amber whispered defiantly. She stared wide-eyed at the display and willed the phone to be quiet. "No way am I answering it. She doesn't deserve a chance to explain anything. There's no way on Earth that I'm answering."

Amber turned angrily and took two shaky steps out of the kitchen.

As the ringing faded, she stilled. After a split second, she whirled around and grabbed the phone before quickly pressing it to her ear.

"Lena?" She asked.

There was a brief moment of silence over the line before an unmistakable voice responded.

"Amber, hello," Lena replied, subdued. "I didn't think you were going to answer my call."

Amber immediately wanted to kick herself. *I knew picking up was a bad idea* she thought in annoyance. *It's always a game to her.* "Yeah, well...You got me," she faltered after a pause. "What do you want, Lena?"

"I wanted to speak with you," Lena replied with a heavy sigh. "I...I haven't been at the hospital."

"Oh, really?" Amber asked, feigning boredom. She certainly wasn't going to admit that she had noticed Lena's absence, however much of a relief it had been.

"Sarah and I, we...we went away together," Lena continued. "We need some time to figure things out. We've rented a cabin for the next two weeks. I thought it would be best to reschedule my surgeries and give you time. I just...I had to make sure there wouldn't be any...difficulty when I get back. At the hospital, I mean. I'm sure we may see each other here and there, but you know that both of us could be in jeopardy if word gets out about the last six months. After this week, my career is the one stable thing I have. I don't want that to also be harmed because of you."

Amber's mouth dropped open. Lena's patronizing tone and refusal to accept any blame made Amber's blood pulse, red and boiling, through her veins. The low buzzing in her temples gave way to a loud hum deep in her ears.

"If word gets out about *what,* Lena?" Amber spat. "What exactly was it to you?"

Lena sighed again. "Do we have to get into this now?" She pleaded. "Darling Amber, I know I've put you through so much. Perhaps I got carried away in the fantasy. For that, I am sorry. That lovely dream of you and I, languid Sundays in bed, evening strolls along the Katy

Trail, rushed and covert lunch hours just to steal a kiss...Perhaps I got too wrapped up. I should have been more realistic with you."

Amber leaned against the kitchen wall and glared at the tile floor. "And what would realistic have looked like?"

"Sex," Lena replied simply. "Sex between two very beautiful people who harbor an undeniably sizzling attraction to one another. Sex without attachments; instead, with reassurances that I am nowhere near keen on the idea of letting go of my partner or risking a successful career for...for a twentysomething newborn photographer who has yet to get her life together."

Pressure pushed against the backs of Amber's eyes and a large lump formed in her throat. She stilled and breathed through her nose for a few moments. She was terrified that if she opened her mouth too soon, Lena would hear her crying.

"You know, I never knew there was so much wrong with my life until I met you," Amber shot back. She hated the wobble in her voice and blinked back angry tears. "I was perfectly happy before you. I was working toward my goals."

"Of course you were," Lena cut in hastily. "Look, the reason for my call was not to hash out the past. I need to make sure that things at the hospital will remain unchanged. I can't be distracted with..."

"God, you really do only care about yourself," Amber interrupted in sudden disgust. Her gut had warned her many times over their six months together. She had stored these thoughts in the back of her mind, always hoping that Lena would prove her wrong. *Except, until now, I was blinded to all the ways she was proving me right.*

"Amber..." Lena started chidingly.

"Don't," Amber interrupted her again. "You won't hear from me. Don't worry. Your career will be just fine."

"My darling Amber, that tone..." Lena tried again.

"Oh, and I am not your darling *anything*," Amber finished hotly. "Have a great vacation. Good-bye, Lena."

With a hard, decisive tap, Amber ended the call and set her phone down. As good as it felt to hang up on Lena Mielkute, she realized that any appetite she'd had was scrapped. With a sigh, Amber grabbed the empty mayonnaise jar and turned to toss it into the kitchen garbage.

As the jar thudded gently against the bottom of the trash can, Amber's phone sounded again. She whirled around in irritation.

"You have *got* to be kidding me," Amber exclaimed. "What is this woman's problem?"

She took a deep breath and pressed the phone to her ear without bothering to glance at the display. "*What,* Lena?" She barked.

A woman, who sounded exceptionally confused, cleared her throat after a moment. "Uh, I'm sorry. I may have the wrong number. This is Bobbi Harold, Executive Vice President of the Key West Chamber of Commerce. I was calling for an, uh, Amber Lucas?"

Amber immediately straightened as her mouth dropped open. "Yes, yes, this is she," she replied quickly. "I'm, um, I'm sorry. I thought you were someone else."

"Oh, that's fine," Bobbi replied politely. "I apologize for calling outside office hours. I was reaching out because you had submitted a series of photos about twelve weeks ago in response to our open call for our end-of-summer exhibition."

"Yes, of course," Amber replied. For the first time in nearly a week, she felt a hint of excitement in her belly. Her mother had informed her of the open call and upcoming exhibition and had encouraged her to submit photos to be included. Amber had visited her mother once in Key West since she had moved, but she had spent most of that time outdoors taking hundreds of photos. "Key West is a photographer's dream."

Amber hadn't realized she had spoken out loud until Bobbi chuckled. "It is certainly a beautiful place to call home," she replied. "Now your application says here that you reside in Dallas, Texas?"

"Yes, that's right," Amber responded. She took a deep breath through her nose. *Play it cool. Don't seem too excited. Act like you have cities all over the world calling you about your photos.* "My mother relocated to Key West about two years ago and I try to visit every chance I get." *Okay, small white lie.* "My primary residence is still Dallas though."

"Wonderful," Bobbi murmured as Amber heard her shuffling

papers in the background. "Well, I do apologize in advance for my short notice. The reason for my call is a bit...*different,* if you will. I see here on your resume that you're a newborn photographer at Parkland Hospital and before that, you worked for six years as the office manager of a Dallas event planning company. In that time, the company doubled in size. Is that right?"

Amber wrinkled her nose, unsure why her years of administrative experience were of interest. "That's right," she confirmed. "When I started, they were still struggling to break out of their start-up phase. They expanded considerably over the years that I was there."

"And, as the office manager, your responsibilities were probably aligned with the company?" Bobbi pressed. "Meaning as they grew, your workload increased significantly?"

Where in the world is she going with this? Amber wondered. "Absolutely," she replied. "In my third year, we brought on two part-time admins who I trained and oversaw. They helped with a lot of the overflow."

"That's *perfect,*" Bobbi exclaimed. "The reason I'm asking about all of this and reaching out when our exhibition is just six weeks away is because we're really in a bind. Our longtime office manager, who normally oversees event coordination and the administrative aspects of our exhibition, quit rather unexpectedly last week. We also have a full-time administrative assistant, but she had a baby only three weeks ago and won't be back from her maternity leave until after the exhibition."

A sinking feeling began somewhere deep in Amber's gut. "Oh, no," she responded lamely.

"Mmhmm," Bobbi hummed. "As you can imagine, we have been scrambling to figure out what to do. Unfortunately, being all the way out here in Key West, there's really no temporary employment office I can contact. Then I realized that I have all of these applications and surely *someone* would have solid administrative experience to potentially help us behind the scenes in a temporary contract role."

Amber swallowed hard as her throat dried. "So, to be clear, you're calling me..."

"To offer you a temporary position as a 1099 employee of the Key West Chamber of Commerce," Bobbi finished. "Your duties will really just be managing the administrative tasks of the exhibition, all those little details that our office manager would have normally overseen. Well, you know I'm sure. After all, you worked with an events management company for six years!"

Amber couldn't believe her ears. She was sure her heart had hit the kitchen floor. "And...And my photos?" She tried, as she waited for this newest disappointment to fully sink in.

"Your photos were lovely," Bobbi continued quickly. "We do have them categorized as stand-by. If any photographer that has been invited to participate must cancel or bow out at the last minute, we may use two or three of the seven you submitted."

I think I've reached my insult threshold for the evening. Hell, for the entire year Amber thought morosely. She opened her mouth to tell Bobbi as politely as she could that she was not interested, but the other woman continued before she could speak.

"The administrative position would be a temporary six-week role," Bobbi went on. "Ideally, you would be here for the three weeks prior to the exhibition, the two weeks leading up to and then one week after to help tie everything up. We operate during standard office hours, Monday through Friday. We're also flexible, so you can choose if you want to work 8 to 5, 9 to 6, or some other variation so long as you get your eight hours in. Oh, and we realize that lodging in Key West can be pricy. Though if your mom lives here, then you may save some money that way. Regardless, we understand that the cost of living here is considerably higher than most areas. Because of that, we're paying $2,000 per completed week of work."

Amber nearly dropped the phone. She quickly padded over to the worn leather sectional in the living room and plopped down hard. *Wait a second* she thought. *$2,000 a week? Granted, I'll have to pay taxes on it next year, but...*She did a few quick mental calculations. *That's a lot more than I'm making now.*

"That, um, sounds great, Bobbi," Amber stammered. "Although I am currently working full-time in Dallas. I...I would have to see..."

she paused and took a deep breath as the wheels began turning. "Could I get back to you by Monday with a final answer?"

Bobbi clucked her tongue lightly. "I understand it's short notice," she replied. "But unfortunately, we're in quite a bind and do need to find someone right away. Would you be able to let me know by lunchtime tomorrow if you'd be able to swing it? With your skillset and experience, it would really be a great opportunity. I'd be happy to write you a recommendation letter at the end of your six weeks. And hey, the island would be yours to enjoy during the times you won't be working. A little R&R away from the same old never hurt anyone, right?"

She has no idea Amber thought as her mind flashed back to Lena, the hospital and the strange rut in which she had seemed to find herself. "You've certainly got me there," Amber replied honestly. "I'll discuss it with my work and my mother to see what I can do. Either way, I'll call you back with a definitive answer before tomorrow afternoon."

"Wonderful," Bobbi replied, her beam evident to Amber through the phone. "I have to be honest, you are the first person I've reached out to. We hope you'll decide to join us for the exhibition."

Amber shook her head in bemusement as they hung up. She had been crossing her fingers in hopes of hearing those words since she had submitted her photos months ago, but not exactly in the way that Bobbi meant them.

She glanced out the living room window at what little bit of the sunset she could see beyond the apartment buildings facing hers and the heat-baked courtyard with its browned, straw-like grass.

I remember what the sunsets looked like in Key West Amber mused. "And they were a whole lot better than what I'm looking at now," she finished with a sigh.

CHAPTER 6

Brooke took a deep breath and hesitantly lifted her fist to knock on her father's door. Just before her knuckles rapped against the hard wooden surface, she turned and smiled weakly at Justin.

"Do you think the wine is too much?" She asked as she gestured to the glass bottle cradled in her right elbow. "I don't even know if she prefers red or white. I can't believe I'm second-guessing myself. I've never been nervous to meet one of Dad's girlfriends before."

"Well, he *did* set the bar pretty high by dropping the L word earlier this week," Justin agreed. He carefully grabbed Brooke's shoulders and waited for her to stop fidgeting. "I think, deep down, you know she could be the real deal for him. And you *are* the most important person in his life, so you know that having a good relationship with your dad means trying for a good relationship with her."

Brooke blew out her breath. "I don't know how you get me sometimes, but you do," she admitted. She glanced at her feet. The standard dress code in Key West was almost always flip-flops, shorts, t-shirts and sunglasses, but Brooke usually preferred a more professional appearance. Soft brown leather boots, skinny khaki chinos and a white half-sleeve button-up that accented her golden tan was about as casual as Brooke liked to be outside of her home.

She had purposely left the ubiquitous rainbow bracelet that she always wore on her right wrist safely at home. She ignored the fact that her wrist looked oddly naked without the thin, colorful beads adorning it and instead decided that she would tackle the heady subject of her sexuality with her father sometime…Just not anytime soon.

Besides, now is the time to focus on the issue at hand. Namely, Sandra Brooke thought. *Yeah, that definitely takes precedence for now.*

"Thank you for coming with me," she muttered. "Just for this first meeting. You know, moral support."

Justin smiled at her knowingly. "Moral support?" He asked, pretending to be offended. "I don't know *what* you're talking about, Miss Adriani. At this point, I want to meet this Sandra just as much as you do!"

Brooke laughed as she knocked once on the front door. She braced herself as she heard approaching footsteps down her father's wide tiled hallway.

"Stop thinking so much," Justin whispered. "You look great. The wine is a thoughtful touch. Dinner will be just fine and you'll realize you've been worried all week for nothing."

"I hope you're right," Brooke murmured. Her face abruptly froze into an expectant smile as the front door swung open.

"Hi, sweetheart!" Dave greeted her happily as he wrapped her into a bear hug. "I'm so glad you could make it. I got the grill out back fired up and some chicken barbecuing now. Shouldn't be much longer. Hey Justin, how are you, man?"

Dave shook Justin's hand and smiled broadly.

"Chicken on the grill?" Brooke asked as they made their way to the open concept kitchen and dining area. A large sliding glass door opened onto a brick patio and in-ground pool, all of which was covered with a thin pool fence and nestled in a grove of tall palm trees.

"Yeah, we got some white meat and some legs out there cookin' right now. You hungry?" Dave replied.

"Starving," Brooke admitted. "Chicken sounds wonderful. I thought for sure you'd be grilling those big, bloody slabs of steak that you enjoy so much. Not that I don't enjoy the occasional steak, but..."

"...It fills your arteries and isn't exactly good for your heart health either," a woman's gentle voice chimed in.

Brooke turned as an older woman about her father's age stepped from the kitchen with a smile. Her hair was a soft auburn that gathered around her shoulders and was held back by a small coral clip. She wore loose khakis and a turquoise top with a simple illustration of the moon phases across it. Her wrists and fingers were filled with turquoise stones and hematite crystals on the nearly dozen bracelets and rings she wore.

"Heart health is so important, especially at our ages," Sandra continued, as she gestured between them. "Not that I would deny anyone the pleasure of a slab of meat once in a while, but I'm sure you know even better than I that it can be quite unhealthy in excess."

Brooke nodded. "Yes," she agreed. She was pleasantly surprised that Sandra seemed to care so much about her father's health. "I've been telling Dad to lay off the red meat for almost ten years now." She took a deep breath and tried a small smile. "But *I'm* sure *you* know even better than I how stubborn that man can be."

Sandra threw back her head and laughed. "It is *so* wonderful to meet you, Brooke," she exclaimed. Brooke immediately liked Sandra's soft, calming tone and the genuine way in which she spoke. "You're as lovely as I'd pictured. Even more beautiful than the photos that your father has shown me."

Brooke blushed. "Thank you. It's really nice to meet you too."

She threw a quick glance at Justin, who smiled encouragingly. "And this is my best friend, Justin Cole," Brooke introduced. "I found him on the side of A1A and invited him to join us for dinner."

Justin rolled his eyes as he leaned forward and quickly shook Sandra's hand. "As you can see, Brooke also has a fantastic sense of humor. It's nice to meet you, Sandra."

Dave cleared his throat. "All right, I'm going to keep working on this chicken," he cut in. He nodded once toward the patio. "I'll let you all get to talkin'. One of you mind bringing me a glass of that wine in a few minutes though?"

Sandra nodded and watched Dave amble through the sliding glass doors with a lingering smile that was not lost on Brooke. *She really does look at him like she loves him* she thought in wonder.

"So how long have the two of you been going together?" Sandra asked politely.

Brooke blinked. "Excuse me?" She threw an incredulous glance at Justin. "You mean…"

Sandra gestured between her and Justin. "You two," she replied. "From what your father has said, you two spend a lot of time together. Has it been very long?"

Justin guffawed loudly and quickly clapped a hand over his mouth. Brooke threw another glance at him as she wondered how in the world anyone could assume he was straight.

"Actually, what my father failed to mention is that Justin is…" Brooke started.

"Gay," Justin cut in quickly with a big smile. "Like, card-carrying, Judy Garland-singing, Cher-loving…"

"I get it," Sandra replied, returning his smile. "Congratulations on Obergefell Vs. Hodges. I was so thrilled when that finally passed. It's been a long time coming. I've never felt that sexuality is something anyone should be ashamed of. After all, it's just one small part of the DNA, experiences, surroundings and energy that make us who we are."

Brooke blinked, temporarily surprised by Sandra's openness. She examined her nails, unsure how to respond, as Sandra carefully uncorked the wine bottle. *Times like these, it would be so much easier just to be out already.*

Justin shot her a knowing look and smiled satisfactorily as Sandra turned to pull four wine glasses from a cabinet.

"Yeah, Brooke, sexuality is nothing to be ashamed of," he whispered gleefully. "You could *really* stand to loosen up sometimes."

Brooke was about to whisper a snarky reply, but Sandra turned and set the glasses onto the dining table. "And *who* are we, anyway?" She continued. "Can anyone really answer that? Are we merely a body, a brain, a soul? Who can answer that? Who am *I* and what is this *I* that we all refer to?"

Sandra poured a glass of wine and handed it carefully to Justin, who stared at her wide-eyed. "My apologies," she went on. "I've been studying with a group through the Key West Tara Mandala and my most recent meditations have brought some fascinating explorations." She handed another glass of wine to Brooke.

"That...That's nice," Brooke replied. "I've never heard of the Tara Mandala."

"Well, you're more than welcome to join me if you'd ever like," Sandra offered. "They have several meditation sessions throughout the week."

"Sure," Brooke replied hesitantly. She didn't feel sure at all. "That sounds nice."

Sandra smiled as she poured wine into a third glass. "You're sweet," she spoke warmly. "I could feel that about you from the moment you walked in the door. Your aura gives off this beautiful orange-red color, which tells me you're very confident and enjoy personal power. However, it also shows a great deal of health and vibrancy toward life. Excuse me for just a moment so I can make sure your dad gets his wine."

As Sandra slid between the glass doors, Brooke turned and faced Justin slowly. "She's...She's..." Brooke tried to come up with the words. *A nut? A living, breathing Throwback Thursday to 1969?*

"She's *fabulous*!" Justin gushed, his voice barely hovering at a whisper. He took a sip of wine and grinned. "Oh my *God*, I love her. I want her to tell me about *my* aura!"

"You're kidding," Brooke replied in a low voice. She narrowed her eyes at her friend.

Justin fixed her with a wounded look. "I am *not*," he huffed. "She's a little left of normal, but aren't we all? She seems kind and utterly fantastic. I *love* that big turquoise ring on her index finger. It *had* to be custom-made..."

They quieted as Sandra stepped back into the open dining area. "Chicken is just about ready," she reported. "Say, what's your sign?"

Brooke paused, taken aback. "What?" She asked. "You mean my astrological sign?"

"Of course," Sandra replied, as though it was a perfectly normal question. "You'd be surprised at how accurate the constellations and planetary alignments can be. For example, I'm a Pisces. You know, the fish?"

Brooke nodded as she wondered where this was going. Out of the corner of her eye, she could see Justin had taken a seat at the dining table and leaned forward. He rested his chin on his fist with rapt attention.

"One of the most common characteristics of most Pisces women tends to be our focus on our inner selves," Sandra continued. "In fact, Pisces are some of the most mystic and psychically-inclined of the whole zodiac. Now, I'm not saying that I could give you the winning lottery numbers or anything. Believe me, I'd be having my retreat built in Sedona right now I knew that..."

"I *love* Sedona," Justin cut in dreamily.

Brooke rolled her eyes at him as Sandra's smile widened. "It is a wonderful, magical place, isn't it?" She replied. "But what I mean is that I can sense things. An intuition, if you will. My grandmother was also a Pisces and I swear that woman was a true psychic. *Horribly* agoraphobic, couldn't leave her house even if Clark Gable himself was outside asking for a dance."

"Clark Gable is fantastic," Justin agreed.

Sandra chuckled. "But I'm telling you, that woman knew everything going on outside those four walls. The *good* stuff too, like who was pregnant or who was having an affair. Hell, the old woman even knew when I'd snuck out to a Rolling Stones concert one weekend. Granted, I came home stinking of a certain plant, and not roses, if you know what I mean. Boy, my parents were livid. More wine?"

Brooke's mouth dropped open. She blinked at her empty glass. "Yes," Brooke replied. "Definitely more wine."

"Me too, please," Justin cut in again as he excitedly slid his glass across the table.

Brooke smiled despite herself. *Just go with it.* "So, um, I'd *really* like to hear about that Rolling Stones concert but to answer your question, I'm a Virgo."

Sandra nodded knowingly. "Ah, yes," she replied. "A Virgo. I'm so glad to hear that. Lou Ellen, my spiritual advisor, told me that there's an Aquarius I need to watch out for. Nothing too malicious, just that this person will cause me some unexpected pain. It's important for me to know who I'm crossing paths with."

"Right," Brooke replied after a long sip of wine. "Totally reasonable."

"You know, my daughter is also a Virgo," Sandra went on. "I just have one child and she's my baby. Twenty-eight, still living in Dallas. That's where I'm originally from, but I've been here in the Keys for the last couple of years. Anyway, I'd like to think that makes me a near-expert in all things Virgo. She had been dating a surgeon for some time, but I didn't have a good feeling about it. I could never say much to Amber though. She would have just gotten mad and told me I'm being nutty."

Brooke held back a snort and nodded instead. "Virgos do like to figure things out on their own."

"Yeah, even if those *things* are the same things that the people close to them have been telling them *forever*," Justin interrupted with a dramatic roll of his eyes.

"That's quite right," Sandra agreed. "I knew from the moment that she told me Lena's birthday was December 5th that the relationship wouldn't work because she's a Sagittarius. But what could I do, besides talk with Amber for over two hours the other night when she informed me that things were over for good? She was very upset."

"I'm sorry to hear that," Brooke replied. And she was. *Lesbian break-ups are never* not *messy. Wait a second...Did Sandra say that Amber was dating someone named Lena and that* she *was a Sagittarius?*

Brooke realized that Justin had caught on too. He met Brooke's eyes and then cleared his throat. "So your daughter is..."

Sandra smiled at the display on her phone and then turned the screen to Justin and Brooke as her bracelets jangled. "Her," she finished. "My daughter is her. In the picture." She tapped the screen proudly. "I'm still trying to figure out how to send photos from my phone, but Amber sends me pictures sometimes. That one was a month or so ago, before a dinner date in Dallas with, well, the *ex*."

"Beautiful!" Justin exclaimed. He took the phone from Sandra's hand and studied the photo. "Your daughter is *beautiful*. Her eyes are such a unique color. Are they light brown, or...?"

"They're a light shade of hazel," Sandra replied. "Very light brown with remarkable emerald tones. Probably the only decent thing she got from her father. That man was *not* the marrying kind. Gave up life on the road with his folk band and realized how much he hated domesticity. He stuck around a while after Amber was born, but his spirit just wasn't meant to be tamed."

Brooke scooted closer to Justin and craned her neck over his shoulder. Justin glanced at her with a knowing smile and silently flicked his wrist so she could see the photo. Brooke raised an eyebrow at the grinning woman before her.

God, she is *gorgeous* she thought. She wasn't sure what she had expected, but natural, unfiltered beauty without the need for a lick of make-up and a sunny smile that beamed through the phone was not it. Long, straight honey-colored hair fell over her shoulders in light waves and naturally full lips made Brooke wonder for a moment why Sandra's daughter had never pursued a career in modeling. She could easily picture that same genuine smile in a United Colors of Benneton or Tommy Hilfiger print ad. *Whoever Lena is, she must have been a real idiot to let her go.*

The sudden clanging of the sliding glass door made Brooke jump as Dave walked into the house. Her face reddened as she realized she had been staring at the photo of Sandra's daughter for just a beat too long.

She smiled politely as Justin handed the phone back to Sandra and stood to help Dave with the plates of food. "She's very pretty," Brooke allowed.

Sandra met her eyes for a moment as Brooke recognized something akin to realization in her friendly gaze. *No* Brooke thought in horror. *I'm just being paranoid.*

"Thank you," Sandra murmured.

Dave, oblivious to the exchange, quickly handed Brooke a plate of perfectly charred chicken. "Got a hot plate, comin' through," he warned her. "Take what you want from it, but be careful with your fingers."

"Thanks, Dad," Brooke replied. She grabbed a pair of tongs from the center of the table and plucked two pieces of chicken from the platter.

"Everything, uh, good, Brookie?" Dave pressed in a low voice.

Brooke glanced up at her father and recognized the question on his sun-burnt face. *He wants to know how talking to Sandra went and what I think of her* she realized.

"Great, Dad," she reassured him with a grin. *...And the truth is, I kind of like her. She's quirky, but Dad is right. She's different. And, from what I can see so far, she truly cares for him.*

Brooke watched as her father nodded once and then sat back in his chair with a relaxed smile that she hadn't noticed before. *Maybe, just this once, Justin is right* she decided. *Maybe I need to loosen up a little.*

~

"EVERYTHING WAS SO GOOD, thank you again!" Brooke called over her shoulder later that evening, as she and Justin said their good-byes to her father and Sandra.

"We'll see you soon, sweetheart!" Dave called back. He waved as he slung his free arm around Sandra's waist. "Drive safe."

Typical of an Adriani meal, nearly three times the amount of food had been cooked than guests present. Brooke shifted the weight of the heavy Styrofoam container of leftovers in her arms as she and Justin reached her Lexus.

Once they were safely ensconced in the car, Justin turned to her excitedly. "Oh. My. *God*," he started. He paused, falling back against the passenger's seat dramatically, and placed his hand over his heart. "*Seriously*, Brooke. Sandra is fabulous. I'm so jealous of you right now. I wish *I* had a Sandra, instead of that miserable witch my father married. Every time I go up to Tampa for a holiday, she *always* asks me where my girlfriend is and if I'd like to join them for Sunday services. Their church, by the way, is very conservative. The woman has *known* I'm gay since the day she met me!"

Brooke threw Justin a sympathetic glance. "I guess when you put it that way, I could be doing a whole lot worse than Sandra for Dad, huh?"

Justin sat up. "You have *no* idea," he confirmed. "Says a lot about your dad too. You know, in case you ever make it a point to tell him that you're a lesbian."

Brooke rolled her eyes. "Justin!" She admonished him. "It's not that I don't want to tell him, it's just that..." she sighed. "I'll say something when I'm ready. Why rock the boat now, especially when he seems so happy?"

Justin sighed. "Your dad is obviously *not* homophobic, Brooke," he replied wearily. "He couldn't be if he's serious about Sandra, given the fact that her daughter likes women. Besides, as odd as their pairing may seem, she and your dad were totally giving each other googly-eyes throughout dinner. There really is a connection there."

Brooke took a deep breath as they cruised past a row of small, pastel-colored bungalows. Palm trees and thick tropical foliage dotted the square yards and wide screened-in porches seemed to invite passerby for a cold mojito and good conversation.

The moon flickered high and bright in the velvety night sky. Brooke tried to recall which phase it was from Sandra's shirt while ignoring the tugging anxiety she felt whenever she considered coming out to her father. Without a cloud above, tiny stars in navy sky twinkled for what seemed like eternity over the vast, still ocean that hugged the island just a few blocks over.

Brooke didn't realize something was amiss until she made her usual left turn down the quiet gravel road that led to her elevated duplex. With the other half of the home owned by a wealthy Cuban family in Miami who used it strictly for vacations and holidays, Brooke enjoyed the privacy of what often felt like a single family home.

Justin leaned forward and squinted out the window. "What's going on? Why are there firetrucks blocking my Mini Cooper in?"

Brooke slowed to a stop as they took in the scene. Two glinting firetrucks, their red and white lights easily slicing through the thick, humid darkness, had parked diagonally in front of the property.

"What the hell…" Brooke murmured. She rolled down her window as a fireman turned. "Excuse me, sir?" She called.

"Sorry ma'am, we can't let anyone cut through," the fireman spoke apologetically. "Pipe burst in the duplex and there's major water damage to the interior. My guys need space to turn off the water temporarily and locate the owners."

"Oh no, a pipe break?" Justin asked incredulously.

Brooke felt a sinking feeling deep in her gut. "I own #2," she replied quickly. "The unit on the right. What happened? How bad is it?"

The fireman sighed and scratched the back of his balding scalp. "We're not sure yet, but major leaks can be common in these older homes on the island," he answered. "Over time, pipes can corrode. Unless someone did some interior construction recently?"

Brooke closed her eyes and sighed. "The owners of #1 took down a wall a couple of months ago," she replied. "I'm not sure which contractor did the work."

The fireman nodded knowingly. "I would suggest getting in touch with them, ma'am," he advised. "Chances are that the superintendent might have accidentally hit a pipe. Hairline breaks, if not corrected right away, can be a ticking time bomb. All it takes is a little time and progression and the whole pipe will open right up."

"Great," Brooke replied faintly. She stared at the red Spanish-tiled roof of the duplex. "How bad is it?"

The fireman looked nervous. "I'd, uh, plan to stay somewhere else if you can for a while," he said with a nod. "I have a list of emergency water mitigation companies that I can give to you. I'd suggest calling your insurance company and getting someone out right away to start drying your unit. You want to avoid mold contamination. They will be able to give you an exact timeframe, but I'd say you may need to give them a few weeks."

"A few *weeks*?" Brooke repeated, louder this time. She quickly glanced at Justin to make sure she hadn't misheard. His wide eyes only confirmed that her hearing was, indeed, just fine. "That's crazy! Over some water? We're *surrounded* by water."

The fireman sighed. "Why don't you go ahead and check it out yourself?" He replied. "Should be fine, but I'll send one of my guys with you to be sure. You'll need to get some things anyway, I reckon. I'll get that list of mitigation companies for you."

Brooke threw herself back against the driver's seat in frustration as she quickly rolled up the window. "I can't believe this," she muttered as she parked. "Those *idiots* next door! You know, for all the money that family has, you'd think they'd have the sense to hire a *good*, reputable construction company. What am I going to do?"

Justin bit his lip. "Well, you have a couple of options," he replied carefully. "You're more than welcome to stay on the couch of my studio."

As much as Brooke loved Justin, the idea of crashing on someone's couch and sharing a tiny bathroom in a cramped apartment sounded less than appealing. "What's my other choice?" She asked reluctantly.

Justin threw her a half-smile. "One of the three spare bedrooms of the beautiful custom home we just came from, of course," he replied, as though the answer was obvious. "Maybe you'll be getting to know Sandra a lot faster than you thought."

CHAPTER 7

Amber idly twirled a lock of hair around her index finger and slumped lower in the hard blue airport seat. She glanced down at her phone and rested her head along the back of the metal chair. A cold breeze blew through the terminal as industrial-sized air conditioning units along the ceiling rumbled to life.

A thin sheen of sweat covered every inch of exposed skin. *I don't think it's dipped below 85 degrees in at least two months* she thought wistfully. *I'm going to miss Dallas, but this will be good for me.*

Amber glanced at the carefully encased Canon Rebel T5 digital camera snug in its padded black shoulder bag. While it was still considered a beginner's camera, Amber had scrimped and saved for weeks to buy it and had proudly used it nearly every day since.

As she triple-checked the side pocket of the camera bag for her extra memory cards, the phone in her lap rang loudly. *I really need to change my ringtone* she thought.

"Hey, Mom," Amber answered as she pressed the phone to her ear.

"Amber, my baby!" Sandra's excited voice flooded her ear from hundreds of miles away. "I wanted to give you a call before your flight. I'm so happy you'll be here soon; I've missed you something awful. I know you're young and it's important to have your own life, but I've so missed having my baby girl right across town."

"I've missed you too," Amber replied immediately. "Did you get my e-mail?"

"Yes, I have all of your flight information," Sandra assured her. "I'll be at Key West International to scoop you up later."

"Perfect," Amber replied gratefully. "I really appreciate you having me stay with you for the next six weeks. I know this was really last minute and your condo only has one bedroom and that little office area..."

"Nonsense, sweetheart," Sandra replied flippantly. "You know you're welcome anytime. But that was actually what I had wanted to talk to you about. Do you remember that man I was seeing? Dave?"

"Yes, you've been talking about him a lot these past few months," Amber replied teasingly. "Will I get to meet this mystery man while I'm there?"

Sandra was quiet for a moment. "Even better, actually," she hedged. "As you know, we've been seeing each other for some time and honestly...I just love him, Amber. I really do. He's a wonderful man and there's a chemistry that I haven't felt with another soul in so long. We click *so* well. Everything is just so *easy,* it all makes perfect sense with us."

Amber looked at her lap. Her comfortable black yoga pants stuck to her thighs in the early summer heat. "I'm happy for you, Mom," she replied with genuine conviction. "I'm looking forward to meeting Dave."

"Well, that's the thing," Sandra went on slowly. "We had a talk early this morning during one of our sunrise walks along the beach. He asked if I'd like to do sort of a *trial* situation in which I move into his house, perhaps for the summer, and we see how it goes. He has a beautiful home on Big Pine Key, just outside of Key West. It's very spacious with four bedrooms, two bathrooms, a gorgeous screened-in patio and pool..."

Amber wrinkled her nose at her mother's dreamy tone. *This is extra dreamy, even for her.* "Are you sure things aren't moving too fast?"

She asked. "I'm not doubting that Dave is great, but you've always enjoyed your independence. It's only been a few months."

So much for healing mother-daughter time, woman to woman Amber thought as she held back a sigh. She hated to be the one to bring Sandra down to Earth, but recent experience had taught her that everything wasn't always as wonderful as it seemed.

"You know, I've asked myself that," Sandra replied thoughtfully. "And I know that if I were the objective person here, I'd be wondering the same thing. But at this age, you just have to go with what feels right. Forget everything that you *thought* you had learned and follow your heart where the Universe guides you, because it will never lead you astray. Life is too short nowadays. What is the kids say, YOLO?" Sandra laughed and Amber couldn't help but smile.

"I'm glad you're happy, Mom," she replied honestly. "If you feel that this is right, then I trust your judgment. Maybe I just need to meet Dave and get to know him while I'm there."

"Of course you will, sweetheart," Sandra replied, a note of puzzlement in her voice. "After all, you'll be staying there now too. He knows you're coming; he was actually the first person I called after you made your arrangements because I was so excited. He helped me wash all the linens and steam-clean the carpets in the guest rooms. Normally, you would have your pick of the three but Dave's daughter has to stay a while because her duplex flooded last week. A pipe broke in the other unit..."

Amber listened for a moment in shock and then shook her head in disbelief. "*What?*" She cut in incredulously. "Wait a second, you're moving into Dave's house *now*? I assumed you would at least stay in your condo until I returned to Dallas. I don't even *know* this man, Mom!"

"Well, he's very excited to meet you, Amber," Sandra started, her surprise evident. "My intuition already tells me that you two will get on very well. Besides, I'd thought you'd be more comfortable there than in my little condo. You can spread out, have a room larger than that tiny office space to yourself and relax by the pool when you're not working. I thought you would have been happy, but you sound…irate."

Amber took a deep breath and then bit her lip. The unexpected and overwhelming feeling of tears in such a public space was unwelcome, but just a split-second away.

Mom and I have always been the best of friends Amber thought morosely. *And here I am, snapping at her because she's happy and in love. I don't feel like I'm going to cry because of her. It's* everything.

"I'm sorry, Mom," Amber said with a sigh. "I don't even recognize myself lately. These past couple of weeks have been so emotionally taxing."

"Oh, sweetheart, you've always had the kindest soul," Sandra replied gently. "You know I don't believe in hate, but I truly abhor the fact that someone has made you feel less than. You get here soon and we'll start healing, yes? Text me as soon as the plane lands in Miami, before you pick up the connection to Key West, just to check in. I'll be waiting for you."

Amber caught her reflection in the large floor-to-ceiling windows overlooking the steaming tarmac and sighed. Her hair was longer than it had been in a while. Natural streaks of blonde shimmered through straight, light brown locks that reached halfway down her back. Her face and arms were kissed a golden shade of tan by frequent exposure to Texas's omnipresent summer sunlight. She blinked and gazed at the view outside as flight traffic controllers in vinyl neon vests jogged around massive planes.

"Love you, Mom," Amber finally replied. "I'll be there before you know it."

As they hung up, she took one last wistful glance out the airport windows. A uniformed flight attendant had taken up temporary residence behind the wide terminal desk and she knew it would only be a few minutes until they began boarding.

Maybe Mom is right. The Universe doesn't lead anyone astray. Maybe Key West is supposed to be my very own Summer of Love. Not that *kind of love though. The love for myself that reminds me I'm worth it.*

Amber carefully stuck one of her earbuds in her ear as she made her way to the boarding line that was forming near the desk. For the first time in just over two weeks, she felt a strange but welcomed sense of calm and confidence. Falling in love again sounded perfect.

~

AMBER BLINKED and smiled lazily from the passenger's seat of her mother's little red Volkswagen Beetle. There had been something strangely comforting about immediately spotting the familiar car and its green and white "Visualize Whirled Peas" bumper sticker in the sea of traffic at the airport.

"Sorry," she yawned and then blinked again. "I'm exhausted. I guess that early morning flight did it for me."

Sandra smiled and squeezed her shoulder in reassurance. "I know, sweetheart," she replied. She slowly edged up a long, paved driveway before gently shifting the car into Park. "Welcome home. I haven't moved many things in yet myself since this is only a trial period for Dave and I. But you're welcome to look around and make yourself comfortable. Why don't you let me make you some toast and then you can pick a room and take a nap? Catch up on some sleep and rid yourself of the jetlag."

Amber nodded as she pushed the passenger door open. She stepped into the bright, moist humidity and peered at the large tropical home before them. Thick palm trees and foliage kept the house shrouded in shade and privacy. Tall white columns held an extended section of red Spanish-tiled roof over the wide porch, while double mahogany doors appeared to promise that the interior of the home was just as breathtaking as its outside.

Mom wasn't kidding Amber thought in awe. *This is one of the nicest houses I've ever seen. This rivals the old-money mansions in Highland Park and it's probably half the size.*

"Sounds good, Mom," she replied. She pushed a lock of hair out of her face before pausing. "Do you think I can get my bags later? I'm so..."

Sandra laughed and led the way into the house. "I know, I know," she interrupted. "You're so tired. My poor baby girl. You look wonderful, though, sweetheart. I can't get over how good your color is! You look very healthy, Amber."

Amber grinned as Sandra gestured for her to sit at a long granite breakfast bar. "You're just feeding my ego because you're my mother," she teased. "You *have* to say those things to me."

Sandra laughed and shook her head as she rummaged through tall white cabinets. "You are something else," she remarked. "Let me just find where Dave stashed those organic raspberry preserves we got from the farmer's market..."

Amber blinked as she realized how at home her mother had become with Dave. She surreptitiously glanced around the house as she eased herself onto a stool. Shining beige marble-tiled floors, impossibly high ceilings constructed from what appeared to be reclaimed wooden beams and bright, open spaces thanks to large windows made the home feel like an island paradise.

"How has your yoga been, Mom?" She asked. She grinned as she watched her fidget with a fancy-looking digital toaster.

I suppose there's something comforting about being with my mom and having her make me toast Amber thought. *Even if we aren't exactly in* our *home.*

"Wonderful, sweetheart," Sandra replied absent-mindedly. "I've never felt more mind-body balance in my life. It's opened up to a lot of self-discovery. I really hope you'll join me while you're here." She glanced up with a knowing smile. "Remember how we used to go four times a week when we lived closer? You even acted as an assistant instructor in the classes I taught in Las Colinas."

Amber smiled at the memory. *God, what happened to me?* Becoming a certified yoga instructor had been another unrealized goal. "And what have you discovered about yourself since getting back in touch?"

Sandra carefully placed two slices of bread in the toaster and opened the small jar of preserves. "There are so many big things that are going to happen in our lives," she replied. "I can feel it. I can't explain it, but it's almost like it's in the air. I'm excited. I'm thrilled to have fallen in love with someone so worthy, I'm excited for this next step in our relationship and I firmly believe there's a reason that you've made it here, Amber."

Amber eyed the glass of cold-pressed juice that her mom placed in front of her and then shrugged. "Sure, maybe it's a career-related thing," she decided. "Even though I'm technically working behind the scenes of the exhibition, maybe I'll make some valuable contacts or ..."

"Or maybe you'll meet a woman," Sandra cut in hopefully.

The crisp wheat bread popped up from the toaster and startled both Amber and Sandra.

"See, even the kitchen appliances think so," Sandra finished with a plaintive smile.

"When it's the right time, it will be," Amber replied after a thoughtful moment. "But I won't know until it's that time, will I?"

Sandra laughed in delight as she handed a plate to her daughter. "Oh, go upstairs and go to bed!" She exclaimed. "You're sounding more and more like me these days. I just hate to see you alone. You deserve a kind, loving partner."

Amber hopped off the stool and kissed her mother on the cheek. "Thank you," she replied. She bit off a piece of toast as she walked out of the kitchen. "You sound like you're trying to marry me off. And besides, the most important relationship is the one you have with yourself," she called as she walked up the stairs.

Sandra shook her head. "That's not a phrase you got from me, that one is from Sex & The City!" She called back. "I knew that! Now get some rest and make yourself at home."

Amber took another bite of toast and giggled to herself at her mother. She gently pushed open a door at the end of the hallway. An inviting queen-sized bed with a thick comforter waited in the far corner. A ceiling fan hung from high beams while a large window overlooked the patio and pool. Lush taupe carpeting was soft beneath her feet as she kicked off her shoes and set her plate on a bedside table. She didn't even have time to consider how foreign the strange bedroom felt as she pulled back the covers.

A loud male laugh echoing outside piqued Amber's curiosity. *The mysterious Dave?* She padded to the window and gently peeked between the long Venetian blinds. A man no older than 35 laughed again as he backstroked through the pool.

Definitely not *Dave* she decided. *That's strange. I could have sworn Mom said he had a daughter earlier, not a son.* Amber watched for another moment as the man rubbed a wet hand over his cropped hair and then gestured to someone out of sight.

"Come *on*!" He called. "You have two hours until you have to show those condos this afternoon. We have to get our mid-day workout in somehow, since you want to lay low from Sun Studios..." his voice faded and he rolled his eyes dramatically.

A figure stepped into the sun and carefully closed the backyard fence behind her. Amber barely registered the second person before she strode to the edge of the pool and decisively dove in. The dive itself was nearly perfect and Amber watched, rooted to her spot, as the distorted, fluid woman swam the length of the pool beneath rippling water.

The woman broke through the surface at the other end and laughed. Amber was taken by her sense of confident freedom as she threw her head back and tipped her face to the sun. Her features were thoroughly Scandinavian, with icy-blue eyes and high, prominent cheekbones giving her an air of cool beauty. Strong, sharp lines across her upper back and shoulders betrayed the toned muscles just beneath smooth ivory skin. The mysterious woman ran a hand through wet blonde hair and stroked her way over to her friend. Her defined arms sliced through the gentle water in slow rhythm and it was then that Amber realized she hadn't taken her eyes off of her.

"Fine, are you happy?" The woman replied with a laugh. "I actually forgot how much I love swimming, but we should make this quick. Sandra will be here any minute with her daughter."

Amber took a surprised step backward and let the blinds fall closed. *Dave's daughter* she thought as the realization hit her like a ton of bricks. *Who does not look Italian, as her surname would suggest, at all.* She shook her head as if trying to clear away the fact that, for possibly a *split* second, she had been checking her out.

Yeah, right she thought as she crawled beneath the covers of the bed. *My mind is loopy from the early morning flight. Mom is right. I just need a serious nap and all will be on its way to well again.*

Amber sighed happily and shifted further into the pile of pillows. *I guess it would be nice to be holding someone* she considered as she closed her eyes and drifted. *Instead of a pillow.* She shook her head again. *Mom is just getting to me. When it happens again, it'll happen. And it will be...*

"Perfect," Amber mumbled to herself as she quickly fell asleep.

CHAPTER 8

Later that afternoon, Brooke gently pushed open a door in the long, narrow hallway of the fifth story condominium she was showing to her newest client. Located just across the street from Smathers Beach, the sun-washed white building had recently been renovated from apartments to luxury condos. With a cursory glance, her eyes swept over the large guest bathroom.

"Here, we have a full bathroom," she turned confidently and spoke. "With a separate shower and jetted tub."

Her client, Adam Valdez, nodded once and stepped into the bathroom. He turned slowly and grinned. "This condo is beautiful," he remarked. "The owners have taken excellent care of it. If I remember from the listing, there's also a second full bathroom?"

Brooke glanced at the neatly-organized file in her arm and skimmed over the MLS sheet. She always preferred showing homes armed with the MLS information because listing agents often included additional notes about the property that wasn't publicly available.

"You're right," she confirmed. Leading the way to the end of the hallway, she gestured into a spacious bedroom. "And this is the master suite. There's a private bathroom in here, also full."

Adam walked slowly through the bedroom as he admired the clean layout and the beach view from double windows. "God, it's like looking out at a postcard or a watercolor," he went on as he gazed at the water. "I can't get over how gorgeous it is here."

Brooke smiled. *I love this part* she thought satisfactorily. *When the client falls in love with the home. I always know when they've found 'the one'. I can see it in his eyes, hear it in that dreamy tone of voice. He's already picturing himself here. It's just a matter of time and some paperwork formalities until we're at the closing table.*

"It *is* wonderful," she agreed. "Where did you say you were relocating from?"

Adam smiled. "Tucson," he replied. "My son and I. He's six and we're looking to make a fresh start. I went through a pretty rough split with my partner recently. As hard as it's been on me, it's been devastating for our son, Trey. My ex-husband can be quite vindictive and I'm certainly ready to get away from all the negativity."

By now, Brooke had heard a million and one different stories from a long list of clients as to why they were packing it all up and moving to Key West. Most of the time, she half-listened to their stories of former lives in places far and wide and smiled indulgently. She was always happy that they were joining the Key West community, but happier still that it would result in another transaction brokered by her.

This time, though, her heart went out to Adam as he described how withdrawn and reticent his son had become in recent weeks and how he hoped this fresh start would bring new beginnings for them both.

"I'm so sorry," she replied sympathetically. "It's tough, but I think you'll find that Key West is an incredibly welcoming and diverse community. There's so much for kids to do here and of course Duval Street is renowned for adult fun for the occasional dad's night out."

"Thank you," Adam spoke as he walked slowly into the master bathroom. "Oh, double sinks. That's a huge plus. Lots of countertop space too." He paused and turned. "I've been doing my research. I love how prevalent the LGBTQ community is here. Granted, almost any city is probably better than Tucson, but the diversity was a huge deciding factor too." He paused again. "God, I can't get over how large the rooms feel."

Brooke glanced at the MLS sheet again. "The master bedroom measures 16 by 12. I don't believe that counts the master bath."

Adam nodded in excitement. "Very large for a condo," he agreed. "And what did you say this one was listed at?"

"Right now it's at 400," Brooke replied smoothly. She didn't need to add the thousand at the end. She knew that most tourists curious about relocating to the Florida Keys often got sticker shock at the home prices. *You'd be hard-pressed to even find a manufactured home, a trailer or a condo out here for under $200,000* she thought ruefully. *Luckily, Adam sounds like he's done his research already.*

"But the listing agent's remarks do say that the owners have already moved back to North Carolina and are motivated sellers," she continued. "I'm thinking we have some flexibility to talk them down a bit."

Adam nodded once. "That's fine," he replied. He glanced around the condo one more time with a smile. "I wasn't keen on going over 375, but I really like this one a lot. As long as it will work for Trey and I, then I don't mind going slightly over budget."

Music to my ears Brooke thought as she breathed a silent sigh of relief. "That's great news," she replied as they walked into the tiled hallway. They paused as she quickly slipped the key back into the small metal lockbox hanging from the doorknob. "I know we've seen about five or six condos this afternoon, so if you'd like some time to think things over then we can reconvene early next week. We can start looking again or, if you end up deciding on any of the properties we've seen today, I can write up an offer."

Adam nodded as elevator doors opened quietly. Its interior was all glass and marble that sparkled off small recessed lights as they descended into the lobby. "I have to be honest, I think this may have been the one," he went on. "I also really liked the second-floor unit of the two-flat in Old Town though. It'll be a toss-up between those properties. When I get back to Arizona, I'll talk to Trey and show him pictures of each. I think we'll have a decision by Monday."

"Excellent," Brooke met his eyes with a grin. She stuck out her hand as they reached the lobby doors. "It was great to finally meet you in person. Can I give you a lift to your hotel?"

Adam shook her hand and smiled shyly. "Likewise, Brooke," he replied. "Thank you, but I have a late flight tonight." He hesitated. "Hey, I don't normally do this, but I was sort of hoping to explore the island before I have to get to the airport. Want to grab an early dinner? If you're free, of course."

Brooke thought for a moment. It wasn't common to socialize with a client even in laidback Key West, but she felt strangely comfortable with Adam and genuinely sympathized with him. *I feel like he could be a friend* she admitted to herself. *What the hell? Can't hurt to get a bite to eat.*

"You know, that's a great idea," she replied. "What do you have a taste for?"

"What do you recommend?" He countered. "From what I understand, the restaurants are plentiful and delicious."

Brooke laughed. "Luckily, I'm a bit of a foodie," she admitted. "There's a huge restaurant scene here, but it all depends on what you're in the mood for. Half Shell Raw Bar is one of the oldest restaurants in Key West. It's a casual place and I personally think they have the best oysters in town. They even hold shucking competitions," she paused. "Or there's El Siboney. It's a little off the beaten path, but they have great old-school Cuban food. And, if nothing else, there's always Seven Fish. Tiny place, but the best seafood on the island. My friend Justin waits tables there a couple nights per week for some extra cash. Sometimes if I'm lucky, he'll bring me a plate of leftovers that didn't get sold."

"That sounds good," Adam decided. "I love shrimp and scallops. I'm sure it's fresher than anything in Tucson."

"Seven Fish it is," Brooke agreed. They paused as they reached her Lexus and she nodded toward the passenger's seat. "Hop in."

~

NEARLY TWO HOURS LATER, Brooke hadn't expected to still be eating, drinking and laughing at Seven Fish. As she twirled another bite of seafood pasta onto her fork, she glanced out the window at the setting sun with a smile.

Who would have thought that Adam was so funny? She thought. *It may be the three mojitos talking, but perhaps I should hang out with clients more often. I bet I'd have a lot more friends. Maybe I'd even meet a cute, single...*

"This has *got* to be the best shrimp scampi I've ever had," Adam remarked, interrupting her train of thought. He took a long sip from his frosty beer. "Easily. Thank you again for the recommendation. I apologize for being so forward earlier. It's just that I'm making such a big move and I'm a little nervous about making new friends. Even though my ex-husband has made my life a living hell, I still have about four or five great friends in Tucson and it'll be hard to leave them."

"You're more than welcome," Brooke replied. "Truly, it's my pleasure. I've had a wonderful evening and would be honored to be your first friend in Key West."

Adam grinned warmly and clinked the neck of his beer bottle against Brooke's nearly-empty mojito glass. "To friends," he announced. "So, you know all about me and my hardships with my ex. What about you? Attached, unattached?"

Brooke shrugged and rolled her eyes. "Unattached," she confirmed. "I've been...enjoying my independence. I haven't been in a real relationship since leaving New York City five years ago."

"Wow," Adam looked impressed. "You don't miss it at all?" He sighed. "Maybe it's because I've been attached *too* long, but adjusting to being single has been tough. I've always been a serial monogamist. I would much prefer to fall asleep with someone rather than alone. I love having a boyfriend to do all of those silly couple things with. You know, cooking for him, going on vacations, that sort of thing."

Brooke pondered this for a moment. "I get it," she admitted. "Though I don't think I've ever been in love. Maybe once, in high school, with the first girl I ever had a serious crush on. You know, typical unrequited straight girl crush. That one felt like love, because it sure hurt a lot."

Adam smiled. "Love doesn't automatically have to equal pain!" He exclaimed. "Look at me. I mean, my ex-husband has been making my life a living hell and I still believe in love. It's out there. I know I'll find it again and I can't wait."

As Brooke glanced at the sunset again, she allowed her mind to wander for a few quiet, comfortable moments. In that split second, she imagined herself sitting on a beach towel spread over the soft white sand. The sun was sinking into the horizon, much like it was now, and candy-colored pastels streaked across the expansive sky. Palm leaves rustled in the distance with an evening breeze and the warm, salty waves lapped just inches from her toes. There was someone else too. A sweet, affectionate and beautiful woman whose face she couldn't picture relaxing contentedly in her lap. The woman's arms were wound around her neck as they lingered in their embrace, moved by the show that Mother Nature was putting on and breathless from something deeper than mere affection for one another that pulsed just below their skin.

"Brooke!" An excited male voice called out. "Hey, I didn't know you were going to be here tonight."

With that, the image in her mind's eye dissolved as quickly as it had appeared. The fantasy had been jarringly intoxicating and Brooke wanted it badly. She pasted a smile to her face and turned to the voice.

Justin leaned in and gave her a quick hug. "Sorry, I was just swinging by to pick up my check," he went on. "And I saw you over at your favorite corner table, so I wanted to say hi." He paused and took a long look at Brooke's dinner-mate. "So, um...Well, hi!"

Brooke, her mind still momentarily clouded by the fantasy, shook her head quickly. Justin's face had reddened and he quickly looked away from Adam before fixing his eyes on the table.

"I'm sorry, I just completely lost my train of thought," she spoke, forcing a laugh. "I don't mean to be rude. Adam, this is my best friend Justin. And Justin, this is my newest client, Adam Valdez. He's relocating here from Tucson with his six-year old son."

Brooke swore that Justin's face slightly fell. "Nice to meet you, Adam," Justin said as he stuck out his hand. "How do you like this place? I may be biased, but Brooke definitely took you to the..."

"Best seafood place in town?" Adam finished with a grin. He wiped his mouth with a paper napkin and shook Justin's hand. "It really is. Probably the best shrimp I've ever *had,* since Arizona isn't exactly renowned for its seafood. Once we've relocated, I can't wait for Trey, my son, to try the key lime pie. That kid has a sweet tooth a mile long."

Brooke laughed and threw a glance at Justin. "Funny, so does a certain thirty-three old *kid* I know!"

"You like sweets too?" Adam asked. There was a short, awkward pause as Justin opened and closed his mouth before the blush that had splashed across his cheeks deepened. "You two will have to tell me where to get the best key lime pie then. My ex-husband *hated* sweets. I think, in moderation or for a treat once in a while, it's perfectly fine to indulge yourself. Right?"

Brooke didn't miss Justin's eyes widening with the realization. *Oh my God* she thought as the meaning behind his odd behavior dawned on her. *Justin is into him. My best friend, who is never off-balance, is totally crushing on my client.*

"Right, yeah," Justin spoke quickly. "Indulging yourself is just fine sometimes."

A strange pause lingered over the table and Brooke watched as Adam held Justin's eyes for a moment. He quickly glanced down at the table with a laugh. "I look forward to hanging out with you two after we move," he replied honestly. "There's a lot to do in the meantime, but would it be okay if I added you both on Facebook? Just to keep in touch and maybe make some plans after Trey and I get settled in?"

Adam glanced at Brooke and then again at Justin, where his gaze swept his tanned face. Brooke forced herself not to roll her eyes. *What he really wants is to keep in touch with Justin* she thought ruefully. *He knows damn well that he and I will be in contact about the condo.*

"Of course," Brooke replied.

Justin blinked in surprise. "I, uh, sure," he stammered and then laughed at himself. "I mean, that would be great. Definitely."

Adam smiled and looked like he wanted to say something else, but decided against it. He grabbed the bill from the table. "I ought to get going so I'm not late for my flight home," he replied, sounding resigned. "TSA was terrible on my way here. I've got dinner. Justin, would you like anything?"

"Oh no, you don't have to do that!" Brooke protested. "I was planning to pick up dinner."

"That's really sweet of you, but I'm all right," Justin spoke at the same time. "Really."

Adam grinned and nodded at the hostess stand as he stood. "Nonsense, you've been so kind in showing me all of these condos," he replied. "Really, I know I have some specific must-haves and you've been great about making sure every place you've shown me meets those needs. Dinner is the least I can do."

Brooke and Justin blinked at each other as Adam ambled away from the table. Justin turned once and watched as he paid the bill.

"Oh my *God*, Brooke!" Justin whispered. "Did you see that? He just *paid* for your dinner and offered to buy mine! That was so sweet."

Brooke was impressed. "It really was," she agreed. "Though I think he may have been trying to be *extra* charming since you showed up."

Justin blushed. "No way," he shook his head vehemently. "Did you *hear* me? I couldn't get an actual word out. You didn't tell me that your newest client was so handsome!"

Brooke shrugged and wrinkled her nose. "I guess."

Justin sighed. "You are *such* a lesbian," he whispered. "*Look* at him. What do you suppose he is? Native American?"

"I think he's half-Hispanic and half-Caucasian," Brooke replied. "He showed me a photo his mom had texted him earlier of her and his dad with his son."

Justin bit his lip and appeared to deflate. "Oh, that's right," he muttered. "His son."

"Justin Cole!" Brooke whispered loudly. "What's wrong with that? A second ago, you looked just about ready to marry him."

"I don't know about kids…" he hedged. They both fell into silence as they watched Adam walk back to the table. For good measure, Brooke gave Justin a light kick to the back of his shin.

"Can I give you a ride to the airport?" Brooke offered. "It's not far. Well, I suppose technically *nothing* is far on the island."

Adam waved his hand. "Oh, that's all right," he replied. "I requested an Uber a second ago. You've already been so great, spending your evening with me. My ride should be here in about five minutes."

"It was nothing," Brooke replied. "It was great to meet you in person. I'll plan to hear from you on Monday or Tuesday about either of the condos you were interested in or I can follow up with you by mid-week."

Adam nodded. "Sounds good. I'm ready to get the ball rolling on this once I've made a final decision. New beginnings and all, you know?" Adam smiled at Justin, who Brooke was sure had melted into her side.

"New beginnings," Justin agreed dreamily.

As they stood at the entrance to the restaurant, they waved goodbye to Adam as his Uber arrived. A balmy breeze washed over Brooke and Justin as they stood for a long moment and watched the car fade into the distance.

Justin laid his head on Brooke's shoulder and sighed dramatically. "I think I'm in love."

CHAPTER 9

As Brooke quietly shut off her car and strolled up the driveway of her father's home, she tried to sort out her thoughts. The silvery moon was full and bright in the expanse of dark, cloudless sky above. The air was humid, still and quiet, without the rustling of breeze or the sounds of insects rummaging through nearby foliage. She felt inexplicably light, lighter than she could remember feeling in a long time, and wasn't quite ready to turn in just yet.

Though that could be the remnants of those three mojitos... She reminded herself as she slipped the key into the lock. From the looks of it, the inside of the house was dark. Brooke suspected that her father and Sandra had already retired to the master bedroom. It was then that she remembered, with a blink, that there was still one more person who may or may not be at the house.

Sandra's daughter she thought with a sigh. Brooke knew she had arrived today and hoped Amber was so jet-lagged that she went to bed early. *Not that I'm averse to meeting her* Brooke reassured herself. *I'll have to soon. But this is all so crazy. Dad with Sandra, Sandra moving in and now Amber staying here for the next six weeks?*

Brooke wondered for a split second if Justin had been right; if she could stand to loosen up and get out of her self-imposed bubble once in a while. She tried not to remember Amber's warm, striking eyes or her wide, contagious smile reflected in the photo that Sandra had shown them. Brooke didn't have much time to mull the confliction she felt as she froze at the sight before her. She blinked once, twice, three times to ensure the odd scene in the living room wasn't a Key West mojito-inspired hallucination.

It wasn't. Sandra turned gently, met Brooke's bewildered gaze and silently pressed her index finger to her lips. Her father was comfortably positioned on his back on a makeshift cot in the middle of the living room. He appeared to be asleep, with his hands resting gently over his slightly-protruding belly and a small beanbag pillow over his eyes. The room was darkened, save for five or six candles of varying colors that were scattered around the cot. The light from their flames danced across the living room walls and a large salt lamp that, to Brooke, resembled a rock cut from a cave gave off a pale pinkish glow at his feet.

"We're doing an energy healing session," Sandra whispered. "We're almost finished. I'm a certified Reiki master and Soul Detector®. Your father will feel much better after this."

"A soul detector?" Brooke repeated dubiously. She glanced at her father and then back at Sandra. "That's a real thing?" For some reason, she couldn't get the image of Sandra, wearing vintage detective gear and searching for souls with a magnifying glass, out of her head. Brooke bit her bottom lip to keep from erupting into laughter.

"Of course," Sandra replied with a smile, as if this was all very normal. "I feel blessed to be able to give healing to those who are accepting. My true calling has always been as a healer."

Brooke watched as Sandra picked up a deep crystal bowl and quickly dragged what appeared to be a mallet around its rim. "This is called a singing bowl," she explained in a whisper. "The sounds lift and remove stagnant energies while encouraging healing."

"Sound can do that?" Brooke asked as she raised an eyebrow. Deep, vibrating sounds emanated from the bowl and filled the living room.

"Sure it can," Sandra said kindly. She carefully set the mallet onto the hardwood floor and picked up a small metal tool. "This is a tuning fork. These create sacred sounds that resonate deeply into our core. If we're open, these sounds can penetrate invisible layers of our bodies to heal and balance."

Brooke opened her mouth to reply, but a loud snore escaped Dave's throat. Sandra glanced at him and then back at Brooke with a sheepish smile.

"Well, I guess his meditative state took him right to sleep," she went on with a laugh. "It's all right. He's new to this. The positive here is that he was able to release some built-up stresses and let go of a lot of those day-to-day emotions that take us from our true selves. He relaxed enough that he went right to sleep like a baby."

Brooke gazed at her father as he snored on the cot. "He *does* look comfortable," she admitted. *Maybe there's something to that* she thought. *I could use some day-to-day stress relief. Like father, like daughter, I suppose.*

Sandra glanced over Brooke's shoulder and her face lit up in an expectant smile. Without looking behind her, Brooke became acutely aware of a presence at the bottom of the stairs. As she simultaneously resigned herself to meeting Sandra's daughter while pondering the nervous drop in her stomach, the other woman padded to Sandra and gave her a brief hug.

Brooke stared at the floor as she watched Amber run a hand through her hair in her peripheral. "Late night healing session?" She asked.

Sandra nodded excitedly. "You can be next, if you'd like," she offered. "As soon as I wake Dave up and get him settled into bed. Give me five minutes?"

Brooke finally gathered the nerve to steal a glance at Amber. She flashed a smile and rolled her eyes good-naturedly.

"I don't think so, Mom" she replied. "Not tonight. I crashed out this afternoon and now I'm wide awake."

Sandra reached out and affectionately touched Amber's cheek. "All right, sweetheart," she replied. "I'm just glad that you're here now."

Amber smiled. "Yes, one layover, four screeching twelve-year olds on the plane headed to cheer camp and a much-needed nap and I'm finally here."

"No, you're *here*," Sandra continued insistently. Her soft smile crinkled the thin skin at the corners of her eyes.

"I..." Amber paused. "Oh, I know what you mean."

"You're *here*," Sandra confirmed. "Don't think about those self-imposed boundaries that we've been conditioned to think in terms of. Remove the label of Key West, or Florida, or even Earth. Take away those labels and where are you, sweetheart?"

Amber appeared to hesitate. "Here?"

Sandra grinned and nodded. "Yes, my daughter. You're finally here in the present moment. I can see clarity returning to your eyes."

Amber shrugged sheepishly and finally glanced at Brooke, who hadn't been expecting the sudden eye contact. She immediately felt a jolt of surprise that seemed to awaken her senses, before quickly forcing her gaze to somewhere, anywhere else in the room.

Sandra smiled knowingly and patted her daughter's hands. "I can see the change taking shape already," she replied. She gently placed her index and middle fingers along the space above and between Amber's eyes. Brooke felt inexplicably proud that she knew Sandra was referencing Amber's third eye. "You may not realize it yet, but keep your eyes open. You'll begin to feel the difference."

Brooke stood, rooted to her spot, as Sandra shuffled over to the cot and quietly began waking Dave. She stole another glance at Amber and decided that she had been bolstered enough by the drinks earlier to break the ice. *Besides, I* definitely *don't feel like going to bed now* she thought as she surveyed the strange scene again.

"There's some wine left in the kitchen from a dinner we had a couple of weeks ago," Brooke realized the words were out of her mouth before she had time to think. "I'm not really tired either. Drink by the pool?"

Her throat felt dry as she sensed Amber gazing at her. Brooke wasn't used to being assessed by virtual strangers, which, she decided, must be why there was that nervous pit in her stomach. She sensed Amber was trying to determine whether Brooke was friend or foe. Almost simultaneously, she realized that she really, really wanted Amber to decide that she was a friend.

After a split second, Amber grinned. "Thanks, that sounds great."

As Brooke led the way to the kitchen, she caught Sandra sneak a contemplative smile in their direction. She took a deep breath. *Yes, having a drink by the pool is simply an act of goodwill to help Amber feel welcomed* Brooke decided. *I'm just trying to be nice. Loosening up, like Justin suggested. After all, it would be rude to ignore her.*

CHAPTER 10

Amber watched as Brooke carefully topped off their glasses with the last few drops deep, maroon-colored liquid. She sat casually along the edge of the in-ground pool. She had rolled her jeans to her knees before gently kicking her feet beneath the clear blue water, relishing the warmth between her toes.

"Thank you," Amber murmured as Brooke handed her one of the glasses. She took a deep breath and gazed out into the darkness just beyond the pool screen. "This is relaxing. You must come out here often."

Brooke appeared to hesitate for a moment and then gently plopped down next to Amber before crossing her legs beneath her. "The pool is my favorite part of my dad's house," she admitted. "I own one half of a duplex in Key West, but it's under construction at the moment. Unexpected water issues. Definitely no pool like this."

Amber smiled and closed her eyes for a moment. The scent of salt from the nearby ocean lingered in the air and the still humidity wrapped itself around her like a blanket. "It's beautiful. Did Dave design it himself? My mom mentioned that he had been in construction."

Brooke nodded. "He did," she confirmed. "In fact, most of this house he designed himself. Built it from the ground up, the crowning jewel upon decades of long hours spent pouring his soul into his company and sacrificing that 9 to 5 life. He owned a construction company in New York City and, after my mom passed away, it really became his major focus."

Amber stole a glance at Brooke, who didn't appear mad or otherwise upset. She hugged her knees to her chest and thoughtfully watched the water lap against the other side of the tiled wall. She didn't have to say anything more; Amber realized the implication.

She must have been so lonely she thought.

"I mean, it's okay though," Brooke continued hastily. She blinked once and appeared to break from her thoughtful reverie. "His hard work and long hours helped him build an incredibly successful company. It allowed him to retire early and sell it for a nice profit. Not too bad for a first-generation Italian kid from Brooklyn."

"Is that how you got your name?" Amber asked with a teasing grin.

Brooke's face lit into an enigmatic smile. "Maybe."

Amber's mind wandered as she contemplated the woman next to her. *Okay, so I'd be lying to myself if I said I didn't find her attractive* she mused. The realization made her tip her glass to her lips and take another long swallow of wine. The crisp, fruity flavor bit at her palate, but was successful in soothing her. *That's the last thing I need. Another gorgeous woman who says all the right things, but is cold as ice in reality.*

Amber shifted uncomfortably. She hated that she noticed the impossibly natural ruby-reddish color of Brooke's lips as she gently tapped the rim of her wine glass against her chin in thought. For a quick moment, Amber's eyes slid down her neck and chest as Brooke leaned back onto her wrists, one of which was decorated with a thin bracelet. Even in the dark of the late night, she easily zeroed in on the rainbow-colored beads. Amber quickly averted her gaze and blinked at the middle of the pool at the unexpected confirmation.

"So, Dallas, huh?" Brooke asked. "That's a long way away from here. Congratulations on the job. From what I've heard, the Chamber can be very selective on their hires, so they must have really liked you." She paused and met her eyes. "That's pretty cool."

"Thank you," Amber replied. "It was time to do something...different. Maybe that sounds selfish, but I had been putting..." she sighed and chose her words carefully. "Someone else first for a long time. And she didn't necessarily deserve that from me, though I'm beginning to suspect blame could be placed on myself too. I had a lot of goals, but I put them on the backburner. I wanted to get my yoga teaching certificate and decide on a career path, but I was too consumed. And then it was easy to set everything aside for her."

Amber rolled her eyes and took another sip of wine. "They say hindsight is 20/20, right?" She went on. "This was a good opportunity to take back my sense of self, I suppose. I love photography. I plan to learn as much as I can about the Chamber while I'm here. Maybe next year, my photos will be chosen for the exhibition."

Brooke thoughtfully twirled the stem of her wine glass between her thumb and index fingers as she processed Amber's words. The buzzing of nearby cicadas and the gentle sound of pool water lapping against the vents created a relaxing background din that allowed her a few extra moments to reflect before speaking.

I wish she would just speak freely Amber thought. *She should really stop filtering herself so often.* Flashes of an unexpected feeling of want briefly touched her, but she wasn't sure exactly for what.

"I always wished I had an artistic talent like that," Brooke responded honestly. "Painting, photography, writing, singing, *something.* Unfortunately, I just never had the knack for the arts, aside from a great appreciation, that I seem to for business. If you have a passion for something, you're already worlds ahead of most people. It means your work will always be true to you."

Amber bit her lip. "I guess I never thought of it that way," she admitted. "If photography wasn't a passion, I would have left it behind long ago. It hasn't exactly paid itself back to me, you know? Still, I can't imagine it *not* being part of my life."

They lapsed into a moment of silence before Brooke slowly stood. "It's so quiet out here, isn't it?" She asked. "Sometimes it's one of my favorite parts of this backyard, sometimes it's one of the worst."

Amber tried to figure out what Brooke had meant by that as she watched her stand on tip-toes next to a stereo system near the sliding doors. It was only then that she noticed the black speakers wired at the corners of the pool screen.

"I've always thought it was a bad idea to let love become a dependency," Brooke continued as she fiddled with the radio dial. "That sort of mindset is dangerous."

Amber bristled. "There's no textbook way to love," she replied defensively. "It's completely unique and that's what makes it special. I don't know how else to care for someone than all the way."

Brooke glanced over her shoulder and fixed her with a look that immediately made Amber feel childish. *Just like Lena* she thought, Brooke's cool attitude well under her skin.

She finally settled on a radio station and took a sip of wine as she walked to the other side of the pool. Amber's mouth dropped open as music filled the patio.

No she thought. *It can't be.*

Brooke stopped short. "Are you okay?"

I didn't ask him his name, this lonely boy in the rain

Fate tell me it's right, is this love at first sight?

Please don't make it wrong, just stay for the night...

"The...The song..." Amber started, flustered. *What kind of cosmic shit is this?*

Brooke looked between the stereo and Amber, perplexed.

...All I want to do is make love to you,

Say you will, you want me too

All I want to do is make love to you

I've got lovin' arms to hold onto...

"I hate this song," Amber finally spat. She glared at the pool. "This is the worst song in the history of all bad songs *ever*."

"I mean, it's not my favorite..." Brooke agreed. Her voice trailed off and Amber realized too late that she sounded crazy. She closed her eyes in embarrassment as Brooke stood again and quickly switched off the stereo. "We don't have to listen to any music." She fixed her with a patronizing smile that Amber decided she probably deserved this time.

"Will you be at the party next Saturday?" Amber asked, trying for a change of subject. She slowly glided her foot back and forth beneath the water and watched the ripples wave until they faded into oblivion. Right then, she sort of wished she was one of them.

"What party?" Brooke asked.

Amber glanced at her. "The summer solstice party," she replied. "My mom mentioned earlier that she and Dave are hosting a get-together next weekend to celebrate the longest day of the year."

Brooke blinked in surprise. "It's the first I've heard of it. My dad always tells me when he's having a party."

Amber immediately realized she had said something wrong. The frown in Brooke's eyes told her that perhaps she was still adjusting to the relationship much like she was.

"They probably only decided today," Amber forged ahead quickly. "I don't know how well you know my mom, but she's infamous for last-minute shindigs and impulsive events. Two weeks' notice is actually pretty good for her."

Brooke stood abruptly and stretched her legs. "I'm sure you're right," she replied evenly. "I'm going to turn in. I have to spend most of tomorrow at my duplex sifting through water-damaged contents for the insurance company." She rolled her eyes. "Not my choice of Sunday activity, but I'm afraid it has to be done."

Amber felt the other woman walk carefully behind her and then hesitate. Seconds later, Brooke was halfway inside the house. Amber listened to the glass door slide into place as she stared at the distorted image of her feet beneath the water.

That went well She thought sarcastically. A streak of irritation flashed through her. *Does Brooke think that she's the only one getting used to changes?*

For a brief moment, Lena Mielkute's face flashed through Amber's mind and further dampened her mood. *Hot and cold* she thought. *I bet Brooke, with that gorgeous face and too-cool-for-school attitude, gets all the girls around here. And I'd bet money I don't have that she pushes them all away too.*

After another moment, Amber stood and hurried into the house.

She ignored the frigid blast of air conditioning against her wet calves as she raced up the stairs. She reached the landing as Brooke was gently closing her bedroom door behind her.

"Brooke." Amber stated her name once, her annoyance evident. It was only after she spoke her name that Amber realized she had no idea what she was going to say. She only knew that she was inexplicably irked by a stupid '80s song and the other woman's all-too-familiar attitude.

Brooke glanced up and held her gaze for a long moment. "Yes?"

The slight surprise in her eyes confirmed to Amber that Brooke was not accustomed to people challenging her. Amber sensed the provocation below the surface and straightened her spine. "They're crazy, you know?" She went on, throwing a pointed glance at the master bedroom suite. "But they're really happy too."

Brooke smiled, though it didn't quite reach her eyes. Amber's gaze didn't waver. *She wants a challenge, then she's got it.*

"I know," Brooke finally responded. Her tired grin appeared somewhat resigned. "Good night, Amber."

"Good night," Amber repeated softly. She listened to the door shut into its frame as she padded down the hallway to her room. Frustration mingled with intrigue as she settled into the guest bed.

An hour by the pool, and I still feel like I know nothing more about Brooke Adriani than before I arrived.

CHAPTER 11

"I can't believe my dad didn't tell me about this party," Brooke went on irritably, as she relayed the whole strange story of last night to Justin. "I mean, I'm staying here too."

Justin was quiet for a moment. "Maybe he was embarrassed."

Brooke scoffed. "Embarrassed? *My* dad?" She wrinkled her nose. "He's had plenty of parties here before. Why would he not want to tell me about this one?"

"I mean, it *is* a summer solstice celebration," Justin hedged. "Not exactly the loud Super Bowl parties or crazy Halloween costume parties that he usually hosts. He probably thought you'd look at him with that same Brooke face that you make whenever something seems strange or out of ordinary to you."

Brooke's mouth dropped open. "I do *not* make a face!" She replied indignantly. "So, what you're saying is that my dad feels uncomfortable telling me the things because I'm judgmental?"

"Well, I didn't mean it *quite* that way," Justin responded. Brooke could tell he was holding back laughter, but she didn't see what was so funny. "Sometimes you can seem a little...*closed off,* how about that? Especially when faced with sudden change or things you're not familiar with, because then you're not completely in control."

Brooke silently chewed her bottom lip. A sneaking suspicion told her that Justin had a point.

"And you do *so* have a face!" He went on, the grin in his voice now evident. "You know the one. Your left eyebrow goes up, there's this dark shadow that flashes through your eyes and you avert your gaze really fast before anyone can catch your expression, but it's always too late."

Brooke caught her reflection in a large rectangular mirror mounted over a heavy oak dresser in the corner of the guest room. Her eyebrow was quirked at least an extra quarter-inch and the tones of blue in her eyes had darkened considerably. She sighed and quickly looked away.

"All right, maybe you're on to something," she admitted. She paced the floor of the guest room. "Tell me you're coming to the party next Saturday. I have no idea what exactly is involved in a summer solstice celebration, but I could use the moral support. Besides, you never miss one of my dad's shindigs. You know they're always good."

Justin was quiet for a moment longer. Brooke didn't like the silence that filled her ear in place of her friend's enthusiastic reply. "I can't," he finally spoke apologetically. "Not next Saturday. I, uh, have plans."

Brooke sighed. "Well, why don't you just drop by after? You know my dad's parties never end early."

"I don't know," Justin replied uncertainly. "I don't think I'll be able to make it, Brooke. I'm not exactly sure when I'll be finished with, um, what I had planned for the evening."

Brooke plopped onto the bed and cradled the phone in her neck as she pulled on her favorite pair of white Nikes. "What gives with all the mystery, Justin?" She asked. Realization dawned on her as she sat up straight. "Wait, do you have a date?"

"Ummm..." Justin hemmed and hawed. He finally sighed. "Adam. From last night?"

Brooke's mouth dropped open. "My *client* Adam?"

"Yes," Justin replied with a touch of nervousness in his tone. "He sent me a Facebook message last night after he got to the airport. We were messaging back and forth for a while before his flight and then we talked on Skype this morning. Just, you know, getting to know one another. Anyway, Adam said he's flying back next Friday for a couple of job interviews and won't be leaving until Sunday. He asked if he could take me out." Justin sighed. "He's so romantic, Brooke. Despite everything he's been through, he still really loves...*love*."

"That's great, Justin," Brooke replied. "But you haven't even known the man for 24 hours."

"And that's why we're getting to know each other," Justin replied defensively. "We plan to keep talking regularly until his move. And then who knows? We'll see what happens. All I know is that there is so much about him that I like so far. He's one of the good ones, Brooke. I can feel it."

Brooke knew Justin was beyond objective logic. But there was also something in his voice that was a little bit contagious. *Who knows? Maybe it could be love* she thought. The faces of her father, Sandra, Justin and Adam flashed through her mind. *Perhaps Cupid has taken up residence in Key West.*

"Hey, you're one of the good ones too," Brooke reminded him gently. "You deserve the best. I'll make do at the party. Hopefully I'll have some great stories for you after."

"Thanks, Brooke," Justin replied happily. "You'll have an ally anyway; won't Sandra's daughter be there? Have you talked to her yet?"

Brooke fell back onto the bed with a heavy sigh. "Oh yeah, I have to fill you in on that too. I don't know what happened last night. It was...*weird*."

"Uh-oh," Justin replied. "Did you do you usual Brooke thing?"

Brooke scowled as she stared at the ceiling. "First I have a face and now I do a thing?"

Justin burst into good-natured laughter. "You know I love you," he replied between breaths. "But yes, you know, purposely maintaining distance and building a mental wall in your head. Brushing her off as soon as you don't agree or hear something you don't like. I've seen you do it a thousand and one times."

"Well, Dr. Cole," Brooke started. "As entertaining as you seem to think your findings on me are, I believe I had a right to be annoyed that not a word was spoken to me about this party. And she wasn't exactly friendly to me either. She has a strange contempt for '80s power ballads."

Brooke shifted uncomfortably as she sat up. *Okay, so maybe I was a bit short with her* she decided. For a split second, she couldn't think of a single good reason to be distant with Amber. Brooke wondered for a moment if her old rules of never giving away too much and keeping distance seemed a little…silly. It was a disconcerting thought.

"Well, save it and come downstairs. I'm pulling into the driveway now. Ready for a fun-filled Sunday listing out your water-damaged contents for Allstate?"

Brooke rolled her eyes. "Am I ever," she replied dryly. "Thanks for keeping me company. Not exactly a Sunday Funday."

"It was either that or a Law & Order: SVU marathon," Justin responded. "As much as I *love* me some Christopher Meloni, I felt like getting out of my apartment today. Though it *was* a narrow margin."

Brooke laughed. "Thanks a lot. I'll be right there."

As she quickly hung up and quietly closed the bedroom door behind her, she didn't notice Amber sitting on the bottom step of the staircase until she was nearly halfway down.

Brooke paused as Amber leapt to her feet. Her worn blue jeans were just a touch loose around her waist, but hugged her thighs. Two large holes had been precisely ripped over each knee and a white tank top showed off her strong, smooth shoulders and golden tan. A hint of nude lip gloss and a long, loose ponytail completed Amber's casual look.

Brooke tore her gaze away with the sudden realization that she found Amber in her jeans and ponytail far more attractive than any yogi in leopard-print pants. *Oh no…* The thought echoed in time with her heart. *Don't even think about it. Nice and welcoming, remember? Even though it didn't exactly end that way last night.*

"You take forever getting ready," Amber spoke plaintively. She smiled. "The morning is halfway gone and I'm guessing there's a lot to do at your duplex."

"Excuse me?" Brooke was sure she had misheard.

Amber sighed. "I'm coming with you," she continued, a little less confident this time. "Look, I know we're both in sort of a crazy situation here. But I thought you could use the extra help and besides, I start my job at the Chamber tomorrow and I'm kind of nervous. Anything to busy my mind and rid myself of those pre-first day jitters would be awesome. Cool?"

Brooke was flabbergasted. She had all but readied herself for a challenging six weeks after the way last night had ended. A flutter of intrigue warned her that perhaps there was more to Amber than she'd originally assumed. She opened her mouth and tried to recover.

"Of course," she replied with a quick nod and then paused. "Sorry. I'm not much of a morning person. It takes me a good hour to fully wake up."

Amber sipped something from a plastic travel mug and grinned. "Lucky you, there's a fresh pot of green tea on the stove," she replied. "I'm sure you're a coffee girl, but green tea has almost as much caffeine and it's packed with nutrients and antioxidants."

She's Sandra's daughter, all right. Brooke held back a laugh at the idea of green tea over black coffee.

"Thanks, but we can head out," she replied. "My friend Justin is helping today too. He's outside. My place isn't too far from here."

"Sounds good," Amber responded after another sip of tea. "Let's go."

As Brooke led the way through the foyer and politely held the front door for Amber, she fought the urge to smile, though she wasn't sure why. There was something oddly refreshing about the undeterred and sunny Amber that Brooke couldn't quite put her finger on, but she decided she liked.

Brooke took a deep breath as she watched Amber saunter down the driveway. *Well* she thought. *What had originally been pegged as a boring Sunday just became a lot more interesting.*

CHAPTER 12

As Amber slid into the cramped backseat of Justin's bright red Mini Cooper, she marveled over what had come over her this morning. Brooke had politely introduced her to Justin, but if he thought it odd that Amber was joining them, he did a good job of hiding it. Amber caught his curious glance in the rearview mirror as he backed out of the driveway, but his smile instantly made her feel more comfortable.

She stole a glance at Brooke in the passenger's seat. As usual, Brooke's body language betrayed nothing and relayed only cool steadiness and a sort of sensual fluidity that Amber tried very hard not to notice. She took a deep breath and ignored the fluttering of attraction deep in her chest.

Remember she warned herself. *Brooke may be beautiful, but she's just like Lena. The only reason you're joining them today is because you feel bad about the contentious end to the evening and allowing past emotions to get to you.*

Amber swallowed hard as she tried to convince herself that yes, she was only joining them to make nice. *Okay, and maybe you* are *nervous to start the new gig tomorrow. But mostly the first thing. And it* definitely *doesn't have anything to do with that undeniable sexiness that Brooke seems to carry.*

As Brooke and Justin continued to make polite conversation, Amber turned her head and watched as they raced past groups of palm trees. Their thick leaves were green blurs as Justin sped to carefully pass a slow-moving van on A1A. She swallowed hard and tried to forget the way she had lingered just a moment longer than necessary before going inside the night before. Just as she was allowing herself a moment to wonder about the searing heat that Brooke's lips could surely leave in their wake, the Mini Cooper abruptly stopped.

Amber felt a blush creeping over her neck, even though she knew Justin and Brooke couldn't possibly know just how far her thoughts had wandered. She blinked out the window and took in the large duplex on thick concrete stilts. Assigned parking spaces were neatly marked in the shade beneath the house. Two short wooden staircases on either side of the duplex led to what Amber assumed were private entrances for each unit. White vinyl siding and a charcoal-colored shingled roof made the home look clean and beachy. Amber couldn't help but smile. To her, it looked like a well-loved and neatly-maintained seaside duplex; something she would have seen on HGTV or in a shabby-chic design magazine.

Justin glanced over his shoulder and grinned as he threw off his seatbelt. "We're here."

As they walked up the stairs to the duplex on the right side, Amber wasn't sure what to expect upon walking into Brooke's home. She briefly tried to guess how many people had been inside her personal space and guiltily wondered if she'd overstepped by inviting herself along. After all, she had spent plenty of time at Lena's penthouse, but didn't realize until that last day just how unwelcome she'd been.

It doesn't take a genius to guess that Brooke is an exceptionally private person Amber thought. She waited as Brooke dug out her keys and unlocked the door.

Justin waltzed through the foyer and put his hands on his hips to survey the damage. Amber could easily tell that he had been there more times than he could probably count. She sighed and hesitated, suddenly feeling like the odd one out.

Maybe this was a dumb idea.

Brooke reached out and held open the door. She met Amber's eyes with a slightly puzzled smile. "Come in."

Those two words were all the invitation that Amber needed. She carefully stepped through the open door and took in Brooke's home. Tasteful and elegant were two adjectives that immediately came to Amber's mind, which she quickly realized could also describe Brooke.

Beige ceramic tile led from the narrow foyer into a spacious and bright living room. The walls had been painted in mute, neutral tones, which accentuated the bright white crown molding and tray ceiling with its recessed lighting.

"They didn't need to take up any of the flooring?" Justin asked incredulously.

Brooke shook her head. "Just in the two bedrooms where there's carpet," she replied.

"I'm going to run upstairs and use the restroom," Justin did a full turn as he surveyed the damage. "I'll see what we're working with in the bedrooms and then we can decide how to split this up."

Brooke nodded as Justin headed for the stairs. She glanced at Amber and half-smiled. "Little known fact. Ceramic tile is non-porous, so it doesn't get ruined by water or mold. It's also a really common type of flooring in Florida homes. I had been meaning to change out all the ceramic in here for bamboo, but I suppose it's a blessing in disguise that I hadn't had the chance to replace it yet. If this was all wood or carpet, this flooring would have been ruined."

Amber couldn't help but smile back. This time, it felt real. "What about the kitchen?"

Brooke made a face. "Yeah, well, the kitchen didn't fare so well," she admitted. "The cabinets will definitely have to be replaced. I think the restoration crew removed most of them already. Almost all of the drywall had to be cut three feet up."

Amber glanced at the eat-in kitchen, which had been cordoned off by long sheets of taped plastic. Brooke carefully peeled back a corner and peeked inside at the few dark brown cabinets remaining. Amber could easily picture how the kitchen had looked before, with the rich wooden cabinets contrasting against tan granite countertops and stainless steel appliances.

"Your home is beautiful, Brooke," Amber realized she had spoken out loud after the words escaped her lips. "I'm sure it will get fixed soon."

Brooke was quiet for a long moment as she gazed at the construction zone of a kitchen before them. She processed the scene much like Amber was beginning to realize she processed everything – With an air of quiet, contemplative coolness.

Brooke finally turned and shot her a small, unguarded smile. "Thank you."

The hallway suddenly felt hot and narrow as Amber realized how closely she stood next to Brooke. As she took a quick step back, her shoe landed on a loosened piece of thick industrial tape that had been used to secure long sections of cord for the fans and dehumidifiers. As the machines whirred loudly around them, she quickly stepped off the corner of tape but became caught in one of the cords. She stumbled as she tried to shake the cord from her ankle.

Instinctively, Amber reached her arms to catch herself against the wall. Instead, Brooke reacted quickly by grabbing one of her arms and placing her palm lightly along her hip to steady her. Even as she regained her balance, Amber felt oddly light-headed by the warm, steady hand on her waist and the sudden concern in Brooke's eyes.

"Are you okay?" Brooke asked.

Footsteps sounded from the stairs as Amber's face burned with embarrassment.

"Yes," she replied quickly, still dismayed by her reaction to the other woman's touch.

Justin cleared his throat. "So, um, where do you want us to start?" He asked. "We're only doing inventory on contents in the rooms with damage, right?"

Brooke nodded. "Right," she replied. "Bedrooms, kitchen and powder room."

"Okay," Justin mused. "So you probably have the most items in the bedrooms and kitchen. Maybe we should knock those out first. I'll start on the kitchen if you and Amber want to take the bedroom."

Amber knew Justin had no idea of the suggestive nature of his words, but her heartbeat immediately quickened. She silently begged her mind not to go there.

"No!" Brooke replied quickly. Amber watched as she stumbled over her words and tried to recover under Justin's curious glance. "I mean, the bedroom, there's so much stuff."

Justin looked thoroughly confused. "That's why I suggested that you and Amber go through all of those contents. I'll get the kitchen done and then help you two finish up."

Brooke looked thoroughly stuck. "All right," she finally responded after a moment. She quickly composed herself and threw a tight smile at Amber. "We got this."

Amber nodded. "We got this," she echoed, though she wasn't entirely sure. *Don't go there, mind* she told herself as she followed Brooke up a tiled staircase. *All you and my heart seem to do is team up and get me into trouble. Not this time.*

ROUGHLY TWO AND a half hours later, Amber felt as though they were nearly finished. The skies had darkened considerably through the wide windows of Brooke's bedroom and threatened an afternoon thunderstorm. Amber had finished inventorying the much smaller guest bedroom, despite the loud noises from industrial fans and drying equipment placed by the restoration contractors. The guest bedroom had been relatively easy, with not many contents. Amber could tell it was a place where Brooke didn't spend much time, which further solidified her theory that not many people ever made it inside her home.

She paused for a moment in the doorframe of the master bedroom. Brooke sat cross-legged on the concrete sub-floor and tapped her pen against the notebook she had been using for her inventory log. Long, straight hair fell over her shoulders like a rich, blonde waterfall and partially hid her look of fierce concentration. Amber watched for another moment as Brooke bit her bottom lip and blinked, her long eyelashes framing the thought in her eyes. In this position, alone and sitting cross-legged over a spiral notebook, Brooke looked almost vulnerable.

Shit. Amber swallowed hard with the knowledge that she found the image before her incredibly attractive. *Anyone with eyes could see that she's beautiful* she thought defensively. *My hormones and libido must be all out of whack after the last few weeks. Besides, her being attractive doesn't mean that we have anything in common and it certainly doesn't mean that I should have some sort of silly crush on her. I'll leave that to all the other lesbians in Key West.*

As Brooke bent her head again and jotted something in the notebook, she cleared her throat. "Is everything okay?"

Amber felt her face redden as she wondered just how long Brooke had known she was there. Brooke didn't meet her eyes, but instead smiled down at her notebook as she silently continued writing.

Double shit. "Oh, yeah," Amber replied quickly. "I'm done with the guest bedroom. Do you need some help finishing in here?"

Brooke finally looked up and briefly met her eyes. "Of course, thank you," she spoke. "Umm…" She looked around as her gaze finally settled on the walk-in closet. "I'm almost done with the closet. There's a couple of cardboard boxes I haven't gotten to yet. It's all old stuff from New York City that I packed away and mostly forgot about. Do you mind glancing through?"

Amber shook her head. "Not at all."

She walked to the closet and pulled out the first cardboard box. It was already open, so Amber dragged it to the edge of a suede chaise positioned near a large window. The sky was an angry gray-black and clouds swirled ominously as gusts of wind pushed them across the horizon.

Amber glanced at the modest stereo in the corner. "I think we're going to need music for this."

Brooke raised an eyebrow. "Music to unpack a box?"

Amber shot her a smile as Janis Joplin's bluesy tone emanated from the speakers. "A little bit of chocolate and the right music can make you do anything."

Brooke laughed good-naturedly. "Do you have evidence to back that statement?"

Amber closed her eyes for a moment as Janis's raw, gritty voice filled the room. "Oh, yes."

Brooke shook her head as she turned back to her notebook, but the smile was unmistakable. Amber took a deep breath and blinked as the iconic image of The Beatles crossing Abbey Road stared back at her from the box. She gingerly fingered the thin, square record cover. "Beatles fan?"

Brooke glanced up quickly, but couldn't hide her excitement in time. "Oh my God, the vinyls!" She squealed. Amber was taken aback at the thrill in her voice. It seemed to go directly against the image of her that Amber had created in her mind. "They didn't get damaged, right? *Please* tell me they aren't ruined. Some of those are my mom's. Original, from the '60s through the '80s. And then I started adding to the collection in college because I realized how much I *loved* the sound of a record. An actual record, played on a turntable with a spindle and an arm," Brooke gushed. "It's gritty and it's so *real*. It sounds silly, but they make me feel closer to my mom. Like the record collection is something we worked on together."

It wasn't until Brooke paused for a moment that Amber realized how much she enjoyed this hidden side of her and how contagious her unexpected show of enthusiasm was.

Amber turned the record over in her hands. "I don't see any damage." She glanced over as Brooke seemed to deflate with relief. "And it's not silly at all. I can't believe you have this record. This is one of my all-time favorite albums *ever*, in the history of, like, ever. I mean, *Come Together? Oh, Darling? Here Comes The Sun?* Easily the best Beatles album."

Brooke gazed at the record thoughtfully and then shook her head quickly. "As much as I love Abbey Road, I don't know if that one is my favorite. There's almost too many to choose from. Rubber Soul, Sergeant Pepper's Lonely Hearts Club Band...No, wait!" She paused and grinned for dramatic effect. "The White Album. For sure. Hands down. The White Album is the best Beatles record."

Amber was already shaking her head. "Wait, wait," she countered, as she felt herself become inexplicably caught up in the excitement of shared musical taste. "I agree, *but* there's no comparison to The White Album. You can't count it as just another of their records. It's massive! There's, like, thirty songs on it."

Brooke nodded in agreement. "You're right. Totally in a class all its own."

Amber carefully placed Abbey Road on the floor and then laughed at the next record in the box. She held it up with a rueful roll of her eyes. "The White Album. Can we at least agree that George Harrison was the coolest Beatle of them all?"

Brooke sat up so quickly that her pen rolled across the floor. "No way," she replied immediately. "They're *all* geniuses, but can you really argue against Lennon? John Lennon is an icon."

Amber considered this. "Sure, but George was always the one who slipped under the radar and then came out with something beautiful like *While My Guitar Gently Weeps*," she countered.

Brooke's mouth dropped open. "Great song, but John Lennon's solo career was *amazing*," she replied. "As a free artist, his creativity was unlimited. None of the others ever matched his solo career and he's been dead for over thirty years."

Amber laughed. "Okay, okay," she conceded. "As much as I love George, I can get with you on this one." She placed The White Album on the floor and plucked Rubber Soul from the box. "Though I was never a big fan of *Jealous Guy*. He's basically apologizing for being an over-possessive jerk."

Brooke sighed patiently. "He was a man hopelessly in love. Can't most people relate to that? All those emotions making you sort of crazy? Doesn't it make you do things you wouldn't normally ever consider?"

Amber bit her lip as her mind flickered over Lena. "Yeah," she replied. "You're right."

She rifled through the next few records and felt Brooke watching her appraisingly from the floor. *I have to admit, Brooke's taste in music is not bad* Amber thought. She squinted at a stained corner of an Adele record before placing it with the others. *In fact, it's pretty good.*

"You said last night that you just got out of something?" Brooke asked casually. She didn't meet Amber's eyes and instead inspected her thumbnail closely.

Amber blew out her breath. "Yeah," she muttered as she added Alanis Morissette's Jagged Little Pill album to the list.

"It ended badly?" Brooke asked.

Amber nodded. "About as badly as it could have possibly ended," she replied. "Without, you know, us ending up on an episode of *Snapped*."

Brooke raised an eyebrow. "That awful?"

"Yeah," Amber muttered again. "I thought it was something special and she, on the other hand, wanted something to distract her from the long-term relationship she was in. I was told they had broken up and I guess believing that was naïve. I think she was attracted to the whole clandestine, secret romance aspect of having an affair. She said all the right things and I wanted to believe her, so I was toast."

Brooke winced. "Sorry," she replied gently. "I hope it wasn't too messy."

"It was," Amber continued with a short laugh. "Her girlfriend unexpectedly came home the morning after one of our nights together. I had to hide in their closet and even then, I got found out because their dog..." She abruptly stopped and wondered if she should continue. She was feeling more comfortable with Brooke, but was still acutely aware of the repercussions for trusting too soon.

Brooke met her eyes questioningly. "Their dog...?" She asked.

Amber laughed and shook her head. "I don't know why I'm laughing," she admitted. "It isn't funny. Maybe it'll be funny in a year or two, but right now it's not. Their dog found an, um, undergarment of mine. And, once again, I was toast." She sighed as the nervous laughter subsided. "Honestly, I'd never hated myself as much as I did leaving their building that morning. And I hated Lena for making me lose my self-respect."

"Lena?" Brooke asked.

"From Lithuania," Amber clarified. "That's her name. We worked at the hospital together. Technically, I'm taking a short-term leave of absence. I haven't even thought about what it'll be like when I go back."

Amber's stomach turned at the thought. She neatly stacked the records together and placed them back into the cardboard box. "You and your mom's collection is phenomenal, by the way. You have just about the best taste in music of anyone I think I've met."

Brooke blinked, but didn't break her gaze. "That's sweet," she replied. "And Amber? Lena from Lithuania was an idiot for not seeing what she had in front of her. What I should've said last night was to not blame yourself for her. If she was selfish before you and selfish with you, then she'll be selfish until the end. You can't blame yourself for people like that."

"That's sweet," Amber replied with a smile, coyly parroting Brooke's words back to her. "But you don't have to say that. I should have seen it for what it was. What can I say? Rose-colored glasses."

Brooke chewed her bottom lip. "But that's a *good* thing, Amber," she replied. "It's great that you still see the world that way. Not many people do. It's one of those unique things that makes you who you are. Don't lose that because of someone else. Find someone who loves that part of you, *all* parts of you."

A stretch of silence lingered between them for just a beat longer than necessary. "What about you?" Amber continued quickly. She glanced pointedly at Brooke's beaded bracelet. "I don't think you've ever mentioned a girlfriend or ex-girlfriend."

Brooke thoughtfully fingered the tiny multi-colored beads that encircled her wrist. "I haven't had a girlfriend since before leaving New York," she admitted. "First, I wanted to establish myself here.

Then I wanted to focus on my career. After that, time just kept going by. I never realized exactly how long, because I've always had plenty of love in my life. From my dad to Justin to extended family…" Her voice trailed off.

"Being with someone doesn't have to equal dependence," Amber replied. "Despite what you may believe. Not that I'm the greatest one to listen to on the subject, considering my recent history." She shook her head. "There's something to be said for real closeness though. That intimacy when you're with someone you truly love. Not just sex. *Intimacy*."

The air in the bedroom seemed to be growing hotter and more humid as raindrops splattered urgently against the windows. "I don't think I'd be a very good girlfriend," Brooke replied with a shrug. "I wouldn't even know *how* after this long."

Amber reached into the box and pulled out a stack of photos. They were the old kind that had been printed at a grocery store and were still kept in a long yellow envelope bearing the Kodak logo. "Good thing these photos don't look damaged," she remarked. Amber carefully flipped through them and paused as one glossy image struck her.

A girl no older than nine or ten was wearing a nightgown and standing next to a large bed. Her blonde hair and ice-blue eyes were a stark contrast to the navy blue of her pajamas and the heavy oak headboard that stretched across the wall. In the bed, a woman had leaned toward the girl and wrapped a thin arm around her waist. The girl's tiny hand held the woman's other hand and their heads were tipped closely together. They both wore wide smiles; the girl's grin missing one bottom tooth.

Definitely Brooke Amber realized.

She held the photo out to her. "Is that you and your mom?"

Brooke took the photo and stared at it for a long moment. "Yes," she replied. "She was already sick here. This was right after we brought her home from the hospital, where she had surgery to remove the tumors from her ovaries."

"She was beautiful," Amber spoke with a smile. "You two look alike. Same features, same eyes and everything. Was she Scandinavian?"

Brooke nodded and smiled faintly. "Her parents had emigrated to New York from Norway before having my mom and my uncle. She was always smiling," she continued with a sigh. "At least, she always was around me. Even though I realize now how much pain she must have been in, she never let me catch her struggling."

"Maybe it wasn't so much that," Amber said gently. "As it was that you actually brought that smile out of her. You were her daughter and she obviously loved you very much. Maybe every time she saw you, she just couldn't help but smile. *Despite* the pain."

Brooke was quiet for a long moment and finally met Amber's eyes. Her gaze was wide and unguarded as she nodded. "I never really considered that," she replied. She took a deep breath and smiled. "That's a nice thought."

A clap of thunder shook the duplex. Amber stood and began carefully repacking the box. "Will this be safe back in the closet?"

Brooke slowly unfurled her legs and stretched as she stood. "The closet is fine. I'm, um, going to keep this one with me."

Amber half-turned and saw the photo still in Brooke's hands. She nodded as an unexpected swell emotion tightened her chest. "You should do that," she agreed and then paused. "Are there any other boxes to go through?"

Brooke shook her head. "There's another box with more old photos, but I'll go through that another day." She smiled, but Amber recognized a brief shadow of sadness behind her eyes that she hadn't seen before.

Or maybe what I was so quick to chalk up as coldness was actually pain. Amber suddenly felt guilty for last night's kneejerk assessment that Brooke was an ice queen. It wasn't lost on her that somehow, during the quiet darkness of the storm, she had begun to crack Brooke's formidable shell.

Amber stole another glance at Brooke as a streak of lightning lit the room in a dazzling glow. She briefly wondered how it would feel to casually pull the other woman to her and gently kiss that dimple at the corner of her mouth. Were Brooke's lips as soft as they looked?

A beat had barely passed before Justin's hurried footsteps clambered up the staircase. "Hey, check it out!" He called in excitement. "I found something!"

CHAPTER 13

Justin paused in the doorframe to catch his breath. "Look, I found Evangeline's twin sister, Ernestine!"

He proudly held the five-inch hula statue in his palm. "By the way, a bottom drawer in the powder room is *no* place for Ernestine. If I had known you were mistreating her, I would have taken her myself..." Justin's voice trailed off as he blinked at them. "You two look so serious."

"Who's Evangeline?" Amber asked at the same time.

"No, this is *Ernestine*," Justin corrected her. "Evangeline is in Brooke's car."

Brooke shook her head as the hula doll bobbed silently in his outstretched palm. "I actually forgot there was a second one."

Amber glanced back at Justin, her eyes falling to his hand, and then cocked her head. "So, let me get this straight," she finally spoke. "You two *named* the Hawaiian doll?"

Justin chuckled. "Brooke's right, there are two," he admitted. "Evangeline lives on Brooke's dashboard. She says it's her good luck charm or something. I always wondered what happened to Ernestine." He sighed sadly. "Now I know. She was relegated to a life face-down in a bathroom drawer." He straightened and then smiled at Amber.

"Long story short, it goes back to the first night that Brooke and I met. She had just moved here from New York and I was bartending at Aqua Nightclub. She would stop by often. She was always alone and would sit at a corner table, near the bar and away from the stage. Brooke would nurse her drinks *all* night. I hadn't seen her around before, so we started chatting and became fast friends."

Brooke caught the quick look that Amber stole at her and felt a flash of uncharacteristic shyness. She grinned at Justin. "And the rest is history, right?"

Justin nodded. "One night we had a drag performer from out of town. He was this crazy queen who arrived dressed in full-on Hawaiian hula garb. He was scheduled to be the first on stage, but became irate because there weren't many people in the club yet. He thought he was a celebrity or something. Anyway, Brooke was in her usual spot at the bar and she and I were discussing suspicions I had that my cousin was gay. Which, by the way, I was correct about. He came out last year and I'm no longer the only rainbow sheep of the family."

"We *are* everywhere," Amber replied. "Good for you."

Justin placed a hand over his heart. "Why, thank you," he replied. "So, this crazy drag queen had a complete meltdown right there on stage. He had a bunch of these cute little hula dolls that he was planning to hand out to the crowd. I think. Or maybe he just always travels with a duffel bag filled with plastic hula dolls. Anyway, he started throwing these dolls into the crowd. Like, *really* chucking them hard. Thankfully, two of our bouncers were able to haul him off stage pretty quickly, but not before poor Brooke got beaned right in the side of the head by a flying hula doll." Justin's voice broke off into laughter.

Brooke smirked as she remembered the wild evening like it was yesterday. "So I took her home with me," she interjected amusedly. "Coincidentally, she's the *only* girl I've ever brought home from Aqua. Justin and I had a good laugh about it and, after a couple more drinks, we decided to name her. Somehow, we came up with Evangeline. She's been on my dashboard ever since." Brooke glanced down at her hands in embarrassment. "It's kind of silly and dumb, but, you know, it was one of those things..."

She glanced up and met Amber's grin. "That's not dumb," Amber replied. "That's an awesome story." She paused and her eyes sparkled with mirth as she held Brooke's grin for a moment longer. "Silliness is okay sometimes, Brooke. I promise I won't tell anyone."

Amber's teasing sarcasm cut deeply through Brooke and hit her square in the chest, causing a fluttering sensation that she quickly told herself was *not* butterflies.

"Oh, and then Justin found Ernestine later that evening," Brooke finished quickly. "He was walking to the other side of the bar and almost stepped on her. Somehow, one of the hula dolls ended up flying all the way over the other side of the bar..."

"...That queen had a damn good arm on her, that's for sure," Justin cut in with a serious nod.

"...So he picked her up and dusted her off," Brooke concluded. "Of course we had to name her too. And that's the whole sordid tale."

Justin gently placed Ernestine on a side table and patted her tiny head. "I'm hungry," he announced as he placed a hand over his stomach and made a face. "Any chance you two are up for grabbing a bite to eat?"

Brooke stood quickly and brushed off her pants. "I didn't realize how late it got," she replied apologetically. "I wanted to take you both to dinner for helping me today. I know there's a million other things you could have done with your Sunday, but I appreciate the company." She paused as her gaze landed on Amber and stayed there for a moment longer. She swallowed hard and tore her eyes away. "I'm sure it would have taken me much longer on my own. What do you have a taste for?"

Justin and Amber looked at each other and then Amber shrugged and smiled. "Something on the water?" She asked. "I can't believe I've been here over 24 hours and I haven't made it to the beach yet. I'm so landlocked in Dallas that anytime I'm near water, I want to be right by it."

Brooke exchanged a glance with Justin. "Are you thinking what I'm thinking?"

"Schooner Wharf Bar," Justin replied with a knowing nod. "You may have heard of it. It's pretty popular with the tourists, but we have a great time whenever we're there. The food is good, the music is live, the patio is casual and you can hear the water just a few yards away."

Amber grinned. "I'm sold."

As Justin led the way down the hallway, Brooke politely paused to allow Amber to pass through the bedroom door first. A sliver of pleasant surprise snaked up her spine as Amber lingered in the door-frame and fell into step next to her. Brooke fought the sudden urge to casually sling her arm around Amber's waist or gently place her palm against her lower back. The thought of touching her seemed to elicit strange bursts of excitement deep in her chest, ones that felt disconcertingly different from the excitement of yoga with Lydia or a casual meeting with someone else.

Brooke took a deep breath and shoved her hands into her pockets instead. She forced her thoughts away from the shy smile playing at Amber's lips and the silly definitely-*not*-attraction she felt.

I barely know her she concluded. *And isn't that how I prefer it?*

CHAPTER 14

As they walked outside to Justin's Mini Cooper, Amber stopped short. She turned her face up to the sky and wrinkled her nose in confusion at the rays of sunlight peeking between clouds.

"Wait a second, wasn't it pouring rain a few minutes ago?" She asked as she turned slowly.

Brooke watched her for a moment, all warm evening sun sparkling off her face and shining from her hair. "Welcome to Florida," she replied with a wry smile. "Where torrential downpours appear at random and then disappear faster than they arrived."

They pulled into Schooner Wharf Bar in what felt like just a few minutes. The restaurant was on a narrow corner that faced a boutique hotel on one side and a harbor on the other. As they parked and walked casually across the street to the restaurant, Brooke stole a glance at Amber. She appeared to be drinking in the sight of sailboats parked neatly at their docks. They bobbed gently over clear blue water, the tops of their sails stretching into an endless deep orange and light pink sky. The sun loomed just out of reach at the horizon as civil twilight blanketed the island.

They walked directly to the patio, where a bored-looking teenaged girl leaned against a modest podium. She snapped a wad of gum and gestured for them to help themselves to an open table. A couple of older men in Bermuda shorts and tie-dyed t-shirts tooled around a low wooden stage that faced the patio. Their necks were bent as they carefully tuned their guitars and strummed test notes.

Brooke led them to a scarred wooden table in the back corner. It faced the left side of the stage, but it was far enough away that it would allow the three of them to hear each other over the band.

"Is this okay?" She turned and asked. *Maybe Amber wants to be closer to the music.* Brooke realized the idea of not being able to continue talking to Amber disappointed her, but she quickly dismissed it.

To her relief, both Justin and Amber nodded their approval and made themselves comfortable along the wooden benches at either side of the table. Tiny paper lanterns strung along the beams of the patio swung gently in the evening breeze and illuminated the tables in twinkling pink, green and blue lights. The scent of salt and seawater hung in the humid island air and Brooke breathed it in deeply.

"This is perfect," Amber spoke, taking the words right from Brooke's mouth. She grinned and picked up a laminated menu from the center of the table. "Seriously. I can't think of anywhere else in the world I'd rather be right now."

Amber's sincerity made Brooke bite back a smile she hadn't been expecting. She quickly flipped over the drink menu and perused the evening's house specials. As she opened her mouth to reply, Amber spoke first.

"Crab cakes," she announced confidently.

"I'm sorry?" Brooke asked in mild confusion.

"That's what I'm having," she clarified. "I bet the crab cakes here are to die for. Dallas has a couple of good fish places, but there's nothing like fresh seafood by the ocean."

Brooke nodded. "Can't go wrong with that," she agreed. "So I take it Dallas is very different from Key West? I've never been."

Amber nodded. "For starters, it's landlocked. There are no palm trees. You can't smell the ocean from literally *everywhere* you stand. It's hot, but the heat is dry." She sighed dreamily. "This is world's away from what I've known. No wonder my mom fell in love with it so quickly."

"Your mom is *wonderful*, by the way," Justin cut in. "I met her a couple of weeks ago when Brooke and I went over for dinner. Sandra is a doll. Really, you both are."

Amber blushed. "Thank you," she replied. "My mom *is* pretty awesome. We've always had a really positive relationship, even when we've struggled. In fact, the times that we struggled a little are actually the times I remember us being the closest..."

Her voice trailed off and Brooke swallowed. She didn't know a thing about struggling financially and, for the first time, she felt acutely aware that others hadn't grown up as fortunate.

She wondered what Amber had thought of the house, the pool, the gaudiness of it all as a belated feeling of embarrassment washed over her. It was quickly replaced, however, by something Brooke didn't give freely: Admiration.

"And just what are *you* so deep in thought about?" Justin's voice cut through Brooke's consciousness as she rolled her eyes.

"Crab cakes," Brooke responded mysteriously. "I'm thinking about ordering them too."

Justin snorted. "Yeah, *right*," he laughed. "Well, I believe I'm well overdue for a margarita. And you know I can't turn down the tuna nachos here."

Brooke groaned. "You get that *every* time," she replied. "Why bother looking at the menu?"

Right then, the band started their set with the instantly recognizable intro riffs to "Sunshine of Your Love" by Cream. Justin's retort was drowned out by the excited cheer from tables closer to the stage.

Amber turned to Brooke and started to say something, but she didn't quite catch it.

"Sorry, what was that?" Brooke apologized, as she ducked her head closer.

Amber leaned in so close that Brooke could smell the gentle strawberry-mint scent of her conditioner. "I asked if you like this song,"

Amber spoke louder. "I didn't see a Cream record among your collection," she finished teasingly.

Brooke laughed. "I love classic rock," she admitted. "What can I say, I was raised on a steady diet of it. It stuck with me."

"I was too!" Amber exclaimed. "I guess that's one thing that your dad and my mom have in common."

Brooke nodded. "That's something," she agreed.

"Uh, Brooke..." Justin started warningly.

"They do seem happy together," Brooke finished after a thoughtful moment.

"Brooke..." Justin tried again. He nudged her ankle beneath the table.

Brooke glanced at him and blinked at the look on his face. Justin's blue eyes were as wide as saucers as he stared over her shoulder.

As she turned to see what he was staring at, Brooke immediately recognized the light sound of flip-flops against the rocky gravel and the tinkling of several thin silver bracelets.

Oh, no... she thought.

Lydia stopped short at the head of their table and fixed Brooke with a pointed look. Both of her hands rested on her hips as she silently glowered.

Amber glanced between Lydia and Brooke, but remained silent.

"Here we go," Justin muttered to the table.

"Small world, isn't it, Brooke?" Lydia started, her voice dripping with sarcasm. "I haven't seen you in yoga in, I don't know, *weeks* but here you are at Schooner Wharf."

"Really, I..." Brooke started and then sighed. *What? I'm busy? Work is crazy? I haven't had the time? The same old excuses sound just like... Excuses.* "I'm sorry. Can I...Can I buy you a drink?"

Lydia folded her arms tightly, but her bravado was quickly replaced with a flash of hurt in her eyes. "Fine," she said after a moment.

Brooke stood and fell into step next to Lydia as they made their way to the bar. Lydia's arms were still folded tightly and she glared at the gravel as they reached the other side of the patio.

"You could've just…You could've just said that was all you wanted, you know?" Lydia finally spoke. "A one-time thing."

The guilt that chewed at Brooke's stomach was an unfamiliar feeling and she disliked it immensely. Since moving to Key West, she had always been clear about her casual intentions but the realization that she had been careless with Lydia was not something she was used to.

"What'll it be?" The bartender asked. He looked between them expectantly as he tossed two paper napkins onto the smooth bar top.

Brooke glanced back at her table in the corner and immediately recognized the back of Amber's head as she and Justin chatted animatedly.

Am I tiring of casual trysts? She wondered. *Or have I felt unfulfilled by them for a while?*

Lydia stuck a hand on her hip and followed Brooke's gaze. "You know," she continued, an edge in her tone. "You don't have to go through the motions of buying me a consolation drink and giving me the speech. You know, 'it's not you, it's me, whatever'. Your eyes say it all." Lydia pointed knowingly at the table.

That got Brooke's attention. "What?" She spluttered. The bartender's lips twitched and Brooke finally glanced at him. "Uh, a rum and Coke. Make that two."

Lydia rolled her eyes. "*I* prefer tequila, thanks for asking," she paused and fixed the bartender with a syrupy-sweet grin. "Can we make that a rum and Coke and a Paloma, please?"

The bartender flushed and nodded quickly. "Yes," he replied quickly. "Of course, *bella donna*."

Lydia smiled, satisfied, and turned back to Brooke. "You don't have to tell me anything." Her eyes were downcast as she sighed. "I get it. It's all over your face."

Brooke felt a flush of indignation at the second person in a day informing her of these suddenly-expressive facial features. "I'm sorry I've been avoiding you," she replied. "But you don't know what you're talking about."

Lydia fixed her with a look. "Yeah, right."

Brooke didn't know what to say. She realized she had somehow become locked in a battle of wills with the young yoga instructor and was relieved when the bartender placed their drinks in front of them.

Lydia bit the inside of her cheek as Brooke placed a $20-dollar bill on the table. "Was it me?" She asked. "Did I do something wrong?"

Brooke hated the guilt that sliced right through her middle. She finally met Lydia's gaze. "No," she replied. She held her eyes for a moment. "I promise."

Lydia nodded slowly. "I waited for you to call. And then you only responded to my texts with short, one-word answers. You never came back to yoga, so I got the drift. I decided to see my ex-boyfriend in Fort Lauderdale next weekend. He wants to get back together."

Brooke stole another glance at the table and wished for a split-second that Amber would turn around. She had *such* a heart-stopping smile…

"I don't want to keep you from your friends," Lydia continued as she pointedly followed Brooke's gaze again. "But don't, like, come running back to yoga in a few weeks thinking you'll have another chance or something."

Brooke picked up her drink. "I'm sorry, Lydia. I really am." It was the first time she had apologized for breaking a heart and she had meant it.

Lydia stood. "Don't bother," she snarled. "If you'll excuse me, I have more important things to do. See you around, Brooke."

Two minutes later, Brooke returned to the table and shook her head. "I cannot believe that just happened," she groaned. It embarrassed her that Amber had witnessed that more than she cared to admit. She briefly recalled Lydia's assumption and quickly brushed it aside.

She has no idea what she's talking about Brooke told herself.

"She must have really liked you," Amber replied, her tone cool.

Brooke shook her head vehemently. "No, it wasn't like that at all," she said quickly. "It was just an unexpected…thing. She, um, was my yoga teacher…"

Amber's mouth dropped open. "Your *yoga* teacher?"

"It just sort of happened," Brooke tried to continue. "It was this uncomplicated thing..."

Amber raised an eyebrow. "Sounds like it was complicated to her."

Brooke sighed as the waiter arrived at the table and took their orders. "I didn't know," she finished. *Or did I choose not to know?*

An awkward silence descended over the table. The familiar contentious air from the night before threatened to ruin the strides they had made. Brooke didn't know why it was suddenly important to her that Amber knew her relationship with Lydia had been purely casual, but she wondered for the second time in as many days just why she and Amber Lucas seemed to get on each other's nerves.

As the band launched into another popular classic rock cover, Amber leaned in. "Speaking of dating, are you seeing anyone special?" She had directed the question to Justin, who squirmed uncomfortably on the bench.

"I...Sort of," he finally relented. "It's too early to say what it is for sure, but I did meet someone recently. He lives in Arizona, but he's moving to Key West soon. In fact, Brooke is helping him buy out here."

Amber turned to Brooke, surprised and impressed. "Wow, real estate!" She exclaimed. "That must keep you busy."

Brooke nodded. "Oh, it does," she replied before glancing down at her phone. "And hopefully Adam will call me tomorrow as promised to let me know which property he'd like to make an offer on. Because the first one..." She paused and quickly scanned through an e-mail. "...Just went under contract an hour ago."

Justin let out a low whistle. "This market is something else."

"The competition here is stiff for anything that becomes available," Brooke continued. "But fortunately, I don't think that's the one he fell in love with."

"I don't think that's the one he fell in love with either," Justin cut in with a dramatic pause. Both Amber and Brooke laughed at his antics.

"Are you excited for his move?" Amber responded with a grin. "It sounds like you really like him."

Justin leaned back as the waiter quickly placed steaming plates of food in front of them. "I am," he answered thoughtfully. "You know, it's weird. I wasn't looking for anything in particular. I was *just* telling Brooke how we're in our prime and then along comes Adam. He makes me re-think *everything* I thought I knew."

Amber stilled as she blew on a forkful of steaming crab cake. "My mom said those exact words just the other day, when she was explaining the trial living situation to me." She looked momentarily stunned.

Justin took a long sip of his margarita. "Adam also has a son," he went on. "Which scares the hell out of me. I mean, what do I know about raising a kid?"

"I think if it's meant to be, it will work out," Amber replied as she recovered. "If Adam is special to you, then his son will be too."

Justin grinned at her before popping a bite of nacho into his mouth. "I love how optimistic you are."

They laughed again before digging into their food. "Say," Justin started thoughtfully. He paused as he swallowed a bite of nacho. "My birthday is this Wednesday. I'm making Brooke go parasailing with me that evening, because what better way to ring in thirty-four?" He smiled. "I'd love it if you could join us."

Brooke almost dropped her fork at his casual invitation. *It's his birthday* she scolded herself. *He can invite whomever he pleases. Besides, what do I care if Amber tags along or not?*

Amber grinned. "I'd *love* to!" She squealed. For a split second, Brooke felt that same odd fluttering she had felt earlier at her house and when glancing at Amber from the bar.

"I've never been parasailing, but it's always something I wanted to do," Amber gushed. "It seems so...*freeing*. Besides, I'd love to help celebrate your birthday."

"Perfect," Justin replied with an easy smile. "I'll add you to the reservation tomorrow."

CHAPTER 15

As they walked casually to the car after dinner, it dawned on Amber that she hadn't thought about Dallas – or Lena – at all that day. The hurt that had dampened her spirits and put her in a dark funk appeared to be much less potent than it had been.

"Thank you both for the day and the evening," she spoke as they reached the public parking lot. "It's been nice to feel like myself again."

Justin threw her a sympathetic smile. "Women troubles?"

Amber climbed into the back seat and settled against the warm leather. "It had been," she admitted. "But that sting finally seems to be fading."

Justin pulled out of their parking space and then quickly hit the brakes as a group of motorized scooters sped by.

"Having a car on this island can be such a pain," he groaned. "I should've just kept my scooter."

As he made a cautious left onto William Street, Amber craned her neck toward the bright lights further down Greene Street. Groups of tourists laughed loudly as they marched down the narrow road in droves, some carrying glass bottles wrapped in brown paper bags.

"They're all headed to Duval," Justin spoke, as though reading her thoughts. "That whole area turns into one big party most nights."

"Like Sixth Street in Austin?" Amber asked, before realizing that neither Justin nor Brooke had probably ever been to Texas.

Justin shrugged and nodded as Amber's gaze fell on Brooke. Her profile was gently illuminated by streetlights as they drove further inland. *Always one step forward, two steps back with her* she thought somewhat wistfully. For all the sudden closeness she had felt with Brooke while alone upstairs in her empty house, it seemed to fizzle away like the day's earlier thunderstorm after Lydia's unexpected appearance.

And I was not *jealous* Amber told herself firmly. The disconcerting feeling of annoyance, however, had dug itself deep beneath her skin after Brooke hurriedly stood to buy Lydia a drink. *Why would I be?*

Amber startled as her eyes met Brooke's in the passenger's side mirror. They held each other's gaze for a long, steady moment as illumination from the streetlights danced across their faces. Amber swallowed hard. The depths of emotion that flickered in Brooke's eyes went deeper than she'd imagined and this both intrigued and terrified her, for what she suspected were the very same reasons.

If there was one thing that Amber had become accustomed to in her relationship with Lena, it had been reading the sub-text. The hours in Brooke's bedroom had been real and unguarded. Despite her best efforts to lump Brooke and Lena together in her mind, her sharpened senses suggested that perhaps there was much more to Brooke beneath her cool exterior.

"So what's your coming out story?" Justin asked conversationally."When did you first realize that you're gay?"

Amber pondered his questions for a moment. "I don't know if I have a coming out story at all," she finally replied. "You already know my mom. She was always careful not to push old-fashioned gender roles onto me. When I got older and have crushes at school, she always made sure to use gender-neutral pronouns or mention him *or* her, rather than assuming it was a him. It helped me to feel comfortable as I eventually realized that these school crushes were not only becoming more intense, but they were all on female peers."

"You're lucky," Justin replied. "She seems so understanding."

Amber nodded. "She is," she admitted. "During my senior year, I finally admitted to myself what I was. My mom, as you can expect, was supportive as ever. In fact, she suggested that my high school graduation party also be a rainbow-themed coming out party. As grateful as I was for her support, I quickly nixed that idea."

Justin snorted with laughter. "I like your story," he replied. "That's how it should be, you know? Knowing you have support from the beginning and being able to figure things out for yourself without pressure or expectation from anyone else."

"What's your coming out story?" Amber asked.

Justin threw her a shy smile in the rearview mirror. "Would you believe it if I told you I was the star wide receiver of my high school football team? We were a top 10 team in Florida all four years that I was there."

Amber's mouth dropped open. "Not that I believe in stereotypes," she started. Justin burst into laughter. "But high school football star?"

Justin nodded. "Justin Cole, number 24 of the Niceville High School varsity football team. I grew up in a small panhandle town, where high school football is life, they host an annual mullet festival and being openly gay isn't an option."

Amber blinked. "A mullet festival?"

Justin smirked. "For the fish, not the haircut," he replied. "Though both were prevalent. You know how it is in the south with high school sports. It just so happened that I picked the right one, because I was actually really good at it. It allowed me to focus on something other than the fact that I knew deep down I was different. Couldn't even *think* the words to myself for the longest time."

"I can't imagine growing up in a place like that," Amber replied, her eyes wide. "When did you finally come out?"

"After high school, of course," Justin replied confidently. "I could at least say the words by then. My mom still lives up there. We visit sometimes. She accepts me for who I am, but I don't think we'll ever be very close. She's...Niceville and I'm...*not.* My dad lives with my step-mom in Tampa and that's worse. My step-mom is your picture-perfect Southern Baptist and my dad, well, he does whatever *she* wants."

"So you're not close?" Amber replied, her tone filled with empathy.

"The funny thing is, I was very close with my dad growing up," Justin said with a sigh. "He never missed one of my games. Sometimes I wish that support could have been unconditional."

Amber was silent for a long moment. "Wow," she replied. She shook her head slowly. "I'm sorry, Justin. I can't imagine the difficulties you've faced."

Justin smiled and quickly waved a hand. "Oh, stop," he replied and then sighed. "Thank God for Key West."

As they pulled up to Brooke's father's house, they said their goodbyes to Justin and then casually fell into step as they walked up the long driveway.

Amber glanced and Brooke and spoke after a moment. "What about you? No coming out story to share?"

Brooke's gaze fell to the concrete and a lock of blonde hair fell over her face. She paused, brushing it behind her ear, and replied carefully. "I don't have a coming out story because I'm not out. At least to my dad."

Amber's mouth dropped open as they reached the porch. "I had no idea," she exclaimed. "I…I just assumed. The bracelet…" she pointed to Brooke's beaded rainbow accessory. "How can he *not* know?"

Brooke threw a glance at her as she dug for her house key. "My father really is that…dense to some things," she replied with a roll of her eyes. "I've known I'm gay for as long as I can remember. It's always been a fine line of hiding it from him and being out everywhere else. I guess it started as a protection thing toward my dad. Even years after my mom passed away, he was still reeling from it and I didn't want to add even one more stressor to his life. Besides, *his* life was the construction company and his hours were endless, so I had a lot of independence once I reached high school anyway."

"And you've never wanted to tell him since?" Amber asked in bewilderment.

Brooke shrugged and headed for the stairs. Amber guessed that it wasn't something she often went into detail about and decided not to ask any more questions, though her mind raced with this information.

"I told myself that when I fall in love and I'm absolutely crazy for someone, once I *know* she's the one, then I'll tell him," she turned from the top stair and replied simply. "Until then, there's no reason to risk..." she paused. "You know."

Amber wrinkled her nose. "Your dad isn't a homophobe," she replied. *My mom wouldn't date him if that were the case.* "He and I get along fine."

Brooke sighed. "I'm *not* scared," she continued. "For a really long time, I was all he had left of my mother. And before Sandra, I was his main person."

Amber was quiet as Brooke turned and walked into her bedroom. She couldn't help but think that the other woman sounded more like she was trying to convince herself that she wasn't scared than anyone else.

As she padded down the hallway to her own bedroom and processed this, she turned as Brooke's door creaked. The other woman stood in the frame, her expression guarded and her hair wavy around her shoulders. The moment seemed to stretch between them until Brooke finally spoke.

"You probably think that's really lame, right?" She asked with a roll of her eyes. "Being thirty-three and not even out to my dad?"

"No," Amber replied honestly. "It's sweet that you want to protect your dad."

Brooke's gaze was intense, but she stood rooted and still in the doorframe. After a moment, she smiled and Amber immediately recognized as one of her "real" ones.

"Thank you," she murmured. "Good night."

"Good night," Amber echoed.

Late that evening as Amber tried to sleep, still images of Brooke burned behind her eyes and defiantly refused her brain's orders to go away. It would be only hours before her first day at the Chamber and, instead, she tossed and turned with thoughts of the other woman and all that she had learned today.

"This is not fair," Amber muttered into the darkness. She glanced at the alarm clock next to the bed. Glowing neon numbers reminded her that not enough sleep before a first day at work was always a recipe for disaster.

She ran a hand through her hair in distress as memories of Brooke leaning over her notebook filled her mind's eye. "What the hell are you getting yourself into?" Amber whispered to herself. "And of all times in my life, why *now*?"

~

"WHY NOT NOW?" Bobbi asked from her seated position at the head of a long glass conference table. She peered at Amber over a pair of fashionable purple and red half-glasses. "Doesn't Terri know that this would be great visibility for her?"

Amber glanced at a thick manila folder before her. It was filled with notes, invoices and other important paperwork for the exhibition that the former office manager had left behind. "When I spoke to her this morning, she said that she's working on a twenty-foot mermaid sculpture for the Fort Myers Beach American Sandsculpting Championship. Unfortunately, it's one week after the exhibition, so she's unable to commit to more than one major event so close together."

Terri Jacobson, the artist in question, was a champion sand sculptor and local Key West resident who Bobbi had been inexplicably desperate to book for the exhibition. After several phone calls and more than a few messages, she had finally returned Amber's call earlier in the day. There was more, but she didn't feel it was appropriate to mention in front of the entire Chamber staff at their planning meeting.

"All right," Bobbi replied with a sigh. "I suppose we'll have to look into other options then. Can you supply me with a short list by the end of the day? Something unique and something artistic that can be done outdoors. Something that will really pique peoples' interest and get them inside for the exhibition."

Amber nodded. "Of course."

As Bobbi moved on to catering, Amber jotted a quick note and then looked around the small conference room. It was her third day at the Chamber and she was surprised at how much she was enjoying it. Her nerves about adjusting to a formal office job versus the controlled chaos of a large hospital were relieved after a smooth transition and a warm welcome from the team.

"Remember, our challenge this year is that the Chamber really wants the local community interested. We're shying away from this being an *art* event," Bobbi used dramatic air quotes around the word art and paused for effect. "This year, it's a family affair. We want parents to bring their kids, tourists to stop by, even the retirees to enjoy all the different visions these photographers are bringing."

Amber suppressed a smile. Bobbi was unlike anyone that she had ever worked with before, but there was something refreshing and oddly likeable about her brightly colored outfits, spiked hair and fire engine red lipstick. Even though she was in her late fifties and had revealed to Amber that she had been with the Chamber for nearly thirty years, she looked more suited for theatre. Amber had no problem imagining Bobbi under the hot lights of Broadway, waving her arms as she spoke and carefully enunciating every syllable.

"We want to casually bring art to the people and make it as kid-friendly as possible." Bobbi paused again and smiled. "After all, they are our future, aren't they? And kids certainly aren't interested in black ties and hors d'oeuvres. If we can successfully rebrand this event and get the whole community engaged, then I believe that we can build on all these possibilities for years down the line."

Amber nodded, along with the other four Chamber employees in the meeting, and murmured an affirmative "got it".

Bobbi clapped her hands together. "Wonderful," she went on. "I'm counting on your ideas to make this a success. Let's consider what each of us can do to make this a cohesive, brand-new event that the Key West community, especially the families and kids, are going to want to visit. No idea is too big or too small. There's a lot of work to be done, but I trust your abilities and look forward to your thoughts."

Amber glanced around the table. The Membership Director, two Tourist Information Managers and the Digital Marketing Director were all nodding their agreement as they reviewed their notes.

"I believe that's all we have for now," Bobbi finally concluded. "I know we all have several individual projects we are working on for this event, so I'm going to update the meeting in Outlook to reoccur twice a week. That way, we can discuss our progress, present ideas and pitch in to help if any issues come up."

As the others filed out of the conference room, Amber was about to follow suit when Bobbi cleared her throat pointedly.

Amber turned expectantly. She had already learned what to anticipate from Bobbi, who managed with a purposeful, direct approach. Amber found that, rather than being put off, she quite admired Bobbi's assertiveness. As long as she kept her end of the bargain – making progress on the exhibition, meeting deadlines and having answers to questions that Bobbi had – she was, for the most part, left to do her work in peace.

"How about all that for a trial by fire?" Bobbi chuckled. "Would you believe it's only day three and you've already been such a big help to us? I'm *so* thrilled you're helping us out, Amber. Speaking of, have you been settling in all right?"

Amber nodded. "I feel as though I've fit right in," she responded honestly. "I'm glad I was able to roll up my sleeves and get to work right away. Really, I'm shocked at how quickly the day goes by!"

Bobbi smiled good-naturedly. "Time flies when you're having fun. Or trying to plan a major event, pick your poison," she laughed. "Say, I had a question about your conversation with Terri. Did she just mention that she was overbooked right now or did she allude to anything else that I should know?"

Shit. Amber opened and then closed her mouth as she tried to decide on the most diplomatic way to relay exactly what Terri had told her.

"She, uh, did seem a little…irritated that I was reaching out to her," Amber started hesitantly. She watched Bobbi's face carefully for any signs of upset. "She said something, um, along the lines of why you were having me reach out if..." Amber paused. "I think she wanted you to contact her, not me."

Bobbi pursed her lips and narrowed her eyes behind her glasses. "Oh, really?" She replied tightly. "What did she say?"

Double shit. Amber knew Bobbi wasn't going to like this, but sugar-coating the strange conversation didn't seem to be softening the blow. She sighed. "She said if Bobbi Harold wants to speak to me, you can take the phone from your, uh, behind and call her yourself instead of having your office manager do it. She said she won't hold her breath, though, and probably wouldn't be, um, inclined to answer your call anyway."

Bobbi's mouth dropped open and Amber quickly rushed ahead. "That was what Terri said, of course," she continued. "I was as surprised as anyone at her, uh, candor when she finally returned my call."

Bobbi nodded slowly. "Yes, I understand," she replied. "I had asked you what she said and you told me the truth. That's important, Amber. We need to be able to trust each other over these next several weeks."

Bobbi continued to speak, but Amber could tell that she was bothered. Her mind seemed far away as she smiled tightly. "Anyway, do you have all that for the exhibition?"

Amber hadn't heard a word. "Yes, of course."

"Great," Bobbi replied as she strode into the hallway. Amber followed and headed for her desk when Bobbi turned once more. "You've really been doing a stellar job in your first few days, Amber. If you wrap up by 3, you can go ahead and head out. I'll see to it that you're still paid until 5. I have an unexpected errand that I'm going to have to take off for, so you may as well enjoy the afternoon."

Amber's eyes widened. "Are you sure?" She felt compelled to clarify. "Thank you."

Bobbi waved a hand. "Thank *you*," she responded. "And absolutely, enjoy your afternoon. Please see to it that you send me your list of entertainment ideas to draw people into the exhibition first thing tomorrow morning and I'll review it right away."

"Not a problem," Amber replied. "Thank you again. I was invited to go parasailing this evening, so it works out well. I really appreciate it."

Bobbi lifted an eyebrow and looked impressed. "Wow, parasailing," she spoke. For a brief moment, her gaze turned far away again. "I had a first date parasailing once. It was...lovely." Amber saw a flash of sadness in her expressive eyes, a jarring contrast to the vivacious woman who oversaw the Chamber of Commerce.

"Oh, well, this isn't a date," she replied hastily. She wondered how to explain her relationship to Brooke in just a few short sentences. It seemed difficult, though she wasn't sure why. "My mom is seeing this guy, and his daughter is going parasailing tonight for her friend's birthday. They invited me along."

Bobbi smiled plaintively. "That's nice," she replied before disappearing into her office. "I'm sure you'll enjoy."

For a moment, Amber wondered if Bobbi's sudden "errand" had something to do with the strangely acrimonious relationship between her and the sand sculptor. She had access to Bobbi's Outlook calendar, where another of her duties involved ensuring her availability and planning meetings and other engagements so they didn't run over one another.

As she settled back into her desk, she opened her Outlook and clicked over to Bobbi's daily calendar. Sure enough, there were no afternoon or evening appointments scheduled. Her mind flitted over the idea that perhaps Bobbi and Terri had a romantic history that clearly hadn't ended well.

Nah Amber thought. A quick glance at the clock at the upper right-hand corner of her laptop told her she had about forty minutes until 3 P.M. *It's not my business anyway. Speaking of, there's enough Chamber business to deal with for the exhibition.* With that, Amber pushed all curious thoughts of Bobbi and Terri aside and reopened her file folder.

"Let's see what I can tackle and get out of the way in an hour or less," she murmured to herself, still pleasantly surprised that she had begun to take to this gig. What had started as an insult – but too good of a financial offer to pass up – had somehow shifted to an enjoyable environment doing something that she was confidently good at.

"Verify the layout of the event space, make sure each photographer is represented and send a final copy to the Chamber's maintenance director," Amber muttered to herself as she pulled a long sheet of paper from the folder. "Perfect. One more thing I can check off the list."

As she set about completing the task, Amber smiled to herself and wondered for a moment if her newfound enjoyment in her work could be attributed to a bit of Bobbi rubbing off on her.

Though it could also be the daily yoga that my mother has been dragging me along to she thought ruefully. Though it was only the third day, Amber had all but grudgingly accepted that, so long as she was staying with her mom, yoga would be a daily part of her life. She smiled as she thought of the pointed complaints she had made on Monday morning as she was roused out of bed after finally falling into a restless sleep and the scowl she had thrown at Sandra upon leaving the house as the sun was rising. On Tuesday, she was less vocal but had still made a point of throwing her blanket back dramatically as Sandra woke her with a cheerful smile and a steaming mug of green tea.

This morning, she had been ready in her yoga shorts and tank top before Sandra could even crack the bedroom door. The look of surprise on her mother's face had caused them to exchange a knowing smile as Sandra silently handed her another mug of green tea.

Amber flexed her right foot beneath her desk, relishing the delicious stretch in her sore hamstring. Though her body was still adjusting to the daily yoga, she realized her mind already felt a little sharper and clearer than it had before her arrival. Another quick glance at the clock told her she had a little under a half-hour to go. She tried to ignore the light shiver of anticipation that snaked up her spine or the growing well of excitement fluttering in her stomach.

I'm beyond just to go parasailing she told herself. *After all, I've never been.* She refused to acknowledge that the anticipation seemed to multiply tenfold at the thought of another evening with a certain tough, cool blonde. *It definitely has nothing to do with her.*

CHAPTER 16

Brooke took a deep breath as she shuffled through three new exclusive buyer representation agreements that had been signed and returned to her that day. The paper of the lengthy contracts was still warm from the office printer and three individual file folders had been carefully created with each buyer's information by the brokerage's office manager.

Her desk phone rang as she slipped each contract into its folder. Brooke picked up the phone and cradled it between her ear and shoulder as she scanned each contract's details.

"This is Brooke," she answered briskly. *2.5 percent commission, okay* she thought. *Not as much what I earn when I'm the seller's agent, but that's normal. Besides, being the buyer's agent is generally the easier gig.*

"I knew you would still be at the office," Justin spoke. "Remember, we're going parasailing this evening. I know you didn't forget my birthday because I got your Facebook message earlier."

Brooke grinned. "To be fair, I was out all morning and through lunch with some heiress who wants to buy a vacation home. Forget the fact that she's five years younger than me." She rolled her eyes for good measure. Though her newest client wasn't nearly as difficult as Brooke had anticipated, she wasn't exactly the sharpest tool in the shed and exclaimed "Oh my *Gawd*!" more times in an hour than Brooke could count.

Justin laughed. "Heiress, huh? Says the woman whose father owned a multi-million-dollar construction business."

"Ah, but therein lies the difference," Brooke replied dryly. "*I* always chose to do *my* thing and make my own way. In fact, staying with my father while my place is being fixed is the first help I've accepted from him in years. Besides, this newest client is on a totally different level."

"Yeah?" Justin asked, suddenly interested. "Like, Hilton level?" He gasped. "Oh Brooke, is she a *Kennedy*? I heard a few of them were planning to relocate from Martha's Vineyard to a warmer climate for the winter."

Brooke laughed. "How do you *hear* this stuff?" She asked, bemused. "And no, not a Kennedy or a Hilton or any famous last name, actually. She's a chicken heiress or something."

"A chicken heiress?" Justin repeated flatly. "Can I ask what that even is?"

Brooke spun in leather chair and carefully filed the new folders into a long cabinet behind her. "You know, chicken," she replied, distracted. She removed the folder for her most recent closing. That would be taken to the office manager for filing in the brokerage's closed properties vault. "Her father is the owner of a national poultry company. Not Purdue, but something like that. A competitor, I think."

"Huh," Justin appeared to ponder this for a moment. "Well, now that you're done with the chicken heiress and you've gotten everything completed at the office, I expect to see you at the Historic Seaport in thirty minutes or less. I already texted Amber the directions because I knew you wouldn't."

Brooke stilled at the mention of Amber's name. She wrinkled her nose. "What's that supposed to mean?"

Justin sighed. "Just meet us there, okay?"

Brooke relented. "All right, all right," she replied. "I'll leave here in a minute, birthday boy."

As they hung up, Brooke wiped her palms on her pressed black pants. She wasn't sure why they had suddenly gone clammy or why the blood was pulsing loudly through her ears.

Humidity she decided as she rubbed her palms against her thighs one last time. *Besides, the air conditioning in the office sucks.*

Brooke thought of the last time she had seen Amber, a few days ago. Amber had recognized Brooke's walls and witnessed her exchange with Lydia, but there were moments when she recognized a certain fire and conviction in Amber's hazel eyes that seemed to sear right through her.

For the first time since Amber's arrival, Brooke had allowed herself to become lost in a moment after she had opened her bedroom door and met the other woman's gaze across the hallway. She had wondered what could happen if she strode down the hall, pushing them both into the guest room and using only the wall for balance as she kissed her hungrily. Brooke wanted to feel Amber's conviction, her belief that Brooke was sweet, as she kissed her back. The thought of letting go and temporarily allowing her walls to crumble with the sheer force of their clashing wills was intoxicating. Brooke wouldn't stop until Amber was putty in her hands – Breathless, sated, sweaty and begging for more.

Instead, Brooke had stood rooted in the doorframe and overwhelmed by the unexpected surge of desire. They hadn't seen each other over the next few days, but it wasn't something Brooke had planned purposely. Her day started late in the morning and ended in the waning evening hours. Amber was already long gone by the time Brooke was awake and she had usually retired to her room by the time Brooke returned. She was genuinely curious how Amber's job at the Chamber was and she had maybe thought about that happy sparkle in Amber's eyes.

Just once or twice Brooke reassured herself silently.

As she strode to the restroom, her duffel bag slung over her shoulder, a small thrill of anticipation quickened her heartbeat.

Brooke unzipped her duffel bag and locked a stall door behind her. As she removed the carefully folded bathing suit, shorts and tank top, she felt unmistakable goosebumps along her forearms. This time, she wasn't so sure she could blame it on the air conditioning.

~

"BROOKE ADRIANI, THERE YOU ARE!" Justin yelled from a wooden table overlooking the marina. He waved emphatically and took a few steps from under the wide white umbrella that shrouded the table in sought-after shade.

Brooke laughed and waved back as she walked across the marina. A small tent branded with the parasailing company's name, phone number and website stood near the table.

Justin loped down the steps and met Brooke. He handed her a ticket. "Okay, this is what you need," he instructed her. "Go to the tent and give them your ticket. They'll check your name off the reservation list and you'll have to sign some waivers. Then just meet Amber and I back at the table. They'll let us know when they're ready for us to board the boat."

Brooke nodded and glanced up at the table. Her breath immediately left her body as she spotted Amber on a wooden stool. Her hair was tied in a loose bun, but the sea breeze had caused a few stray pieces around her face to escape. The deep golden tan of her skin was a reminder that Amber was a born and raised southerner who was likely used to the hot sun and spiking temperatures.

She swallowed hard. Amber's pink and navy blue bikini was worn with tight white swim shorts that barely covered enough of her to be practical. Brooke quickly realized she wasn't the only one who noticed her. A guy from the parasailing company stood nearby, desperately trying to win her attention. From the eager smile on his face and his open body language, Brooke knew right away that he was trying to flirt.

Brooke glanced down at the ticket and turned toward the tent, but not before accidentally catching Amber's eyes. She smiled and raised her hand in a short wave before turning her attention to the paperwork handed to her.

Why do I care if some beach bum wants to flirt with Amber? She told herself. *It doesn't bother me.*

Still, Brooke couldn't shake a lingering sense of irritation as she signed the waivers. She paused before placing her initials in a box next to one line that stuck out in particular.

"Um, excuse me," she spoke.

The girl in the tent smiled expectantly. "Yes ma'am, do you have a question?"

Brooke nodded. "I do," she confirmed. "It says here that you need my initials to absolve your company of any trouble if I encounter grievous bodily harm, including death. Um, how many people exactly have died parasailing?"

The girl sighed. "It's just something that our attorney says has to be there. It's standard for any water sports company."

Brooke glanced back at the table. Justin met her eyes and shot her a questioning glance. "Okay, but do people normally get hurt doing things like this?" She prodded. "I mean, I'm not trying to be a stick in the mud but that's some pretty serious legal stuff you're asking me to sign away..."

Justin cleared his throat pointedly. Brooke hadn't seen him leave the table. "Is everything okay, Brooke?" He asked.

"Yes," she replied. "I'm just a little concerned that I'm very literally initialing my life away, should something go terribly awry..."

"All of our boat captains are *very* highly-trained, ma'am," the girl cut in hurriedly. "They go through intense training and are all quite experienced. I'm sure you'll have no problems..."

"Can I get *you* to write that down and sign that statement, then?" Brooke cut in.

"Hey, hey," Justin interrupted. He turned to the girl in the tent with an apologetic roll of his eyes. "Excuse us for one moment."

He turned back to Brooke and guided her by the elbow around the tent. "*What* is going on with you?"

Brooke swallowed hard and then sighed. "I'm terrified of heights."

"What?" Justin asked incredulously. "You can't be serious, Brooke. Why did you agree to go parasailing? And how have I known you for five years, but I don't know this? We could have just as easily gone to dinner for my birthday."

Brooke closed her eyes. "Justin, that's not fair. You were so excited when you suggested parasailing and it's *your* birthday. I didn't want to dictate what you should or shouldn't do on your special day. I was *trying* to take one for the team, but did you read that waiver?"

Justin took a deep breath. "Brooke, they have to have stuff like that in the waiver," he replied patiently. "It doesn't mean..."

"Is everything okay?" A soft voice that Brooke recognized instantly came from behind them. She took a deep breath.

Great she thought. *As if it's not lame enough that I'm not out to my dad, let's add terribly-fearful-of-heights to that too.*

"Brooke is terrified of heights," Justin replied. "She freaked out at the part on the waiver that acknowledges the company will not be held responsible for any serious bodily harm or death."

"I did *not* freak out," Brooke started.

Justin fixed her with a knowing look and she sighed miserably. "It just took me by surprise, that's all," she muttered.

Amber looked between them for a moment. Finally, she turned and met Brooke's gaze. "Think of it like one of your real estate contracts, you know?" She began. "I mean, those are, like, ten pages long sometimes, right?"

Brooke nodded and wondered where she was going with this.

"And in your real estate contracts, you want to cover every angle and protect yourself and your buyer or seller from every possible situation, right?" Amber went on. "Even though the likelihood of those situations happening are slim to none. It's the same thing here, just a different industry. Situations like that are so rare, just like the situations you want to cover in your contracts are incredibly rare."

Brooke found herself searching Amber's eyes. "You're right," she finally sighed. "I just hate heights."

"How about this?" Amber offered. "Why don't you and I parasail together? That way, I'll be next to you and you can talk to me the whole time."

Brooke raised a dubious eyebrow. "You would do that?"

Amber shrugged. "Of course," she replied. "I'm just excited to get up there and experience it. Besides, it'll be more fun to have someone to enjoy it with."

Brooke nodded and then followed Amber back to the front of the tent. The disconcerting feeling of following someone else, having another woman reassure her and not always being in total control was not lost on her. She glanced back at Justin, who stood in the same spot with a look of mystification.

As Brooke finished initialing the waiver, another man with the parasailing company was waiting outside the tent. He looked about forty, with short blonde dreadlocks, tanned skin that resembled leather and grayish scruff along his jaw. He nodded to them with a grin.

"You ready?" He asked. "I'm Jeff. I'll be helping out, getting you guys in and out of your harnesses and making sure everyone has a great time. Our captain is getting the gear ready, so if you want to come with me then I'll get you on the boat and situated. Sound good?"

"Yeah!" Justin exclaimed. He rocked on the balls of his feet in excitement.

"Awesome," Amber said with a smile, before Brooke caught her stealing a glance in her direction. She unconsciously took a few steps closer to Amber as they clambered down the pier and followed Jeff.

She implied I could stick with her, right? Brooke thought. *I'm slightly nervous, that's all. Everything will be fine.*

As they approached the speedboat, she caught sight of the large parasail canopy spread along its back. The nerves flared in her gut again and she paused as Jeff and Justin hopped into the boat.

Amber stopped too and looked at her with concern. "Are you okay?"

Brooke nodded quickly. "Just nervous."

Amber smiled again and, without a word, she weaved her fingers between Brooke's and carefully stepped into the boat. Without letting go of her hand, Amber turned and helped Brooke hesitantly climb into the boat behind her.

"It'll be okay," Amber replied. "Remember, we're doing this in tandem so I'll be with you the whole time."

As they sat on a bench along the right side of the boat, Brooke realized that she was still holding Amber's hand. Under normal circumstances, Brooke would have felt patronized, insulted even, at the sweet and careful way that Amber spoke to her. She would have been more determined to parasail alone so she could show herself and everybody else that she didn't really need anyone's help.

But this was no ordinary situation, Brooke decided, as she took a deep breath and became acutely aware of how warm and soft Amber's hand was. As the boat's engine whirred to life and Jeff stood at the front of the vessel to review the safety rules, Brooke relaxed slightly.

Maybe this won't be so bad she thought. *There could be worse things.* She glanced at Amber out of her peripheral and swallowed as she realized their thighs pressed together as the boat accelerated over a wave.

Yes Brooke decided as her eyes slid over Amber's stomach. She blinked as her gaze reached supple breasts held tightly by the thin fabric of her bikini top. *Despite the fact that I'm at risk for, what did the waiver say? Grievous bodily harm? There could be much, much worse things.*

CHAPTER 17

Amber laughed in delight as the boat skipped over another wave in the water and light spray hit her face. It felt refreshing in the sticky humidity of the early evening. She glanced over at Justin, who had somehow managed to find enough cellular service to FaceTime Adam. As he held his phone in front of him and chatted excitedly to his maybe-boyfriend, Amber glanced down at her left hand. It was still loosely intertwined with Brooke's slender fingers, resting gently atop their knees side-by-side.

Brooke's fear of heights was only the second time that Amber had seen the other woman vulnerable. She had enjoyed being the one to appease her fears more than she cared to admit.

It's nice to feel needed, that's all she told herself firmly.

"There's Brooke and Amber, say hi!" Justin called as he turned the phone towards them. They both grinned and, as they waved, Amber realized she immediately missed holding Brooke's hand. She ignored the disappointment and turned her face to the water. Without a cloud in the sky and the sun sinking lower into the horizon, Amber decided that this was like an Impressionist painting, only better because she was living it.

"This is amazing," she called over the loud engine. The boat cut a clean path over clear blue water. Amber couldn't help herself – She reached over the side of the boat and trailed her fingers along the water. At such rapid speeds, the water felt like velvet skimming over her fingertips and she closed her eyes. She wanted to remember this feeling forever.

As Amber opened her eyes, she blinked as she met Brooke's gaze. Something akin to intrigue flashed through her eyes and sent a shiver down Amber's spine, despite the nearly ninety-degree evening.

"Worlds away from Dallas yet?" Brooke called over the engine.

Amber nodded. "It's exhilarating," she replied. "I feel free."

"You *are* free," Brooke replied. "Well, as free as anyone else."

Amber pondered this as Justin ended his call with Adam and put his phone in his bag. *She's right* she realized. *I'm not suffocating anymore.*

"Who's going to go first?" Jeff clapped his hands together eagerly. "Right now, we're in a national marine sanctuary off Key West. In fact, the entire area surrounding Key West is a national wildlife refuge and marine sanctuary. This is great, because we want to keep Key West beautiful and this ensures that certain regulations are met to keep our water unpolluted and our environment healthy. Just a little further out, and we'd be in the Gulf of Mexico. Now who's brave and ready to get high?"

He laughed at his own joke as Amber wondered how many times so far that week Jeff had done as much. Justin's hand shot into the air as relief washed over Brooke's face.

"It's his birthday today," she told Jeff. "So he should definitely go first."

"Pretty sweet, bro," Jeff grinned at Justin. "Happy birthday, my man. Captain Joe here is going to idle the engine for a few minutes and I'll get you hooked to the canopy and show you where to hold."

Amber noticed Brooke watching very carefully as Jeff guided Justin to the deck of the boat and directed him how to stand as he hooked lines and ropes around his waist and legs.

"He'll be fine," Amber said in a low voice. "Look how excited he is. You totally made his birthday by agreeing to go parasailing."

"If he knew how much I hated heights, he never would have

wanted to go," Brooke admitted. "I didn't want to be the reason he wouldn't do what he really wanted for his birthday."

They watched as Jeff helped Justin into a bright blue life jacket and then hooked the harness around him. *She really isn't as bad as I'd thought* Amber realized.

"Will you take some photos on your phone and send them to me?" Justin asked Brooke. "Mostly so I can send them to Adam and show him how much fun Key West is. Then he'll never want to leave after he moves here."

Brooke laughed. "You got it." She snapped a quick photo of Justin grinning and giving the camera the "hang ten" sign before Jeff gave a thumbs up.

"All systems go," he said. "Captain Joe, we're ready to roll with our first one. Just take a seat here on the deck..." he paused as he helped Justin sit. "And put your legs flat in front of you. Hold on here..." he placed Justin's hands on a long, round handle in front of him. "...And you are good to go, my man! Everything feel all right?"

Justin shifted once and nodded. "Feels great."

Jeff nodded at the captain, another fortyish man with scraggly brown hair and a pair of black wraparound shades, before clapping him once on the back. "Let's hit it."

With that, the engines revved once more and the boat gained speed as it flitted over the waves. Justin laughed as he slid from the deck of the boat. The canopy caught the wind and opened to its full bright blue-and-yellow-striped shape, lifting Justin into the air before his rear end hit the surf. He splashed his feet once in the water and then floated higher and higher into the air.

Brooke shaded her eyes and squinted into the setting sun. "Oh my God, he's so high!"

Justin's laughter echoed down to the boat. "He's having the time of his life up there," Amber replied. "Look, he loves it."

Brooke glanced dubiously at the metal parasail towline, which squeaked as the rope quickly unwound. By now, the canopy was too high and far behind the boat to make out anything.

"This is *great*!" Justin's gleeful voice floated down to them.

Amber watched as Brooke snapped more pictures on her phone. Satisfied that she seemed more at ease, Amber was about to sit back on the bench when the boat hit two large ripples in the water, one right after the other.

Amber's butt hit the bench hard. Before she could register any soreness on her backside, Brooke tripped over her own feet and fell back against her. Amber tried very hard not to notice that Brooke was suddenly in her lap. She tried even harder to dismiss the fact that she had briefly wondered how it would feel to tighten her arms around Brooke's waist and casually rest her chin on her shoulder.

The fantasy had dissolved even before Brooke quickly bolted upright. "I'm sorry," she apologized. "I wasn't ready for that wave."

Amber shook her head. "It's okay, neither was I," she replied. "At least you didn't hit the bench. I may feel that tomorrow." She grimaced as she reached around her hip and rubbed her lower back.

To her complete surprise, Brooke burst into laughter. She crossed her legs beneath her on the bench and paused before falling into another round of giggles.

"I'm glad you think it's so funny," Amber muttered, feigning annoyance. "*You* got to fall back on cushion. I, on the other hand..."

Brooke grinned, barely containing her laughter. "Do you suppose this is the grievous bodily harm they tried to warn us about?"

Amber laughed, taken again by how beautiful Brooke was when she truly let herself go. Brooke shook her head and gazed over the water. "I swear, I laugh so much when I'm with you," she admitted.

Amber flushed. "It's okay to laugh, Brooke," she replied. "I told you I wouldn't tell anyone," she finished teasingly. As Amber met Brooke's eyes, she realized too late that her teasing was beginning to sound suspiciously like full-on flirting. The moment disappeared as quickly as it had arrived as Jeff reeled Justin back onto the deck.

"Did you see that?" Justin asked in excitement as he bounded to the bench. "I was *so* high! I could see *everything*, it was amazing! This has been the best birthday ever." Justin sat and sighed happily. "That was an experience unlike any other."

Jeff high-fived Justin and then nodded at Amber with a smile. "You gals ready? Let's get you hooked up to the tandem gear."

Amber glanced at Brooke, who appeared to have gone paler than what was normal even for her. "Remember, you don't have to do this," she told her quietly. "I can go myself if you're not comfortable."

Brooke took in the vast blue water that surrounded them and quickly tied her messy, salt-and-windswept hair into a ponytail. "No," she replied. "I want to do this. After all," she paused and turned to Amber. "You only live once, right?"

Amber nodded her agreement. "Like my mom always says, the present moment is all we have. Let's do it."

Amber ignored a longing to hold Brooke's hand again – to be comforting and helpful, of course – as Brooke planted her feet on the deck. She appeared quiet and contemplative as she watched Jeff expertly maneuver ropes and harnesses around her legs. He quickly directed Amber where to stand and gently pushed her closer to Brooke.

"Got to get a little closer, ladies," Jeff went on as he hooked the harnesses around them. "This is a two-person harness, so you'll have to do this side by side." He chatted casually as he hooked them to the canopy, but Amber barely heard a word. Her heart thumped loudly as she tried to ignore that she was once again pressed up next to Brooke.

They sat carefully on the edge of the deck. Brooke's legs were long and lean, her skin a creamy-ivory that extended all the way to her arched feet and forest green-painted toenails. Amber looked at her own legs, which were slightly more muscular no thanks to her recent yoga regimen. Their tan color betrayed her love of nature and her toes were manicured but unpainted.

A study in opposites she thought.

Amber had been nearly forgotten that they were about to be parachuted into the atmosphere when the noise of the engine drowned out her thoughts, all of which seemed centered on Brooke.

"Here we go!" Jeff told them with a grin.

Amber could practically feel Brooke's heartbeat thudding against her ribcage on the side that was pressed to her. Brooke stared steely but terrified at her toes and gripped the handlebar so tightly that her knuckles were bright white.

"Sayonara, ladies," Jeff told them as he leaned down and yanked at the rope around the towline. "Have fun!"

Amber laughed as they slid quickly from the deck and landed with a soft plop just atop the frothy surf. Warm saltwater tickled her ankles and she kicked her feet playfully beneath the surface. In seconds, the canopy had lifted them six, ten, then twenty feet off the water as they continued to glide higher.

She closed her eyes for a moment against the salty sea breeze. When she finally opened them, a brief glance at her legs dangling helplessly above the water told her that the canopy had taken them even further above the azure-blue expanse below.

An excited shiver raced up Amber's spine as she took everything in. She hadn't expected it to be so...quiet. In fact, the only sound was of the breeze whooshing past her ears and gently caressing her neck.

A long, thin rope was all that connected the canopy to the boat below. The vessel looked tiny to Amber from her vantage point. Her gaze traveled over the clear blue water that surrounded them on all sides and eventually gave way to a deeper, darker navy blue. Amber suddenly felt incredibly small, though the feeling of exhilaration didn't go unnoticed. She briefly remembered how, just weeks ago, she had been miserable many miles away and felt trapped in a growing rut.

I'm leaving that behind a sure, steady inner voice decided. Memories of the stress that constantly sat on her shoulders as she stretched each paycheck to the dollar, the sick feeling at having to place her expenses on her credit card and the desperation at trying in vain to pay down the mounting monthly balance flitted through her mind's eye. She thought of the boredom at work, the lack of motivation it had caused and the feeling of emptiness at falling just short of so many goals. Finally, there was a fleeting image of Lena. She thought of their first date and the many late nights binge-watching Netflix in bed.

It wasn't all bad the inner voice concluded. *But it wasn't enough. It's time to move on.*

There was an immense sense of peace as Amber as she watched the boat forge through the waters ahead. She welcomed the uncharted territory and, with silent acknowledgement of all that had hurt her before, she took a deep breath and let it go.

Amber smiled at the smooth ripples along the water below. Every once in a while, she spotted a dark shape beneath the surface, which Jeff had explained were natural reefs. The sun had begun its descent into the horizon, a clear, straight line directly ahead that seemed just out of reach. Golden rays colored the sky and sparkled across the water.

"The universe sure likes to show off sometimes," Amber spoke dreamily, her gaze never leaving the horizon ahead. She shook her head of all thoughts and, with a deep breath, she sat with the present moment. As it passed, Amber exhaled and blinked. She wondered if the new feeling of lightness was simply an effect of being strapped to a canopy at 500 feet in the air, but she decided that maybe, just maybe, it had something to do with releasing her baggage too.

"What did you say?" Brooke's voice cut into Amber's wandering thoughts. "I couldn't hear you over the wind."

Amber laughed. "I said that the universe likes to show off sometimes," she replied. "This is amazing. Words don't do it justice."

"Uh-huh," came Brooke's dry reply after a moment.

Amber stole a glance to her right. Her mouth fell open at the sight of Brooke. Her fingers were clenched tightly around the handle and her eyes were squeezed shut.

"Wait a second, have your eyes been closed this entire time?" Amber asked incredulously.

"Umm..." Brooke hedged. "I just...All I can think about is if something were to happen and I hit that water. How I'd break every bone in my body. You know, the grievous bodily harm that I signed away on."

Amber rolled her eyes good-naturedly. "I'm glad you didn't leave your wit down on the boat," she replied wryly. "Brooke, you have to see this. You'll regret it forever if you don't. It's beautiful up here. You can see...*everything*."

Brooke wrinkled her nose, her eyes still closed. "Okay," she finally replied uncertainly. She took a deep breath at the same time that Amber slipped her hand back into Brooke's.

Amber could feel her pulse racing just below the delicate skin of her wrist. With their fingers locked tightly together, Brooke slowly opened her eyes and then blinked.

"Wow," she breathed after a long moment.

"I know," Amber replied softly. She knew there weren't adequate words.

"The universe really does like to show off sometimes," Brooke agreed. She was quiet as Amber watched her take in everything. For a moment, the sure, confident woman who quickly and coolly sized up every situation was gone.

She really is beautiful Amber thought again. Desire swelled deep in her stomach as tiny alarm bells sounded in her head. She suspected it had everything to do with the way Brooke's eyes lit up at the view and the dimples that appeared on either side of her mouth when she really smiled.

"You can't go through life with your eyes closed all the time," Amber went on. She turned her gaze back to the horizon. "I mean, look at all the stuff you would miss out on. When you open your eyes, you can see what's right in front of you and so much more."

Brooke opened her mouth to reply, but they suddenly drew closer to the water. Amber peered down at the boat and could spot Jeff's figure as he slowly cranked the towline to reel them in.

As they descended upon the deck, Brooke turned in her harness and met her eyes. "Thank you," Brooke paused and smiled. "You're right. I would have never forgiven myself if I hadn't that."

Amber nodded. "It was too good to miss."

In less than another minute, they were brought back to the deck and quickly unclipped by Jeff. As he removed their harnesses and directed them to step out of the wet ropes that had landed around their feet, Justin stood expectantly.

"What did you think?" He asked with an eager grin. "*Amazing, right?*"

Amber opened her mouth to answer, but faltered when she saw Justin's eyes fall to their hands. He raised his eyebrows and looked as though he wanted to say something, but decided against it. She followed his gaze to her hand, still tightly in Brooke's, and flushed.

Oops Amber thought. The revelation felt as though it came entirely too quickly on the heels of her growing attraction: *But I really like holding her hand.*

CHAPTER 18

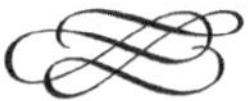

Brooke quietly eased her sleek Lexus up the driveway of her father's home. She glanced in the rearview mirror and spotted the familiar round headlights of Sandra's Volkswagen Beetle cutting through the thick darkness behind her. Brooke guessed that Amber had been using her mother's car to get to and from work, while Sandra and her father shared his heavy-duty pick-up truck.

She smiled to herself at the thought of Sandra trying to navigate the large Chevy Silverado. Since she and Amber had driven separately to the seaport, Brooke had told Amber to follow her back to the house.

Brooke listened to the sound of a car door being slammed across the long driveway. She moved to exit the Lexus, but not before the colors of a familiar beaded bracelet caught her peripheral. She glanced down at her ubiquitous rainbow bracelet and sighed as she quickly removed and pocketed it.

How much longer? She thought. *How much longer are you going to sneak around and hide from Dad?*

Brooke wasn't sure why, but she was suddenly immensely weary of the constant watch she had to keep on herself to avoid accidentally revealing her secret.

Brooke wondered if her sudden distress over staying closeted from her father had anything to do with Amber's unrestrained freedom. Her father didn't seem to have an issue with it; in fact, Brooke could tell that he liked Amber. Regardless, the roof hadn't seemed to cave in or the house implode under the weight of Amber's sexuality.

I'm just not used to living at home anymore she thought defensively. *Having my duplex gave me at least a shred of privacy.*

Brooke glanced at Evangeline as she tried to sort out her thoughts. The dashboard hula doll swayed slightly as she exited her car.

"You looked…deep in thought," Amber spoke after a moment.

Brooke smiled and shoved her hands into the pockets of her shorts. She rubbed the smooth beads of her bracelet with a fingertip. "Just tired," she fibbed. "All that sunshine and excitement did me in."

Brooke thought briefly of confiding in Amber, but the loud music that poured from the home as she opened the front door muted her thoughts. Amber glanced at her and wrinkled her nose as they exchanged confused glances.

"Get on-a up,
stay on the scene
Get on-a up,
like a sex machine..."

The suggestive lyrics were not lost on Brooke as they looked around the foyer and finally found the source of the fast-paced funk song.

"What the…" Amber murmured as she stopped short in the living room. Brooke nearly walked into her back as James Brown continue to sing and shout in his familiar gritty, primal tone. The loud music shook the walls and vibrated the windows in their frames. Brooke grimaced as she covered her ears.

The living room sectional had been pushed to the wall, which opened up a large floor space. Dave and Sandra were dancing without a care in the world, their fingers lightly intertwined as Dave pulled away and spun Sandra in time to the beat.

Brooke had never seen her father dance before, but now she was fairly sure why he didn't make it a habit. He crouched slightly forward, stepping to the song, as Sandra shook her hips suggestively. His face was red and a thin trail of sweat snaked down his temple, but he beamed with joy.

"Shake your moneymaker,

Shake your moneymaker..."

James Brown continued to sing and screech along to the twanging guitar as Sandra swayed back and forth to the rhythm and shimmied her way into Dave's arms. Brooke and Amber watched in bewildered silence as he gently dipped her. Sandra let out a delighted laugh.

"Shake your moneymaker,

Shake your moneymaker..."

"Nope," Brooke decided out loud. She quickly turned away from the spectacle and hoped to make a quick escape to her room, but Amber caught her arm.

She reluctantly turned back as Amber nearly doubled over with laughter. "I don't know if there's enough therapy in the world to bleach this from my memory."

"Oh stop, look how much fun they're having!" Amber exclaimed as she pointed into the room. "They didn't miss us at all tonight."

As Sandra spun again, she caught sight of them across the room. She reddened and laughed before quickly tapping Dave's bicep and pointing at them.

Dave turned the volume of the stereo down and ran a hand through his thinning hair in rueful embarrassment. "Oh, hey girls," he started, breathing heavily. "You, ah, made it back pretty early."

Brooke raised an eyebrow at her father, his face red from exertion and his expression sheepish. She crossed her arms sternly. "We work tomorrow."

"Of course," Sandra cut in breathlessly. "Right, it's a Wednesday. We forgot. We'll keep it down for you."

Brooke wasn't sure that she enjoyed feeling like the rigid stick-in-the-mud while Dave and Sandra exchanged smiling glances.

"Have you eaten?" Sandra asked as she absent-mindedly smoothed her hair. "There's a few Boca burgers left in the kitchen."

"Boca burgers?" Brooke asked in confusion.

"Mmm, I'm *starving*," Amber replied. "Can I heat one up?"

"Sure, sweetheart," Sandra replied. "Come on, there's a little iceberg lettuce and sliced tomato in the fridge that you can dress it with."

Amber turned and followed her mother out of the living room before they disappeared from view in the kitchen.

Brooke turned to her father. They faced each other across the room for a long, awkward moment.

"So..." Brooke started, unsure what to say. "Um, what are Boca burgers?"

Dave laughed loudly, his slight belly jiggling as he threw his head back. "They're, ah, veggie burgers," he replied. "Made from soy or somethin', Sandra says. Pretty good though. I didn't mind it once I got enough celery salt on the thing."

Brooke laughed. *That sounds more like him.* "Oh, Dad, she just wants you to eat healthy."

Dave smiled and shook his head. "This woman, Brookie," he replied. He shook his head again. "Boy, she can really cut a rug."

Brooke raised an eyebrow. "I'm not sure how I feel about that."

Dave sank back onto the sectional and wiped a hand across his forehead. "I got to tell you, Brooke, I feel young again," he went on. "Younger than I've felt in years. Decades, even. You know we found my old James Brown 8-track and listened to it for the last hour? Just laughing, sharing memories..."

"Dancing," Brooke supplied. "But what's an 8-track?"

Dave nodded and laughed. "Dancing," he repeated. "8-tracks were long before your time, Brookie," he paused and glanced up as she eased perched on the arm of the sectional. "How was parasailing? Justin had a good birthday?"

Brooke couldn't hold back her grin as she remembered the exhilarating view from the parasail. She briefly remembered the way in which Amber had held her hand and the sense of calm it had brought. She couldn't remember the last time she had felt that way by simply holding someone's hand. Brooke's grin widened as the brief memory caused a light fluttering somewhere deep in her chest.

"It was great," she replied confidently. "Justin loved it. He said afterwards it was his best birthday yet."

"Good," Dave replied with a nod. "And you? You didn't go up there, did you? I know how much you hate heights."

Brooke laughed. "I'll have you know that my fear was appeased and I did, in fact, parasail as well," she went on. She was proud of herself for conquering what seemed like impossible task. "Amber was nice enough to do a tandem parasail with me, so we went up together. It helped a lot. I don't think I would have been able to do it on my own."

Brooke paused and realized her father was studying her face. She shrugged. "In fact, I actually enjoyed it," she finished. "It was an amazing experience."

Dave sat back against the couch and thought for a moment. "I think that's the first time I've ever heard you admit you couldn't do something on your own." He paused and rubbed his chin. "You and, uh, Amber have been hanging out, huh? She's a sweet girl."

Brooke suddenly felt slightly defensive, as if she had given too much away. "Not really," she quickly backtracked. "I mean, we're both been busy with work. It's the first I've seen her since Sunday night."

Her heartbeat quickened as Dave glanced at her. *He can't possibly know* she reassured herself. *You're being paranoid.*

"No, I mean it's nice," he went on off-handedly. "I'm glad that you and Amber are getting along. It's real nice of you to help her feel at home while she's here. She was kind of thrown into this situation like you, but, you know, she doesn't have any friends or a life established here, really. I'm glad you're reaching out. That's my girl." Dave patted her shoulder proudly and smiled.

Brooke stood and forced a smile. Guilt tugged at her gut, but she couldn't pinpoint why. *Am I taking advantage of Amber?* She wondered, before dismissing the thought. *No, that's silly. We haven't done anything that could be construed as taking advantage.* Still, there was guilt at developing...what? A silly attraction to her father's girlfriend's daughter? It was as though she had done something wrong, though she couldn't figure out exactly what.

"Thanks, Dad," she replied, before leaning down to give him a quick hug. "I'm exhausted. I have another closing tomorrow, so I'm heading to bed."

"Good night, Brooke," Dave's voice echoed after her as she took the stairs two at a time.

You do *have a crush on Amber* a small voice piped up. As she again recalled how she had felt holding Amber's hand earlier, there was an unmistakable sinking feeling deep in her gut.

As Brooke gently closed the bedroom door behind her, she nearly lost her breath at the thought of the scandal that could erupt upon Dave and Sandra finding out.

"Like it wouldn't be enough to come out and say I'm gay," Brooke whispered. "But to also come out and tell Dad that I'm into his girlfriend's daughter? He'd never forgive me." She imagined the look of horror and disappointment that would surely disappear Sandra's serene smile. "And if she found out I had completely inappropriate feelings for her *daughter*? Forget that pleasant relationship we've established. She'd hate me."

Brooke glanced at her laptop bag. She knew she should review the file for tomorrow's closing to ensure nothing was missing that could hold up the transaction. She sat on the edge of the bed and blinked slowly. Amber's face and the setting sun causing evening light to sparkle from her gaze as they floated hundreds of feet up filled the dark space behind her eyelids.

There's only one thing to do, and it's what I do best Brooke decided firmly. *Avoid, avoid, avoid.*

~

Two evenings later, Amber strode up the driveway as she felt around in the pocket of her navy blue slacks for the house key. After completing her first week of work at the Chamber, she had a newfound appreciation for Fridays. The work kept her busy for the entirety of her day, with little time for boredom. She had, however, carved out time during her lunch break to call Visa and pay off the balance that had been lingering on her credit card for nearly a year. It had felt fantastic to pay it off in one fell swoop, thanks to the temporary raise she had received by accepting the job at the Chamber of Commerce.

Sure, I might be a little broke until next Friday Amber thought ruefully. She swung open the front door and kicked her shoes off in the foyer. *But with my experience making those dollars stretch? It'll be no problem. Besides, it feels great to have that finally off my back.*

The house was quiet as Amber wandered into the kitchen and perused the contents of the refrigerator. With next week's paycheck, she planned to set aside enough money to pay her half of next month's rent at her apartment in Dallas. That would cover her through her return, though there was only about two and a half months left on the lease.

Amber settled on a carton of organic orange juice and turned to grab a glass from one of the tall cabinets. She briefly wondered if she could set aside enough money to cover her half of the rent through the end of the lease while she was here. As she turned back to the fridge, however, all thoughts of budgeting immediately disappeared. She nearly dropped her glass as her gaze landed on a bikini-clad figure lounging poolside.

Despite Brooke's designer sunglasses shielding her eyes, Amber could tell that she was awake from the way her thumbs typed furiously on her phone. Brooke relaxed along the chaise and rested her phone on her bare stomach for a moment.

It's not fair Amber thought miserably. *Why does she have to be so sexy?*

Amber bit her lip and, after a moment of thought, she opened the sliding glass door. Brooke startled as Amber padded around the perimeter of the pool before sinking into the chaise next to her.

"TGIF," Amber remarked. "One week at the Chamber down."

Brooke sat up quickly and glanced at the clock on her phone. She had lost track of time after her late-afternoon client had rescheduled and hadn't expected Amber home so quickly. She stretched her legs and crossed them loosely under her.

"I'm still working," she replied, hoping that Amber would go back inside. "The nice thing about real estate? You can do most of the work from your phone."

She glanced up pointedly and immediately regretted it. Amber wore a dash of gloss that accentuated her full lips and made Brooke momentarily forget all about the comps she was trying to pull in Old Town.

Amber smiled but appeared to be looking everywhere but at her. "Lucky you," she replied. "Where's my mom and Dave? I thought they'd be home."

Brooke wondered for a moment if Amber was flustered. Deliciously, she allowed her mind to wander for a split second to the possibilities of Amber's low flush being the result of Brooke's bikini and bare skin, heated and warm from the late afternoon sun.

This is dangerous she told herself. *It's risky to be home alone with Amber, but even worse when she's sitting right next to me.*

"They're on their weekly date night," Brooke replied with a shrug. "Apparently they have more of a Friday social life than either of us. I think they went to dinner and then shopping at the Key West Greenmarket. Farmers' market, so, you know," Brooke's gaze fell to her lap. "I imagine they'll be preoccupied for a long while.

I should go inside Brooke thought. *To shower and finish my work in the bedroom.* As Amber leaned back in the chaise and gathered her soft hair into a loose ponytail off her neck, however, Brooke wondered why she would ever want to be anywhere but right there.

"Good for them," Amber replied after a moment. "Do you get a lot of new clients around this time of year?"

These kinds of thoughts are dangerous Brooke reminded herself. She glanced down at her phone. *What did Amber ask? About clients? Yes, work. Focus on that.*

"It's the busy season," she answered with a nod. "But I get all kinds of clients, so it keeps it interesting. My newest client is some kind of millionaire poultry heiress. And yesterday I helped a retired couple close on a condo they plan to move into once they sell their family home in Indiana."

Amber nodded, seemingly satisfied with that information. Brooke waited a beat to see if she'd go inside, but nearly groaned with frustration when Amber drummed her fingers against her thigh instead.

Brooke stared pointedly at her phone, her thumbs frozen over the keypad. *What was I doing? Oh, right. Comps. Now do these sellers have three or four bedrooms again?*

"So, what else is there to do on a Friday night in Key West?" Amber asked pointedly. She squinted at the sky.

"Hold on, let me finish this..." Brooke muttered.

Focus she reminded herself. It really wasn't fair that Amber had the uncanny ability to distract her. Brooke was sure she saw Amber make a face from the corner of her eye.

What was the price range for those comps? She wondered. *700 or 800,000?*

"Is work all you do, even on Friday nights?" Amber asked. She sounded suspiciously close to pouting. Brooke finally glanced at her to make a pointed remark, but the words died on her lips when she met Amber's imploring smile. She had turned her body toward Brooke and gazed at her with a disarming grin that made Brooke forget all about the Key West real estate market for good.

After a moment, Brooke realized she was smiling back. *There's nothing wrong with putting my phone away and taking a break* she thought defensively.

"Come on," she said as she stood. "I want to show you my favorite place in Key West."

For the briefest of moments, she was sure Amber's eyes had widened imperceptibly as her gaze swept over Brooke's body.

Trick of the light she thought as Amber blinked.

Brooke started toward the sliding glass door. She was oddly excited to put work away for the evening and focus on something more, rather some*one,* much more...

Interesting she thought, turning once and sneaking an appreciative glance at Amber. *Much more interesting.*

Brooke cocked her head as Amber stared back at her. She was all wide eyes and messy hair and it made Brooke swallow quickly.

Beautiful she added silently, before she could stop it. *Much more beautiful too.*

Amber finally stood. "Sounds fun," she replied, her voice somewhat faint. "Let's go."

Brooke smiled again and raised an eyebrow. "Oh, and you'll need your bathing suit."

CHAPTER 19

Brooke had no idea what in the Universe had compelled her to invite Amber on an impromptu beach trip. As she waited in her car and pondered the ease with which the other woman had distracted her, she glanced at Evangeline on the dashboard.

The hula doll stared blankly back at her. "Shut up," Brooke muttered.

She glanced up as Amber sauntered down the driveway. Her camera was slung over one shoulder and her hair was long and loose over her shoulders. Cut-off denim shorts and a simple striped tank top over her bathing suit left just enough of Amber's golden skin exposed. Brooke blinked to keep herself from staring.

God, I wish this was a real date the thought was alive in Brooke's head before she had a chance to stop it. She took a deep breath and quickly reminded herself that this was completely, *definitely* not a date. As if to prove her point, she leaned over the middle console and cracked the passenger door for Amber.

See? She thought satisfactorily. *Totally unromantic. If this had been a date, I would've gotten out of my car and opened the door for Amber.*

"Where to?" Amber asked as she climbed into the passenger's seat.

She leaned back and smiled. "I'm excited to see what constitutes as Brooke Adriani's favorite place on the island," she finished teasingly.

"I'll tell you," Brooke countered as she pulled onto Roosevelt Boulevard. "Smathers Beach."

Amber looked confused. "Smathers Beach?" She asked. "But isn't that..."

"Where all the tourists hang out?" Brooke answered for her. "Yes. It's the largest public beach on the island, so it's a huge draw. But Smathers Beach at sunset, after all the tourists have packed it in and left? Easily the most beautiful place in the continental United States."

"Wow," Amber replied, impressed. "I should warn you that you're setting the bar pretty high. I've been to some beaches myself, you know, like South Padre and Galveston..." she paused and grinned. "As cool as they were, I don't know if I'd say it was the most *beautiful* place..."

Brooke shot her a look. "Do you trust me?"

Amber's teasing grin faded into something unreadable as she met Brooke's eyes. "Yes," she answered hesitantly.

Brooke smiled. "Good," she replied as she eased into a public parking space. There were only a handful of other cars parked nearby. *Quiet now, just as I thought.* "Because we're here."

The expansive sky looked ethereal as they exited the car. Pale yellow light from the setting sun illuminated the horizon and gave the entire sky a magical, otherworldly glow. Thin, wispy clouds that had always reminded Brooke of eclectic brushstrokes gently rolled past as Amber's sharp intake of breath caused her to still for a moment.

"It's *gorgeous*!" She exclaimed.

Brooke bit her lip to avoid the response that was poised so easily on her tongue – *Yes, and so are you* – and instead nodded at the car. "I have some extra towels in the trunk," she said. "The best part of this beach is all the way at the end. Under that palm tree over there."

Amber craned her neck and turned back with a grin. "This is incredible, Brooke," she replied. "You weren't lying about this spot at sunset."

Brooke strode past Amber and shot her a teasing half-smile that said *I told you so.* She tossed her one of the thick beach towels slung over her forearm. "I'd never lie to you," Brooke responded cheekily as she continued walking.

She grinned to herself as she heard Amber padding through the soft sand behind her. *I'll let her figure that one out.* Brooke knew she was hopelessly flirting with Amber, that she already felt lighter and more relaxed than she had all week and that she was edging into dangerous territory.

So much for avoidance she thought with a sigh as they set up their towels beneath the large palm tree. It was Brooke's favorite spot, at the end of the beach and away from the groups of tourists and rows of beach volleyball nets. It was close to where the sand curved gently into the ocean and met a rocky outcrop that jutted about thirty feet into the water. The tall palm tree rustled with the evening breeze. Its trunk had long ago curved toward the ocean at such an angle that its long green leaves provided a small patch of protection from the elements.

Brooke took a long sip from the clear plastic cup she had purchased from a vendor near where they had parked. The crisp taste of Corona with freshly squeezed lime quenched her suddenly dry mouth. The hard salted rim scraped against her lips as she stole a glance at Amber.

"Mmm," she murmured as she dug into an Italian ice. Amber sucked the sticky-sugary mixture of tart lemon juice, ice and sweet cane sugar from a plastic spoon and shook her hair off her neck. "This is refreshing."

Keep your thoughts PG Brooke warned herself sternly. *Fantasizing about kissing the half-melted Italian ice off your father's girlfriend's daughter's lips is the exact opposite of avoiding this...this silly crush. Or whatever it is.*

To Brooke's relief, Amber set the cup of Italian ice onto the sand and fiddled with her camera. A look of focus set her jaw as she adjusted the lens and checked the aperture.

"So why photography?" Brooke asked. "What is it about photography that you love so much?"

Amber gazed thoughtfully at the foamy tide and then took a deep breath. "Okay, so the way I see it?" She started. "Go with me here. Our entire lives are a series of moments. They define us and shape who we are and what we become. These memories live in our mind's eye and deep in our hearts for a lifetime. I mean, everyone has certain moments they wish they could freeze and relive on this happy loop forever, right?"

Brooke paused. For some reason, she thought of her mother and the picture that Amber had stumbled across at her duplex. "You're right," she replied carefully.

"So, being able to have those moments and give others those moments is incredible," Amber's eyes lit up as she continued. "Memories fade and even the most vivid images in your mind will eventually become fuzzy over time. Photography gives you the ability to give people their beautiful moments, their most cherished memories, in a tangible form that will live forever and can be revisited anytime. I mean, even after the physical body is long gone, the generation after you will still have these pieces of a life...*Your* life. It's proof you were real. It's *magical*," She paused for a breath and then, suddenly shy, she met Brooke's eyes. "What?"

Brooke was taken by Amber's unbridled passion and the fiery, confident way in which she described what photography meant to her. There was something intoxicating and contagious about it. "I never thought about photography like that," she replied honestly. "And now I don't know if I'll ever think the way I did before about it," she finished with a laugh.

Amber grinned. "You want to see how the camera works?" She offered. "There's a lot of pieces and moving parts. Took me forever to figure it all out, but I'm self-taught."

Brooke placed a hand over her chest in mock surprise. "And you're going to reveal all of your tricks of the trade to *me*?"

As they laughed together, there was a brief pause. "Yeah, well, you're special," Amber replied with a teasing gleam in her eyes. Quickly, she glanced back at her camera and scooted closer to Brooke on the towel.

Brooke swallowed hard and tried to keep her thoughts on the impromptu photography lesson. She was relaxed with Amber. Nothing about the evening felt forced. In fact, when Brooke thought harder about it, avoiding Amber was what felt forced. Uncomfortable. Unnatural, even. But laughing together on the beach and getting to know the passionate, free-spirited woman she had been so quick to write off in the beginning was one of the better ways Brooke could recall ending her week.

"See, if you hold it," Amber went on and paused as she handed the camera to Brooke. "And get used to the feel of it in your hands? Then it's much easier to take high quality photos. I've used this camera so much that it's practically an extension of my own hands. It's weird," she shook her head. "Even though I haven't used the camera as much lately, my brain and my body still remember exactly which buttons are where and how to navigate."

Brooke turned the camera over in her hands. "It's heavier than I thought."

Amber nodded. "That's because it's a DSLR," she replied. "They're usually heavier and larger than other cameras."

"Maybe you could show me your work sometime," Brooke said as she handed it back to Amber. "I'd love to see it."

Amber smiled. "I'd love to show it to you," she replied. "*If* I liked anything I've shot recently. That's the thing about passion. That energy, it's contagious. It's transcendent and it shows in everything you do. You can see the difference between some of my earlier photos, when I was younger and didn't care so much about the rules, and now. In the last year, I started to second-guess myself a lot." She took a deep breath and looked out to the ocean again. "I wasn't feeling secure in my relationship or my career and that chipped away at the passion. I know I'll find it again. It doesn't fade." Amber shook her head gently, but didn't take her eyes off the water. "I just hate the wasted time."

Brooke nodded slowly, no longer sure if Amber was taking about photography or love or both. The beginning of a jealous fire sparked somewhere deep in her stomach. The imaginary flames heated her as she tried not to notice Amber's nearness.

You're jealous she realized. *Jealous of what? That Amber loved somebody else?*

Brooke couldn't help it. She touched Amber's hand comfortingly and waited until the other woman met her eyes. She was surprised when Amber's fingers curled tighter around hers as she tried to sort out the confusing mess of emotions coursing through her body.

She's holding your *hand now* Brooke told herself as she scoffed at the sudden streak of jealousy.

"Brooke?" Amber's voice was soft and quiet, a question in the way she spoke her name.

Kiss her Brooke thought. With a start, she realized this was achingly close to her brief fantasy while at Seven Fish with Adam. Just as she leaned forward to give in to her curiosity about Amber's soft lips, a soccer ball bounced across their towel and skidded to a stop in the sand.

"Sorry!" A younger man in swimming trunks ran after the ball and waved. He grinned sheepishly as he plucked it from near the surf. "Sorry about that."

Brooke reddened with embarrassment as she watched as he loped back across the beach to his friends. There had been a split-second, but it had passed and now she felt awkward and vulnerable.

Say something she told herself. *Anything.*

"The photographer that my brokerage outsources all our home photos to has something like that," Brooke continued as she deftly scooted back on the towel and pointed at Amber's camera. Work automatically came to mind as a safe, benign subject.

"What?" Amber asked. She raised an eyebrow and tried to search Brooke's gaze. "Wait, I…"

Don't say anything Brooke pleaded silently. She knew Amber had felt the moment too and immediately cursed herself for letting it get nearly out of hand. *Please don't say anything.*

"Yeah, I always wondered how he takes such great photos of our homes," Brooke forged ahead quickly. "Hey, that's it!" She snapped her fingers as an idea hit her. "Our photographer is freelance and he's been slammed. He works with several other brokerages in the Keys *and* does weddings too. Maybe I could talk to some of our agents and have you shoot a few houses."

"Really?" Amber asked slowly. "You would do that?"

"I mean, if it's something you'd be interested in," Brooke replied. She slowly raked her fingers through the soft sand next to the towel. "I know you said you hadn't been feeling inspired lately. It's not, like, *Better Homes & Gardens* or anything, but it would be paid photography work and something you could add to your portfolio. Maybe it would help you to get back behind the lens."

"That's really sweet, Brooke," Amber replied with an excited smile. "Thank you. I really appreciate it."

In one sip, Brooke drained the last of her Corona. With a safe distance between them, her head was beginning to clear. "I can't believe I didn't think of it before," she admitted. "Besides, it's the least I can do. You helped me *parasail* earlier this week. I've been afraid of heights for as long as I can remember. Never in a million years did I think I would do something like that." She paused and smiled triumphantly. "I'll help you too."

NIGHT HAD WASHED over the island as Amber settled into the passenger's seat of Brooke's car. She had apologized profusely for the sand she'd tracked into her pristine vehicle, but the other woman wouldn't hear of it.

It was an odd contrast, as Amber remembered how obsessive Lena was with her own vehicle. *One thing about power lesbians* she thought. *They certainly love their cars.*

As she settled into a comfortable silence, Amber replayed the evening in her mind. Something she had never admitted out loud was that one of the reasons she loved photography was because it relaxed her. It allowed her solitude with her thoughts and brought her back to that all-important present moment. She stole a glance at Brooke in the driver's seat, confident, poised and *so* casually sexy, as passing streetlights splashed over her sun-streaked blonde locks and highlighted the dimples on either side of her mouth.

That would be a picture she thought told herself before forcing her eyes back to the road ahead. Amber held back a wistful sigh as she wondered about that near-kiss on the towel. *I didn't imagine that, right?* Brooke's walls had been so quick to go back up that Amber thought it may have been wishful thinking. *But I've been kissed by so many unsure women before. And I'm always the one who ends up hurt in the end because I tell myself that I can make them love me back, even though they never will.*

"I never realized there was so much to photography," Brooke spoke, her voice jarring Amber from her thoughts. Her hand dangled casually over the steering wheel as she glanced at her with a quick smile. "I think I have a newfound appreciation for the art."

"Really?" Amber asked dubiously.

"Of course," Brooke replied, her eyes on the road. "I took an elective photography class in high school, but I wish it had been more hands-on. I mean, it's hard to get students engaged when you just talk at them and click through slides, you know? Let them get involved instead. Show them how to take apart and put a camera back together, let them play with the settings, teach them tricks in Photoshop. I think it would have been much more interesting if the class had been structured that way."

Amber's head snapped up as the wheels began turning in her brain. She blinked as the seeds of an idea began to take root. "That's it!" She exclaimed. "Oh my God, Brooke, that's *it*!"

Brooke glanced at her from her peripheral. "Sorry, I'm lost."

Amber twisted in her seat and faced Brooke eagerly. "The expo! At the Chamber of Commerce," she tried to explain. Her brain seemed to be cranking out thoughts faster than her mouth could keep up. "They're trying to rebrand it from being a formal affair to a family-friendly event that kids will be interested in." Amber paused and lightly smacked her palm against her forehead. "We've been racking our brains trying to figure out how to remodel the whole event on such short notice."

Brooke raised an eyebrow as she pulled into the driveway. "You want to make it more interactive?"

Amber nodded so quickly that she nearly got dizzy with enthusiasm. "Exactly," she replied. "I mean, *duh*! Kids have short attention spans and everything so interactive these days already. They need to touch and do things on their own. *That's* how you get them engaged and pique their interest."

Brooke nodded as her smile grew. "That's a great idea, Amber," she agreed. "That leaves so many possibilities for what you could do."

Amber grinned. "It was *your* idea!" She exclaimed as she threw off her seatbelt. "Photo booths, interactive contests, iPads in the expo hall for immediate digital photo purchases. The theme is *The Best of Key West* so the sky is really the limit."

As they walked into the foyer, Amber shook her head slowly. "I have to get on my laptop," she went on. "I need to work through these ideas and get them shaped, so I can put together a slideshow. I need something coherent for Bobbi first thing Monday morning."

Brooke paused as they reached the top of the stairs. Without a second thought, Amber whirled around and hugged her. "Thank you so much," she whispered. She had meant the gratitude to be casual, but her voice caught instead and the words came out soft and hoarse.

Amber quickly pulled away before the danger of hugging Brooke could catch up to her. *Haven't you embarrassed yourself enough today?* She thought, thinking again of their near-kiss.

As she gently shut her bedroom door behind her, Amber spied her laptop on the nightstand. She woefully tried to console herself with a reminder that Brooke Adriani was quite possibly the most emotionally unavailable woman in the Florida Keys, but the thought didn't seem to help as well as it did before.

Amber sat cross-legged on the bed and waited as Windows booted up. The blue glow of the screen illuminated the dark bedroom as she anxiously tapped her index and middle fingers against the worn trackpad. Infused with a frenetic energy thanks to conflicting, smoldering thoughts of Brooke, jumbled ideas for the exhibition and the need to get them all out of her brain and onto a slide deck, Amber glanced at the digital alarm clock and smiled to herself.

It was going to be a long night.

CHAPTER 20

The early Sunday afternoon sun was high in the sky, beating down on Brooke's back in hot, sticky beams that seared through her spandex tank top and caused a trickle of sweat to snake between her shoulder blades.

She paused in the parking lot of the local fitness center, where she was meeting Justin for a high-intensity spin class, as another bead of sweat ran the length of her spine. Though Lydia certainly wasn't the only instructor at Sun Studios, Brooke thought it best to find another fitness center and had wheedled Justin to cycling class instead.

Her phone jangled loudly in her duffel bag and she crouched as she fished through it. Brooke had spent nearly all day yesterday with the chicken heiress, narrowing down fifteen potential homes to five. Considering just how high maintenance the heiress, Kelsey DuPont, had been, Brooke considered that a win.

Please be her Brooke sent up a silent prayer as she grabbed her phone. *Please tell me that she's decided to make an offer.*

"This is Brooke," she answered matter-of-factly.

"Hey, it's Michael," the vaguely familiar voice replied.

She wrinkled her nose as she tried to place the friendly tone.

"From First Stop Restoration?" He continued uncertainly into the silence that stretched over the line.

Right, the superintendent who has been overseeing the reconstruction at my duplex Brooke quickly recalled. "Michael, yes!" She exclaimed, hoping to keep the disappointment from her voice. "How's it going?"

As Brooke dreaded the idea of going to see another ten-plus houses that Kelsey would undoubtedly turn her nose up at and complain loudly about, Michael cleared his throat.

"Great, thanks," he replied. "I'm at your duplex now to check our crew's progress and I wanted to give you an update. They've been working real hard and it looks like they're going to finish ahead of schedule. The cabinets and flooring have been reinstalled and the only thing we're waiting on is a final clean-up. That's scheduled for tomorrow. I'll stop by again in the evening, but I'd say you should be able to move back in on Tuesday."

Brooke leaned against the back bumper of her car and processed this. It was about a week ahead of the original estimate's schedule, which she knew was nearly unheard of in the construction industry.

I should be elated she thought. *Jumping for joy at getting out of Dad's house a week early and having my duplex back.* Brooke wondered why she instead felt rather...underwhelmed.

"That's wonderful news," Brooke forced cheer into her voice. "Thank you."

As Michael launched into a full overview of each line item on the estimate, the odd feeling of disappointment didn't sit well. She had been so distracted with...other things...that the prospect of eventually moving back into her duplex had completely escaped her.

While her mind immediately went to work and closings and difficult new millionaire clients named Kelsey, a single face flashed behind her eyes. With a sigh, Brooke knew deep down exactly *who*, not what, she had been so distracted by.

"I'll give you a call tomorrow after the final clean-up," Michael continued. "Unless something unexpected comes up, you'll be good to move in no later than Tuesday. Will it be okay to give you a confirmation call then?"

"Sounds good," Brooke replied, half-listening. The idea of not being under the same roof as Amber was one that Brooke didn't like. As she chewed her bottom lip thoughtfully, she realized she wanted more time.

Time for what? She wondered.

"Great," Michael went on. "Talk to you late tomorrow then."

"Sounds good," Brooke repeated. She squinted in the sun as she gazed across the parking lot. The heat was getting to her now. Her back was soaked and she could feel droplets of sweat forming along her hairline. "Thanks you for everything."

As they hung up, Brooke pushed herself off her bumper and walked into the gym. The thick heat made quick movements difficult and her legs felt as though they were moving through molasses as she finally pushed open the door of the fitness center. An icy blast of air conditioning shot out and immediately made her shiver.

"Brooke!" Justin's familiar voice called. She glanced up and grinned at his expectant face as he waited outside the low-lit cycle room.

She waved back and promised herself that she would reexamine her conflicting feelings for Amber later. For now, she welcomed another distraction – Exercise and conversation with her best friend.

TWENTY MINUTES into the spin class, and Brooke's sweat had returned with a vengeance. She and Justin had quickly learned that the instructor was a professional mountain biker and not someone who was going to take it easy on a Sunday group exercise class.

"Are you excited?" Brooke panted as she stood from the bike seat for a moment and continued to pedal. "Adam is coming to town this weekend. Yesterday, I submitted the offer for the condo he decided on before the chicken heiress bogarted the rest of my day. I haven't heard back from the sellers yet, but they're very eager to offload according to their listing agent. I suspect it'll be a smooth negotiation."

Justin was quiet, a look of fierce focus in his eyes as he stared ahead. "I'm excited, yeah," he replied off-handedly. "But he's bringing

Trey this weekend too. He wants him to finally see the island, so he can be excited for the move."

"That makes sense," Brooke reasoned. "After all, that's a hell of a cross-country move for a kid. I'm sure it will be hard to leave his school and friends."

Justin nodded and was quiet again. "Adam and I have been Face-Time-ing every day," he went on. "And when we're not video chatting, we're either talking on the phone or texting." He paused and sighed. "Adam is amazing, Brooke. I've never met someone so genuine. He's a great person. Even if I could have designed my perfect man, I don't think I would have come close to Adam."

Brooke raised an eyebrow and stole a glance at her friend. "That's great, Justin," she replied carefully. The burn in her calves grew as the instructor told the class to increase their gear. "So why do you sound so serious?"

"The kid thing," Justin replied, looking torn. "The last couple of times we've video chatted, Adam had Trey talk to me too. I know they're a package deal and I knew from the beginning that Adam has a son, but..." he paused and swallowed hard. "It's just a lot. I never thought about kids, really. And now I feel like I'll automatically become a dad if I'm with Adam. I'm not trying to be selfish, I'm really not. I just...never thought about being a dad."

Brooke glanced at him as he grunted on the bike. "It's fine if you're not ready, Justin," she replied. "But it's something you should decide sooner than later. It sounds like you're falling for Adam and you're right that he and Trey are a package deal. It wouldn't be fair to either of them or to yourself to string them along for a few months, become attached and then decide the relationship isn't for you."

"I know," Justin responded miserably. "Trust me, I know." He sighed and then tried a small smile. "Trey is a pretty cool kid though," he went on. "Wicked smart. He told me he won the entire first grade science fair earlier this year."

Brooke smiled at her friend as they lowered the gear on their bikes and prepared for a sprint. "You know," she started as she began to pedal faster. "Just because something is different doesn't mean it's bad.

You're falling for Adam and, as your best friend, I think it's adorable. I can picture it. You, Adam and Trey, a family of three. You just have to let it happen and trust that Adam is the one."

They sprinted harder and the room was silent, save for the sounds of flywheels cutting through air. After a moment, Justin shot her a knowing glance.

"What?" Brooke asked.

Justin opened and then closed his mouth and shook his head. "I can picture it too," he replied honestly. "And what about you? Any women on your radar?"

Brooke laughed, a short sound that she hoped relayed how crazy that notion was. "Yeah, right," she responded. "Like I have the time."

Justin threw her a sideways glance. "What about Amber?"

Brooke's heartbeat kicked up a notch at the mention of her name, but she tried to blame it on the sprint. "What about her?" She replied as casually as she could muster.

Justin rolled his eyes. "Don't play dumb, Brooke," he went on. "I know you too well. First off, she's easily one of the nicest and most personable people I've met," he paused and sat up on the bike, taking his hands from the handlebars and ticking off on his fingers. "Secondly, she is drop-dead gorgeous. Even *I* can see that. Third, she lives with you. Well, technically with your dad. But still, since you guys are playing The Brady Bunch this summer, you might as well recognize that a great woman is right there, under your nose, and wake up. Do something about it! Fourth, she brings you out of your shell and *that's* hard. I've been trying for years. Oh, and fifth? Amber is *clearly* crazy about you, Brooke."

Justin met her eyes, grinned and waggled his fingers at her. "Need I say more?"

Brooke couldn't remember the last time she had been rendered totally speechless, but she blinked as she tried to process Justin's words. One sentence in particular stuck out the most, and it caused an excited flutter deep in her stomach.

"What...What do you mean, Amber is crazy about me?" She

started, rolling her eyes and hoping it gave her an air of playing it cool.

Justin fixed her with a look and cranked the gear on his bike again. "Trust me, anyone with *eyes* can see how she looks at you," he replied. "She likes you."

Brooke tried to fight the warm flush that spread over her neck and chest. "She likes everybody," she scoffed and then shrugged. "Some people are just that kind and unjaded."

"Why are you argui..." Justin started and then stopped short. He glanced at her with wide eyes as his bike nearly sputtered to a stop. "Oh my God, *you* like her too!"

"What?" Brooke started hastily. She immediately shook her head and tried to backtrack. "That's crazy, I..."

"I *knew* it!" Justin crowed. Two cyclists in the row of bikes ahead turned back and glanced pointedly at them.

"Would you be quiet?" Brooke hissed. "You *don't* know!"

"I do too," Justin went on, his tone softer this time. "I had a feeling. I recognized it that first day at your duplex and then again when we went parasailing. You're falling hard for her, Brooke."

"I...That's...No, I mean," Brooke spluttered. She wondered when she had become so transparent and then remembered that Justin knew her better than most. It was silly to lie to him. "I just..." Brooke blinked and bit her lip before meeting his eyes. "What do I do?"

Justin smiled proudly as he shrugged. "You talk to her," he started. "You open yourself up, bit by bit, and let her see the real you. After all, wasn't it you who advised me that just because something is different doesn't mean it's bad?"

"It's hard to stop thinking about her," Brooke admitted. "Sometimes the strangest or most random thing will make me think of her, and I immediately want to text her just to say hi. I've *never* felt compelled to do that before. Or...Or...If I'm having trouble falling asleep at night, I'll sometimes picture her in her room. Nothing creepy, of course, but I'll picture myself sleeping next to her or, you know, her in my arms. It relaxes me so much that I fall asleep right away." Brooke paused and took a deep breath. "That's weird, right?"

Justin laughed. “Not weird,” he confirmed. “You only just described every person that’s ever been in love.”

As the instructor directed them through their cool-down exercises, Brooke quietly considered this. It felt good, freeing even, to speak openly with her best friend. She couldn’t deny that it felt as though some sort of boulder had been removed from her shoulders.

Now what exactly do I do about Amber?

CHAPTER 21

Amber rushed into the Key West Chamber of Commerce offices at exactly 8:29 A.M. on Monday morning. She had spent most of the weekend working on her presentation, reviewing all of the details, researching information from vendors and trying to anticipate any of what 'what ifs' that Bobbi would surely throw at her. Not wanting to risk any superstitions, Amber had taken care to ensure that the morning was so far perfect. After her usual sunrise vinyasa flow with her mother, Amber had dropped her off at the house and then stopped at the nearest Starbucks for a pick-me-up and a final review of the slides she had worked so hard on. She loathed coffee, but decided to make an exception just this once. She wanted to be fully caffeinated and ready for the impromptu meeting.

The espresso tasted thick and bitter on her tongue as she settled in at her desk and booted up her computer. Bobbi's sturdy SUV was already in the parking lot

At 8:36, she knocked on Bobbi's partially-ajar door. The older woman was clear about her open-door policy when it came to employees, so Amber wasn't worried about bothering her boss. Besides, she had a feeling that Bobbi would be just as thrilled once

Amber launched into the details that she had spent the weekend smoothing out.

"Good morning," Amber said warmly, as she rapped her knuckles against the frosted glass of Bobbi's door. "I was wondering if you had a couple of minutes to chat about the exhibition."

Amber strode halfway into Bobbi's office and then stopped short. The other woman looked small behind a large bouquet of fruit cut into flower shapes.

Bobbi nodded and smiled wanly. "Of course," she replied. "Come, sit down." She gestured at a chair in front of her desk. "What's on your mind?"

Amber was thoroughly thrown off by the presence of the edible arrangement and the sadness in Bobbi's eyes. "Wow, where did *that* come from?" She asked, with a nod at the fruit bouquet.

Bobbi blinked back at the arrangement. "Actually, myself," she answered and then picked a sliced strawberry on a thin wooden stick from the center of the bouquet. "Berry?" She asked.

Amber shook her head uncertainly. "Oh, uh, no," she replied, feeling more confused than ever. "I had a croissant at Starbucks earlier."

Bobbi popped the strawberry into her mouth right from the stick and shrugged. "Well, if you get hungry in a bit and decide you want some fruit," she continued, spreading her hands across her desk. "I have plenty of it to go around."

Amber nodded slowly. This wasn't how the presentation was supposed to start. Bobbi looked crestfallen and the mysterious fruit bouquet loomed between them.

She opened her mouth to steer the conversation back to the exhibition, but Bobbi shook her head silently and turned to the window in thought.

"You know, do you ever..." she started and then sighed as she crossed her arms. "Have you ever cared for someone so deeply and then something happened to tear the two of you apart, but it wasn't your fault? Do you ever feel as though the Universe is conspiring against you?"

Amber wasn't sure how to respond. She blinked as the awkward silence stretched between them and then Bobbi quickly shook her head.

"I'm sorry," she apologized. "That's not what you came here for. You had something you wanted to discuss and here I am, bothered by my personal life. Or what used to be some semblance of a personal life. My apologies."

"I have," Amber replied quickly and then paused. "Felt that way, I mean. I have felt that the Universe was conspiring against me. And that frustration doesn't just go away because you walk through the doors of your office. I understand. We're all human."

Bobbi smiled. "Terri," she finally admitted.

"Terri?" Amber asked. "The sand artist?"

Bobbi nodded. "We were together for fourteen years. Fourteen lovely, crazy, imaginative and challenging years that were cut short right after Christmas."

Amber's heart went out to the other woman. "Oh Bobbi, I'm so sorry."

"The last year or so had been very trying," Bobbi went on as she picked a daisy-shaped piece of pineapple from the bouquet. "All long-term relationships go through their rough patches, that's normal. Expected, even. But this one seemed to be never-ending. Lots of arguing, getting onto one another's cases for minor things which naturally then became bigger things. But in all that time, giving up on her was never an option."

Amber nodded, waiting for Bobbi to continue. *The presentation can wait* she thought.

"Then the office manager happened," Bobbi said with a sigh. "She was a friend of mine. We'd go out for happy hour here and there, perhaps a working lunch. As far as I've always known, she was straight. When she learned that Terri and I were having problems, things changed. She became...interested. Curious. Started confiding her own problems with her boyfriend to me." Bobbi's eyes looked far away as she shook her head. "I suppose that was my fault. I should have recognized the signs. Despite what felt like a blossoming friendship, it wasn't necessarily appropriate due to the fact that we were colleagues."

Amber nodded again. She had a feeling she knew where this was going.

"Anyhow, the office manager eventually quit," Bobbi went on briskly. "It came as a huge shock to me. I had never considered our relationship as anything more than platonic. My heart was always with Terri. However, during the office manager's exit interview, she confided to H.R. that she was hopelessly in love with me and couldn't stand to work together any longer while having to deny that her feelings existed. She was under the impression that, if she quit, her and I would be together."

Amber's mouth dropped open. "That sounds..."

"Crazy," Bobbi finished with a nod. "And it was. Absolutely. Despite the fact that I've never had any infractions during my tenure with the Chamber, H.R. was required to look into this to find out if anything against policy had taken place."

Bobbi glanced at the fruit bouquet bitterly. "It destroyed what was already a troubled relationship and ruined any chance for us to mend things. Even though H.R. eventually closed their investigation and ultimately sided with me, it had already ruined Terri's trust in me. I don't know that she ever truly believed that nothing happened. *Especially* because we had already been having such a rough go of things."

Realization washed over Amber. "So you sent the edible arrangement..."

"To Terri, yes," Bobbi replied. "I promised her in the beginning of our relationship that I would never give up on her and I haven't yet. But..." she sighed and gestured at the fruit. "It's becoming very disheartening. She's put up this wall and it's impenetrable. She won't even hear me. She acts as though I don't exist."

"Maybe she just needs time," Amber offered. She felt highly unqualified to give her boss any relationship advice.

"One can only hope," Bobbi replied. "Sitting back and waiting has never been a strong suit of mine."

"Fourteen years is a long time," Amber replied.

"Now that I've talked your ear off about everything *not* work-related, what was it you had wanted to discuss?" Bobbi asked. "Something about the exhibition?"

Amber blinked as she tried to reel herself back into professional mode. "Yes," she answered with a quick nod. "I know how we can rebrand this event and make it into a cohesive, successful affair that accomplishes all of the objectives you've put forward."

Bobbi slid her glasses onto her nose from the colorful chain dangling around her neck. "Well, I like what I'm hearing so far," she spoke matter-of-factly. "How are we going to do this? Let's see what you've got."

As Amber clicked over to the PowerPoint presentation on her laptop, thrilled at having piqued Bobbi's interest, she launched into her ideas. They were all backed with details, facts, costs and estimated returns, thanks to her research and hours of conversation with associated parties.

After nearly thirty minutes, Amber finally reached her final slide. She glanced at Bobbi and in hopes of any small clues to gauge her reaction. Bobbi sat back in her chair for a long moment, her eyes still on Amber's laptop screen, as she thought.

"I love it," she finally spoke. "This is great."

Amber had to practically restrain herself from jumping for joy, but she couldn't hide her wide smile. "I know there are still some minor details to be ironed out, but I wanted to come prepared with some well-rounded ideas," she replied. "Instead of simply throwing them out there. Now, as for an official event photographer..."

Bobbi met her eyes and shot her a look, as though the answer was obvious. "Why don't you do it?"

"I, uh...I mean, that would be very cool, but," Amber stammered. She hadn't expected that. "But I'm not really a professional. Yet. I..."

"Well, why not?" Bobbi asked. "You have the gear. And the experience. Tell me, what exactly constitutes a professional photographer, anyway? You originally submitted photos for the exhibition, correct?"

Amber was surprised that Bobbi had remembered. "Yes, I did."

"And if I recall, we put them on standby," Bobbi went on. "In the event that any of our chosen photographers were unable to commit to the event. Do you have any idea how competitive this exhibition is? Over fifteen *thousand* applicants, Amber," Bobbi paused. "We rejected a lot more than we accepted or put on standby."

Amber considered this. *When she puts it like that, then...Why not?*

"I'd love to do it," she replied excitedly. "It would be an amazing opportunity to be part of the exhibition in another way. I just..." she paused. "I guess I'm a little rusty. I don't want you to be disappointed."

Bobbi threw her head back and laughed. "Amber, you have not disappointed me yet," she replied and gestured at the slideshow. "Now, give me tonight to meet with the rest of the Chamber Board and discuss these options. You've certainly given us a *lot* to work with and I don't see a single idea on your presentation that may not go over well. Once I have full approval, I want to run with this. I especially love the idea of having professional chalk artists along the walkway leading to the entrance."

Amber nodded enthusiastically, taking that as her cue to leave. "Okay," she replied. "We'll move forward soon then."

"Absolutely," Bobbi continued. She turned to her computer as Amber slipped halfway through the door. "Oh, and Amber?"

She turned as Bobbi met her eyes over the top of her glasses. "Yes?"

"Excellent work," Bobbi replied. "Great job. Thank you."

Amber grinned in response and quietly shut Bobbi's office door behind her. She slowly sat down at her desk and bit back the urge to let out a thrilled squeal. She glanced at her phone and read a text message from Brooke, sent about ten minutes ago.

Hi, how are you? Two agents here each have a condo that they would like to set up photos for this week, if you're available. But more importantly, how did your presentation go?

Amber was pleasantly surprised that Brooke had remembered her ideas. A smile played at her lips as she thought of Brooke, sleek and cool, in her office at that very moment.

The weeks are so busy she thought wistfully. *And this week is about to get even crazier.*

A brief feeling of disappointment washed over Amber as she realized it might be nearly a week until they had any real time together. It seemed far too long, but she told herself that the extra money from the real estate shoots would be helpful.

At this rate, I'll have my half of the rent set aside for the rest of the lease Amber thought. *And then I can really start saving.*

An idea began to take shape in her mind as she remembered that the summer solstice party was Saturday evening. She knew Brooke would be there and the delicious, wicked idea spread its wings further as Amber opened her web browser and searched for local spas, hair salons and clothing boutiques.

There's nothing wrong with using some of this extra money to splurge a bit Amber told herself firmly. *Or with wanting to look nice for the first party I've been to in ages.* She glanced at her shadowy reflection in the window opposite her desk. Her hair was longer than it had been in years and could use a deep conditioning.

Maybe even some subtle lowlights Amber thought. *And then an outfit. Definitely something that I'll feel special wearing, but something that fits the evening too.*

As Amber contemplated looks and hairstyles, she knew that there was only one head she wanted to turn on Saturday night. With a devilish smile, she leaned over her desk and jotted a couple of nearby addresses onto a Post-It.

"If I have anything to do with it, Brooke won't even know what hit her," Amber whispered gleefully. She had no time to wonder where her newfound confidence was cropping up from. The long week stretched before her and there was a lot to be done before Saturday's fun.

CHAPTER 22

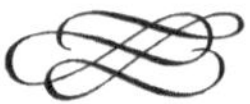

The weekend couldn't come fast enough for Brooke, who took the rare opportunity on Saturday morning to sleep past 9 A.M. By the time she had rolled herself out of bed, Amber was nowhere to be found. Her father was on the patio, sweating profusely under the hot morning sun, as he cleaned the pool and added chemicals.

Brooke poured herself a steaming cup of black coffee and slid into a chair behind the kitchen table. She smiled at Sandra as her father's girlfriend studied two long trays of hors d'oeuvres ready for the oven.

"Those look good," Brooke spoke, nodding at the trays. "What are they?"

Sandra turned with a flourish. "Tomato ombre on toasted flatbread. We got these amazing heirloom tomatoes from the farmers' market that are just delicious. I have a homemade ciabatta recipe that's been handed down my family for generations. Toast it with a little olive oil and garlic, slice up the tomatoes and add a dash of sea salt and black pepper. Pop them into the oven for no more than three to five minutes to get that crunch. Simple, but a perfect dish for summer solstice."

Brooke was positive her mouth was watering at the casual

mentions of garlic, tomato and homemade ciabatta. She realized she must have been staring just a beat too long at the trays as Sandra laughed.

"Would you like to try one?" She asked. Before Brooke could answer, Sandra glided effortlessly across the kitchen and carefully handed her one of the tomato ombres. "You'll have to tell me if it needs anything. After all, I could use a taste-tester. Amber was out of here by eight this morning and said she had a bunch of errands to do before tonight. And your father? Well, he tells me *everything* I make is delicious. Diplomatic, yes, and certainly very smart, but I could use some feedback in the kitchen."

Brooke crunched down on the tomato ombre and closed her eyes for a moment as she savored the heady taste of garlic against the dewy tomatoes. "Wow," she mumbled as she swallowed hard. "This is *really* good."

Sandra winked at her. "I'll put a couple to the side for you," she replied as she turned her attention to a large bowl of shredded crab meat on the counter. "Speaking of, you'll be here for the party, right? It would be a shame if you weren't able to make it."

Brooke nodded. "I'll be here," she confirmed. "I have most of my clothes and things already packed to move back into my place tomorrow."

"And you did the final walk-through with the contractor?" Sandra asked. "Everything looked good?"

"It did," Brooke replied. "The walk-through was on Wednesday morning, but the week, uh..." she faltered as she realized she had no real answer for why she had been procrastinating on the move back. Sure, her week had been busy. *Today* was going to be busy too. She had agreed to pick Adam and Trey up from the airport around lunchtime so they could be present for the inspection at the condo. Still, Brooke had the strange sense that Sandra could always see through her.

Just because she knows the color of my aura doesn't mean she knows everything about me Brooke thought stubbornly and then paused, in disbelief that things like auras were now common ideas.

"Um, but the week just got away from me," she finished lamely. "I thought we had finally found a house for Kelsey DuPont. She even had me write up an offer, only to rescind it the next morning. Then, we found *another* house and she put an offer in on that one. My fingers crossed that everything will go smoothly."

Sandra smiled sympathetically. "She sounds like a tough client."

Brooke nodded. "One of the neediest I've had," she replied. "But that's to be expected when you work with high-income clients and more expensive homes. It's nothing I can't handle."

"I don't think there's much that you can't handle," Sandra agreed with a knowing nod.

Brooke wondered where Amber had gone and what important errands had demanded she leave the house so early on a Saturday morning. They hadn't seen much of each other this week, but Brooke knew some of that was her fault. The other brokers, however, were thrilled with her listing photos and had already begun recommending Amber around the office.

"Say, tequila sunrise or berry vodka spritzer?" Sandra's question cut into Brooke's wandering thoughts as she tried to shake the remaining cobwebs from her brain.

Brooke blinked. "Now?"

Sandra threw her head back and laughed. "No, silly!" She exclaimed. "For tonight. Tequila sunrise goes with the theme of summer solstice, but everybody loves a vodka spritzer. I can cut up these limes, blueberries and raspberries, add them to the berry-flavored vodka we have with a splash of club soda and *voila*! We have a refreshing, adults-only drink."

Brooke half-listened as her mind wandered back to Amber. For a moment, she wondered if Amber had met someone. Her stomach lurched as she realized the idea wasn't totally outlandish. It wasn't as though Key West was lacking in lesbians.

And with her smile? Brooke thought as she struggled to ignore a sudden streak of jealousy. *She could meet someone anywhere.*

"Earth to Brooke," Sandra called, laughing. "I didn't realize the choice between tequila and vodka was so tough."

Brooke shook the thoughts away, but an uneasy feeling remained entrenched in her gut. "Both," she replied. "They each sound perfect. Tequila sunrise is classic and vodka spritzers would be good for anyone who doesn't particularly care for tequila." She waited a beat and took a deep breath, hoping to sound as nonchalant as possible. "So, did Amber mention what she had to do today?"

"Mmm," Sandra replied through a small taste of crab. "I like your thinking. We'll have tequila and vodka. Besides, I have a feeling your father will have a stash of Heineken somewhere in case someone wants a beer instead."

Brooke waited patiently for Sandra to continue. She had already grown accustomed to her free-flowing train of thought and happy-go-lucky energy.

"Oh and Amber!" Sandra went on after a moment, as if remembering Brooke's question. "You know, I'm not sure. I think she said something about going shopping. Wanting to find something to wear for tonight."

Brooke nodded, feeling only slightly appeased. "Oh, that's cool," she replied off-handedly. She smoothed her thumb along the edge of the kitchen table.

Maybe I just sort of want to see her Brooke thought, resigned.

Sandra turned halfway from the counter and met her eyes. She raised an eyebrow and searched her face for a long moment. Brooke shifted uncomfortably before averting her eyes to her nearly-empty coffee mug.

"Were you expecting her for something?" Sandra asked slowly. She turned back to the counter. "If so, you can always give her a call or send a text. God knows Amber always has that phone glued to her somewhere."

"No, no, nothing like that," Brooke replied. She felt silly for pressing Sandra for details on her daughter's whereabouts. "Just curious."

Embarrassed, Brooke stood from the table and began washing her cup at the sink before spotting another mug on the drying rack. She fingered the misshapen handle and smiled at the thick clay.

Geez, someone could kill a person with this thing she thought as she turned the mug over in her hands. *My third-grade art teacher failed to tell me that I was using way too much clay.*

The smooth glaze had dutifully not chipped over the years. It was a crudely-designed cup – sculpture had certainly not been one of Brooke's strengths – and she was pleasantly surprised that it had survived the years. She stopped short as she turned the mug over once more and spotted a small, barely legible inscription that had been thinly carved into the clay before it was fired dry.

Brooke Adriani. Grade 3. To Mommy, I love you.

Brooke's peripheral blurred with unexpected tears. She gently set the mug back onto the drying rack and felt a light arm around her waist before she could turn away.

"I'm sorry," Sandra apologized gently. "I hope you're not upset that I had my morning tea in that mug. I didn't see the inscription until I was washing it out."

Brooke shook her head. "I'm not upset," she replied as she swallowed and composed herself. "Truthfully, I had forgotten about this mug." She smiled and then pretended to flex an arm while holding it. "It certainly is unique, isn't it?"

Sandra laughed and then quickly reached over to dab a tear from the corner of Brooke's eye. "Hey, you had a vision when you created your art. Even if you were only eight or nine years old. I think it's beautiful."

Brooke smiled despite herself. Sandra turned and dropped some sliced strawberries into a blender.

"Here," she went on matter-of-factly. "I'm sure you have plenty to get done before tonight. Let me make you a smoothie to go, a little pick-me-up to give you some extra energy today."

"Oh, you don't have to do that..." Brooke started. She had already planned a run through the Starbucks drive-through for a double shot before picking up Adam and Trey.

Sandra poured orange juice into the blender and added a handful of ice. She waved a hand as she flipped the machine on. Its loud whirring filled the kitchen as the strawberries and ice melded into the swirling juice.

"Nonsense!" Sandra shouted over the blender. "Did you know that the flavonoids in orange juice stimulate the brain naturally through improved blood flow? This will save you a trip to Starbucks and five dollars, or whatever obscene price they're charging for their beans these days."

She shut off the blender and pulled a plastic travel cup from the cabinet. "Not to mention…" Sandra shouted and then paused. "Oh, that's right. Not to mention," she repeated in a quieter voice. "That this smoothie is much better for you than any syrupy, sugar-filled, mass-produced coffee drink."

Brooke wanted to argue that, despite the empty calories, she actually liked those syrupy, sugar-filled, mass-produced coffee drinks, but thought better of it. A strange sense of comfort replaced her earlier unease as Sandra carefully screwed the lid onto the travel cup and handed it to Brooke.

Is this what it feels like to have a mom? She wondered. Of course she had memories of her own mother, cherished recollections captured in her heart that would often replay in her mind's eye, but they abruptly stopped after the age of ten.

Without another word, Brooke leaned over and embraced Sandra tightly. She knew it was uncharacteristic behavior and grinned at the cautious way in which Sandra hugged her back.

"Thank you," Brooke spoke quietly, before straightening and grabbing her smoothie. "I have to run to the airport and then complete a couple of appointments. What time is the party? Should I be here early to help you set up?"

Sandra shook her head. "No, no, don't worry about that," she replied as she pointed to the patio. "I have your father all day long and, believe me, I'll be putting him to work. You do what you need to do and be back by 6. Party starts around 7, but I'm sure you'll want to get ready."

Brooke nodded as she headed for the front door, slightly disappointed she wouldn't see Amber until then. "Sounds good. I'll be here."

~

As Brooke gently pulled her car to the curb of Key West International Airport, Adam's smiling face was suddenly in view through the passenger's side window, his other hand clutching that of a small boy wearing a green Lego™ Ninjago t-shirt and baggy blue jeans.

Brooke immediately waved back and hurried around the car so to help them transfer their bags into the trunk.

"How are you?" She called. "How was your flight?"

"Not bad," Adam replied, waving her hand away as he lifted his bag into the trunk. "Too early for a Saturday." He winked. "Oh, and this is my son, Trey."

Brooke crouched on the balls of her feet and stuck her hand out. "Hey, Trey," she spoke with a smile. "Welcome to Key West. Are you excited?"

Trey nodded and politely shook her hand, but sank further against his father's waist.

Adam ruffled his hair affectionately. "He's a little shy," he replied. "And probably still waking up. He slept through the *entire* flight."

Brooke nodded at the car. "Well, come on in," she went on. "I think we'll have to head straightaway to the inspection," she continued as they buckled their seatbelts. She paused as she carefully navigated them back into the endless loops of airport traffic. "We may have a few minutes if you'd like to stop somewhere fast for a bite to eat. I don't know how hungry or thirsty you are."

"I'm all right, thanks," Adam replied. He glanced in the backseat at Trey. "I think he'll be okay too. I'm mostly excited to get the home inspection completed. A little nervous too, since there's always the chance there could be something terribly wrong hidden in the condo somewhere."

Adam laughed as Brooke shook the empty travel cup in her middle console. Sandra hadn't lied, the smoothie had been refreshing and sweet. Brooke couldn't be sure, but the natural energy that flowed through her veins might have even been preferable to the jittery coffee buzz she was used to.

"I agree," she replied. "It's the last major step before your closing date, so it's an exciting time. In my professional opinion, I don't think you should worry too much. There may be minor issues that come up, but this building was recently rehabbed from rental units to luxury condominiums. Any major internal issues, such as problems with the electrical, plumbing or HVAC, would have been noted and fixed during that process. It doesn't appear that the current owners did much more than cosmetic remodels, so I don't believe we'll be in for any major shocks."

Brooke pulled quickly onto Government Road and then glided the Lexus around Little Hamaca Park. "Right here is one of seven official city parks on the island," she continued as she gestured out the window. "There are also two children's parks right on the beach. Higgs Beach Children's Park has a playground, swings, the whole works. Trey will love it. And Astro City Park is just a few blocks from the famous Southernmost Point concrete buoy. You know, 90 miles to Cuba?"

Adam nodded excitedly. "That's where everybody takes photos, right?"

Brooke laughed. "It's easily one of the most visited tourist attractions on the entire island. Sometimes there are lines of people all the way down the corner waiting to take pictures by the buoy."

Adam turned toward the backseat again. "What do you say, Trey?" He asked. "Should we take a picture by the big buoy before we leave on Monday?"

Brooke glanced in the rearview mirror in time to see a tentative smile cross Trey's face as he nodded eagerly.

As they pulled up to the condo building, Trey pointed from the backseat and grinned. "Hey, that's cool!"

Brooke followed his small finger as it pointed directly at Evangeline. She bobbed gently on the dashboard as Brooke carefully pulled into an empty space.

"Yeah, I like your hula doll," Adam said as he playfully tapped her head. "I noticed her the first time we were out looking at properties. She's cute."

Brooke met Trey's eyes with a knowing smile. "That's my Key West good luck charm," she spoke conspiratorially. "I found her right after *I* moved here from all the way across the country. She's been hanging out on my dashboard ever since."

Trey's eyes widened. "Do you think I could find a Key West good luck charm?"

Brooke nodded. "Sure," she replied easily. "Maybe you could find a really cool seashell on the beach."

"Yeah!" Trey exclaimed. He looked at his dad. "Maybe Justin will help me find a seashell later."

It was strange hearing her best friend's name from the mouth of a child, but it was also endearing. She smiled as they exited the car and strode across the parking lot to the entrance of the building.

Justin, I sure hope you know what you're getting yourself into Brooke sent up a silent prayer. *Breaking a lover's heart is terrible, but breaking a child's heart is unforgivable.*

As Brooke held open the door for Adam and Trey, her gaze settled on the beach across the street. It had been just over a week since her and Amber's impromptu beach trip, though it felt like a small eternity to Brooke. Somewhere in the back of her mind, she knew her feelings for Amber had developed into something more than the fleeting crushes she'd had before. She smiled to herself as she thought of the evening sun splashing across Amber's face and the way the frothy ocean surf had washed over her feet.

She's different from anyone I've ever met Brooke thought, allowing a moment of private honesty.

It was true. Amber, with her sunny gaze. Amber, easily approaching the world with deep compassion and an open heart despite being hurt. Brooke had spent her adult life placing importance on things that were tangible and measurable. Things like career success, physical fitness and, yes, even pleasure. The feeling, however, that filled her chest whenever Amber was near was equally powerful.

I have to talk to her Brooke realized as she, Adam and Trey waited patiently for the elevator. She recalled Justin's advice to open herself up to Amber, but immediately tensed at the idea. Brooke reminded herself that Amber was not in Key West to stay. It simply didn't make sense. This…*thing* between her and Amber was not black and white. It wasn't something she could quite define, much less easily measure.

"Amber is clearly crazy about you, Brooke" Justin's words rang in her head. *"Anyone with eyes can see how she looks at you."*

As Brooke pondered whether or not this was true, her heárt raced with pride and anticipation. While she waited for Adam and Trey to step into the elevator, she caught sight of her distorted reflection in the glossy marble walls of the lobby. There was a brightness, a clarity even, behind her eyes that hadn't been there before. Everything else except that moment seemed to temporarily disappear. Brooke nodded and, in that moment, her decision was made.

Tonight she told herself. *I have to talk to Amber.*

CHAPTER 23

Amber stared at herself in the long mirror that hogged an entire corner opposite her bed. She swallowed hard and wondered how to feel as confident inside as she appeared on the outside. The day had been busy. She hadn't expected it be quite so time-consuming to find the perfect outfit for the party. Despite several shops in Key West, the majority catered to tourists and beach bums. She soon realized that formal wear was generally considered a tye-dyed wrap to cinch over your bathing suit or a pair of leather sandals versus rubber flip-flops. She had briefly wondered how it could be then that Brooke was always dressed so smartly. She thought of texting her to find out where she did her shopping, but decided against it. Amber wanted to catch Brooke completely off-guard, to see the intrigue and intensity flash through her eyes before she could catch herself.

As the clock struck 6 P.M., Amber studied every angle of herself in the mirror and decided the day had been a success. She had stumbled upon Green Pineapple, a hip, eco-friendly clothing store on Duval Street – Unsurprisingly in the gay mecca of Key West. There, she had found The Dress. A mini tube dress that reached just above her knees, the white linen garment with its large, navy blue bohemian flower pattern was comfortable and seemed to fit like a glove around her curves. A thin chain hung an oversized gold cut-out of a daisy in the hollow of her throat. Given its price, she was sure the necklace wasn't real gold but its color and style had fit the dress perfectly.

Her hair was another big change and Amber slowly ran her brush once more through the straight, glossy locks as she tried to get used to the difference. It had been colored just a shade darker brown and cut so it barely grazed the tops of her shoulders – A "lob", the heavily-tattooed and ultra-hip female hair stylist had called it. The milk-chocolate shade of brown had tiny hints of deep, shimmery red. The stylist had said it would "add dimension", something that Amber had no idea her hair could do. Regardless, she had layered it so it was slightly shorter in the back and softly fit the shape of her face.

A touch of deep brown eyeshadow just under her delicate brow bones and a light dusting of blush across the tops of her cheeks did wonders for playing up the slender angles of her face and bringing out her eyes.

Finally she thought as she added a quick coat of mascara. *Done.*

She blinked once as a knock on the bedroom door roused her from her thoughts.

"Amber?" Her mother called. "Is everything okay?"

Amber opened the door for Sandra, who gasped and blinked. "Sweetheart, you look *fantastic*!" She exclaimed. "That dress is beautiful. Oh, and your hair! Did you darken it? It looks wonderful."

Amber blushed under the unexpected praise and dabbed a touch of clear gloss across her lips. "Do you really think so?" She asked. "Is it too much?"

Sandra shook her head vehemently. "No, you're perfect," she replied. "I was going to ask if you'd help me take some trays out to a table, but I'll let you be so you can finish getting ready."

Amber smiled. "It's all right, I'm just about done," she responded. A thought crept into her mind as she followed her mother out of the bedroom. "Has, uh, Brooke been back yet?"

She had been so focused on getting ready that it was entirely possible that Brooke had slipped back into the house without her hearing the footsteps she had already memorized. Her stomach did nervous flips as they made their way down the stairs.

Sandra glanced over her shoulder at Amber. She searched her eyes for a moment and then smiled. "No, I haven't seen her yet," she replied. "I imagine she'll be here any minute though. When I spoke to her this morning, she planned to be back around 6."

Any minute. The words rang in Amber's ears as another wave of nerves closed her throat. *This is silly* she accused herself. *You've never been this nervous around Brooke before.*

"Any particular reason why you decided to doll yourself up for the party?" Sandra probed as they reached the kitchen. "Not that you need a reason to spoil yourself, of course," she continued cheerfully. "Have you invited any friends to the festivities tonight?"

Amber knew what her mother was really asking. "No," she answered off-handedly. "I don't really know anybody well enough yet."

"And the closest one to your age that you *do* know best will already be here," Sandra supplied as she helped Amber lift a long tray.

There was that fluttering in her stomach again. "Right," Amber replied. "Should be a fun night."

She felt her mother's gaze linger on her for another moment as they carried the tray out the sliding glass doors and to a table at the far corner of the back patio.

As they approached the table, Amber heard the sound of the front door opening resound through the house. "Hey, Brooke!" Dave's voice boomed a few moments later. "You're right on time."

"Say, there's Brooke," Sandra spoke to Amber. "I knew she'd be home shortly."

"Sorry I'm a few minutes behind," Brooke's voice echoed through the open windows and doors. "The seller for the house that Kelsey put an offer on responded with a counter, so we had some last-minute negotiations. It took some back-and-forth, but we finally have a contract. Thank God."

Brooke's voice sounded nearer and Amber imagined her walking through the house, getting closer to the sliding glass doors. In just a moment...

"Oh, Amber!" Sandra exclaimed at the same time that Amber lost her grip on the tray. Her fingers slipped from under it and the hors d'oeuvres slid into a jumbled heap at one end.

"Crap, I'm sorry," she apologized. They quickly steadied the tray and placed it onto the table, working together to reorganize the neat lines of appetizers. "I'm so sorry. I just spaced out for a minute."

Sandra gently rubbed Amber's arm. "Don't apologize, sweetheart," she replied. "These things happen. I probably should've asked Dave to help with the heavier trays of food."

Amber sighed. The weight of the tray hadn't been the issue and she had a nagging feeling her mother knew that too. Her cheeks burned with embarrassment and then she felt Sandra's cool hand on her shoulder.

"Why don't you go say hello?" She spoke gently. "Get rid of some of those jitters. I'll fix you a quick drink before our friends arrive."

Amber nodded silently. *A drink sounds good* she thought. *Especially if it numbs these nerves.*

As she walked back into the house, Amber was as aware of each footfall bringing her closer to what she really wanted, what she had been waiting for, as she was of the pounding in her chest. Brooke was in the living room bantering with her father as Amber stepped closer.

She suddenly felt shy as she wondered how to say something as simple as hello. For the life of her, she couldn't remember how she had said it to Brooke before. A casual "hey, how are you" seemed an awkward contrast against the rapid beating of her heart. Conversely, a quick hug was dangerous territory – Amber wasn't sure she would be able to keep herself from lingering in Brooke's arms.

Fortunately, she didn't have to ponder it any longer. Brooke, probably sensing another presence in the room, turned expectantly and then froze. She blinked once, twice, three times. Amber stopped short halfway across the living room and forced what she hoped was a nonchalant smile.

Brooke's mouth dropped slightly open and then Dave followed her gaze directly to Amber. He grinned and spoke first.

"Amber, you look great!" He exclaimed. "That's a real nice dress. You get it here in Key West?"

Amber nodded quickly as she floundered for her voice. Brooke's eyes were still locked onto her and were filled with an intensity that seemed to drive the temperature in the room up at least ten degrees.

"Yes, at a boutique called Green Pineapple," she replied. "The necklace too."

Dave nodded. "Green Pineapple, huh?" He continued. "That's one I haven't heard of. Sandra on the patio? I'd better see if she needs any help before she calls for me."

His easy grin relayed his love and Amber watched him disappear through the sliding glass doors.

With a deep breath, she turned back to face Brooke, who had stuffed her hands into the pockets of her skinny black chinos and appeared uncharacteristically shy.

"You…" she started and then paused. She met Amber's eyes and held her gaze for a long moment. "You look amazing," Brooke finished softly.

Amber felt the flush and the smile before she could find the words to respond. As she opened her mouth, the sound of the doorbell chimed through the house.

"Amber, honey, can you get that?" Sandra called from the patio. "We're trying to set up plastic cups, but this darn breeze keeps knocking them over!"

Amber and Brooke both laughed. Amber opened and then closed her mouth again before nodding at the front door.

"I'd better grab that," she finally spoke quietly. "And thank you, Brooke."

Amber hurried to the front door, telling herself not to sneak a glance over her shoulder. She could still feel the other woman's eyes on her. The searing heat flushed across her skin in the exact places where Brooke's gaze had fallen.

She pulled open the door. "Hi, come on in!" Amber greeted the party-goers. "I'm Amber Lucas, Sandra's daughter."

"Nice to meet you," the older woman smiled and then tipped her fedora politely. "I'm Terri and this is my brother, Ken."

Amber stilled for a moment as realization caught up to her at the same time her mother did.

"Terri, how are you!" Sandra exclaimed. She hugged her and then Ken, kissing air around each of their cheeks. "I'm so glad you could make it. You're actually the first here, but I suspect the others are nearby."

"Can we help with anything?" Terri asked politely. "Thank you for the invite. Ken tells me that your parties are not to be missed."

"Oh, you're too kind," Sandra replied with a wave of her hand. "I think we're all set. Food and drinks are poolside, on the back patio. Powder room is just on the other side of the kitchen. And I see you've met my baby girl, Amber. She's visiting us for six weeks while she fills in at the Chamber of Commerce. She's helping plan and execute that big photography exhibition they host every year."

Terri's weathered face, framed by floppy blonde hair, turned back to Amber with sudden interest.

Shit she thought. *What are the odds?*

"The Chamber, huh?" Terri replied conversationally. "Must be an interesting gig."

Double shit.

"It's been fun so far," Amber replied diplomatically. "Photography is a passion of mine, so I'm excited to help with the exhibition."

"Amber, Terri is a local sand sculptor who does amazing work," Sandra went on. "Maybe she could get involved in some of the Chamber events!"

Terri made a noise in her throat and blushed slightly. Amber wondered if the other woman felt as awkward as she did. The elephant in the room loomed invisibly between them.

"Really, it's true!" Sandra exclaimed. "Beautifully detailed art. Her brother, Ken, is retired from the Armed Forces. He and I became fast friends in our weekly meditation group and then Terri joined a few months later."

"Your mom is a wonderful friend," Ken spoke. "I sought the Tara Mandala because I recently lost my wife. Sandra has been so great. She's helped me with my practice and it's led to a certain peace of mind that I didn't think would ever be possible."

"I'm so sorry," Amber murmured. "I'm happy to hear that my mom could be a friend to you."

"Let's get a drink, shall we?" Sandra spoke. "Dave is on the patio getting that first pitcher of tequila sunrise mixed. I hope you've arrived hungry and thirsty."

Terri and Ken dutifully followed Sandra onto the patio and disappeared into the night. As Amber began gently closing the front door, two more pairs of bright headlights cut through the sticky night air and paused at the base of the driveway. She sighed and re-opened the door as she waited for the next guests to arrive.

It was going to be a long night.

CHAPTER 24

The cool air from the refrigerator teased the goosebumps along Brooke's arms. She hadn't been sure what exactly to expect from a summer solstice party, but this was not it. First off, she hadn't been expecting Amber, stunning as she was, to meet her halfway across the living room in what felt like a moment when time had suddenly stood still. Brooke had almost forgotten her dad was standing right there. She realized too late how close she had been to reaching out and touching Amber's hand, gently tugging her closer and pressing her lips to Amber's perfectly glossed mouth.

A thought struck her as she took a cold bottle of water from the fridge before firmly shutting it.

Did she do that for me? Brooke wondered and then immediately shunned the thought. *There's that ego again. Amber wanted to look nice for the party. That's it.*

Brooke leaned for a moment against the fridge and took out a bottle of cold water. She had stopped speaking to her father in mid-sentence. Somewhere in the back of her mind, she had been slightly aware of the way he followed her gaze to see what had so immediately commanded all of her attention.

She shuddered, glad that Dave could not, at least, read her

thoughts. The party had grown quite a bit in the last several minutes. At least fifteen more people had arrived and quickly made their way to the back patio, where the festivities were in full swing. Brooke, grateful for a few minutes to collect herself, was sure that Amber had joined them. She glanced at the shadowy reflection of her lower half in the glass of the oven door across the kitchen. She hadn't had time to change after Kelsey had again stolen precious time from her.

Dressed in her professional business best wasn't how she wanted to approach Amber. As Brooke mentally inventoried the clothes she had already packed away for something…party suitable, she recalled a purple halter top that tied around her neck and left her shoulders bare. The top hadn't seen light in years; in fact, the only light it ever saw were the bright strobes at Aqua Nightclub.

Perfect she thought as she raced up the stairs. *Party suitable.*

As she closed the bedroom door behind her and stripped off her business clothes, Brooke recalled her promise to talk to Amber tonight. Nerves chewed at her stomach as her mind raced with the implications. After all, there was always the chance that Amber didn't feel the same way.

"Anyone with eyes can see how she looks at you" Justin's words echoed in Brooke's mind. A smile played at her lips as she thought again of the sudden intensity behind Amber's eyes just a few minutes before.

God, how could I have not recognized that earlier? She thought with a swallow. *We may have had a rocky start, but...*

Brooke's phone rang, sounding loud and unwelcome in the quiet of her bedroom, and jolted her from her thoughts.

"This is Brooke," she answered sternly as she turned from the mirror.

"Oh, Brooke, thank *God*," Kelsey's Southern drawl immediately grated on her nerves. "So, I was thinking…"

Brooke glanced impatiently at the digital display on the alarm clock next to her bed. "Yes?"

"I have to take a quick flight back to Louisiana first thing tomorrow morning," Kelsey went on. "I'll be back by the end of the week, but I'd really like to get the signed contract before then."

Brooke rolled her eyes. "Of course," she replied, her chipper voice a contrast to the aggravation she felt as the seconds ticked by. "I have a scanned copy that I'll e-mail to you first thing in the morning. I'll see to it that you have it before you step onto your flight. Now, I hate to have to cut this short, but..."

"Oh, you're a dear, Brooke," Kelsey went on, her voice syrupy-sweet as ever. "I really do appreciate that, honey. However, I'd like to get a printed copy to take with me. My daddy wants to have his counsel review the contract. You know, *legal* stuff," she continued with a little sigh. "And you know these old men, they don't have the patience for e-mails and PDF documents and what have you. I know this is last minute, so how about I just drop by and grab a printed copy?"

Brooke bristled at the easy way in which Kelsey commanded what she needed of her. She was a woman that Brooke knew had very rarely, if ever, been told no in her life.

"I'm not at the office, Kelsey," she replied, struggling to keep the frustration from her voice. "And I won't be for the rest of the evening. It's nearly 7 o'clock on a Saturday night."

"Oh, of *course*!" Kelsey exclaimed. "My apologies Brooke. I didn't mean to imply that you'd still be at the office. Of *course* you're at home, probably settling in for a movie or feeding your cat."

Brooke's mouth dropped open. *I'm only thirty-three* she thought indignantly. *I could be getting ready to head out to a club right now. Maybe. And I* don't *have a cat.*

"Actually, there's a party going on at my home right now," Brooke replied smugly. It didn't matter that it technically was her father's party or that, if not for summer solstice, she probably *would* be settling in for a movie right about now. "So I'm a little busy," she finished, rather unnecessarily.

"Oh, I *love* a good party!" Kelsey shrieked over the phone in excitement. Brooke carefully pulled the phone away from her ear and blinked. "That's wonderful! I'll just stop by to grab that contract then. I promise I won't be a nuisance or take you away from your guests for too long."

Brooke silently let her head fall back in frustration as she glared at the ceiling. "Okay, sounds great," she replied as she injected every ounce of warmth she could muster into her voice. *Anything to get her off my back.* "Do you have a pen and paper? The home is on Big Pine Key."

As Brooke finished her conversation with Kelsey, she rifled through her laptop bag and pulled out the signed contract. She carefully set the crisp, stapled sheets onto the dresser and turned at the sound of her father's voice.

"Brookie!" He called up the stairs. "You there? We got the bocce set up in the backyard. You in?"

Brooke smiled despite herself and hurried out of the bedroom. Her father's face relaxed into a grin when he spotted her at the top of the stairs.

"Come on!" He gestured. "Let's get you something to eat and drink."

Brooke followed her father through the living room, where small throngs of people sat on the sofas talking and laughing loudly.

Dave turned as they reached the sliding glass doors. "Sandra know how to put on a good party or what?" He went on. "We almost got Monty to jump into the deep end of the pool in his boxers. We got him up to forty bucks and he said he'd do it. He was taking off his jeans before I finally told him I was kidding and that I'd give him the forty bucks to keep his clothes *on*," Dave laughed loudly. "Don't nobody want to see that."

Brooke smiled and thought of the lead foreman who had overseen the build of this very house. He and Dave became fast friends, given their expertise in construction and shared New York City background. While her father was Brooklyn all the way, Monty was born and raised Queens. Anytime the Knicks played the Nets, Dave and Monty were together to rib each other and shout at the television set.

As they continued through the sliding glass doors, Brooke immediately spotted Amber at the opposite corner of the patio. An older lesbian who Brooke didn't recognize spoke quietly to her.

Brooke immediately wondered if Amber was being hit on, but it didn't appear that way. She stopped short behind her father as he paused to introduce her to a group of friends. Brooke smiled, half-listening and shaking each of their hands, all too aware of Amber just yards away.

As one of the men launched into a story about how his car had nearly been rear-ended on the way to the party, Brooke stole a glance over her shoulder. Amber's eyes were somewhere just beyond the older woman. She glanced across the clean blue water of the pool and then her attention settled on Brooke. Their eyes met in the low light across the long patio. They held each other's gaze for a slow moment as everything else became muted and still. Brooke took a deep breath, suddenly aware of the flush of desire that made her heart pound against her chest and her throat to suddenly become dry.

All of these people here and she's looking at me Brooke thought. There may have been a time during which this realization would have made her smug, but tonight she was lost in the wonderment of it all. There was no longer any doubt in her mind. *Amber wants me too.*

It was then that Brooke realized she was grinning, because Amber's face lit up in a smile back.

~

"I WANTED TO APOLOGIZE," Terri spoke quietly. She glanced thoughtfully down at her drink. "I realized as soon as you introduced yourself that you were the new hire at the Chamber and you had left me those messages about participating in the exhibition."

"It's okay," Amber replied. She was dreading this conversation. "Really."

"No, it's not," Terri went on. "I was rude when I got back to you. That wasn't right. You were just doing your job. It was wrong of me to take it out on you simply because of a...history."

Amber shook her head and took a small sip of her vodka spritzer. "It's completely fine," she reassured her. "Misunderstandings happen."

Terri shot her a small smile. "I'm glad we were able to clear the air," she replied. "I certainly didn't want there to be any weirdness hanging over the party."

Amber laughed. "Not any more weirdness than a summer solstice party already brings."

Terri grinned. "Your mom really is wonderful though. I joined my brother at meditation at his request. He was in a terrible state after losing his wife. Granted, I don't think he'll ever be fully *over* my sister-in-law, but he's certainly in a better state of mind than he was," Terri sighed. "And then I went through a loss of my own, though nothing compared to his. A bad break-up, really. He encouraged me to join him and at first I thought it was a little..." Terri stuck the tip of her tongue out and made a silly face. "Well, you know. A little odd. But your mom is one of the kindest souls I've ever met. And wouldn't you know, the regular meditation has helped me with some of the break-up issues *I* was struggling with."

Amber nodded and briefly recalled how she had felt after Lena. It seemed so far away now. "That's understandable," she replied. "Break-ups are awful."

Terri shook her head. "My ex and I, we were together for fourteen years," she admitted, her eyes faraway. "And it all ended because of a horrible misunderstanding. I know you're young yet, but no communication will kill a relationship every time. Take it from me."

Amber bit her lip and wondered what to say. It was obvious that Terri, despite her stubborn refusal to acknowledge Bobbi's attempts at reconciliation, still cared deeply for the other woman. "Maybe you two should sit down and talk," she suggested. "Clear the air. At the very least, it might give you both some closure."

Terri shook her head. "You know, all I want from my ex is a simple apology," she replied. "She's made some gestures. Tried to send fruit baskets, that sort of thing. But it's never direct contact."

Amber immediately felt guilty for all the fruit she ate at the office the week before.

"That's one thing she was never good at," Terri continued. "Apologizing. For some reason, simply saying the words I'm sorry seem to be the biggest challenge for her. A simple ownership of responsibility for it and saying I'm sorry was all I wanted and she couldn't even do that."

Amber filed this seemingly-important information away and glanced across the pool again. She had openly longed for Brooke a few minutes before. The taut muscles in her upper back and her strong, smooth shoulders had been on full display. It teased the slow-boiling passion that Amber tried to tamper down with a fruity drink and a breezy spot in the corner.

Ken gestured for Terri to join him at the other side of the table. "Everything happens for a reason, I suppose," Terri finished. "But I'd better head back to my brother. He may just eat all those spring rolls over there."

Should I say something? Amber wondered. *After all, she has no idea that I know she's talking about Bobbi.*

"Terri?" She called.

The other woman turned and looked at her expectantly.

"She still cares," Amber started and then paused at the look of confusion on Terri's face. *Crap, back-pedal.* "I mean, I'm sure anyone would. Nobody could get over a fourteen-year relationship with a snap of their fingers. Some people just have, you know, odd ways of communicating."

Terri smiled and nodded once. "Thank you," she replied. She looked as though she wanted to say something else and then decided against it. With a wave, she turned back to the table and laughed with her brother.

Amber lightly shook her plastic cup and drained the last of the liquid from between melting ice cubes. Cold, watered-down vodka hit her tongue as she glanced around the back patio. Her mother was busy regaling a group of four with quite an entertaining story, judging by her animated hand gestures and big smile. Another group hovered around the bocce game in the backyard and cheered as Dave tossed a ball.

She looked around again as she crushed her empty cup in her hand. With a sigh, Amber tossed the cup into a nearby trash bin and paused at the table. Another drink from the row of full plastic cups in front of a large punch bowl would surely help relax her. Without a second thought, Amber swiped another cup from the table and took a long, refreshing sip. Somewhere in the back of her mind, she knew that she should probably slow down, that she tended to be a bit of a lightweight and back-to-back drinks would certainly give her a vodka-induced buzz, but it temporarily distracted her from the dilemma of how to talk to Brooke.

Amber stepped around groups of people socializing on the patio and approached her mother. She turned as an older man in neon shorts whizzed past her.

"Whoops, sorry!" He called over his shoulder as he jogged to the food table. Amber blinked, feeling slightly off-balance.

A split second later, Sandra wrapped an arm around her waist and squeezed affectionately. "And this is my daughter, Amber!" She introduced her to the group. "Isn't she beautiful?"

Amber smiled and blushed as she politely waved around the group. After a moment, she turned to Sandra. "Mom, have you seen Brooke by any chance?" She asked quietly. "Do you know where she went?"

Sandra paused and then shrugged. "Sorry, no idea, sweetheart," she replied apologetically. "I saw her out here a few minutes ago."

Amber nodded. "I did too," she said with a sigh. She took another swallow from her drink and was surprised that it was already empty. Amber frowned down at the cup in confusion and chewed an alcohol-soaked raspberry that had sunk to the bottom.

Sandra cleared her throat. "She may have gone inside," she went on. "You might find her there if you're looking for her."

Amber shook her head quickly, but her face flushed with embarrassment. "Oh no, I'm not," she replied. "I'm not, like, *looking* for her or anything."

Smooth she thought, refusing to meet her mother's dubious gaze. *Real smooth.*

"All right," Sandra shrugged. "Well, I'm sure she'll make her way back outside."

Amber nodded and was grateful as her mother changed the subject. "I was just telling my friend Mindy that you had been going to sunrise yoga three times a week with me," Sandra went on as she gestured to an older woman with a beaded navy blue shawl wrapped across her shoulders. "Mindy was my morning yoga buddy for, gosh, how long now?"

"It was at least a year," Mindy supplied.

"Yes, a year!" Sandra exclaimed. "She had to undergo shoulder surgery about six weeks ago, so she's been unable to join and I miss her so very much." Sandra reached out and proudly touched her friend's forearm. "But she has been rocking and rolling through her physical therapy and is nearly recovered, right?"

Mindy nodded again. "Doctor thinks maybe another four weeks to be safe, but then I'll be right back to our morning yoga."

Amber smiled. "Wow, congratulations," she murmured, along with the rest of the group. Out of the corner of her eye, she swore she spotted a flash of blonde through one of the open living room windows. Turning, Amber craned her neck but the thick plantation blinds blocked much of her view indoors.

"Excuse me," she spoke and then squeezed her mother's hand. "I'm going to run inside for a moment."

Amber could feel her mother's eyes on her as she hurried across the patio and through the sliding glass doors. Her heart hammered in her ribcage as she surveyed the living room. A group of men relaxed along the couches as they laughed loudly.

Just then, someone put a Sly & The Family Stone record on the stereo outside. Groovy music blasted from the patio and into the house as guests clapped along and laughed. The vodka buzzed through Amber's temples for a long moment before she decided to get a glass of water. The drinks had been sneaky, but Amber began to loosen up as she continued for the kitchen.

She paused and placed a hand on the refrigerator door to steady herself before blinking at the sudden glare of light as she searched for a bottle of water.

"God, this is a *really* good song," Amber murmured to herself. She realized somewhere in the back of her mind that it was more than likely the vodka talking, but dancing seemed a better and better idea.

As the first sip of icy water hit her lips, the doorbell rang. While Amber contemplated if she should get it or continue jamming to the oldies – because jamming to the oldies was *really* fun right now – a shadow swept from the dining room into the foyer.

With a start, Amber realized it was Brooke. She wiped the back of her hand across her mouth and swallowed the water with a gulp. Brooke strode across the foyer, cool and collected as ever, and opened the front door. Desire emboldened by vodka surged through Amber as the water bottle nearly slid from her suddenly-clammy grip.

She stood frozen in place as Brooke greeted a young, vivacious redhead in a little black cocktail dress.

"Kelsey, hi!" Brooke spoke enthusiastically.

"Good evenin', honey," Kelsey drawled with a wide grin. "I believe you have something I'm looking for."

Amber's heart pounded harder as she stood dumbly in the middle of the darkened kitchen. *What does that mean?*

Brooke laughed good-naturedly. "I believe I do," she agreed. "Can I get you anything to eat or drink while you're here? As you can see, the party is in full swing so you're welcome to stay and enjoy."

Kelsey smiled. "That's a real sweet offer, honey," she replied. "But I don't want to intrude any more than I already have."

A tingle of something – was it jealousy? – crept into Amber's chest. *If she calls Brooke "honey" one more time...* Amber stopped short. *Or what? You're going to emerge from the shadows of the kitchen and claim what you've decided is yours?*

"I understand," was Brooke's reply. "You can come upstairs with me then."

Amber watched as Kelsey and her large chest followed Brooke up the stairs and then disappeared into the darkness. Her heart had dropped into her stomach as Amber tried to comprehend what she had just witnessed.

No wonder Brooke has been spending so much time with this client she thought dully. *It's not because she's some rich, difficult princess. They're... They're...*

Amber tried not to picture Kelsey on Brooke, Brooke's fingers lingering along Kelsey's skin or what they might be doing in her bedroom at that moment. Her gaze settled on a half-empty bottle of Absolut that had been left behind on the kitchen counter. At that moment, Amber would take anything she could to erase the images from her mind's eye.

CHAPTER 25

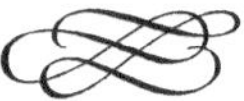

As Amber contemplated taking a shot before returning to the patio, Sandra walked into the kitchen and flipped on the light. She blinked at Amber and looked between her and the vodka bottle.

"Hi, sweetheart," she spoke. "Having a good time?"

Amber shrugged, more confused than ever. Beneath the confusion, disappointment had a chokehold through her core. *How could I have misjudged everything so much?*

"Amber?" Sandra asked. Her eyes flicked over her, concern in her gaze. "Say, do you know where Brooke snuck off to? Dave wanted to know if she wanted in on the next game of bocce. I think they were going to set up the horseshoes too."

Amber knew exactly where Brooke had snuck off to and the reminder of her alone with Kelsey was too much. "Mom, is Brooke dating anyone?" The question escaped before she could stop it.

Sandra looked closely at her. "I don't think so, though I can't be sure," she replied with a shrug. "I've never heard her talk about a man."

That shot of vodka was sounding better and better. Amber leaned back against the counter and shook her head. "You probably won't *ever* hear her talk about a man," she replied quietly. "Brooke is gay. Dave doesn't know."

Sandra's eyes widened. "I had a feeling, sweetheart," she replied carefully. "But that's not something for you or I to discuss, especially here and now. That's private business that she'll have to talk to Dave about once she's ready." Sandra paused and looked Amber up and down. "Amber, are you feeling all right? Do you want to head up to bed?"

Amber bit her lip as she remembered sitting closely with Brooke on the beach. Her skin felt electrified every time Brooke brushed against her. "Do you think…" She paused and sighed. "Do you think she'll ever fall in love?"

Sandra opened her mouth to respond, but closed it as Brooke and Kelsey came down the stairs. Amber's gaze fell back onto Brooke as she politely opened the door for her client.

"Thanks again for this," Kelsey called over her shoulder. "You're wonderful!"

Brooke smiled and waved. "No problem," she replied. "Have a good night."

Amber was aware that Sandra had followed her eyes to Brooke. She knew her mother understood why she was asking questions. At the moment, she didn't care. She wasn't trying to hide the longing in her gaze anymore.

"Earth to Amber," Sandra finally spoke gently. She quickly waved her palm in front of Amber's eyes. She blinked and, in that moment, she knew that her mother knew.

"I didn't know I'd fall for her," Amber quickly answered the silent question. "Honestly."

Sandra studied her face for another long moment and smiled softly. "You love her, don't you?"

"It wasn't supposed to happen this way," Amber mumbled with a sigh. "I swear."

Sandra enveloped Amber into a brief hug. "She's lucky then," she whispered into her ear. "It'll be okay. I promise."

As Amber hugged her mother, her eyes met Brooke's across the short hallway. She took a step toward them and then another. Amber realized that each hair of Brooke's loose bun was in place and that her halter top was still tied exactly the same as when Amber had watched her back retreat slowly up the stairs.

"Is everything okay?" Brooke asked as her puzzled smile swept over them.

Sandra took a step back and nodded. "Yes, just girl talk," she replied. "I should be getting back to the guests. Come find me on the patio."

With that, Sandra left Amber and Brooke in the quiet of the kitchen. Amber suddenly felt vulnerable as she placed a hand on the counter for balance. Brooke took a tentative step toward her.

"Are you all right?" Brooke asked. "You seem a bit out of sorts."

"I'm fine," Amber replied. She nodded at the vodka bottle. "You want to take a shot?"

Brooke ignored her question and took another slow step closer. "Look at me," she said firmly. She waited as Amber finally met her gaze.

Brooke searched her eyes for a long moment. "Are you tipsy?" She asked incredulously.

Amber shook her head too quickly and blinked against the sudden spin. "What does it matter to you?" She asked, rolling her eyes. "You're…you know."

Brooke raised an eyebrow and shook her head. "No, I don't know."

Amber gestured and started to give a snarky reply when her elbow knocked the vodka bottle from the counter. It sailed to the floor, crashing in a puddle of sharp shards and clear, sticky liquid.

"Okay, I think you've had enough," Brooke started. She reached for her arm at the same time that Amber crouched to her knees.

"*Shit*, I'm so sorry," Amber apologized, embarrassment burning her ears. "You didn't get hit, did you?"

Brooke crouched at Amber's level and firmly held her arms before she could reach the broken glass. "It's okay," she replied firmly. "Accidents happen. But you *must* be tipsy if you think I'm going to let you touch that broken glass."

Amber fell silent and met her eyes. Brooke's cheeks colored as she quickly looked away.

"There's a broom and dustpan in the linen closet upstairs," Brooke spoke as she stood and carefully pulled Amber up with her. "I'll grab it and get this cleaned up before anyone even notices. Maybe you should sit down for a minute."

Amber chewed the inside of her cheek and then followed Brooke up the stairs. "It's my mistake," she replied. Her short buzz was finally starting to wear off. "You shouldn't have to clean it."

"The only thing you should be doing right now is sitting down and sipping some water," Brooke reminded her as they reached the upstairs landing. "Besides," she turned abruptly and gently touched Amber's palm. "I don't want you cutting up these hands."

The linen closet was spacious, but Amber stood in the doorway and crossed her arms. She watched as Brooke knelt over a shelf and grabbed a thick bath towel.

"That's not fair, you know," Amber replied stubbornly.

"What isn't fair?" Brooke asked as she tapped a finger against her lips and scanned the closet. "I swear the broom is here somewhere."

"This!" Amber held up her hand and then sighed. She felt like a fool.

Amber froze as Brooke brushed past her and then quietly closed the closet door, shutting them inside. It was then that Amber realized her voice had been carrying.

"You're going to have to be more specific," Brooke replied slowly. Her gaze betrayed the same curious intensity that Amber had witnessed before. Each time, that fluttering feeling returned.

One thing Amber was certain was that the temperature in the small space seemed to have spiked at least ten degrees. The air was steamy with subtext and she told herself to breathe in through her nose and out through her mouth – Just like she'd relearned how to do in yoga.

Bad idea she thought belatedly. *To follow her upstairs. What in the world was I thinking, chasing after Brooke right into a cramped space that forces me so close that I could reach out and touch...*

Amber blinked. How quickly logic turned to fantasy when she was near Brooke. She had to get out of the walk-in closet, had to step away from the searing heat and temptation inches away.

"Never mind," she muttered. She backed away, gripped the door-knob and turned. There was nothing.

Amber took a deep breath and hoped that Brooke couldn't hear how loudly her heart beat against her ribcage. Amber turned the knob again and nudged the door with her shoulder. It seemed as though it wanted to move, but something was keeping it stuck in place.

Oh my God Amber thought. *I'm stuck in the closet. Again.*

"Um, Brooke..." she started, turning to the other woman with a slight frown. She decided that being stuck in a closet two times – three times if you counted before she was out - was already two times too many. "Something is wrong with the door."

"Shit," Brooke muttered. Amber stepped aside, her heart still pounding at Brooke's nearness, and watched as she tried the knob. "Damn it, I should've remembered."

Brooke pushed her full weight against the door and shook the knob in her hand.

"Damn it!" She cursed again, breathless. "My dad has had problems with this door since it was installed. It's always sticking. Something with the size of the doorframe not being measured correctly. He explained it to me a while ago. Basically, any sudden heat, humidity or moisture will cause it to stick."

Amber wondered what exactly that meant. Surely the heat between them had been imagined, right? It was just another fantasy in her mind, wasn't it? There was no possible way it could have been responsible for spurring an existing structural issue in the house.

Brooke stepped back from the door and tucked a piece of hair that had fallen loose from her bun behind her ear. "My dad has been meaning to get it fixed forever," she continued, resigned. "But since it's just a linen closet, I suppose he's been putting it off."

Amber nodded as she tried to keep up, but the most important facts seemed to be stuck on a loop in her mind. *I am stuck. In a closet. With Brooke. I am stuck...With Brooke.*

"Do you have your phone?" Amber suggested. "Mine is still in the kitchen."

Brooke bit her lip. "I left mine in the bedroom."

Amber rolled her eyes, unable to stop herself. "Oh, right," she muttered. "You were busy with Kelsey."

Brooke threw up her hands. "What does that even mean?" She asked. "Yes, busy in that I was giving her a printed copy of her signed sales contract. She's my client, after all. What on Earth did you *think* I was doing up here with…"

Brooke's voice trailed off as realization dawned on her. Her expression shifted to something unreadable as Amber quickly averted her gaze. Her eyes fell to the soft carpet as she refused to meet Brooke's steady stare. *Nailed.*

Brooke blinked incredulously. "You think I'm…doing something with Kelsey?" She asked. "You honestly think that?"

Amber was aware of her heart racing in her ears as her gaze fell to Brooke's lips. *Just once* she thought. *I want to feel that side of Brooke. Does the passion and intensity translate to her kisses?*

"I…I don't know what I think," Amber stammered as she shook her head. "Though I *do* think her flirtations are entirely inappropriate for conducting business and you inviting her upstairs made it look even worse."

"Kelsey stopped by for a printed copy of her purchase contract," Brooke spoke in a low voice. "That was it."

Amber swallowed hard. "You mean it?"

A smile played at Brooke's lips. "I mean it," she replied. "But even if I *did* have some sort of arrangement with Kelsey, why would that upset you?" Brooke took a step closer in the small closet and searched Amber's eyes. "Why would it matter to you?"

Amber took a deep breath. "Because *I* like you, Brooke," her voice was barely above a whisper. "*We* have something. You know it and I know it. Maybe it's not up to us anymore. If it's meant to happen, then that's it. Because I *know* you feel it too."

Without breaking eye contact, Brooke reached for Amber's hand and held it tightly. The energy in the small space was palpable as

Brooke's eyes flashed.

"It's always been you," she finally replied, her voice barely audible. "Not Kelsey, not Lydia, not anybody else. Since the day you arrived, it's been you."

The words were music to Amber's ears, though she struggled to process them through the torrent of heat and energy. She swallowed hard as Brooke's fingertips gently grazed her cheek. Brooke was closer and then, as though they had a mind of their own, Amber's eyes closed against the soft, full lips that met her own. Brooke's mouth was hot and soft and her kisses sweetly delicate, as though begging for permission to go harder.

Amber couldn't resist any longer. She wound her arms urgently around Brooke's neck and opened her mouth to deepen the kiss. Even as her pulse pounded loudly in her temples, Amber wasn't oblivious to the warmth that spread through every cell in her body.

There was something strangely familiar about the way that Brooke gently wrapped her arms around her, always carefully searching her face for even the most fleeting emotions that Amber knew allowed the other woman to read her more accurately than anyone had. She had no idea just how perfectly Brooke's lush mouth felt against her own or how it was possible that the other woman's touch was so familiar, so desired and so new all at the same time.

Amber buried one hand in Brooke's hair, her loose bun already half out, and craned her neck to give her better access to skin that hadn't been thoroughly kissed in far too long.

Have I ever been kissed like this? Amber briefly wondered, before letting her eyes fall closed and giving herself to the sensations. Her thoughts slowed to a trickle as she realized with an unconscious shiver that Brooke truly was a perfectionist in all aspects. The other woman had no intention of doing anything too quickly or sloppily. Brooke languorously made her way back to Amber's lips. She seemed to be enjoying the build, focused completely on Amber and translating her simmering, fiery passion through deep kisses and white-hot caresses.

Amber pressed her body closer as the world spun around her. She had been kissed and touched before, but was taken by how much more she felt with Brooke. As they continued to explore each other's mouths, a light whimper escaped and she felt Brooke smile against her lips.

Heaven she thought. *It must be.*

CHAPTER 26

With a sudden jolt that Brooke wasn't sure stemmed from her semi-coherent thoughts or from the fact that Amber had begun gently nibbling along the corner of her bottom lip, one realization was louder than all the others.

Happy she struggled to form full thoughts as Amber's warm mouth wandered from her bottom lip to the sensitive spot just below her right ear. *This is what totally, completely happy feels like.*

Finally, Brooke gave herself over as the sensation she'd come to recognize as unshakeable *happy* continued to flood her veins. It was too intoxicating, too much of what she'd been missing for so long, and she unconsciously wrapped her arms tighter around Amber.

Brooke took a couple of steps backward, momentarily surprised when her back hit the closet wall. Her legs felt like jelly and she slowly sank down the wall until she sat on the floor. Amber, never breaking their heated kisses, crouched down with Brooke and then finally tilted her chin for a breath.

As she leaned against the closet wall for support, Brooke unfolded her legs in front of her, one knee on either side of Amber, and intertwined the fingers of her right hand in Amber's left.

"I like you too," she finally whispered. She took a deep breath. "A lot."

"Hey," Amber murmured. She slipped a finger under Brooke's chin and gently forced her gaze up to meet her own. "Look at me. Say it again?"

The warm, tingling feeling that seemed to start from her stomach and spread through her chest was unfamiliar territory as she blinked into Amber's hazel eyes. There could only be one possible explanation.

"I think I'm falling for you," Brooke admitted in a breathless whisper. She reached over and ran the tip of her thumb along Amber's cheekbone. "You're beautiful."

Even as the words escaped her lips, Brooke wished she had a better way to articulate how she felt in that moment. She knew phrases like "you're beautiful" were often used and discarded, but she had meant the words from the very bottom of her heart. As she watched the corners of Amber's wide eyes crinkle with a self-conscious smile, Brooke wondered again how anyone could let someone with such a kind heart and gorgeous face go.

"Wow, Brooke," Amber replied after a moment. "Keep it up and I might be ready to break out of this closet with you," she finished with a teasing smile. Brooke closed her eyes as Amber's thumb grazed her lips, followed a split-second later by her sweet mouth.

"Impossible," Brooke murmured, hoping to lighten the intensity of the last few minutes. "You're already out of the closet."

Amber rolled her eyes through her grin and then fought back a yawn.

"Bad joke," Brooke conceded. "But they sort of write themselves in this situation."

"You're not kidding," Amber cracked. "This is the longest I've been in a closet since I was sixteen years old."

They both laughed and then Amber clapped her hands over her mouth as another large yawn overtook her.

"You're tired," Brooke observed. She paused as Credence Clearwater Revival's bluesy version of *Heard It Through the Grapevine* floated up the stairs. A few cheers from the living room followed. "Why don't you take a nap?"

"Here?" Amber looked around the darkened closet. "Oh my God, what if we're stuck in here all night?"

Brooke laughed. "We won't be stuck all night," she reassured her. "Eventually someone will notice we're missing. The way I see it, we can either pound on the door, shout until we're blue in the face and *not* be heard over The Greatest Hits of 1969 or you can take a nap and we can wait for someone to come upstairs."

Amber chewed the inside of her cheek as she appeared to consider this. She blinked and then nodded. "You may have a point," she admitted. "Fine," she went on as she settled herself along the floor of the closet and laid her head in Brooke's lap. "When you put it that way, a nap sounds good."

Brooke smiled and unfolded the bath towel. She draped it over Amber as a makeshift blanket in case her dress rode upward.

"I guess that will have to do for now," Brooke spoke uncertainly. Unconsciously, she ran her fingers through Amber's hair.

Amber grinned and wrapped an arm around Brooke's leg. "I'm actually beyond comfortable," she replied sleepily. "Especially when you do that. Just wake me up..." she paused and yawned once more. "...In a few minutes, okay?"

"Okay," Brooke replied. She gently stroked Amber's back and watched as her breathing slowly deepened and evened. Brooke swallowed hard and leaned back against the closet wall as the seconds silently ticked by. She wondered if it had been two minutes or ten since Amber had closed her eyes, her gaze never leaving the sleeping woman in her lap.

Brooke wasn't sure how much time had passed when she finally began to nod off. The buzzing energy had subsided into a warm, pleasant feeling that had settled deep into her core.

I'll close my eyes for just a minute she decided. *The party will die down soon and then we can bang on the door until someone hears us.*

For reasons that Brooke now recognized, she was not at all concerned about being stuck inside the linen closet for a little longer.

In fact, she realized, she would just as happily fall asleep right there with Amber soundly curled into her if it meant hours of uninterrupted affection between them.

Brooke smiled into the darkness at the idea and then sat up a little straighter as she heard footsteps on the stairs. She froze and listened carefully before shaking Amber awake.

"Hey," she whispered loudly. "Amber, wake up. Someone is on the stairs. Maybe we should try banging on the door."

Amber sat up with a start and rubbed at her eyes. "Wow, I really fell asleep," she mumbled, her voice husky. She blinked and smiled at Brooke. "I was *really* comfortable."

Brooke couldn't help herself. She leaned forward and planted a kiss on Amber's warm lips. "I'm glad you were *really* comfortable," she replied teasingly. "I didn't want to wake you."

Amber opened her mouth and looked as though she might kiss Brooke again, but the footsteps were firmly in the hallway now. Brooke was sure she saw the same slight disappointment at getting out of the closet reflected in Amber's eyes.

With a deep breath, Brooke stood and rapped her knuckles against the door. "Hey!" She called. "Is anyone there?"

Amber joined her and hit the door with her open palm. "Hey, in here!" She shouted. "Help, we're stuck!"

The footsteps paused and then Brooke could make out Sandra's confused voice just outside the door. "Girls?" She asked. "Hold on just a second."

They took a step back and watched as the knob rattled. Sandra sighed at the other side of the door and tried again. Brooke pulled at the knob as the door shook in its frame. She guessed that Sandra had pushed her shoulder against the door in an effort to loosen it.

After another few seconds of struggling, the door popped open with force and bounced off the closet wall with a resounding thump. Someone had changed the music downstairs to the Jackson 5. Michael Jackson's high-pitched voice flowed up the stairs and sounded much louder with the closet door open. Sandra blinked at them, a vodka spritzer in hand, and laughed as she shook her shoulders to the music.

"Oh my God, I think my mother is tipsy," Amber murmured under her breath. "She only does that awful shoulder-shake thing after two or more drinks."

Brooke stifled a giggle as Sandra opened her arms to them. "Oh, my!" She said breathlessly. "Come here, what happened?"

Amber opened her mouth to explain, but closed it as Sandra rolled her eyes dramatically. "Would you *believe* that someone spilled a drink all over the kitchen floor? Glass shattered and everything, and they didn't clean it up!"

Brooke and Amber exchanged glances, but remained silent.

"I know things happen at parties," Sandra went on with a wave of her hand. "But to leave broken glass and a sticky mess all over the floor? That could be dangerous! I came up here to get the broom and dustpan before someone gets hurt. Sorry for barging in."

Sandra's voice trailed off and a look of confusion wrinkled her forehead. "Wait, *did* I barge in?" She asked. "I didn't, you know, interrupt anything, did I?"

Amber's face went beet red at the same time that Brooke wondered what that meant.

"Oh my God, Mom, *no*!" Amber exclaimed as she shook her head vehemently. "We, um, came up here to clean the mess in the kitchen and the door stuck. We couldn't get out."

Sandra frowned. "Oh, sweetheart, I'm sorry," she replied. "I know how you are with small spaces. That's odd, I didn't hear you shouting or banging on the door though. Not until I came upstairs, at least."

Brooke swallowed hard and knew that Sandra's questioning was entirely innocent by the look of genuine confusion and concern in her eyes. However, she knew her father probably wouldn't find the situation so innocent if he were to find them all upstairs and then learn that she and Amber had been locked in the closet together.

"It was the music," she blurted out. She forced a shrug as both Lucas women's confused gazes landed on her. "I mean, it was so loud. We tried. Shouting, I mean. But the music was really loud..."

Shut up she thought and then shook her head and faked a yawn. "I'm actually exhausted," she went on. "But I can't thank you enough for helping open the door. We were afraid we'd be stuck in here forever."

Sandra waved her hand again. "Of course!" She exclaimed. "But you can't go to bed already, Brooke. Your dad has been looking for you for bocce and the conga line just started a minute before I came upstairs."

Brooke laughed. "As much fun as that sounds, I'd better head to bed," she replied. "I'm actually *really* sorry I'm missing the conga line though."

Sandra turned to Amber. "Are you in?"

Amber looked between Brooke and Sandra. "Fine," she replied, dragging the word out. "I can hang out for another half-hour or so, but then I'm heading to bed too."

Sandra threw up her hands dramatically as the spritzer sloshed dangerously in her cup. "Ugh!" She exclaimed. "Fine then. Hold this." Sandra handed her cup to Brooke and grabbed the broom and dustpan. "Young people these days..." Her voice trailed off with an affectionate laugh as she went down the stairs.

Brooke glanced at the cup still in her hand and then turned to Amber. "Your mom is awesome," she stated matter-of-factly.

Amber burst into laughter and shook her head. "She *never* drinks," she replied quickly. "That's why she's such a lightweight when she *does* imbibe." She sighed and took the drink from Brooke's hand. "I'd better fulfill my promise to hang out a little longer. I'll take this to her. Are you sure you want to go to bed already?"

Brooke's face heated at Amber's question. Of course she didn't mean it in the context that Brooke heard it, but goosebumps appeared on her arms nonetheless. The comfortable sleepiness that had enveloped her in the linen closet had all but disappeared, shaken away by Sandra and the security of the shut door.

"I'd better," Brooke replied softly. She knew if she ventured downstairs for even another half-hour that something was... different. Her father would see it on her face, hear it in her voice and recognize it with every glance she snuck in Amber's direction. Now that the floodgates had been wrenched open, she didn't know how to go back and she wasn't certain she wanted to.

"All right," Amber conceded. She touched Brooke's hand and then squeezed her fingertips. "Get some rest then. Have a good night."

Brooke fought the urge to press her lips against Amber's. A quick glance down the stairs told her it was too risky, that anyone could walk by at any moment and see them embracing. *Anyone*, of course, included her father or one of his buddies.

"Thank you," she replied and then dropped her eyes to their adjoined hands. "You have a good night too."

Awkwardly, Brooke turned for her bedroom. As she gently shut the door behind her, she listened to Amber's footsteps floating down the stairs. Brooke immediately wanted to kick herself for not kissing her. It frustrated her immensely that her own lack of courage had held her back.

How long has it really been holding you back, though? An inner voice of reason piped up. *You know the answer. Too long.*

Brooke wrestled with her thoughts as she scrubbed her face and changed into pajamas. As she settled into bed, she rolled onto her back and stared at the ceiling. She pined for Amber and replayed their heated kisses in vivid detail in her mind's eye, even though she was only downstairs. Sleep no longer felt as though it was coming anytime soon.

CHAPTER 27

Hours later, Brooke wasn't any closer to sleep than she had been before. The sounds of the party had trickled into silence and she had listened as Dave and Sandra finally helped each other up the stairs after seeing the last guests out from the foyer. She had briefly dozed off after flopping onto her stomach, but thoughts of Amber kept her mind wide awake.

I should've kissed her good night when I had the chance Brooke thought ruefully. With a sigh, she finally threw back the covers and sat up. Her tousled hair fell over her face and the air conditioning felt cold against her skin without the warmth of the blankets. She slowly opened the bedroom door and swallowed hard, praying that it didn't creak loudly in its hinges.

As she padded down the hallway to Amber's room, she paused outside the door. It wasn't completely closed. The inch of space served as an invitation to Brooke, but she wondered if Amber would feel intruded upon.

All I want to do is kiss her good night Brooke thought firmly. *She wouldn't mind if I snuck in for that...Right?*

As Brooke continued to rationalize in her mind, she gently pushed Amber's bedroom door further open and stepped into the frame. She stopped short as her breath caught low in her throat. Amber looked impossibly young as she slept soundly. Her hair was spread along the pillow beneath her head and her oversized t-shirt was wrinkled around her. Soft beams of moonlight filtered between the blinds and washed her profile in a pale, dewy glow. One hand rested along her side and the other was near her head, stuffed beneath a pillow.

Brooke wasn't sure when the lump in her throat had started forming or why a wave of sudden emotion had taken her, but she decided right then that Amber looked far too peaceful to be woken for a kiss.

Swallowing hard, she turned and then froze as Amber whispered to her.

"Brooke?" She repeated, a little louder this time. Brooke turned just in time to see Amber stretch slowly beneath the blankets. "Come here."

The sleepy satisfaction in Amber's voice was more than enough for Brooke. She slowly made her way to Amber's bed and perched along the edge.

"I'm sorry," Brooke whispered. "I just couldn't sleep and, you know..." She paused and swallowed. "Honestly, I couldn't stop thinking about you and..."

Amber struggled to sit up further. "It's okay," she murmured with a smile. She reached out and cupped Brooke's face in her hand. "Shh, it's okay. Come here."

Brooke lapsed into silence and let Amber draw her close. The short distance between their lips was quickly closed and, for a few quick moments, Brooke felt as though she was slowly spinning in the darkened room.

"I missed you," Amber whispered breathlessly. "I mean it. Is that crazy?"

Brooke shook her head and felt herself relax as Amber rested her chin on her shoulder. They sat like that for a moment and held one another tightly as the silence of the large house washed over them.

"If that's crazy, then I guess we both are," Brooke replied softly. "I missed you too. I haven't slept at all. I've been tossing and turning all night."

Amber smiled again and leaned in to explore Brooke's lips once more. "Poor thing," she murmured teasingly. "Come on."

Amber scooted over and pulled back the covers. She patted the open spot for Brooke and raised an eyebrow as she met her eyes across the bed.

Hesitating, Brooke bit her lip. There was nothing more she wanted than to cozy up with Amber and kiss until they finally fell into a blissful sleep, but the risks of being caught in Amber's bed resounded at the back of her mind.

"Please?" Amber whispered again. "Just for a minute," she finished, as if reading Brooke's mind.

The almost-desperate plea for closeness hinged in Amber's voice spurred Brooke's body into action before her mind could rationalize otherwise. In seconds, she settled next to Amber and tucked the sheets around them as they sunk back into the pillows.

Without a second thought, Brooke leaned over and kissed Amber with abandon. Their kisses grew deeper as they continued to seek out every inch of each other's mouths and then Brooke felt Amber shift beneath her.

Amber sighed happily as Brooke's mouth wandered from her lips to her neck. Brooke didn't flinch as Amber's short fingernails dug into her shoulder blades and her body sought purchase somewhere, anywhere, along Brooke's legs.

Brooke ran her palm along Amber's side, pausing at her waist. The warmth of Amber's body just beneath the hem of her t-shirt intoxicated her. Her fingers itched to explore further and caress the soft skin that teased her through Amber's sleepwear. Brooke nibbled at her collarbone as her fingers trailed lazy curves lower along Amber's waist.

Unconsciously, Amber lightly bucked her hips; a silent plea for more. Brooke felt her own arousal between her thighs as she realized just how close Amber was to climax. She gently traced a fingertip along the warmth that seeped through Amber's underwear. As her fingers passed a certain area, Brooke watched as Amber's breath caught and her back jolted a few millimeters from the mattress.

"We shouldn't," Brooke finally breathed. The scent of Amber's arousal made her feel lightheaded. She shifted on the bed in hopes of ignoring the throbbing between her own legs. "Not right now."

Amber blinked up at Brooke. Her eyes were lidded and her pupils were dark with desire. "I'll be quiet," she whispered. "Can *you* be quiet?"

Brooke grinned and then met Amber's lips with another kiss. "When I move back into my duplex," she replied breathlessly. "We won't have to be quiet."

Brooke's head was swimming. She had only meant to give Amber the good night kiss that she had been obsessing over since going to her bedroom. With a start and another uncomfortable shift, she realized that Amber wasn't the only one who had unexpectedly been brought to the brink of climax.

Amber nodded after a moment. "Okay," she agreed. "You're right." She ran a finger along Brooke's jaw. "I don't know if I can promise silence."

Brooke shivered and kissed Amber again as she hurriedly climbed out of the bed. If she stayed wrapped under the covers a moment longer, she wasn't confident she would be able to stop what they had inadvertently begun.

"I'll see you in the morning," Brooke murmured as she slowly ran a hand through Amber's hair. "Try to get some sleep, yeah?"

Amber rolled her eyes but didn't move away from Brooke's gentle touch. "Yeah, thanks a lot."

Brooke grinned again and leaned down to kiss her forehead.

Amber defiantly lifted her chin so that Brooke's mouth met her lips instead. "You know, those dimples won't *always* get you out of trouble with me," she stated with a teasing glare.

Brooke tried to quiet her laugh and squeezed Amber's fingers. "Maybe I won't get into trouble with you because I'll make you happy," she replied as her mind wandered to all the ways – physical and not – she could try to see that sweet smile. "Sweet dreams, beautiful."

She tried not to look back as she carefully left the bedroom and returned to her own. It was the first time she had hinted at wanting more than simply casual to any woman in recent memory, but the prospect didn't scare Brooke as she settled into bed.

With a glance at her closed door, Brooke touched her fingertips to her mouth as a smile played at her lips. She still had no idea how she was going to get any sleep tonight.

~

AMBER WOKE up earlier than she had expected the following morning. She knew today was the day that Brooke was moving back into her duplex and sounds from the kitchen suggested that somebody was already awake.

She assumed it was her mother, who had always been an early riser, as she pulled on a pair of loose-fitting sweatpants. As she quickly clasped her bra beneath her t-shirt, Amber listened as a kettle whistled and then stopped abruptly as someone grabbed it from the stove. She didn't smell the usual rich, bold odor of Brooke's coffee and grinned to herself as she bounded down the stairs.

Just in time for Mom's green tea she thought satisfactorily. A dull ache pulsing at her temples was a gentle reminder that too much vodka was never a good idea, but she didn't feel much worse for the wear.

Amber stopped short at the entrance to the kitchen and blinked. Brooke stood over the stove with her back to the door as she carefully poured steaming yellowish-green liquid into two mugs. Amber allowed herself a long moment to unabashedly drink in the sight of Brooke and each minor detail that she found irresistibly attractive. Her heartbeat quickened in response.

Brooke was stoic and confident in her tight tank top. Her shoulders and arms appeared impossibly strong as the early morning sunlight highlighted the length of her back. The sun bounced off her mussed blonde hair, which was still messy from sleep.

Only after Amber had decided how unfair it was that Brooke was still unbelievably sexy, even first thing in the morning, she finally leaned against the doorframe and gently cleared her throat. She crossed her arms casually as Brooke turned and grinned.

Her bright smile washed over Amber and nearly made her forget an important observation. "You're drinking green tea," Amber stated. She raised an eyebrow, impressed. "No coffee in the pantry?"

Amber was sure she witnessed a nearly imperceptible flush color Brooke's face as she glanced down. "No," she replied coolly. Her eyes danced as she met Amber's gaze. They shared a knowing smile. "There's coffee."

"I thought you'd be asleep still," Brooke continued. She leaned back against the kitchen counter and handed Amber the second mug. "I was going to leave this by your bed."

Amber shook her head. "I planned to stop at the Chamber for an hour or so," she explained. "I have to make some last-minute updates to the overall budget spreadsheet for the exhibition. Bobbi needs it first thing tomorrow morning for her final pre-event meeting with the Board."

Brooke nodded as she took a long sip of tea. "Well, you know where I'll be," she replied with a nod at the foyer. Amber finally noticed the four sleek black suitcases lined neatly at the front door. "Maybe you could come over tomorrow after work. If you're not busy," Brooke finished hurriedly. "I know it's the last week before your exhibition."

Amber bit her lip. "I promised my mom I'd go to Mindful Monday with her," she replied with a sigh. "It's a meditation workshop that her Tara Mandala group is hosting." She thought for a moment and then perked up. "You're more than welcome to join us and then I can go home with you. If you want to, of course. It's probably not your thing..."

Brooke nearly choked on her tea at the words *I can go home with you*. "I'll go," she replied quickly and then recalled her very first dinner with Sandra. "Besides, your mom invited me to join her for meditation a while back." She paused and tried to shrug it off. "I meant to go."

Amber smiled. "My mom asked you to go to meditation?" She asked. "She must really like you."

Brooke blushed again, something that Amber found impossibly cute, despite it being a rare occurrence. She met Brooke halfway across the kitchen and met her lips in a fast, hurried kiss. It felt like they had been locked in a heated embrace for only seconds when the familiar sound of the master bedroom door bouncing open sounded all the way down the stairs.

Amber took a few shaky steps back as Brooke closed her eyes and let out a frustrated groan.

"How is it possible that I can't wait to get back into my own home to have privacy but, at the same time, I don't want to leave because I won't be under the same roof as you?" Brooke asked as she blinked at the ceiling in irritation.

"Girls?" Dave's voice boomed from upstairs. "You up already? I'm going to make some eggs, you in?"

Amber blinked and met Brooke's eyes. There was a promise in her gaze as she whispered two words: "Tomorrow night."

CHAPTER 28

The following evening, Brooke drummed her fingers against her thigh in anticipation. The Tara Mandala hadn't been difficult to find, since the group primarily met at the Key West Tropical Forest and Botanical Gardens. The meditation itself had been interesting, if not slightly frustrating. The first twenty minutes had been dedicated to sitting meditation at an area that the group had reserved on a flat concrete terrace facing an impossibly still lake. The terrace was surrounded by tall, lush palm trees and rich green grass, which proved problematic for Brooke during the fifteen-minute walking meditation.

She had followed Sandra's lead but after a long minute or two of wondering how quickly she'd roll her ankle and what the odds were that she would walk herself face-first into the hard trunk of a palm tree, Brooke had opened an eye. The others in the group walked slowly and purposefully, their eyes squeezed tightly shut and their faces serene as they took one gentle, assured step and then another.

The hour-long session had ended with a fifteen-minute open discussion and then a final ten-minute seated meditation. Brooke took a deep breath as she sat straight and still with her legs neatly crossed in front of her. Perhaps it was the rush of being in such close proximity with Amber or because it was her first go at real meditation, but the fact that she couldn't seem to focus frustrated Brooke. She disliked not being able to accomplish something right away.

Brooke opened her eyes again and blinked. Her gaze landed on Amber, who appeared relaxed as ever in loose linen pants and a tank top that Brooke noted hugged her very best curves. Amber's hair was down around her face and a hint of light pink lip blush accentuated the lushness of her face.

Amber turned suddenly and her eyes met Brooke's. A warm smile immediately crossed her face at the same time Brooke felt herself flush for being caught staring. Amber bounded over and, for a slow, enticing moment, Brooke was sure she was going to kiss her right there in the middle of the botanical garden. In that split second, Brooke was torn between her raw desire to feel Amber's lips against her own and her fear of Sandra seeing them together. Still, she was slightly disappointed when Amber stopped just short of meeting her face and instead sat down opposite her.

"What do you think?" Amber asked. "Did you feel anything differently?"

Brooke sighed. "I don't *get* it," she admitted. "I tried, but between being terrified that your mother was going to walk-meditate herself right into the lake and making a mental list of what new clients I need to reach out to tomorrow, I couldn't focus."

Amber smiled and leaned forward. "It's not about *getting* it, Brooke," she replied. "There's no manual for being with the present moment. You just *are*. It's okay. It takes practice. I can help you try one more time if you want. Can I show you something?"

Brooke swallowed hard and nodded. She knew Amber didn't even realize the power that her smile held over her and that she would have allowed her to show her just about anything in that moment. "Okay," she replied softly.

Amber took a deep breath. "Okay," she responded brightly. She straightened her spine and gently clasped Brooke's hands in her own. "Take a big breath in and let your eyes fall closed."

Brooke nodded and did as she was told. Amber's hands were soft and warm, so she focused on the gentle way that her thumbs caressed her fingers.

"Slowly exhale," Amber's voice was quiet. "Be mindful of your breath and how you're taking each one in. When you inhale, recognize how it fills your lungs. As you exhale, imagine yourself breathing out all of the day's stresses. In goes energy, mindfulness, positivity and all of the good things you can imagine. Out goes the staleness, the negativity, the things that upset you and take you further from yourself."

Brooke felt herself relax as she shifted focus to her breathing, still conscious of the gentle warmth holding her hands.

"Just keep breathing, Brooke," Amber's voice sounded further away, though Brooke knew she hadn't moved. "In. And then out. Thoughts will come and go, fleeting things will pass through your mind. It's only natural. Let them go instead of wondering why they're there. Thoughts only breed more thoughts. Breathe in and imagine light filling you as the oxygen fills your lungs."

Behind her eyelids, Brooke could see the warm yellow light casting the inside of her body aglow with goodness and energy. The sounds of the garden had all but faded from her consciousness, her awareness only on the present moment - slow, mindful breathing as she exhaled stress and fear from deep inside. Amber's hands gently grasped her own as her voice carefully broke through invisible walls into her consciousness.

After what felt like only a moment, Brooke was aware of Amber embracing her tightly.

"You did great, Brooke," she whispered into her ear. "You look amazing."

Brooke blinked. The evening light seemed unwelcome and bright. "I felt…relaxed. What you were saying really helped ease me into the moment."

Amber grinned. "That's called guided meditation," she replied proudly. "It's helpful for those just beginning."

Brooke couldn't help herself as she smiled back. "So I tried for an entire hour and that's all I needed? You to hold my hands and guide me?"

Amber glanced up and held her eyes for a moment. "You should let your guard down more often," she countered gently. "Having a deeper connection doesn't always have to be scary."

Brooke and Amber regarded each other silently for a long moment. It was only after Sandra lightly cleared her throat from behind that Brooke realized they were still holding hands opposite one another on the concrete. From an outsider's perspective, Brooke knew exactly what this looked like: Two people falling in love.

As she looked around, Brooke realized that most of the group had already departed. Amber didn't look concerned and, for the first time, Brooke didn't feel scared either. In fact, she felt safe with Sandra. It was a strange feeling she had never known with any of her dad's girlfriends.

"Are you girls about ready?" Sandra asked. The bracelets on her wrist jangled as she lifted a hand to shade her eyes. "Amber, sweetheart, you'll drop me off at Dave's house?"

Amber nodded as she stood and held out her hands to help Brooke up. "Of course," she replied.

They fell into step together as they walked to the parking lot. The air was cool and tinged with the scent of the sea as palm leaves rustled overhead with a gentle evening breeze. Brooke inhaled deeply, still in wonderment about what had transpired during those last few minutes of the meditation.

Sandra stopped short as she reached the Volkswagen Beetle and turned to them. The older woman perfected the ability to look both puzzled and deep in thought. The knowing depths behind her eyes briefly made Brooke wonder if she was nearly headfirst out of the closet. She didn't have to wait long for her answer.

"I've always suspected..." Sandra began and then shook her head. "No, *suspected* is the wrong word. It implies wrongdoing." She took a deep breath and started over. "I've always *sensed* an energy between the two of you. At first I thought, well, perhaps it's because I'm so in tune with my daughter even though we live thousands of miles apart. But I sensed it from you too, Brooke. Almost immediately."

"I...I'm sorry," Brooke apologized. She wasn't sure what Sandra was trying to say, but felt that an apology was necessary.

Sandra smiled at her. "Now, whatever for are you apologizing?" She asked. "I'm sensitive to the energies around me, but even someone who understands nothing about soul connections could sense something between the two of you. I didn't realize just how deeply it went until this evening. Seeing you," Sandra paused and turned to Amber. "Guiding her. Holding her hands and helping her reach another level of consciousness, of awareness. I believe you two may have a soul connection. I just...I can't believe I didn't see it before." Sandra paused and tapped a finger against her lips. "The two of you...Of course."

Amber met Brooke's eyes and shot her a look, before rolling her eyes in embarrassment.

Brooke hugged Sandra back as she embraced her and bid her good night. "Everything is going to be okay, Brooke," Sandra murmured. "I promise. I can feel it."

She wondered about Sandra's words as Amber slid into the driver's seat and waved good-bye after confirming she would meet her back at her home shortly.

What does she mean that everything is going to be okay? Brooke puzzled as she opened the door of her own car. *What could possibly go wrong?*

~

A LIGHT SHIVER ran up Brooke's spine despite the searing evening temperature. The implications and possibilities of what could happen between now and the next morning played in her mind's eye as she glanced at the dusky sunset in the rearview mirror. Amber pulled into the driveway behind her, the tires of the Beetle crunching to a stop as its bright, round headlights penetrated the evening.

The air was uncharacteristically warm, even for South Florida, and the humidity made Brooke's hair stick to the back of her neck. Her hand dangled out the open window, but she cranked the air conditioning higher anyway. She smiled as she watched Amber eagerly jump from the driver's seat, a messenger bag slung over one shoulder.

Amber leaned casually through Brooke's window and rested her elbows along the weather strip. "That air feels good," she remarked with a grin. Amber nodded at Brooke's air vents and then reached over and tapped Evangeline on the arm. "Hey Evangeline," she laughed as the hula doll bobbed back and forth on the dashboard. "Anyway, I didn't know humidity like this existed until I came to Florida."

Brooke turned off her car and fumbled with her keys as she walked up the stairs with Amber. "It takes getting used to," she replied and then smirked. "And a lot of really good hair products."

As she finally unlocked the door, two arms slung loosely around her waist from behind and hugged her tightly. Brooke felt Amber rest her head against her back as the now-familiar scent of clean mint and sweet strawberry wafted into her consciousness.

In one quick motion, Brooke turned in Amber's arms and held her close. She wasn't sure if it was the meditation, the intoxicating effects of the warm, salt-tinged air or some combination of the above, but she was buoyed by a certain clarity. It seemed to heighten her awareness and make her conscious of every detail, like the way the gentle breeze caused tiny hairs to stand up on the back of Amber's neck or how her small, satisfactory sigh was enough for Brooke's heart to race inside her chest.

After a long moment, Brooke slipped her hand into Amber's and led her into the foyer. "Would you like a drink?" She asked as she walked into the kitchen. Brooke bent as she squinted into the bright refrigerator light. "I have mineral water, orange juice, Sprite..." Brooke's voice trailed off and she stood uncertainly. "There may be some wine in the pantry."

She could sense Amber behind her again. The other woman was all in her personal space and grinned easily as she placed a casual hand on Brooke's hip. Amber bent slightly and pulled a glass bottle of mineral water from the fridge before straightening. She didn't make any effort to move from where she stood, millimeters from touching Brooke again. Instead, Amber flashed her a smile.

"I'm good with water, thanks," she replied. There was a gleam in her eyes as she finally took a step back and then sauntered across the kitchen. "Keeps you hydrated."

It was then that Brooke realized she was being mercilessly teased. Amber seemed to get a thrill out of her momentary off-balance and the fact that she had been struggling to keep herself in check since the meditation they had shared.

Brooke steeled herself as she walked across the kitchen to where Amber had leaned against the counter and taken a long sip of water. She wasn't accustomed to being nervous and had all but believed she'd mastered the art of seduction long ago. *She wants to flirt, huh?*

She paused and, without missing a beat, softly kissed Amber's neck. Brooke felt her first stiffen and then relax into her mouth as she continued to work over the soft spot where Amber's neck met her collarbone. Brooke wound a hand in the fine hair at the base of Amber's neck and nipped at her throat as she gulped the water in her mouth.

"If you're going to tease me, you'd better be able to back it up," Brooke murmured with a grin. "Do you have any idea how much I want you?"

Amber's breath seemed to hitch in her throat. "Tell me," she managed to reply.

"I haven't been able to stop thinking about you," Brooke replied softly. She glanced up from Amber's neck, flushed pink from kisses and heat, and nearly lost her nerve as she met Amber's eyes. "You drive me crazy."

Amber looked as though she wanted to say more, to ask more questions about her feelings for her. At that moment, however, Brooke's instincts had taken over. She would make love to Amber so thoroughly that the other woman couldn't possibly have any questions about where Brooke stood. She would never need to wonder if Brooke's heart belonged to her again.

Quickly, she met Amber's lips and kissed her deeply. A lascivious thrill shot through Brooke's body at the ease in which Amber opened her mouth to her.

She wants me too Brooke thought blissfully. Her heart pounded with pride as she smiled against Amber's eager mouth.

Amber let out a muffled moan of approval as the tip of Brooke's tongue gently massaged hers. Soon, their tongues were exploring lips, mouths and necks as the kisses drew longer and grew in intensity.

Brooke kissed her confidently and relished the feeling of Amber slowly becoming undone under her gentle touch and lingering kisses. After what seemed like several minutes of Amber's tongue gliding in rhythm with her own, the other woman pulled back, took a steadying breath and whispered words that were magic to Brooke's ears.

"Take me upstairs."

CHAPTER 29

Most of the times when Brooke bedded a woman, it was hard, fast and satisfying. Fervent lust filled the room and fueled their salacious appetites as kisses and caresses lingered longer. Momentum and need made fingers, tongues and libidos impatient. Soon enough, the goal had been achieved and desire quickly subsided – Until next time, of course.

This was different. Brooke wanted to take her time with Amber. She wanted to use the entire night to memorize her body, her breaths, the things that made her move and stretch along the length of the bed as she silently asked for more. Brooke wanted to listen to her whimpers and moans as she buried herself in Amber's warm wetness and made love to every inch of her body. The heady feeling of teasing lust and temporary desire was missing and it had been replaced with something new. Something deep and undefinable, something that Brooke could feel inside and out.

Intimacy she realized as she recalled Amber's words from the afternoon at her duplex. It already felt like long ago. *I feel so much more for her.* Brooke swallowed hard at the revelation, but Amber's naked body was too distracting. Amber's wide eyes implored her from the pillow as she watched Brooke breathlessly and trusted her implicitly.

Brooke's lips left Amber's breast and she slowly trailed the gentle, lazy circles her fingers had begun teasing her most sensitive areas lower and lower. Her fingertips were covered in Amber's desire and Brooke knew then that it was time.

Brooke lowered her mouth to Amber's wetness, which elicited an encouraging moan from the other woman. As her tongue and lips explored Amber, Brooke quickly deduced that slow, firm pressure was her favorite. Amber writhed against the sheets, breathing hard and arching her hips further into her mouth, as she desperately grabbed Brooke's fingers in one hand and gripped the corner of a pillow in another. Brooke unconsciously curled her fingers around Amber's hand in assurance. Her mounting pressure was tangible and it would only be a matter of seconds until...

Amber's high-pitched moans pierced the room as her body shook against Brooke's tongue. Brooke smiled as Amber squeezed her fingers tighter and didn't move from between her thighs until she was sure that Amber rode out the last wave of her orgasm. As Amber collapsed against the pillows, sated and breathless, Brooke scooted next to her and wrapped an arm around her waist.

"I..." Amber started. She blinked as she took another deep breath. "I don't think I've *ever*...That hard..."

Brooke felt another rush of pride as Amber rolled over and into her side. "You are the *sexiest* woman alive, Brooke Adriani," she murmured into her shoulder. After a moment, she lifted her head and blinked again. "And I hope you don't think you're going to sleep yet..."

AMBER WASN'T sure what she expected in bed with Brooke. If she was honest with herself, she had probably been too excited, too lost in the chemistry to speculate. Whatever she had expected, gentle Brooke was not it. She seemed almost shy in her intimacy and it cut to Amber's very core. There was an inherent sweetness in the way that Brooke looked at her and placed soft kisses along the warmest areas of her body. Amber wanted to make Brooke feel what she had just felt and she had a feeling it would start with *her* taking control this time.

As she deftly straddled Brooke, who appeared mildly surprised by her burst of energy but far more intrigued with her sudden show of dominance, Amber leaned over and kissed her deeply. Brooke's back arched into Amber, seemingly craving the skin-on-skin contact that had driven Amber crazy just minutes before. She worked her way down Brooke's neck as she kissed along her ears, her throat and, finally, her strong shoulders. Brooke murmured sounds of approval and shifted beneath Amber's firm body as her light explorations continued.

As Amber gently took Brooke's nipple between her lips, her moans grew louder and more pointed. Amber felt another slow wave of excitement rise inside her chest as she teased Brooke below with two searching fingertips. Brooke responded by fisting her hand in Amber's already-mussed hair and pushing her hips further into her touch. Amber knew she was desperately seeking purchase, that Brooke needed to be touched, but she selfishly wanted to keep her wanting for longer. She quickly realized, however, that she was bringing the other woman dangerously close to the edge.

She carefully pulled her fingers back and grazed her lips across Brooke's chest as she languidly lavished attention on her other breast. Brooke's grip grew tighter and Amber couldn't help herself – She silenced her breathy moans with another deep kiss. Brooke's hips desperately pushed and arched against her own as their tongues explored each other's mouths for a slow, heated moment that made it hard for even Amber to think.

The friction between their hips and thighs, as they shifted as one along the bed, was arousing Amber all over again. She blinked and bit her lip as Brooke's body pulsed into her own. She was no longer certain the wetness between them was solely Brooke's excitement.

She knows Amber realized. *Is that how Brooke keeps control, even when someone else is on top?*

Amber swallowed hard as she tried to ignore the searing pleasure against her body. *There will be time for more* she told herself. *Right now,*

I want to make Brooke come the way that she made me. She doesn't get to be in control all *the time.*

With that, Amber wrenched herself from Brooke's hips and lowered herself between her thighs. She bit back a cry as her own body screamed at the sudden loss of contact. Without a second thought, she stroked her tongue into, over and around as Brooke trembled into a shaking, moaning orgasm that seemed to last for several long seconds.

Amber gently kissed Brooke's smooth inner thigh as her after-shocks dissipated into the dark stillness of the bedroom. She watched as she took a deep breath and then let herself be gently tugged into Brooke's arms. Exhaustion washed over Amber so quickly that she didn't have time to realize she was falling asleep with her lips pressed protectively to Brooke's jaw or that she was more sure than ever that she would never be able to turn back after tonight.

CHAPTER 30

Morning came far too soon for Brooke's liking. She blinked and slowly felt awareness wash over her, despite her best efforts to stay asleep a little longer. The white-hot morning sun blazed the bedroom in a glowing heat. Brooke settled back against the pillow and enjoyed the satisfying knowledge that she didn't have to be at the office until lunchtime and only had only scheduled herself a half-day of general marketing and client calls. The backlog of warm leads that were automatically deposited into her inbox, as well as the creation of listing brochures and the mailing of a fresh stack of Just Sold postcards, could sometimes be tedious but today Brooke was glad she had planned only busywork.

It's been a long night she thought with a mischievous smile. *I don't think I have the energy for a closing or a day out with multiple buyers.*

Her smile deepened as she tried to roll over and away from the bright sunlight. Her right arm was buried beneath Amber's warm body and she detested the idea of accidentally waking her. Brooke dropped a quick kiss onto her temple and gently tried to wrench herself free. The slight movement caused pins and needles throughout her arm and finally Brooke flopped back against her pillow in defeat.

Another glance at Amber gave her an opportunity to unabashedly drink in the sight of her. She was sound asleep and Brooke relished the quiet moment to watch her. Amber's chin was tucked slightly into her chest and her face was half-buried in Brooke's shoulder. A lock of hair had fallen over her face, blocking out the morning sunlight. One of her fists was balled up beneath a pillow while the other hand rested firmly...

Brooke's eyes widened in surprise and a swell of desire immediately tightened her chest as she realized Amber had fallen asleep with her hand boldly between her thighs. She tried not to think about the fact that Amber's slender fingers were just millimeters from her most sensitive area or even of the delicious sensations that would tease her with the slightest of shifts.

Swallowing hard, she focused instead on the bedside table just beyond Amber's tousled head. The numbers on the digital clock told her that it was time to temporarily push the fantasy to the back of her mind, because Amber still had a full day ahead at the Chamber of Commerce.

With a reluctant sigh, Brooke gently brushed the errant lock of hair across Amber's face and curled it behind her ear. She couldn't help but grin as Amber frowned in her sleep. Her eyebrows furrowed in barely-conscious disapproval of the sunlight.

"Amber," Brooke whispered. She carefully shook her shoulder. "Hey, it's almost 7:30." She paused, unable to help herself, and pressed her lips to Amber's ear. Brooke nuzzled the soft area behind her ear and took a long, deep breath as she inhaled her light scent. "As much as I adore waking up with you, I don't want to be the reason you're late to work, love."

Amber was awake now and grinned, her eyes still closed, as she arched her neck further into Brooke's lips. "Love?" She replied, the deep pleasure in her voice overtaking her mock surprise. "And to what do I owe that designation?"

Brooke flushed. "Sorry," she automatically apologized. "It just sort of...slipped out."

It was true. She hadn't mean to call Amber "love", but the word had dropped from her lips as naturally as the real estate terminology that took up most of her life.

"No," Amber replied, her voice more insistent. She reached beneath the covers and squeezed Brooke's hand. "I liked that," she went on, smiling again. "I love love."

Brooke laughed and kissed her again. "I know you do."

With that, Amber rolled onto her back and stretched. She blinked a few times and then met Brooke's eyes. "Do we have to get the day started?" She asked.

Brooke gave an unenthusiastic nod. "We do," she confirmed. "Technically, *I* don't have to get the day started for another couple of hours, but you do. I'm not going to let you be late on the last week before this big exhibition that you've been pouring your heart and soul into."

She stood, the realization that she had also fallen asleep topless dawning on her only after she had given Amber a full, sweeping view. Amber took full advantage, Brooke noted, as her eyes lingered along her bare stomach and chest before finally meeting her gaze with a cheeky grin.

"So, you don't think there's time to..." Amber started.

"I really, *really* wish there was, but not without you being late," Brooke replied. She fastened the wrinkled black bra that she vaguely recalled tossing over her shoulder late last night. "But there's always tonight. And the next day. And the day after that. And the day after that..." Her voice trailed off as she leaned over the bed and kissed Amber.

"I like the sound of that," Amber replied. "And I *really* like those kisses too."

Brooke smiled as she pulled a faded Rolling Stones t-shirt over her head. The feelings of peace and happiness were so much simpler than she'd imagined. They were certainly far more enjoyable and much less complicated than the feelings of frustration, distress, anxiety, boredom, sadness and fear that had plagued her throughout her adult life.

"The kisses are yours as long as you want them," she confirmed with a wink. "Go ahead and do whatever you need to get ready. I'll make some green tea to go for you."

As Amber climbed out of bed and threw her a look of pure gratitude, Brooke turned and padded down the stairs. As she stepped into the kitchen, she couldn't help but marvel over the change in perspective that had taken place over the last several weeks.

Why don't more people just be happy and at peace? She wondered. *If I had known it was this easy, I would have tried to turn that corner long ago.*

Brooke realized that post-coital bliss probably accounted for a big chunk of her positive outlook, but she also knew permanent, long-lasting change had begun taking root too.

First things first she thought as she turned the dial on the stove to heat a stainless steel pot of water. *One fresh green tea to go and one for here.*

~

THIRTY MINUTES LATER, and Amber was already on her way out the door. Brooke, despite her lack of motivation to get her own morning started, politely walked her to the foyer and handed her a travel mug filled with steaming green tea.

"Thank you so much," Amber said as she opened the front door and turned. "You really didn't have to go through the trouble of making my tea."

Brooke smiled and touched Amber's face affectionately. "I have to admit, there may be something in it for me," she replied conspiratorially. "I've kind of gotten hooked on the green tea too," she whispered. "Don't tell anyone though. Might be bad for business."

Amber laughed and then leaned in even closer. "I won't tell anyone," she teased back. "Don't worry, your green tea secret is safe with me."

Brooke watched as Amber took a step onto the front porch and turned again to wave good-bye. "Wait," she started and then followed her onto the porch. "You forgot something."

Amber cocked her head and shot her a quizzical look. "I did?"

Brooke nodded and then met her lips. The kiss itself was dizzying and Brooke wasn't sure if it was from the heat of the morning sun or the whirlwind of emotion that started low in her belly, but it served its purpose in giving Amber a preview of what was to come that night.

She'll come tonight Brooke thought satisfactorily. *Again. I'll make sure of that.*

Amber blinked and took a deep breath. "And now you're sending me off to work for an entire day with that kiss fresh in my mind?"

Brooke grinned and squeezed her hand. "I'm already looking forward to it. You'll text me when you leave the Chamber?"

Amber shook her head. "You're evil, Brooke Adriani. Totally evil." She paused and smiled. "I'll let you know as soon as I leave work. I may need you to pick me up and be my chauffeur though, because I don't think my mom will let me keep the car overnight two nights in a row."

"That's fi…" Brooke started and, with a single glance at the parking spaces directly in front of her duplex, the words died on her lips. The sinking feeling of horror was slow to wash over her, but her heart immediately began thumping against her ribcage. As the magnitude and the sheer, unexpected terror of the moment dawned on Brooke, she suddenly felt very close to throwing up.

Amber watched her for a moment with concern and then turned to follow Brooke's eyes. From her peripheral, Brooke saw Amber still for a moment and then turn back to her quickly.

"Brooke, there's no way to know if he saw anything," she started, her voice low. "Calm down and wait to react until you know for sure whether he saw us kiss."

Brooke dragged her eyes away from her father's familiar truck that had been idling in direct view of the porch. The look on Dave's face in the driver's seat all but confirmed that he had just witnessed his only daughter making out with his girlfriend's daughter in broad daylight.

"He saw," she replied tightly. She was sure her stomach had dropped to the soles of her feet. Waves of emotion threatened to crack her voice at any moment. "There's no way he *didn't* see. Oh my God, I didn't even know he was planning to stop by."

Amber reached for her hand, but Brooke quickly snatched it away. She ignored the temporary flash of her hurt in Amber's eyes and glanced back at the truck. Her father had gotten out and stood awkwardly against the door, his face unreadable.

I'm going to be sick to my stomach Brooke realized through the buzzing in her ears.

"Look, let's just take a second, okay?" Amber continued, her voice urgent. "Close your eyes and take a deep breath. Let it out through your nose. Do it again if you have to. It'll help you calm down and then we can talk to him..."

Brooke took a step back and ran a hand through her hair in distress. "Nowhere in the history of being told to calm down has it *ever* helped anyone to calm down!" She snapped. "You've been out to your mom for *years*. You have no idea what this means for me."

Amber swallowed hard. "Neither do you until we talk to him. But we can't do that until you're..."

"Until *we* talk to him?" Brooke asked incredulously as her mind raced. "You have to be at work."

Amber rolled her eyes and shook her head. "I don't care," she replied. "I'll tell Bobbi there was an emergency. This is more important to me. *You're* more important to me."

Brooke took another step back as an unexpected lump in her throat rendered her temporarily speechless. "No, Amber, you have to go. I can't...I need to figure this out."

The hurt in Amber's eyes was raw. She tried reaching for Brooke's hand again. "But I want to be here for you," she pleaded. "I...I can go into another room if you want to talk to him privately. I just want to make sure you're okay."

Brooke recoiled from Amber's touch and glanced helplessly at the spot where her father stood. He shoved his hands into his pockets and, with his head down, he walked slowly toward them. "Amber please, just go!" She finally cried in desperation. "I want you to *go*."

She couldn't bring herself to meet Amber's eyes. The other woman stood, frozen for a long moment on the porch, as if she had been slapped. There was a sound deep in her throat, a low, strangled cry, that felt as though it cut Brooke's chest wide open. Amber quickly covered her nose and mouth with her hands and then turned, rushing down the stairs and to Sandra's Beetle.

Dave paused as Amber flew past him. He looked after her, concern filling his face, as she peeled out of her parking space and disappeared from view. He turned, meeting Brooke's eyes, and cleared his throat as he reached the front porch.

Brooke wanted to look away from her father's steady gaze as her years of pent-up fear reached an all-time crescendo, but she couldn't. Everything in her peripheral, from the pink tulips in hanging baskets to the still-open front door, swayed and fizzled. For a moment, Brooke wondered if she was going to faint.

Instead, it was her father's voice that brought her back to the present. "Brooke, I, uh..." he started and then swallowed hard. "I know what's, ah, going on here, but I need to hear you explain what I just saw."

CHAPTER 31

Dave sat on the edge of the couch, his head in his hands. His beet-red face and the look of sheer dismay was exactly what Brooke realized she had been so frightened of for so many years.

She sniffled and averted her gaze from her shaking hands to the box of doughnuts on the kitchen counter. Doughnuts, of all things, had brought Dave to Brooke's duplex. She shook her head at the silliness of it all. Her father knew that she wasn't going to the office until later, as he had explained, and figured that she hadn't had much time to grocery shop yet. The special at Glazed Donuts in Old Town had been too good to pass up, and he thought he'd drop by to bring a dozen to Brooke.

"So…You're gay," Dave stated, still slightly in disbelief. "I mean, like, *gay*-gay, or, you know, you still like men too?"

Brooke closed her eyes. It was too hard to study her father's face right now, to read the shock and disappointment across his familiar features. "I believe the term you're looking for is bisexual," she replied slowly. "And no. I'm not that."

"So, you're gay," Dave repeated. He blinked, but his eyes didn't appear to focus anywhere in particular. "When did you decide this?"

Decades of frustration steadily rose in Brooke's chest and she knew it was just a matter of time until it spewed from her lips and she said something she'd later regret. Instead, she took a deep, steadying breath.

"It's not something you just *decide* one day, Dad," she replied through gritted teeth. "Like what shoes to wear or whether or not you want coffee. It's something I've...struggled with for as long as I can remember."

Dave shook his head slowly as he blinked at the tile. "I mean, I..." he paused. "Is this because I didn't give you a strong female role model to look up to, you know, after your mother? A step-mom or something?"

Brooke wanted to scream, but she knew her father's question was genuine and, misguided as it was, he meant no offense. *Older generation* she reminded herself.

"No, Dad, it's not because you didn't remarry," she bit off the words bitterly. "Mom was more than enough of a role model for me in ten years than any other woman would have been in a lifetime. Sandra has been the closest to a maternal figure since Mom."

Dave nodded. "I just...I just don't understand any of it, Brookie," he spoke as his voice cracked. "I mean, you could have any man you wanted. I don't understand why would choose this instead."

Brooke closed her eyes again in frustration. "Dad, it's..."

Dave held up a hand. "No, hear me out," he went on. "You know Roberto, Monty's son who still lives in Queens? He's seen a couple photos of you on my Facebook page and, uh, he likes what he sees. He's been asking Monty for an introduction the next time he visits him in Florida. My point is, you could have any man you wanted, Brooke. You're a beautiful, smart and successful young woman..."

"Oh, Dad, leave it alone already!" Brooke snapped. *Here come the years of frustration.* "Why on Earth would I want some greasy, macho, gold-chain-wearing, old-school Italian who's never left the bowels of New York City and can't even speak proper English?"

Brooke was acutely aware of the look of shock and then hurt that crossed her father's face. It occurred to her that she could just as easily be talking about him, but she was too angry at the moment to care. "Besides," she continued. "I'm *gay*. It doesn't matter how many men are interested in me, because I'm not *straight*. Their attraction is a non-factor."

"I...I'm sorry," Dave spoke quietly. "I've clearly upset you."

The guilt coursed through Brooke and angered her further. *Why do I feel guilty?* She wondered. *I didn't do anything wrong. I won't feel guilty for who I am anymore.*

"Just stop it, Dad," Brooke spat. She threw up her hands. "What did you expect? How did you *think* I'd feel? I've been terrified to tell you for the last twenty years and...and...instead of comforting me or telling me that it's okay, that there's nothing to be afraid of, you're questioning *why* I'm this way or implying that if a man might be interested, then there's no way I could be gay."

Dave shook his head. "I didn't mean it that way," he replied. "I just...I didn't know..."

It was Brooke's turn to shake her head, but she couldn't see through the tears that blurred her vision. "You said exactly what you meant," she responded. "That's that you'd rather I was straight."

Dave averted his eyes. He looked lost and completely out of his element. In any other situation, Brooke would have felt bad for him. He opened and then closed his mouth.

Seconds that felt like hours ticked by. Brooke folded her arms. "Only one thing has changed between now and all those times you've told me you're proud of me, and that's that you know the truth," she spoke. Her voice sounded higher than usual and her heart drummed against her chest. "So it's true then, isn't it? You'd rather have me be straight?"

Dave looked back at her, his face white. "I don't, uh, know how to answer that..." he started hesitantly.

Brooke didn't want to hear anymore. "Go!" She shouted as she jabbed her finger at the door. "Get out!"

"Brooke, come here," Dave pleaded as he stood. "Please, sweetheart."

She shook her head vehemently. "There's nothing left to talk about, so long as you wish I was straight instead of…" she tried to control the sobs that rose in her throat. "Instead of who I am."

Dave took a few steps toward her, but Brooke held out her arms and moved away. "I told you to get out!" She repeated. "You've caused me so much heartache," Brooke choked out as the tears overcame her.

"Brooke, let's talk," Dave tried again. He took another step toward her, but Brooke pushed against his shoulders.

She finally met his eyes. There was no anger, only concern. *Concern because I'm gay* Brooke thought. *Concern because he thinks I'm troubled, that there's something defective about me. Concern because, in his eyes, gay will never be as good as straight.*

The tears coursed freely down her cheeks and she didn't bother to swipe them away. "I want you to leave," she spoke, her voice steely. "I never want to see you again."

After a moment, Dave nodded. "Fine," he replied dully. "If that's what you want, then I'll leave."

Brooke nodded. "That's what I want."

"Fine," Dave repeated, his voice rising. The front door swung open with his strength. He turned. "When you get yourself under control and you're ready to have a conversation, you know where to find me. Until then, I'll let you be."

With that, Dave shut the door behind him. A few minutes later, Brooke heard the familiar sounds of his truck engine as it sped away from the duplex. She slid down the living room wall as waves of gasping, shaking sobs paralyzed her. Hot tears dripped off her chin and into her lap, leaving wet polka-dots on her jeans.

With her forehead to her knees, Brooke rocked back and forth as she cried. Through her tears, she couldn't help but marvel at how quickly the day had turned on her. In a matter of a few hours, she had somehow lost the two people that meant the most to her – Amber and her father.

She finally recalled the hurt in Amber's eyes and the disbelief that Brooke, someone she had trusted, would reject her so easily. The pain that pierced her chest made it difficult to breathe, but Brooke finally stood on shaking legs.

What she truly wanted to do was fall asleep and start the day over again. Instead, Brooke fell back into bed and curled up against the pillow as a fresh wave of tears hit. Somewhere in the back of her mind, Brooke realized that this would be the first time she cried herself to sleep since her mother died. Her half-day of playing catch-up at the office was no longer in her plans as exhaustion eventually took over. Thoughts and tears faded and then everything was dark.

~

AMBER RUBBED her eyes for the third time in two minutes and blinked at her computer screen. Her eyes had been dry all day after a good cry in her car on the way to the Chamber of Commerce. She had surprised even herself that she had been able to make it to 5 P.M., but she also knew that Bobbi sensed something was off.

She glanced at her phone and massaged her index and middle fingers against her temples. A quick mid-morning text to Brooke to see how she was doing had gone unanswered. Amber had hoped that, once the shock of recent events had lessened, Brooke would respond. She had even let herself hope that perhaps she could still stop by that evening and they could talk. She thought about popping in unannounced on her way home, but Brooke's lack of response made Amber rethink that idea.

With a heavy sigh, she shut her computer down and began gathering her things. Work had provided a paltry distraction but now that there was nothing to busy her mind with, Amber feared she'd be checking her phone every five minutes instead of every twenty or so.

Her head snapped up at the short knock on her door. Bobbi crossed her arms authoritatively and shot her a smile.

"All of the food trucks are confirmed and good to go," Amber spoke. She tried to force a tired smile, but the act of feigning happiness was positively draining. "The last contract I was waiting on was for the shaved ice truck, but I received that this morning. They all know where they'll be parking on Saturday and that an agreed-upon percentage of proceeds will be donated to the Chamber of Commerce."

Bobbi nodded. "That's great, thank you," she replied. "I have total faith in you, Amber. You've taken control of this exhibition and allowed me to focus on all of the other Chamber activities. I can't thank you enough."

Amber sat back in her chair. "You're welcome, Bobbi," she replied. "I'm glad I could help. After all, that's what you brought me on board for, right?" She took a deep breath. "I've enjoyed my time here."

Bobbi smiled again. "I'm glad," she replied. "In fact, there's more I'd like to speak to you with about...*that,* but I have to wait until after the exhibition. However, that's not why I stopped by. You seem...off today. Are you feeling ill? I'm sure we could have you work from home tomorrow if you're under the weather. I'd rather have you healthy and ready for Saturday."

Amber shook her head. "I'm okay," she replied and then sighed. "Well, not really. Some personal issues, I guess. I'll be fine to work though, I'm not sick."

"I understand," Bobbi said with a nod. "I'd better let you get out of here. Big plans tonight?"

Amber shook her head as she rose. "No," she replied. She paused and weighed her options. "Well, maybe relaxing poolside," she corrected herself. A glass of wine and some quiet time by the pool sounded fantastic.

"Good," Bobbi responded as she patted her arm. "You deserve it." She took a deep breath. "It would have been Terry and I's fifteenth anniversary today, so I've just been burying myself in work and avoiding going home for as long as possible. I may take a long, hot bath and listen to my NatureQuest albums." She paused and then shot Amber a pointed smile. "Also excellent medicine for a broken heart."

Amber smiled weakly. "Thanks, Bobbi," she replied. "I'll see you tomorrow." As she turned to leave, she wondered if it was that obvious that romance troubles had taken their toll today. She recalled her brief conversation with Terri at the solstice party. As far as she knew, Bobbi was unaware that she and Terri had met.

They still care deeply for each other Amber thought. *How can it be possible that two people who still love one another end up spending their lives apart?*

"You know, maybe if you apologized to her," Amber said, turning back suddenly. "I mean, obviously the past can't be changed but a sincere apology can still do wonders sometimes."

If they still care for one another, there's always a chance Amber thought determinedly. *Hell, even if I can't ever seem to help myself in love, the least I can do is help someone else. Karma points, right?*

Bobbi paused. "But apologizing would be accepting blame," she countered, crossing her arms. "Admitting fault. The thing of the situation was that I *didn't* do anything wrong."

"It doesn't always have to mean that," Amber replied. "Not if you're simply apologizing for, you know, your part in everything that led you here." She shrugged. "It can't hurt to try, right?"

Bobbi pursed her lips. "But that's what I *have* been doing. Leaving flowers on the porch, sending fruit baskets, trying to tell her that I never did anything..."

"But have you apologized directly to her?" Amber asked gently. She remembered how Terri seemed to think a lack of communication was what destroyed their relationship. "You never know. That might be what she's waiting for."

"I suppose it can't hurt to try," Bobbi replied after a moment. "We'll see if she even picks up the phone for me, but I'll try. Now get out of here, it's almost 5:30. Go on home and I'll see you tomorrow."

Amber waved on her way out the door, her spirits temporarily buoyed by helping someone else.

As she started the car, a call from her mother sounded. The mechanical ringtone had been preloaded onto her phone, but anything was better than Heart. Amber cradled the phone between her ear and shoulder as she maneuvered out of the Chamber's empty parking lot.

"Hey, Mom," she answered.

"Amber?" Sandra asked. "Amber, is that you?"

"Yes, Mom," Amber replied with a good-natured roll of her eyes. "You called me."

"Right," Sandra replied and then took a deep breath. Amber immediately sensed something was wrong. Her stomach churned as she wondered how much more she could take today.

"You're out of work now, right?" Sandra continued. "Since you have the car, can you come to Dave's and pick me up? I've decided it's best if we stay at my condo for a few days. I have my things and yours ready to go."

Amber's stomach dropped to the floor of the Beetle. With everything that had happened so quickly in the morning and then being preoccupied with checking her phone all day for word from Brooke, she hadn't even considered the fact that she was going home to Dave's house and would have to face him directly at some point. Fantasies of poolside relaxation vanished as she processed her mother's words.

"What...What do you mean, stay at your condo?" Amber asked. "Is everything okay? Where's Dave?"

"Sitting in the backyard and refusing to speak to me," Sandra answered matter-of-factly. "He came home very upset this morning. He usually goes out for coffee, but he's been sneaking in a doughnut every once in a while. I had no idea he was going all the way to Glazed Donuts or that he was stopping at Brooke's duplex. How are you doing, honey? How is she?"

Amber opened and then closed her mouth. "I'm...okay," she replied as she tried to keep up. "I, um, don't know about Brooke. Wait, are you saying that Dave kicked us *out*?"

"No!" Sandra exclaimed. "God, no. He said it's unnecessary to leave, but I won't stay here while I'm this upset. After explaining to me what he saw and that Brooke told him she's gay, I asked how he was feeling. Then I told him that there was no reason to feel badly, that there's nothing wrong with Brooke and that you two make a beautiful couple."

Amber swallowed hard. She wasn't even sure if they were a couple. "And then what?"

"Oh, he was livid!" Sandra went on. "He realized that I had known it before him and was very upset that I hadn't said anything. I tried to explain that it wasn't my business to tell and that Brooke needed to speak to him on her own terms, but he's been huffing and puffing ever since. I told him I had my suspicions, but they were only confirmed last night. Nonetheless, he feels betrayed and thinks I should have talked to him right away. I asked him if he really thought you sleeping over there so soon after she moved back in wasn't the least bit telling, but at that point Dave just wasn't hearing logic."

"Oh my God, I'm so sorry, Mom," Amber replied. Guilt filled her chest. The day was quickly going from bad to worse. "I never wanted this to upset your relationship. Please tell me that you two will be all right."

"Well, I don't know," Sandra sniped. "Can I be with somebody so stubborn? Can I be with someone who has a hard time accepting his daughter's sexuality? He relayed some of his conversation with Brooke to me and his reaction to her coming out was all wrong. I know he didn't mean it to be that way, but Brooke deserved better from him in that vulnerable time." She sighed. "Please don't apologize, Amber. He's stuck in his ways and it's hurting everyone around him. There's too much tension here right now. It's upsetting my throat chakra and I am wearing *all* of my turquoise jewelry. The emotion is debilitating any chance at clear communication. I just want to shout at him and shake him until he understands, but he's so damn obstinate!"

Amber turned the corner onto Dave's street. "No shouting or shaking necessary. I'm pulling into the driveway right now."

"Thank you," Sandra replied. "I need my energy cleansed. I made sure to pack my chakra stones and essential oils. Tonight, we'll fight this by meditating on unification and by sending positive thoughts into the Universe."

Amber fought the sudden urge to cry all over again as her mother waved wildly to her from the front door, looked at her phone and then waved again. *How much worse can this possibly get?*

"Oh, I see you! There you are!" Sandra spoke breathlessly into the phone. "I'm in the doorway, do you see me?"

In any other situation, Amber would have laughed at her mother's inability to fully grasp cellular technology. As she ended the call and hurried out of the car to help her mother, the ache in Amber's heart intensified with the realization that she still hadn't received a response from Brooke.

CHAPTER 32

Amber sighed as she finished washing the last of the dinner dishes in the small galley kitchen of her mother's condo on Friday evening. The final week of preparation for the exhibition was over and tomorrow she would be up at 7 and at the exhibition hall by 8 for the long but satisfying day that all their work had culminated in.

She quickly dried her hands on a kitchen towel and peeked into the living room. Sandra sat in the middle of the sectional, her feet curled beneath her, and wrapped a crocheted blanket around herself. She flipped listlessly through television stations.

Amber cautiously stepped around her and perched on the edge of the sectional. "Anything good?"

Sandra sighed and gestured helplessly at the flat screen. "All this junk on television," she replied. "Most of it really does rot your brain."

Amber sat in silence for a moment and then cleared her throat. "Haven't heard from him?"

Sandra pursed her lips. "Oh, he tried to call," she replied. "Once. But I told him I would continue to give him space until he had a chance to fully think things through. He's been a bachelor for a long time. He forgets that his actions don't just affect him, they affect others as well."

"Oh, Mom…" Amber started.

"His response to Brooke's coming out, however unexpected, was inappropriate," Sandra went on, holding up a hand. "I told him that if he can't accept Brooke as she is then I have to assume that, deep down, he has an issue with *every* member of the LGBTQ community and that includes my daughter. I will never be with a man who has a problem with my daughter's sexuality."

Amber swallowed. She wasn't sure if the lump that had suddenly formed in her throat was a result of her mother's unwavering loyalty – really, she was the only person who had shown Amber loyalty throughout her life – or if it was due to guilt.

Not only did things between Brooke and I get ruined, but Mom and Dave's relationship is in turmoil now too she thought. *Everything went so wrong, so fast.*

"Maybe it was just the shock of seeing us together," Amber offered. "I mean, he didn't even know Brooke is gay, much less that she and I are…*were*…developing something."

Sandra shook her head. "He said it's different because it's his own daughter," she replied. "I don't buy that. So it's okay for everyone else, but not good enough for your child? Besides, he had no right to be upset with me for not immediately tattling to him. It was a day or so that I kept it from him, not *years.* I feel awful for Brooke. I tried to call her a couple times but I didn't get through."

Amber looked down at her hands and tried to blink back the tears she felt pushing behind her eyes.

"Oh, honey," Sandra said after a moment. "Haven't heard from *her*?" She smiled gently as she parroted Amber's original question back to her.

Amber shook her head and gazed out the living room window into the night. "Nope," she replied with a deep breath. "And I doubt I will. I fly back to Dallas a week from tomorrow, so you know…" her voice trailed off. "We didn't even get around to talking about the future. Maybe it's just easier that way for everyone."

Sandra reached over and clasped her hand. "I'm sorry she hurt you, sweetheart," she replied. "It wasn't right for her to do what she did, but

Brooke is going through a lot right now. She may just need some time."

"How *much* time?" Amber spluttered. "It's been three days and I haven't heard a word! It's not fair for her to completely distance herself and leave me wondering what's going on. I know she's going through a lot, which is why I haven't pushed myself on her. But if she wanted to make it work as badly as I do? Then now would be the time that she'd be leaning on me, turning to me and wanting love and support. Instead, she's turned her back on me and it *hurts*. This hurts too."

"I know, honey," Sandra leaned over and embraced Amber. "I know."

After a moment, Amber sighed and stood. "I'd better head to bed. Long day tomorrow. Will I see you at the exhibition?"

Sandra nodded. "Of course," she replied. "You know I like to support artists and the community. It's just an added bonus that my baby girl helped put the whole thing together."

Amber smiled as an overwhelming feeling of gratitude for her mother washed over her. She padded down the hall to the small study that had doubled as her bedroom since Tuesday evening. She had managed to build a makeshift bed using the study's loveseat, a few extra pillows and an old sleeping bag that Amber distinctly remembered from early sleepovers with school friends.

Her phone blinked on the small computer desk. She quickly glanced at the new text message as hope bloomed that perhaps Brooke had decided to reach out. Anticipation shattered as Amber re-read the text two more times in disbelief before setting her phone down with a clatter.

It was from Lena. It read: *Darling, I've flown to Key West. I'm staying at the Casa Marina Waldorf Astoria on Reynolds Street. It's over for good between Sarah and I. I need you and must see you right away. Please consider meeting me. Xoxo.*

Amber realized the text had been sent nearly an hour ago, while she and Sandra had been eating dinner. She took a deep breath and felt…nothing. Aftershocks of disappointment that it was not, in fact, Brooke contacting her was all that Amber recognized.

As she plugged her phone into its charger and washed her face, Amber mulled the text. Sure, there was a time when she had wished, hoped and fantasized about a situation just like this but that time had long passed. She wondered how Lena had learned she was in Key West.

My roommate, probably she mused. *Thank God I didn't leave an exact address.*

The thought of Lena and her drama showing up uninvited to either her mother's condo or Dave's house grated on her nerves. She took a deep breath as she tried to get comfortable along the loveseat and in the threadbare sleeping bag.

Before closing her eyes for the night, Amber quickly typed out a reply to Lena: *I'm unable to meet you. You should have told me before flying to Key West; I would have let you know not to bother and saved you the time, money and energy. Good luck to you.*

Amber wondered if her response was a bit harsh, but she didn't much care. She couldn't seem to muster up any of the old feelings she'd had for Lena and had no inclination to see or speak to the handsome surgeon.

As she relaxed into sleep, her mind wandered back to Brooke. Amber's heart seemed to simultaneously speed up and skip a beat as she languidly recalled the details of her smile and the deep dimples that would appear when she just couldn't hold her grin in any longer.

Desire quickly turned to hurt, however, as she remembered how quickly Brooke had closed off and how immediately she had turned on her. Finally, Amber twisted herself into a confused, fragile sleep that left her tossing and turning against the pillows.

~

"So, let me get this straight," Justin said, his eyes wide. He sat cross-legged on Brooke's bed and spoke to the mostly-closed closet door, where she rummaged through racks of clothing. "First off, you're *not* straight. At least as far as your dad knows. In a week's time, you hooked up with Amber, your father caught you with Amber, you came out to your father and then you broke things off with Amber?"

He shook his head in disbelief. "You have been one busy woman," he went on. "I guess that's what happens when you don't talk to your best friend for a few days. How have you been holding up?"

Brooke's muffled voice rang out from the closet. "You know, I think I'm okay," she replied honestly. "Now, at least. The first couple of days I felt numb, like I was living in this crazy, surreal world. But I've been busy all week. I was able to finagle that quick closing on the house for Kelsey the Chicken Heiress, so that was a nice distraction. Then I was able to meditate a few times on it all."

"Meditate?" Justin asked, raising his eyebrows in surprise.

"Yes," Brooke replied. She poked her head out from the closet door. "I haven't had the guts to show my face at the Tara Mandala group in fear of running into Sandra, but I've been meditating here. In the living room. Usually after work. It's helped me feel a lot more…clear-headed."

She stepped around the closet door and gestured at her outfit. "What do you think?" She asked. "Fitting for a photography exhibition?"

Justin wrinkled his nose at Brooke's sleek suit, the short-sleeved black silk blouse tucked casually into a pair of black and gray pinstriped pants.

"Maybe if this was, like, a formal thing in New York City or something," he replied. "But this is family-friendly, it's outdoors and it's casual. Plus, it's going to be ninety-something degrees today. You'll die in all that black."

Brooke sighed. "It's too much?"

Justin nodded. "You look like a Realtor®."

Brooke shot him a confused glance. "But I *am* a…"

"Just try those cute cropped jeans you have and a tank top," Justin cut in, waving his hand dramatically.

"Okay," Brooke replied, rolling her eyes as she disappeared back into the closet. "But I think the suit would have been just fine!" She called through the door.

It had been four mornings since that fateful Tuesday when everything had come crashing down. Four days since Brooke had seen Amber, which, she realized, was the longest stretch of time since Amber had arrived on the island and turned her world upside-down. She missed her terribly. She hated the icy ache that had settled into her chest and the fact that she couldn't feel Amber's warm body against her own when she woke up in the mornings.

After a few days of solitude, there was no doubt left in Brooke's mind as to how she felt about Amber. The hard part had been mustering up the courage to reach out earlier that morning. She knew she was risking Amber telling her to shove it or to never speak to her again, but Brooke knew she couldn't let another day go by without seeing her.

She pulled on the dark blue cropped jeans, rolled at her calves, and a black tank top. A smile played at her lips as she re-read the short text message exchange they'd had this morning. Brooke had a lot to say, a great deal of explaining to do and much that she had come to terms with over the last several days, but she felt it was best to talk to Amber in person. *Besides* she thought wistfully. *I just want to see her.*

Holding her breath as she had quickly and decisively tapped the Send button, Brooke's message to Amber had been simple and to the point. *Hi* it had read. *I know we have a lot to talk about and I'm sorry it's taken me this long to reach out. Please know that I haven't stopped thinking about you. Can I stop by the exhibition today?*

After an excruciating thirty-minute wait for a response, Brooke begrudgingly accepted the fact that Amber was probably punishing her. When her phone had finally sounded with a reply, she had closed her eyes and sent up a quick prayer that Amber hadn't all but given up on her.

Yes, you're welcome to stop by. See you then.

The reply was short and missing the multi-colored emojis, excessive exclamation points and words of affection that Brooke had learned to associate with Amber's text messages, but she didn't mind. She'd take what she could get, so long as it wasn't Amber kicking the door closed before they even had a chance to let their potential flourish.

As Brooke quickly buckled a fashionable black leather belt, she closed her eyes and enjoyed the shiver of anticipation that ran up her spine. *It's not too late* she told herself again. *She hasn't given up on you yet. Today is your chance to get Amber back.*

Brooke emerged from the closet and ran her brush through her hair a final time. She glanced at Justin in the mirror, who was fiddling with his own phone.

"Can't go more than five minutes without a text to Adam?" She asked teasingly.

Justin bit his lip, but forced a laugh. "No, nothing like that," he hedged. "Just replying to an e-mail."

Brooke immediately sensed something was amiss. She turned from the mirror expectantly. "What's going on?"

Justin sighed and seemed to deflate. "We're sort of…taking a break, I guess," he admitted. "He…It's just…He's everything I want, you know? And Trey is so awesome. We just *fit* together, the three of us. We're becoming this little family and it's everything I didn't even know I wanted. In, you know, another ten years. I think."

Brooke's mouth dropped open. "Justin, why didn't you tell me?"

He shrugged. "Oh Brooke, you've had so much going on in your life," he replied. "The last thing I wanted to do was drop my problems on you when you're already going through so much. Trust me, I remember coming out to *my* parents. It wasn't easy."

Brooke swallowed hard, but was unwilling to let him off the hook so quickly. "Where did you two leave things?"

"Adam is upset with me," Justin answered. His face was downcast and Brooke was sure she had never seen her upbeat friend quite so distraught before. "I understand why. He's, you know, ready to get married and be a family."

"And you're not?" Brooke asked, raising an eyebrow. "I know you had a *plan*, but love doesn't follow any sort of plan. If everything you want is right in front of you, how can you turn that away just because it doesn't follow some silly timeline you had in mind?"

"Adam has been hurt before," Justin continued shakily. He shook his head and glared at his phone. "He doesn't deserve to go through that again."

Brooke crossed her arms. "Then don't put him through it again," she responded, as though the answer was very simple. "You care about him and Trey. That much is crystal clear. Show them just how amazing of a man you are and don't doubt yourself. Love comes to us for a reason, Justin."

He nodded as he appeared to consider this. Finally, he met Brooke's eyes and smiled. "You seem very optimistic for someone who is experiencing heartache of her own," he replied. "Maybe I should try this meditation thing too."

Brooke smiled back, despite the nerves she felt at seeing Amber again. "I love her," she admitted quietly. "I want her to know she's never been just another woman to me. She has my heart."

Justin's eyes shone with excitement. "You're in love, Brooke," he agreed. "I didn't think I'd ever see the day." He stood and held out his arm to her. "Come on. Let's go get her back."

Brooke hesitantly took his arm. "You're coming with me?"

"Of course," he replied. "Did you think I *really* just came over to help you pick an outfit and eat stale doughnuts? No ma'am. You're going to need moral support, so let's go and make our presence at this exhibition known."

As they headed down the stairs, Brooke felt overwhelming gratitude for Justin. *He really is one of the best people I know* she thought. *And once I've fixed the mess between Amber and I, I'm going to do everything I can to get him and Adam back together. Everything is going to work out.*

She turned to quickly lock the front door behind them and took a deep breath as the hot sun pulsed against her back.

...I hope.

CHAPTER 33

"Okay, that's perfect," Amber spoke warmly, her eyes trained on the viewfinder of her camera. "Now, if I could just get a smile...Amazing!" She grinned as she snapped three photos in quick succession of the young family that had just arrived at the Chamber's exhibition. She handed them a plain white business card with a URL, where they could later find complimentary digital copies of their photos. They thanked her and then moved on as the younger of the two boys sprinted to the festivities.

Amber shaded her eyes with the palm of her hand and looked around the exhibition with pride. It was only 10:30 and already dozens of families, many with children, had arrived. Getting a solid number of people in before the heat of the day hit had been a crucial measurement for success, as attendance was expected to wane in the scorching early afternoon hours.

Much of the expo took place in the long, rectangular parking lot of the Chamber of Commerce. Student volunteers from Key West High School stood on opposite corners of the main intersection near the Chamber and waved the iconic Conch Republic flag to entice passing motorists.

At the opposite end of the parking lot, four food trucks stood in a neat line against the curb. Amber could already smell the Vietnamese tacos from one and the hot Cuban sandwiches from the other. The scents of fresh food and spices floated through the humid air. It made Amber's stomach audibly growl as she wandered through the exhibition and snapped a few more photos.

A shaved ice truck and a cupcake truck rounded out the food. In between the trucks and the parking lot entrance, people milled about and soaked up the creativity at every turn. The outdoor festivities led to the Chamber's indoor exhibition hall. A group of local chalk artists lined the sidewalk to create mind-bending murals along otherwise dull swaths of concrete. The top ten prize-winning photographs had been blown up into large, interactive jigsaw puzzles. Each had been attached to a large stand and cut into jumbled, uneven pieces. Amber watched with a smile as kids and their parents laughed and tried to decipher the images so they could place the puzzle pieces in their correct order.

She turned again and took a few photos of a toddler running through a line of large squares fixed onto poles in the ground. He traced his chubby hand along the squares as he ran between them and giggled with high-pitched delight as they gently spun. Each side of the square had a different featured image printed onto it, but they all followed a sub-theme of Key West foliage. Amber snapped more photos of the boy, laughing and surrounded by beautiful spinning greenery, and then marveled over how beautifully the exhibit encapsulated Key West's nature. It was a microcosm of the larger environment that surrounded the child and the unbridled joy on his face reminded Amber exactly why she had fallen in love with the transformative magic of art years ago.

She strolled back to the rows of picnic tables set up near the food trucks. As she trudged back to where her mother sat for a bite to eat, she scanned the faces in the crowd.

No Brooke she thought with disappointment. She blew out a breath and told herself that it was still early. *She wouldn't blow you off hours after asking to talk. Right?*

Amber eased onto the scarred wooden bench next to where her

mother had dug into a Cuban sandwich. Just beyond the picnic tables, a local Jimmy Buffett tribute band had been hired to provide light, happy music for the exhibition.

"No sign of her yet?" Sandra asked between bites of her sandwich. A large sun hat shaded most of her face. "Sweetheart, you're too anxious. Brooke is a woman of her word. She'll be here."

Amber felt silly checking her phone for what felt like the tenth time in a minute. "What if...What if it's bad though?" She couldn't help but ponder out loud. "I mean, we didn't exactly end things positively. What if she's decided that she can't be with me? At the end of the day, we're still from two completely different worlds," she shook her head. "It really sucks, because as much as I *want* to hate her right now, I can't. I know how amazing Brooke really is. I was never supposed to fall for her, I know that."

Sandra wrapped her arm around Amber's shoulders. "That's how you know it's real, isn't it?" She replied thoughtfully. "I've seen how Brooke looks at you, Amber. I've witnessed the way her face lights up when you're nearby and the way she studies you as though you're this beautiful, mystical puzzle that she can't quite figure out. My guess is that Brooke *can't* go back from where she is now. And why would she want to? You love with your whole heart and nothing less. Everyone should have the guts to love like you."

Amber smiled. "Are you just saying that because you're my mom and you have to?"

Sandra chuckled. "Of course not," she replied. "Although it *is* my job to lift you up when you're down, just like it was my job to change your dirty diapers as a baby." She paused. "Speaking of, did I tell you whose daughter had twins a few months ago?"

Sandra opened her mouth to launch into what Amber was sure would be juicy gossip gleaned from her mother's occasional e-mail exchanges with friends still in Dallas, but she was abruptly cut off by the singer of the tribute band.

"I have a special announcement to make," he spoke gently into the microphone. Amber was momentarily surprised by how much deeper his speaking voice was than his singing voice, but the surprise quickly faded into panic.

Special announcement? She thought in horror. *The Chamber didn't approve any special announcement or impromptu emceeing.*

Amber's mind raced over the possibilities of just how terribly the situation could unfold, each one worse than the last and sure to hammer the Chamber's reputation. *Obnoxious self-promotion to hawk CDs and t-shirts?* She wondered. *Unhinged discussion about the woman who wronged him? Political rant? Oh God, please no.*

As Amber scanned the crowd for Bobbi, the singer continued with a grin. "We don't usually do this, but we had a special request from someone in the crowd. It's not typically our genre of music, but it was important that it got a certain lady's attention. So, Sandra Lucas, if you're here..."

He paused for a moment and glanced around the picnic tables and growing crowd of onlookers. It took Amber about three full seconds to process that the singer had said her mother's name. Wide-eyed, she turned to her mother. Sandra was frozen in disbelief. Her mouth hung open and a corner piece of sandwich crust dangled between her thumb and index finger.

"What in the..." Sandra murmured, barely audible.

The classic ballad started slow and gentle as one of the guitarists pitched in the familiar backing vocals. The drumbeat rolled steadily as the two musicians harmonized the old Temptations hit.

"Each day through my window I watch her as she passes by
I say to myself, "you're such a lucky guy"
To have a girl like her is truly a dream come true
Out of all the fellas in the world, she belongs to you..."

Amber glanced dubiously between the Jimmy Buffett cover band, which had suddenly begun crooning Motown classics, and her mother, whose eyes were misty and faraway.

"Um, Mom?" She tried.

"But it was just my imagination
Running away with me
It was just my imagination

Running away with me..."

Sandra gently swayed on the bench and reached up to quickly swipe a tear that had escaped. Amber blinked at her and followed her gaze once more, this time recognizing a familiar figure that had begun walking toward the picnic table from the nearby stage. Dave's gaze didn't leave Sandra's face.

As the band continued to play, he stopped, suddenly hesitant, just a few yards from where they sat. It was then that Amber could see how much pain and sorrow filled Dave's normally cheery eyes. In spite of the public atmosphere, Amber couldn't help but feel as though she had suddenly intruded on a private moment.

After a few seconds, Dave cleared his throat. "It's, ah...It's been real quiet at the house without you."

Sandra crossed her arms and looked away. "Perhaps that silence is a good thing," she countered. "To help you reflect and make some sense of things."

"Sandra, I...I'm tryin' to tell you that I miss you," Dave said. He spread his hands helplessly at his sides. "I'm lost and miserable without you."

Amber snuck a glance back at her mother. Sandra met his eyes again and Amber could tell that her willpower was fracturing. Her lip trembled and her eyes filled with tears.

"I miss you too, Dave," she finally whispered. "I miss our walks and our talks..." She paused and laughed through her tears. "And our long talks on our walks! I miss the fun we'd have doing even the smallest things and the joy we'd find in the simplest moments."

Dave swallowed hard. It was as near tears as Amber had ever imagined the gruff, rough-around-the-edges New Yorker. He shoved his hands into his pockets in a way that reminded her too much of Brooke and then Amber was suddenly overcome by a lump of emotion in her throat.

"Why don't you come on home then?" He asked as he kicked at the ground. "You and..." he finally glanced at Amber and attempted a small smile. "You and Amber both."

"And what about Brooke?" Sandra asked.

The second reminder in so many seconds was almost too much for Amber. The pit in her stomach deepened with the realization that Brooke still hadn't shown and her phone hadn't alerted her to a text message or call.

Dave glanced somewhere far in the distance. "Brooke and I, you know, we..." he sighed and waved his hands emphatically. "We've had our own relationship dynamic for a long time. She can be hot-headed sometimes, even though she does a better job of hiding it than me. She, ah, she's a little more like her old man than I guess even *I* thought."

Sandra opened her mouth again but closed it as Dave took a few tentative steps toward Amber. "I...I've never had an issue with you, Amber," he started. "I hope you know that. I've enjoyed you being here and having the chance to know you. And I've especially enjoyed you here because I see how happy it makes your mom. I've had, ah, time to think and during that time, I haven't been able to think of a single thing that makes me happier than your mom and her happiness. Besides, of course, my Brookie and *her* happiness." He took a deep breath. "I've had my...suspicions about Brooke through the years. But I always buried my head in the sand, you know, thinking that if she didn't tell me nothin', then, you know, it wasn't real and I could keep denying what should've been obvious all along. That's my fault. She needed support. She needed to know it was okay to talk to her old man about anything and I failed her."

Amber immediately shook her head. "No, don't say that..." she started.

"I'll make it right with Brooke," he continued. "But I want you to know that the compassion and love that you and your mom show to people is so rare. It's refreshing, you know? Everyone should have the chance to experience love like that, especially my Brooke. When I... When I think about it like that, I realize that, you know, there's nothing else that makes sense more than you and her bein' together. If you love her..." he paused. "And I mean *really* love her. You know, beyond the sharp edges and the reticence and the fact that she lives and breathes real estate – because she can work on all those things – then I would be *proud* and happy and..."

Amber cut him off as she threw her arms around him in an unexpected hug. His voice trailed off as he awkwardly patted her back. "I do," she replied, the words tumbling out over one another. "I love her. You have my word."

She turned as her phone vibrated on the table with a text message. After practically pouncing on it, Amber was mildly disappointed to see that it was from Bobbi. Once she read the message, however, her heart soared with hope. *Could it be?*

As Amber excused herself under the guise of attending to work, she read over Bobbi's text again with a smile.

Please meet me at the main entrance. A guest just arrived and is asking for you.

CHAPTER 34

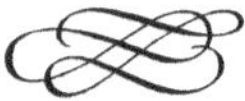

Amber hurried to the entrance of the Chamber building and wondered why Brooke wouldn't just walk the exhibits and find her. After all, it was part of her job to be throughout the exhibition all day.

Maybe she spotted Dave Amber thought. She realized that must be it. *She might not be ready to see him. She probably wants to have a private conversation with him first.*

As Amber reached the entrance, she wondered how the portion of the exhibition inside was progressing. Jealously, she wished she had volunteered for a task in the air conditioned comfort of the Chamber's exhibition hall instead of circling the humidity for photos during the hottest parts of the day.

Inside, all of the selected photos were displayed in a purposely mish-mash fashion. Some were blown up large and took up floor-to-ceiling space, while others were in rows of standard 8X10-sized frames. The different sizes, shapes and layouts were meant to draw more engagement than the identical, neatly-organized rows at most exhibitions.

Two of the meeting rooms were scheduled out for interactive Skype interviews with some of the photographers. A half-hour was allotted for each interview and allowed attendees to ask questions. The Chamber's Digital Marketing Director and his Marketing Assistant acted as moderators.

As Amber wondered why she never went into marketing, if for nothing more than to have the ability to sit down and enjoy air conditioning during events like these, she stopped short a few feet from the double entrance doors. Bobbi, looking fresh as ever in her pressed business suit and identifying Welcome tag on her lapel, spotted her a moment later.

She grinned and waved Amber over. *Come on* she mouthed.

No Amber thought, refusing to believe the image before her eyes. *No, it can't be. Anything but this. No, no, no.*

No matter how many times she blinked, the sight of Lena standing tall and solemn next to her smiling boss wouldn't fizzle away and disappear. *This is real life* Amber realized as her stomach sank to the steaming concrete. *Lena is actually here. How the hell did she find me?*

Once upon a time, the sight of two power lesbians, both so sure and confident that it blurred the lines of arrogance, would have intimidated Amber beyond imagination. At the moment, however, the only emotion she recognized boiling inside her was annoyance. Brooke, though also confident and successful, was far more understated. As a result, Amber realized, she held a much more powerful spell over her.

Amber trudged the last few steps to the doors and folded her arms. "Bobbi, I got your text," she spoke plaintively. She refused to look at Lena. "Is everything all right?"

Bobbi nodded, oblivious. "Oh, yes, of course!" She exclaimed. "Everything is *fantastic*. Look at this event!" She gestured to the crowds of people still arriving in the parking lot. "This is *huge*, Amber. I'm going to go out on a limb and say we probably don't even need to count official attendance before noon because I believe we've surpassed the goal we had and then some."

Lena cleared her throat pointedly. The sound grated tremendously on Amber's nerves. She took a deep breath and closed her eyes.

Compassion, remember? She told herself. *And if that doesn't work, just keep breathing. In and out...In and out...In and...*

"Ah, yes, and there's a visitor who is looking specifically for you," Bobbi continued. She glanced at Lena curiously. "A Dr. Mielkute?"

"Thank you," Amber spoke through gritted teeth. She turned to Lena and didn't return her expectant smile. Instead, Amber grabbed her by the elbow and stomped a few paces around the corner of the building and away from the hordes of people strolling around.

"Amber, you have become strong..." Lena started, sounding impressed. She glanced down at her elbow and then back at her, making a point of rubbing her arm with a smile.

"*What* are you doing here?" Amber hissed.

Lena's smile dropped and Amber recognized her quickly cut to the innocent act instead. Though it had been some time now, she still knew how to read the deceitful doctor by recognizing her cues and facial expressions. It made Amber feel cold all over.

"What, I do not deserve a holiday?" Lena spoke as her voice rose in displeasure. "I cannot wish to leave the grind of Dallas and travel to a beautiful tropical island? Did you not read my text completely? Sarah and I are *over*. We are done for good."

Amber felt nothing. "I read your text," she replied, her tone hovering above a whisper. The last thing she needed was an ex-lover's quarrel at the signature event she had been planning for weeks. She refused to let this overshadow all the hard work she had put into the project. "It didn't mean anything to me. I'm sorry that you two couldn't work things out, but what did you expect? For me to come running back into your arms and to live happily ever after? That might happen in some stories, but not mine. You *hurt* me. You lied to me," Amber began ticking things off on her fingers as resentment got the best of her. "You took away my self-worth and made me feel less than. How can I forget that?"

Lena looked astonished as she opened and then closed her mouth. "I just thought...I thought coming here would show you..."

Amber shook her head in frustration. "You did, didn't you?" She asked miserably. "You really thought I'd come running back into your arms that easily. You thought I would wait forever and you *still* don't understand how wrong you were to treat Sarah and I the way you did."

Lena ran a hand through her spiked hair in distress. "I…I found out you were in Key West from your roommate," she tried to explain. "And I remembered you said your mom lived here. I didn't know you were working or how to find you until I saw your post on Facebook this morning. I…I thought you were pretending to be mad in your text message to teach me a lesson. I thought if I came to see you, things would be different."

Amber swallowed hard and made a mental note to update her privacy settings on the ubiquitous social network. She and Lena had never been Facebook friends because Lena had always said it was too risky and that a social media connection would cause more trouble than it was worth. She hadn't realized the other woman purposely sought out her profile for clues to her whereabouts.

She refused to be Facebook friends because she never wanted to get caught in her lies Amber thought miserably. *Plain and simple. But she'll still use it to find information about me.*

The realization made Amber feel slightly sick, but mostly numb. Truthfully, she just wanted to get away from Lena.

"I don't care," Amber finally spoke, throwing up her hands. "Really. I don't care how you found me." She hesitated, wondering if she had made herself clear. With Lena, she was never sure. "You should go," she finished pointedly.

With that, Amber wrenched herself away from the stucco wall and slipped back into the bustle of people and exhibits throughout the large parking lot. Face-to-face with Lena Mielkute was not what she had anticipated and it jarred her. As she gripped her camera, Amber took a deep, steadying breath with the knowledge that she had done the right thing. Even if Brooke would never be in the picture again, Amber understood that she couldn't go back.

CHAPTER 35

"Amber!" A voice called out. She half-heartedly turned to see Bobbi striding quickly to her. "Amber, I didn't get a chance earlier to thank you."

She assumed Bobbi was referring to the early success of the exhibition and forced a smile. "No thank you necessary," she replied. "It's my job, after all."

Bobbi held her eyes for a moment. "Yes, but listening to me lament about Terri and giving me advice is not," she replied quietly. "You're wise beyond your years, Amber. It's just another testament to the natural ability you have to make people comfortable around you almost immediately. It's a gift and it's something that I am incredibly thankful for, because it worked. Your advice worked!"

Amber blinked in confusion. "What advice?"

Bobbi reached out and touched her shoulder excitedly. "You know, the apology!" She went on, her face aglow. "You were spot-on. I reached out to Terri and did exactly what you said. I apologized, I took ownership of my part in the demise of our relationship and I let her know how truly awful I felt that things had reached such a negative point. And I did that all without feeling as though I had to admit to something I didn't do."

Amber smiled slowly as she followed Bobbi's pointed gaze over her shoulder. Across the parking lot, a familiar figure stood tall and casual against the back of the Vietnamese taco truck. Terri lifted her left hand in what was barely a wave and shot them a warm smile.

Bobbi leaned in conspiratorially. "We're going to get an early dinner after the exhibition has wrapped," she spoke in a hushed voice that Amber could tell she was having difficulty containing. "Perhaps go for a walk on the beach later. That was how we ended our very first date, you know. Parasailing and a moonlit walk on the sand." Her eyes were faraway for a moment.

Amber was pleasantly surprised. "Good for you, Bobbi," she replied. "I'm happy for you both."

And she was. *Even if my advice doesn't work so well in my own love life, I can at least console myself with the knowledge that Bobbi and Mom are working their relationships out* Amber thought as she tried to ignore the sadness camped in her chest.

"Well, I'd better go see if she wants to grab something to drink," Bobbi went on, clapping Amber on the back affectionately. "I can really only take about a twenty minutes. Have you had a break yet? I know you've been out in this heat all morning."

Amber nodded. "Yes, I sat with my mom for a few min..."

The words died on her lips as she spotted Brooke just a few feet away. Two older children chased each other nearby as their shouts added to the background cacophony. To Amber, it was all muted as the blood rushed in her ears. Brooke watched her patiently, but the intensity in her bright blue eyes was almost too much for Amber to bear. There was a clarity and confidence that surrounded her and appeared to take the place of the cool steadiness and hard unflappability that had once seemed to define Brooke.

Amber hadn't realized she was frozen in place until Brooke took a few steps toward them. She didn't break their gaze as she approached.

"Can I talk to you for a moment?" Brooke asked. "Or whenever you have some time." Her eyes darted to Bobbi and then settled back on Amber. "I won't be long."

Bobbi pushed her glasses up the bridge of her nose with one finger and fixed Amber with a mildly amused look that seemed to say *another one?*

"You could probably use another break," Bobbi spoke smoothly. She patted Amber on the shoulder. "Why don't you take five?"

Amber shot Bobbi a grateful look and toyed with the camera around her neck as the silence stretched between her and Brooke. Her boss quickly turned and made a beeline for Terri.

"You came," Amber finally spoke. "I didn't know if you'd make it."

Brooke chewed the inside of her cheek in thought. "Of course I came," she replied. "Regardless of anything else, one thing you should know about me by now is that I always keep my word. Besides…" she paused and took a deep breath. "I've missed you so much."

Amber glared at the ground and then finally met Brooke's eyes again. She was surprised at the emotion that bubbled to the surface. "You threw me out of your house," she responded. The hard edge in her tone betrayed the upset she still felt about that morning. "You were so quick to turn on me the second that things got tough. Life will *always* take unexpected turns, Brooke. You can't just shut everybody out when it does."

Brooke's face reddened as a passing couple glanced at them in curiosity. She nodded at a large banyan tree just beyond the rows of picnic tables. Its long green leaves and thick, twisted roots provided a spot of shade and privacy on the far outskirts of the exhibition.

"I understand why you're upset," she finally replied. "Give me a chance to explain. Please?"

Amber blew out her breath and nodded. She fell into step with Brooke as they walked to the banyan tree, but was mildly surprised when the other woman quickly whirled around after they reached its shade.

~

"It's not fair," Brooke spoke through gritted teeth. She hated how the emotion seemed to overwhelm her and cause her voice to quaver. "It's not fair," she repeated. "You can't expect someone who has spent a lifetime learning how to shut people out to suddenly be able to be wide open."

Amber was quiet as she met her eyes. "I thought..." she paused and folded her arms. "I had this stupid notion in my head that I had somehow cracked your shell. That the Universe conspired to put us in each other's lives at exactly the right time and that maybe it was something really special. I...I care about you, Brooke. I care about you not despite of, but *because* of all the things that make you who you are. Even the things that make you shut out the rest of the world. And that..." Amber paused and sniffled once. She averted her gaze, but Brooke had already seen tears glimmering at the corners of her eyes. "And that's a shame. You're going to miss out on so much."

Brooke squeezed her fists together at her sides, her nails leaving sharp half-moon imprints in her palms. Her chest ached sharply at the thought of missing out on Amber. She had experienced the joy, the peace and even the ecstasy that the other woman could so easily bring out of her.

"My entire life has been a lesson in keeping your distance," she replied in a low voice. "I learned it when my mom was sick and I realized that, no matter what, people you love are going to leave you. I learned it when the kids at school would tease me for only having one parent. Anytime I felt tears creeping in, that helpless feeling of wanting to cry..." Brooke paused, the irony of that same feeling washing over her now not unnoticed. "Anytime I wanted to cry, I'd silently yell at myself. I'd tell myself to stop it, stop it *right* now and quit being a baby. That if they see me cry, then they'll know I'm weak. I didn't want to cry in front of my mom and make her feel worse and I refused to cry in front of those kids, because they didn't deserve the pleasure of knowing they'd hurt me. And since then, that's *always* been me."

A single tear snaked down Amber's cheek and she blinked. "I'm not crying because I'm hurt," she started shakily. "Even though I am. I'm crying for *you*, Brooke. I'm picturing that ten-year old girl in my mind, learning how to shut out the world and relying on *that* for protection. I'm crying because I want to hug her and tell her it's going to be okay."

Despite all of her quick flings and shallow relationships, Brooke was fairly sure no one had ever cried for her. She was overcome with the aching desire to wrap her arms around Amber, kiss her tears away and promise that they could figure out anything.

Instead, Brooke scuffed the toe of her shoe against the fine dirt beneath the tree. "Do you still think that whatever woman captures my heart is very lucky?"

Amber laughed, but nodded. "Of course I do."

In that moment, something clicked inside of Brooke. A conversation from weeks ago nudged its way back into her mind.

"Remember the night we came back to the house after Schooner Wharf? I said I'd come out once I fell in love and was absolutely crazy for someone," Brooke spoke. Her throat felt dry and she struggled to find the right words. "I said once I was sure a woman was the one, that I'd tell my dad I'm gay. Remember?"

Amber nodded. "I remember."

"I'm beginning to think that everything happens for a reason," Brooke continued. "Coming out was unplanned, but I can't help but wonder why it happened now. Why with you."

Amber took a deep breath. "What does that mean to you?"

Brooke smiled and sent up a silent prayer that it wasn't too late for them. "I love you, Amber," she finally admitted. "But it's more than that and maybe that's what I've been so scared of. You're right, you know? I can't fight what was supposed to happen all along. I love you and I…I can't picture being without you."

Amber opened her mouth and then suddenly stilled. Brooke turned in confusion as the tall woman approached them. Suddenly, there was an unexpected shift in the energy. Confused, Brooke looked between Amber and the woman, who took a protective step closer to her.

"Darling, I have been looking for you," the older woman spoke, her words dripping with a thick accent that sounded strangely Eastern European. "What are you doing beneath this big tree? We must finish our conversation. I cannot leave. When I told you I was in Key West, I was hopeful we'd have more time together..."

Brooke felt as though she had been simultaneously kicked in the chest and punched in the gut. She stumbled back a few steps as she wondered where all the air in her lungs went. Amber's eyes were wide and filled with shock. They all but confirmed who the unexpected intruder was. Still, Brooke wanted to hear her say it.

"Lena from Lithuania?" She asked, her voice shaking and low. She didn't meet Amber's gaze.

"Lena from Lithuania," Amber confirmed quietly. "But Brooke, it's not what you think..."

Brooke wasn't listening anymore. She turned quickly before Amber and Lena could see the hot tears that blurred her vision. She didn't want to hear Amber's flimsy excuses or desperate attempts at explaining away what she realized was quite possibly the biggest betrayal of her life.

She hadn't realized she had somehow made it halfway through the exhibition until she spotted Justin near several large, spinning squares. He looked disappointed as he shoved his phone into his back pocket.

"Let's go," Brooke spoke abruptly as she reached him. She ignored his look of disbelief as he took in the sight of her.

"Oh my God Brooke, what happened?" He asked, his concern obvious. "Did you find Amber?"

It was all Brooke could do to nod. "I found her, all right," she muttered. "Amber *and* her ex-girlfriend from Dallas."

Justin's mouth dropped open. "No!" He exclaimed. "What did she say?"

Brooke hadn't realized the tears had been snaking freely down her cheeks until she glanced at the ground and felt them drip off her chin. "I don't know," she admitted. "I physically could not stand the sight of them together. I took off. If Amber called after me, I didn't hear it."

Justin shook his head slowly. "I don't understand," he went on. "Amber wouldn't do that. I *never* saw that coming."

Brooke felt humiliated, stupid for even thinking that Amber felt as deeply as she did, and wondered numbly at how quickly Amber had rushed back into Lena's arms. The brief thought of Amber in *anybody's* arms but her own made her sick to her stomach.

"Can we go?" She choked out. "I want to go home. I can't be here anymore."

Justin nodded and casually wrapped his arm around her shoulders. "You got it."

Brooke's head pounded so hard that she was sure the kids they quickly passed on their way to the car could see her temples pulsing. *Amber knew Lena was coming to Key West.* Her thoughts fired a mile a minute and none brought her any solace. *Did she invite her? What did she do, call her as soon as she left my home on Tuesday?*

"What are you thinking?" Justin asked nervously as he waited at the passenger's side door for Brooke to unlock the car. "Surely there must be *some* sort of explanation."

Brooke scoffed and swiped angrily at the tears on her face. "Honestly?" She replied bitterly. "I'm thinking that this is exactly why I don't do relationships. This is why I've always kept love at arm's length. At least then I never had to feel the way I do now."

CHAPTER 36

Amber sat back in her desk chair and surveyed the empty space. It was her last day at the Key West Chamber of Commerce, capping off a busy final week of post-exhibition activities that ensured Bobbi could close this year's event file with no issue. All vendors were paid; prints were either been donated to the many local galleries that dotted the island or shipped back to the photographer at their cost; post-exhibition marketing e-mails were drafted and sent to everyone on the Chamber's mailing list; all event photos were downloaded, edited and branded with the Chamber logo and final costs and ROI was carefully calculated.

The week had passed in a blur, which was fine by Amber. Brooke had all but disappeared after Lena's surprise appearance at the exhibition. Her calls and texts had gone unanswered and even a text exchange with Justin had given her only a short response advising that perhaps Brooke just needed some time. It didn't, however, seem to betray any confidence that the relationship could be salvaged.

After Brooke took off, Amber wasted no time in again telling Lena to leave. She had hoped to avoid a scene at the exhibition and was surprised when Lena quickly put her hands up in a mock conciliatory gesture, smirked at her and walked off. Over her shoulder, she had remarked that Amber was making a terrible mistake and that one day she would regret not recognizing what a catch Lena was. The irony was not lost on Amber, who had replied that she highly doubted it. Only after reliving the events of the day with her mother did Amber realize that Lena's return to her side had likely been only to spite her and hurt Brooke.

"She had probably seen you two talking," Sandra had explained. "She read the body language. After all," she had continued with a wry smile. "It doesn't take a surgeon to figure out that you two are crazy about one another."

Amber's thoughts were abruptly interrupted by the ringing of her desk phone. She straightened with a start, glanced at her Inbox and answered the call.

"Oh great, you're still there!" Bobbi's voice chimed through. "Say, do you mind stopping by the conference room? I'm letting everyone leave early this afternoon because of that storm they're saying turned course and is now headed for the Keys. It was a tropical depression this morning, but they're thinking it may become a tropical storm watch by dinnertime."

"I already received an automated notice on my phone that my flight tomorrow afternoon is cancelled," Amber replied dryly. "I'm probably going to have to push my return to Dallas back a couple of days, but it looks like there's a flight on Monday I can switch onto. If it doesn't storm all weekend, of course."

"It's always better to be safe than sorry," Bobbi replied. "Anyway, come on over to the conference room. I had a couple questions on costs listed on the final budget. There's an invoice that doesn't seem to match up."

Amber wrinkled her nose in confusion. *That's odd* she thought. *I went over those final costs and each invoice with a fine-tooth comb. I must have reviewed that budget at least three times before I submitted it to Bobbi.*

"Sure, I'll be right there," she replied. With one last sweeping glance over her newly cleaned desk, Amber stood. All that remained on the bare wooden surface was her laptop and her phone. All files had been neatly color-coded and organized so Bobbi could quickly review any aspect of the exhibition once Amber was gone.

As she strolled down the long hallway to the conference room, Amber couldn't help but bite her lip at the nagging feeling deep in her stomach. *When I'm gone* she repeated to herself. *I always knew it was going to be six weeks, right?* Despite reminding herself that it was only ever a reprieve from her life in Dallas, Amber couldn't shake the overwhelming feeling that she wasn't quite ready to go yet.

She took a deep breath as she pushed open the conference room door and immediately froze in place. The rest of the office staff shouted "Surprise!" with exuberant smiles. Bobbi stood at the head of the conference table with a large frosted sheet cake before her.

Amber took a few more steps into the room and grinned as the Chamber's Digital Marketing Director shook her hand and clapped her on the back.

"We're going to miss you," the Marketing Assistant added as she leaned in to give Amber a quick hug.

"Oh my God, you guys," Amber started. She realized she was at a loss for words and it only made the nagging feeling in the pit of her stomach more noticeable. "This is amazing. You didn't have to do this, really. Thank you."

She met Bobbi's eyes and they exchanged a smile. "Thank you, Bobbi," Amber finished quietly. The shock of the moment was finally wearing off and Amber swore she wouldn't let herself get emotional. "I wasn't expecting this at all. This was really nice."

As one of the men from Human Resources began cutting small squares of cake for everybody, Bobbi swiped the first paper plate and handed it to Amber. "We should thank *you*, Amber," she replied. "You've been an excellent team player these last six weeks. The expo wouldn't have been the same without you and your ideas. I'm sure it would not have been nearly as successful."

Amber automatically began protesting through her first bite of cake, but then paused and glanced at the slice on her plate. "This is *amazing*," she said in wonderment. The yellow cake was moist and spongy. Flecks of green dotted thick white frosting and gave it a clean, tart taste. "I don't think I've ever had cake like this. What is it?"

"Key lime, of course," Bobbi replied with a quick grin. She closed her eyes as she brought the first bite to her mouth. "Delicious."

After a few minutes of small talk and well-wishes from the rest of the office, the staff began filing back to their desks. Bobbi placed her empty plate on the conference table and pulled a cream-colored envelope from her inside jacket pocket. She slid it gently across the smooth tabletop.

"For you," she spoke, with a nod at the envelope.

Amber threw her a curious glance and opened the envelope. "What's this?" She asked. She scanned the contents of the letter, a single typed sheet on official Key West Chamber of Commerce letterhead that was signed by both Bobbi and the Human Resources Manager.

After a moment, Amber's mouth dropped open. "You...You're offering me a permanent position?"

Bobbi nodded proudly. "Remember when I mentioned that there was something I wanted to speak to you about, but I had to get the necessary approvals first?" She began, barely able to contain her smile. "Unfortunately, despite being the Chamber, we're still part of the overall Key West government so it took a little longer to get the position and pay rate approved. But once they saw how successful the exhibition was? *They* were asking *me* how quickly we could transition you into a permanent employee."

"I...I would love to," Amber stammered. "Thank you. I just..." She swallowed as the wheels began spinning in her head. *Could I do it?* "I have my entire life in Dallas, you know, and a lot of logistics to consider and..."

Bobbi held up a hand. "I understand," she replied. "And I'm sorry to wait until the very last day to present you with an offer, especially when you have plans to return to Texas so soon. Is your girlfriend going back to Dallas with you?"

Amber's head snapped up. "My...What?"

Bobbi blinked. "Your girlfriend," she repeated. "You know, the woman at the exhibition? I'm sorry, I had just assumed she was..."

Amber shook her head quickly. "No, no, Dr. Mielkute..." she paused and took a deep breath. "*Lena* and I are not together. And, for the record, I wasn't expecting her at the exhibition either. I apologize if it was a distraction."

"Dr. Mielkute?" Bobbi asked, sounding confused. "Oh, no, no, *no*! Not her. The other woman, the second one who arrived. I had just assumed you two were...I mean, there was quite a palpable change in your energy when she arrived..." Bobbi's voice trailed off and she shook her head. "Well, never mind. I..."

Amber stared at the tiny yellow crumbs on her plate. Bobbi was suddenly sounding a whole lot like her mother. "No," she finally answered. "No, it, um, didn't work out between us."

The silence stretched between them for a long moment. "You know, a very smart young lady once gave me some great advice," Bobbi started off-handedly. "She helped save the relationship between my love and I. It's very simple, actually. Why don't you just try apologizing to her?"

Amber glared at the table. "But I didn't do anything wrong!" She exclaimed. "It looked bad, yes, but I would *never* do what Brooke is thinking I did..."

She met Bobbi's knowing smile and then took a deep breath. "Oh," she mumbled. "I get it."

After a long moment, Bobbi raised an eyebrow and ran her tongue along her top teeth. "Well, I understand that you have quite a lot to consider," she began, all business once again. "I know the offer came in a bit last minute, but I hope you've enjoyed working with the Chamber as much as we've loved having you. Per the last paragraph of the letter, we'll need an acceptance or decline by 9 A.M. on Monday morning. Of course we understand that you may need some time to make the move official, if you were to accept. Think about it and let us know. You've fit right in on our team and we hope that you'll become a permanent part of our little corner of the island."

Bobbi smiled as she stood. "Either way, I'll make sure to e-mail a recommendation letter to you sometime next week."

Amber's mind was reeling. "Okay," she replied automatically.

Bobbi reached the door and turned. "Oh, and Amber?" She continued. "Make sure you leave fairly soon. The weather people are now saying to prepare for a tropical storm. It can get nasty here, especially if you're not used to them. Terri and I lost a Jeep to Wilma back in '05 and had to evacuate up to Miami. Now, a tropical storm certainly isn't a hurricane but I'd rather my employees err on the side of caution when it comes to this crazy Florida weather. Head on home and be safe, yeah?"

Amber nodded. "Okay," she repeated. She glanced back down at the offer letter, out the wide windows of the conference room and back at Bobbi before blinking.

Bobbi chuckled as she left the conference room. "All right then," she replied. "We'll be in touch."

~

"You'll need to sign here," Brooke spoke gently. "This is just an acknowledgement from the condo association that you have a copy of the rules and by-laws for the property." She rifled to the last page of a thick stapled document and pointed to a blank area at the bottom.

Adam nodded, his brow furrowed in concentration, and quickly scrawled his signature across the line. "I forgot how much paperwork there is to sign," he replied. He grinned as he slid the sheaf across the long table. "I can't tell you how excited I am to officially be here though."

Brooke smiled as she carefully organized all of the closing paperwork. It was a good sign, she had decided, that Adam's closing was taking place in her favorite conference room at the title company. Joy had greeted her as enthusiastically as ever and an e-mail received shortly before the meeting let Brooke know that she was a top five agent at her brokerage for the second quarter in a row, in terms of transaction volume.

Today is going to be a good day she thought determinedly.

Yesterday's final walk-through with Adam had been quick and painless, with no last minute crises. The closing had so far been flawless and now it was nearly over. Paperwork had been signed, checks had been exchanged and the buyer, sellers, attorneys, real estate agents and mortgage brokers had all been in harmony throughout the nearly two hours seated at the familiar glossy table. She was oddly relieved for the minutiae of the process she knew so well and the ease with which the settlement was becoming finalized.

By sticking close to the things that brought her a sense of normalcy, Brooke found that the sharp, suffocating pain had begun to fade into a dull ache that she could mostly ignore. Except when it was late at night and her thoughts started to wander. Or when she first woke in the mornings, emerging from that gentle place between sleep and consciousness, when she craved the feeling of Amber. Or when she was at home by herself and…

Brooke shook her head to avoid deepening the ache. She had to remain professional, at least until the closing was completed.

"I'm excited for you too," she replied warmly. "I suppose this is where I should say welcome to Key West, but I've spent so much time with you that it feels like it's already your home. When do your movers arrive from Arizona?"

Adam sat back in his tall leather chair and frowned. "They were supposed to arrive tomorrow morning, but I'm not sure if they'll make it. With this tropical storm watch, they may have to wait it out. I'm not sure how I'll fare without my Mac desktop." He rolled his eyes. "Sorry. Tech geek here. And I haven't even *told* Trey yet that he may be without some of his favorite toys for a while."

Brooke glanced at the youngster, who was sitting quietly in a corner chair across the room. He had been quiet for most of the proceedings and instead opted to stuff his nose into a book.

"Tropical storms can be pretty unpredictable," Brooke admitted. "Did you bring the essentials with you?"

Adam nodded. "Yes," he replied. "It was a great tip, thank you. It was a *long* drive from Tucson with Trey plus a bunch of boxes in the car, but now I'm glad you advised us to do that. At least we'll have most of our clothes and toiletries to get us through until the movers arrive."

"Good," Brooke responded. She glanced up expectantly as Rick, the title company's closing agent, rejoined the meeting.

"You're all set, young man!" He boomed excitedly. He reached across the table to pump Adam's hand. "Everything is ready. Here is your official mortgage note." He handed Adam a single sheet of paper. Brooke leaned over his shoulder to quickly scan the content and, satisfied that there were no errors or issues, she sat back against her cool leather chair.

"And here is a copy for you," Rick turned and handed the printed terms of the mortgage to the lender's representative. "Joy is cutting a check for you," he pointed at Brooke and then turned to the seller's agent. "And also for you, for your commission disbursements. You're with ReMAX, am I right?"

As the seller's agent nodded, Rick handed Adam two sets of keys. "Welcome home," he finished with a grin.

Adam took the keys and turned them over in his hand for a moment. He finally glanced up as Brooke opened a folder before them. It was emblazoned with her brokerage's logo across the front and filled with all of Adam's closing paperwork.

"You'll need to keep this in a safe place," she instructed. "The first document here..." she paused as she gestured to a long list of dollar amounts. "...This is your closing summary. It shows all of the costs associated with buying your condo that were paid today. We went through this earlier, but if you have any questions or if something looks confusing then give me or my office a call. The official association documents for the condo building are here too. And of course the terms of your loan, the mortgage note, the attorney's contract and the exclusive buyer broker agreement you signed with me way back when..."

Adam nodded absent-mindedly, but his eyes had fallen again to the keys in his palm. Brooke smiled ruefully and snapped the folder closed before pushing it across the table.

"Okay, I get it," she went on. "You're over this and you're ready to get to your new home. I have to stick around here for a few minutes, but you and Trey are free to head out. We're all done here."

Adam glanced up with a faraway smile. "I'm sorry, I was paying attention," he replied quickly. "I was just...I couldn't help but be reminded that one of these sets of keys was supposed to be for," he paused and sighed. "You know. Justin."

Brooke bit her lip, unsure what to say. She seemed to be fresh out of relationship advice and positive thoughts when it came to love. She had, however, had a long talk with Justin about his fears and misgivings just a couple of days ago over crepes at the Banana Café.

"You know when you fall for someone so quickly that it seems like the world is spinning?" Adam went on. "And it doesn't make any sense, but the chemistry is undeniable? I guess I should have known better than to let things move so quickly, but I've never felt such a strong, immediate connection with someone."

Brooke touched his arm. With the closing confirmed earlier in the week, she had taken it upon herself to let Justin know exactly when and where it would be. She wouldn't force her friend to show up. Deep down, she knew she wouldn't have to – She had a feeling that he would know what to do.

Besides she thought with a deep breath. *Life just hasn't been as fun with both of us depressed and nursing broken hearts. At least I can help Justin get his love back.*

"Why don't I walk the two of you out?" Brooke suggested. "This rain is going to start any minute. It'll be torrential compared to what I'm sure you're used to in Arizona."

Adam agreed and stood, motioning for Trey to follow them.

"Now, there's a K-Mart over on North Roosevelt," Brooke started as they turned a corner into the tiled lobby. "If you need to get some groceries, I'd suggest swinging by now before the storm hits..."

Her voice trailed off as Adam stopped short. Justin sat anxiously in one of the overstuffed chairs in the waiting area, worry written all over his face. He jumped to his feet as he spotted them and wiped his palms nervously on his brightly-colored board shorts.

Adam blinked incredulously and opened and then closed his mouth. "You…You're here," he spoke in disbelief. "But how…"

"Justin!" Trey called excitedly. He took off full speed and laughed as Justin quickly caught him and hoisted him into the air. "Hi! Are you coming to see our new home?"

Justin laughed and mussed Trey's hair affectionately. As he gently set him back onto the tile, he met Adam's gaze. "Adam, I…" he started and then took a deep breath. "Can we talk? I had to see you. I…I really messed up. I've had some time to think and I promise it'll never happen again. I've just…I've missed you and Trey so much."

Brooke quickly put a hand on Trey's shoulder and deftly guided him to the other side of the lobby. "Hey Trey, why don't you come with me for a minute?" She asked as she exchanged a knowing smile with Justin. "Let's give them a moment or two. Besides, I happened to know for a *fact* that Joy keeps freshly-baked chocolate chip cookies in the cabinet under the coffee station…"

She threw a glance over her shoulder after she and Trey took several steps. Adam had wrapped his arms around Justin's waist and the two shared a meaningful embrace. Justin raised his face from Adam's shoulder, blinked at her and then smiled slowly.

Thank you he mouthed to Brooke.

She nodded her acknowledgement and then turned to the portable coffee station that Joy carefully set up each morning for guests. Kneeling down to Trey's miniature level, Brooke opened a cabinet door and felt a sense of peace wash over her. Things were becoming right in her world again.

Maybe she thought. *Just maybe that means there could be hope for Amber and I too. One day.*

CHAPTER 37

It had only been a little over an hour since the closing had wrapped, but the skies had already turned a menacing near-black as Brooke quickly peeled out of her brokerage's parking lot. She had only meant to drop off her commission disbursement to their office manager, but she had become distracted with replying to a bevy of new client leads that had arrived in her Inbox.

Pizza and Netflix tonight she decided. *Good thing I bought those frozen pies yesterday.*

Between her own thoughts and the loud howl of the wind that had quickly picked up, Brooke almost didn't hear her phone ringing. For a long moment, she considered sending the call to voicemail. A quick glance, however, at the display made her fight back a groan.

"Sandra," she murmured. Brooke knew that Amber's mother had moved back in with her father and that things had been resolved between them. Briefly, she wondered if Amber had moved back as well or if she'd opted to stay at Sandra's condo. The only issue was transportation, but it wouldn't be unheard of if Amber had rented a car for her last week on the island.

Brooke's heart hammered in her chest and she swallowed hard. She didn't want to think about Amber leaving. On one hand, she wondered if Justin had a point – that there had to be an explanation – for Lena from Lithuania's unexpected appearance. On the other hand, she wondered what kind of explanation there could possibly be. Amber had to have known that Lena was coming all the way from Texas.

The thought that perhaps Amber and Lena had remained in contact throughout her time here didn't escape her. *We never even got around to talking about the future* Brooke thought in frustration. *What that looked like or what exactly we were.*

"Hello?" Brooke answered the call in a tone much sharper than she had intended.

"Brooke?" Sandra's voice sounded strangely muffled and faraway.

"Hi, yes, it's me," she replied quickly. Tiny alarm bells went off in her head as she realized that Sandra sounded as though she had been crying. "Is everything okay?"

There was a long pause that only served to heighten Brooke's sudden anxiety.

"Um..." Sandra started and then sniffled. "No, I'm afraid it's not. Where are you right now, sweetheart? At home?"

Brooke's stomach did flips as she quickly pulled into a gas station parking lot and waved off an indignant honk from the sedan she had cut off. "No, I just left my office. I'm headed there now," she replied. "Sandra, what's going on?"

For a slow, horrible moment, Brooke prayed that something awful hadn't happened to Amber. The anger, confusion and feeling of betrayal dissipated into the humid, stormy air. Concern and fear overrode everything else. She would never forgive herself if something happened before...

Before what? Brooke wondered silently. *Before we make peace? Before I admit to Amber that I'm completely crazy about her and I meant every word at the exhibition?*

"Pull over," Sandra told her firmly. "Please."

Brooke swallowed hard and glanced around the empty parking lot. It looked as though most had already filled their gas tanks and extra containers to wait out the storm.

"I have," she replied. "I pulled over at a gas station."

"It's your dad, sweetheart," Sandra finally spoke and then dissolved into tears. "I...I'm sorry. I'm a mess right now. We're at the Lower Keys Medical Center. He...He had a moderate heart attack earlier this afternoon, Brooke."

Brooke's entire body felt as though it had gone ice cold. Her heart pounded rapidly as she tried to blink away the sudden dizziness. Somewhere at the back of her mind, she could hear Sandra still talking but she couldn't make sense of the words. Myocardial infarction, cardiologists, a blood clot that they suspected traveled to the heart and blocked an artery. It was all too much. Thrombolytic therapy to dissolve the clot and emergency angioplasty surgery to place a coronary stent in the blocked artery – The information swam through her head as she tried to make sense of it.

"Brooke?" Sandra's worried voice brought her back to the present moment. "Are you still there?"

Brooke realized she hadn't spoken in several minutes, but she was too afraid she would burst into tears the second she opened her mouth.

"I'm here," she replied, her voice low. Brooke quickly threw the Lexus into gear and sped out of the gas station. She turned hard onto Truman Avenue without a turn signal or a thought in her head, except to get to the hospital as quickly as possible. "I'm on my way. I'll be there in a few minutes."

A thunderous crack sounded as though it came from just outside her car as Brooke hung up with Sandra. She peered out the windshield at the wispy clouds above. They rolled through the sky faster than she had ever seen. A few fat raindrops splattered against the hood and she knew more – a lot more – would soon follow.

I just have to get to the hospital she told herself. *And then I won't leave until Dad can.* Sandra had said that he had just been taken back into surgery a minute before she called. The nervous tension had made her voice high-pitched and Brooke knew she was barely hanging on by a thread.

Brooke blinked away the tears that pushed against the backs of her eyes and focused on the road before her. As she raced toward Stock Island and the raindrops grew heavier, a gripping, suffocating fear that she hadn't felt since her mother was sick now threatened to overwhelm her. Her father would be okay. He *had* to be, there was no other choice.

~

As Amber reached her mother's condo and climbed the two sets of concrete stairs to reach the third-floor unit, she wasn't surprised that the Volkswagen wasn't in its assigned space. After all, Sandra had all but moved back in with Dave this week.

Amber had finally broken down and opted to rent a small Toyota for her last week. She only supposed to have it through tomorrow morning, she recalled. She made a mental note to phone Enterprise and extend the rental for a few more days.

She shut the front door of the condo behind her and made a beeline for the study to change out of her business casual clothes. With the blinds closed and the only noise coming from a single wooden ceiling fan above, Amber couldn't help the loneliness that washed over her. She paused in the doorway of the study and gazed at her luggage, all carefully packed and neatly stacked in a corner of the small space. Everything had been organized and ready to go for her now-cancelled flight back to Dallas the following day.

Amber perched on the far corner of the loveseat and pulled on the soft cotton tank top and worn jeans she had left folded for this evening. As she tossed her gray slacks in the general direction of her luggage, she remembered the offer letter that had been folded into their back pocket. Amber carefully picked up her slacks, pulled the letter from its pocket and gently tried to smooth it along her lap.

She read the letter once, twice and then three more times as the words blurred before her eyes. The same question that had snuck into her mind earlier wiggled its way back into her thoughts: *Could I do it?*

Amber gazed again at her luggage. Her job at the Chamber had allowed her to save her half of the rent for the apartment in Dallas for the next two months until the lease was up. It had also helped her pay off her credit card and start saving a modest nest egg. It wasn't much yet, but it was a good start and could be used to help her smooth transition.

Mom would say to stay she thought with a smile. *In fact, she would probably rent this condo to me for a good deal.* She took a deep breath. *But my friends would say to come back to Dallas* she admitted silently. *They'd question what kind of future a younger person – especially someone who wants to break into photography – could have on the island. They'd remind me of the limited job market, the high cost of living and the fact that the nearest big city is about three and a half hours away in Miami.*

Inevitably, her thoughts turned to Brooke and how she had found success even after leaving her life and all that she knew in New York City. Amber briefly imagined Brooke begging her to stay, another of the bittersweet fantasies that she always seemed to find herself caught up in. The aching pang in her chest was a reminder that Brooke was, in fact, probably thrilled that she was leaving.

Amber glanced at her luggage again. *But what about* you? She thought. *What is it that* you *want to do, regardless of everyone else's thoughts and opinions?*

She uncurled her legs from beneath her and carefully lit a candle on an accent table near the door of the study. Just as she had suspected, her mom had an extra package of frankincense in a nearby drawer. Amber knew from experience that the sweet, earthy scent would help to center her.

Whether or not Brooke and I ever speak to each other again, I need to make this decision for me, in my own way she thought determinedly. With that, Amber gathered herself into a comfortable seated position on the floor, allowed her eyes to fall closed, took a deep breath and began to meditate.

~

NEARLY AN HOUR HAD PASSED before Amber blinked. She felt more steady, confident and sure than she had in a long while. With a deep breath, she opened her eyes and grinned at the quiet study. She had reached a decision; really, the only option once she had allowed her mind to clear and the thoughts of everyone and everything else to fade away. She was confident in her decision regardless of any other circumstances and knew in her very core that it was the right one for her.

As she slowly stood and blew out the candle, she noticed her phone blinking impatiently on the small table. The frankincense had long burnt out, leaving a line of light, feathery ashes in its place. Amber grabbed her phone and wasn't surprised to see a missed call from her mother. However, an icy feeling of dread began to grip her gut when she saw that she had actually missed seven calls from her mother. They were followed with a solemn text message that simply read: *Please call me ASAP. It's an emergency.*

"Shit," Amber whispered. She quickly dialed her mother, who answered the call on its first ring.

"Amber!" Her tone was quiet and subdued, but she sounded relieved to hear from her.

"Mom, what's going on?" She asked quickly. "I'm sorry, I was meditating and had my phone on silent. Where are you?"

"I'm at the hospital, sweetheart," Sandra replied. Her voice was thick and Amber could tell immediately that she had been crying.

Double shit she thought.

"We had to rush Dave here earlier this afternoon," Sandra continued. "He…He's had a heart attack." She paused and cried softly into the phone. "We had just gone for lunch and decided to take a walk down the White Street Pier and he…He just *collapsed*."

"Oh my God," Amber heard her voice before she realized she had spoken. She grabbed her car keys and headed for the door. "What hospital, Mom?"

"Maybe it's my fault, you know?" Sandra sobbed quietly. "We had just had a big lunch and I was the one always pushing him to stay active. I suggested a stroll to walk off some of that lunch. If…If his body couldn't handle it, then I should have known…" Sandra dissolved into tears and Amber felt her own throat close up at the sound of her mother crying helplessly into the phone.

"It's *not* your fault, Mom," Amber replied firmly. "Don't you start thinking that way. I'm headed wherever you are. Have you spoken to any of the doctors?"

Sandra sniffled. "Yes, the doctors have been wonderful," she replied. "They've taken him back for an emergency angioplasty and they've been keeping Brooke and I updated as much as possible. It's just…It's a heart surgery, Amber, and I'm so scared for him. What if…"

"No," Amber cut her mother off sternly. "No. Don't say that, don't think it. What is it that you tell me? 'Don't even put the possibility out into the Universe'. Tell me where you are. I'm coming there now."

As Sandra tearfully rattled off the name and address of the hospital, Amber raced to her car. She thought of Brooke and her mother, anxious and terrified, sitting in an uncomfortable waiting room by themselves. As urgency flowed through her veins and she peeled out of her parking space, Amber could think of nothing except being with them *right now*.

CHAPTER 38

Brooke crushed what she was sure was the fourth empty paper cup of what had been dark, sludgy coffee in her hand. Fluorescent lights loomed over the linoleum tile floor and hard plastic waiting room chairs. A muted flat-screen television in one corner was set on CNN, but closed-captioning told her all about a prop plane that had crashed in the cornfields of Iowa.

Not much has changed in the design of hospital emergency rooms since Mom was sick she thought wearily. *Apparently, making them as anxiety-inducing as possible is part of the blueprint.*

Sandra sank back into her seat after hurrying into the parking lot to take a call. Her face was tear-stained and drawn, finally betraying her older age.

"Amber got back to me," Sandra started. She took a deep breath and closed her eyes. "She's headed here now."

Brooke nodded silently, though her heart began beating even faster. It wasn't exactly how she had planned to see her again, but there were more important things at hand.

"You know..." Sandra went on and then paused. She appeared to be thinking over her next words carefully. "Brooke, I know what happened at the expo was bad. You have every right to be upset. And

Amber may be a lot of things at times, but a cheater she is not. She would have *never* personally invited Lena to the Keys. She's not one to quickly jump to someone else like that, even during hard times."

Brooke nodded again and looked down at her hands. "I cared for Amber very much," she spoke softly. "I *still* care for her. It crushed me to see her with another woman."

"Amber told me that Lena only contacted her after she arrived in Key West," Sandra replied after a moment. "She told her she wouldn't see her and then Lena figured out where Amber was through her Facebook page. She took it upon herself to show up uninvited. Amber wouldn't lie to me about that. Even if one of us were to make a mistake, we've always been honest with each other. I know what she tells me is true."

Brooke glanced up. "So she wasn't still talking to Lena this whole time?"

Sandra shook her head. "Not to my knowledge," she replied. "Besides…" she paused and took another deep breath. "Amber loves *you*, Brooke. It's quite clear to me. In fact, she promised your father at the expo shortly before your arrival that she loved you. I probably shouldn't tell you that, but I thought maybe you'd want to know."

Brooke took a deep, shaky breath as she tried to make sense of Sandra's words. *She promised Dad that she loved me? She had nothing to do with Lena's arrival?* The questions swam in her mind.

"Regardless, I want you to know that no matter what happens between you and Amber, you'll always be like a second daughter to me," Sandra finished. A trace of a smile turned her lips up for a moment. "I hope you understand that."

Brooke opened her mouth to respond, but was interrupted by the whoosh of automatic doors parting in the emergency lobby. Without even looking up, she knew exactly who it would be.

~

AMBER STOPPED short as she reached the waiting room. The first person her gaze landed on was Brooke. The other woman looked exhausted. Her eye make-up had been mostly rubbed off and her face was a shade of waxy pale. Amber desperately wanted to go to her; she was overwhelmed by the desire to wrap her arms around Brooke, kiss her face all over and hold her tightly until everything was right in their world again.

Instead, she took a deep breath, averted her eyes and quickly sat next to her mother. Leaning over, she embraced Sandra and gently rubbed her back for a moment.

"How is he?" She asked in a low voice. "Any word?"

Sandra shrugged helplessly and shook her head as an older man in baby blue scrubs paused in the entrance to the waiting room. He met Sandra's eyes and gave her a quick nod.

"Ms. Lucas?" He spoke. "Ms. Adriani? I have some news. Is this a good time?"

Sandra nearly flew out of her chair, with Brooke close behind her. "Yes, yes," Sandra replied quickly. Her eyes had already filled with anxious tears. "Oh God, please tell us something good. Will Dave be all right?"

Amber followed them into a hallway just outside the waiting room. She felt breathless, as though she might throw up, and prayed to every god and goddess she could think of for Dave's health.

Much to her nearly overwhelming relief, the doctor smiled. "The angioplasty went well," he replied. He paused as Sandra practically fell to the floor with emotion. Even Brooke seemed to deflate against the wall as she closed her eyes closed and placed a hand over her heart. "We were able to successfully place the stent inside the blocked artery. Luckily, he only needed one. As you know, he did suffer a moderate heart attack but because the coronary artery disease is still in its early stages, I don't believe there's any need for a bypass or anything of that nature right now."

"Oh, thank God," Sandra responded. "Will he be okay? Can we see him now?"

"We'll need to keep him overnight for monitoring, possibly into Sunday," the doctor continued. "But I anticipate Dave being released by Sunday evening at the very latest. He'll be on blood thinners, so it's really important to make sure he takes his medicine as directed."

Sandra nodded. "I can do that."

"Now, there are things that he can and should start doing once he's back at home," the doctor went on. "A few lifestyle modifications can make managing this condition much easier. I see here that he's not a smoker?" He glanced down at his clipboard and then scanned their faces.

Brooke shook her head. "He's never smoked."

"All right, that's good," the doctor continued. "A heart-healthy diet will be imperative..."

Sandra closed her eyes. "Those damn steaks..." She took a deep breath and her voice wavered. "I've told him about those damn steaks. No more of those."

"Exercise, even if it's light or low-impact," the doctor went on. "Getting exercise each day is important. So is maintaining a healthy weight."

Brooke sighed. "He's had those extra 20 pounds for as long as I can remember."

After a few more minutes of discussion with the doctor, they were told that he had been transferred from the recovery room to his hospital suite.

"Take the elevator up to the second floor and check in at the nurses' station," the doctor directed. "They'll give you a nametag and point you to Dave's room. He may be a bit groggy right now, but he should begin to regain his strength soon. I'm sure he's looking forward to seeing all of you."

As they made their way to the elevators, Sandra turned suddenly toward a heavy door at the end of the hallway. "I'm going to take the stairs," she announced.

Amber stopped short. "Are you okay?" She asked. "Are you sure you don't want to get in the elevator?"

Sandra shook her head. "No, I...I need to take the stairs, sweetheart," she replied. "I need a minute or two to compose myself before we see Dave. You two go on and I'll meet you up there."

Amber turned uncertainly back to the elevator as its doors lurched open. She and Brooke were silent as they stepped into the small space.

Amber took a deep breath as the doors closed behind them. Brooke hit a button for the second floor. Memories of what had happened the last time they were stuck in an enclosed space were close to the surface and threatened her composure. She remembered Bobbi's advice – really, it had been her own advice given back to her – and gently cleared her throat. Besides, she had already made her decision for her future.

"I know that this is a really bad time, but I…" Amber stopped and stared at the elevator doors. "I'm sorry, Brooke. I didn't invite Lena here, I promise. I have nothing to do with her."

I love you! Amber finished silently. *Don't you see that?* You *have my heart,* you're *the one I'm crazy about and it's* you *who I can't stop thinking about reaching over to hug and kiss right now. I want you, all of you!*

"I just wanted to tell you that I'm so, so sorry that all of that happened," Amber concluded. The quaver in her voice betrayed what she had hoped would be a steady coolness, much like Brooke always portrayed. Just then, the elevator doors gently whooshed open with their arrival on the second floor. "But that's not important right now. Let's go see your dad."

Amber walked quickly from the elevator, though her wild heartbeat made her feel like she was practically running from it. She didn't give herself time to hear if Brooke had replied and instead made a beeline for the nurses' station. After a few moments, she felt Brooke's presence beside her as they checked in and received their nametags.

Finally, Amber stole a glance at her as they reached Dave's room. "You should go ahead first," she spoke and then held her breath for a moment. "Are you going to be okay?"

Brooke shrugged one shoulder, but didn't tear her eyes away from the half-open door. "I have to be, right?"

Amber shook her head. "No," she replied softly. "You don't have to be."

She was surprised when, after a moment, Brooke's cool hand grasped her own. Amber squeezed back and told herself that it was just a friendly gesture, that Brooke was scared and seeking support and that it certainly didn't mean anything else.

"I'll be right here, Brooke," Amber murmured.

Brooke turned back and met her eyes for the first time since she had arrived at the hospital. Amber felt as though all the air had been sucked from the hallway at the raw emotion in her gaze.

"I...I told him I never wanted to see him again," Brooke spoke so quietly that Amber strained to hear her. "I didn't mean that. I...I was so upset. *He* was so upset. I can't believe that was the last thing I said to him..."

Amber took a few steps and wrapped her arms around Brooke. She held her silently and listened as her rapid breathing slowed back to normal.

"It's okay," she whispered. Amber hadn't realized she'd pressed her lips to Brooke's ear until she spoke. "It's okay, Brooke. He's stable. He's awake. Go see him, talk to him, tell him everything you want to say. He knows you didn't mean it."

After a moment, Brooke straightened and took a deep, shaky breath as her eyes locked onto Amber. "Would *you* forgive me if you were him?"

Amber shrugged helplessly. "I already have," she replied as she forced a smile. She blinked quickly and hoped the sudden pressure behind her eyes would disappear. "I'm sure he has too."

Amber wasn't sure if she had imagined that Brooke lingered for a moment longer, looking as though there was much more she wanted to say, but she didn't have time to dwell on it.

"Thank you," Brooke finally murmured. A split-second later, she turned and quietly disappeared into Dave's room.

CHAPTER 39

"Hey, Dad," Brooke spoke quietly as she perched at the end of his hospital bed. She reached over and touched his wrist. She hated the I.V.s taped into the top of his hand and the slow beeping of machines near the head of the bed. "How are you feeling?"

Dave blinked a few times, but smiled as he focused on Brooke. "Brookie?" He asked. "Damn, Brooke, I had a scare."

Brooke laughed despite the quiet, somber moment. "That's the understatement of the year," she teased. "Why did you have to go scaring us like that, huh?"

Dave's smile widened and he blinked a few times. "I didn't mean to, kiddo. I bet Sandra already said no more steak, yeah?"

Brooke smiled. "Actually she did," she confirmed. "But those are doctor's orders, Dad. A small sacrifice to make for…" her throat closed as another wave of emotion swept over her. The realization of how close she had come to losing her father was overwhelming. "… You know, being healthy. Because you're not going *anywhere*, Dad. You hear me?"

"Aww, Brookie, don't cry," Dave replied. He grabbed the hand that had been resting over his and squeezed her fingers. "I'm sorry I scared you. You know how much I love you, right?"

Brooke closed her eyes, but the tears fell down her cheeks anyway. "Dad, we don't have to do this right now..."

"Yeah, we do," Dave cut in sternly. "*Yeah,* we do. Look how fast life can change or how quickly it can be taken from you. I would never, *ever* find peace if..." he swallowed hard. "...Somethin' happened and I didn't get to tell you how much I love you. I don't care if you're gay or straight or somewhere in between. That don't matter. What matters is that my daughter is happy and healthy. You thought I'd rather you were straight than gay, but you're wrong, Brooke. You're my kid and you're perfect in my eyes, whatever that looks like."

Brooke nodded once as the tears dripped from her chin into her lap. "Thank you," she whispered.

"There has been no greater accomplishment in my life than havin' you and raising you," Dave said quietly. He squeezed her hand again. "You're the best thing I ever did, Brooke."

Brooke leaned over and carefully embraced her father. She couldn't remember the last time she had cried onto his shoulder – if any – but the moment felt cathartic.

She quickly straightened as the door opened again. Sandra stood uncertainly in the frame.

"Can I...Is it okay if I come in?" She asked. "I've been so worried."

Brooke nodded quickly and stood from the edge of the bed as she motioned for Sandra to join them. In a flurry, Sandra was at Dave's bedside and hugging him tightly.

As Sandra switched between tearful protestations that he'd better never do that again, sweet words of love and questions about how he was feeling, Brooke took a seat in a guest chair near the window. The rain beat down in sheets so thick that she almost couldn't make out the parking lot below. Amber entered a few moments later and then for nearly forty-five minutes until visiting hours were over, Brooke had the overwhelming sense that everything was going to be okay.

After visiting hours had expired and they had been kindly booted from Dave's room by the nurses, Brooke paused beneath a wide canopy over a side exit door. Thin, bright streaks of lightening split the sky and were followed by booming cracks of thunder. She wasn't looking forward to driving home in this.

She felt Amber's presence at her elbow before she turned. Brooke swallowed hard. She didn't want them to simply go their separate ways; she desperately wanted more time with Amber.

"Want to grab a cup of coffee?" Brooke asked, trying to keep her voice casual. She blinked at the parking lot through the rain. "I know it's late, but there's a Starbucks across the street. Besides, I doubt I'll be sleeping much tonight anyway." She shot Amber a small smile.

Amber glanced at her and their eyes locked for a brief moment. "Sure," she agreed after a short pause. "I'm a little nervous to drive in this weather. Maybe an espresso will help to motivate me."

Brooke shrugged. "If you'd like, I can give you a ride home," she offered. "And you can pick up your rental tomorrow. It might be raining still, but it should be much lighter than this. I'm sure I'll be here first thing in the morning, so it wouldn't be a big deal."

Amber nodded. "Okay," she agreed. "Thank you. I'm supposed to drop off my car tomorrow, but I'll have to extend the reservation by a couple of days."

Brooke stole a glance at her. "You're leaving Sunday then?"

Amber nodded again and Brooke was positive she felt her heart splinter inside her chest. *No, damn it* she thought as she fought back another wave of emotion. *It wasn't supposed to end like this.*

"Monday," Amber confirmed. "If the weather is clear and my flight doesn't get cancelled again."

Brooke watched Amber roll her eyes from her peripheral and then felt the other woman's gentle gaze study her for a long moment. Brooke fought the overwhelming urge to turn, kiss Amber hard and slow, press her back to the glass door behind them and never let her go. The image was so vivid that it was practically tangible and Brooke felt the space between her legs grow warm with the fantasy. She took a deep breath and willed herself to speak, to convince Amber that she couldn't possibly go, but the other woman beat her to it and continued after a moment.

"And then I'll be back in Key West on the following Monday," she went on, her tone far too casual for the words that Brooke was hearing. "And then I officially start full-time at the Chamber of Commerce next Wednesday. It'll be a whirlwind, but at least I'll have a week to pack, get my things together, load up my car and make the drive back here. Luckily, I don't have much furniture. I'll only need professional movers for a few pieces."

Brooke blinked as she tried to process this. "Wait...You...You're coming back?"

She turned and was met with Amber's proud smile. "I'm staying, Brooke," she replied. "I got an offer for a permanent position from Bobbi. It was an easy decision to make for myself. Although I'm really banking on my mom renting her condo to me, since she's moved back in with Dave. Besides, I've always said that Key West is a photographer's dream. I'm excited to embark on this new path for myself."

Brooke nodded slowly. It sounded as though Amber had all but decided to move forward in a life that didn't seem to have much room for picking up where they had left off. "It sounds like you've figured it all out," she replied after a moment and then mustered a smile. "I'm happy for you."

Stinging disappointment surged through Brooke as she ducked her head and hurried into the rain. Brooke stilled as she reached her car and listened to Amber laughing as she splashed through puddles behind her. Despite her best efforts to hurry, she was already soaked through her clothes.

I want the girl that laughs in the rain Brooke thought, the realization hitting her hard. Amber reached the car and grinned as she tried in vain to run a hand through her wet hair. *I want the girl that makes me drink green tea and teaches me to meditate. The girl whose smile that makes me melt...*

Brooke opened her mouth, but was surprised how quickly the tears came. She blinked and was grateful for the dark as she let them intermingle with the rain on her face. She couldn't tell teardrops from raindrops by the time Amber rushed over to her. Another loud clap of thunder shook the parking lot and set off a distant car alarm. Through the window, she could barely make out Evangeline's form as she swayed for a moment on the dashboard.

"Brooke, what's wrong?" Amber asked, her voice all genuine concern. "What's going on?"

Brooke took a deep breath, but her throat was dry and she struggled to find the right words. After all, there were only six that kept coming to mind. "I'm in love with you, Amber," she finally replied. "The truth is, I've been in love with you practically since we met. I... I'm crazy about you. It's so hard being away from you, but it's even worse to be with you when it's like *this*. I..."

Amber shook her head and cupped Brooke's wet face in her hands. It was then that Brooke noticed the tears shining in her eyes. "You need to get used to talking to me so unfiltered and being your truest, most honest self."

Brooke swallowed hard. "And why is that?"

Amber let out a small sigh. "Because you're going to be spending forever with me," she replied simply. A smile crinkled the corners of her eyes as she met Brooke's gaze again. "We're going to be together for a really long time, so you'd better..."

Brooke couldn't take the centimeters of distance separating them any longer. She took another step and quickly closed the gap between their rain-soaked bodies. For several seconds, she let herself relish the feeling of Amber in her arms as she held her close. Amber had buried her face in her shoulder and wrapped her arms around her neck as the rain continued to patter against them. Brooke inhaled the intoxicating scent of Amber as she kissed her shoulders, smoothed her damp hair and dropped gentle kisses along the cool skin of her cheek and the shell of her ear. She felt dizzy with emotion and slowly tightened her arms around Amber's waist.

"Consider it done," Brooke whispered between kisses.

"Oh, and Brooke?" Amber murmured. "I love you too."

It dawned on Brooke that perhaps this was that elusive present moment that had so escaped her for most of her life. She took a deep breath and wished with all her might that it would last just a little longer.

"Too bad there's not a photo of this," Brooke murmured with a slow smile. "This is one of those moments you were talking about. On the beach, remember? This is going to be one of those times I'm going to want to relive on a happy loop forever."

"We have a lifetime for these moments," Amber responded before soundly meeting her lips with a happy sigh escaped. Amber relaxed against her again, her wet skin pressed to Brooke's warm body. "Believe me, I will make sure there are *plenty* of pictures along the way."

EPILOGUE

1 Year Later

Brooke Adriani couldn't help but stare. Her yoga teacher was *so* hot. She snuck a glance up from her downward dog and openly admired the woman at the center of the semi-circle.

That smile she thought as she enjoyed the gentle stretch along her calves. *Should be downright illeg...Nah* Brooke corrected the strangely familiar thought. *That smile is the best part of my day.*

The instructor glanced up and met her eyes across the dark-stained wood floor. Brooke realized she was glowing even before she registered their shared grin.

"Eyes on the floor, Brooke," the instructor spoke with a knowing smile. "To get a proper downward dog, the neck should be lengthened. Allow your head to hang and get a good stretch through the spine." She turned and spoke to the class. "If it's difficult to remember how to hold your head, always try to keep your ears in line with your inner arms. When you're in the correct position, you should feel a nice stretch through your trapezius, triceps and hamstrings all at once."

Brooke let her head hang and briefly closed her eyes. She didn't hide her grin, however, when she felt the warm, familiar hand on her lower back.

"I love you," Amber whispered as she passed Brooke's mat.

"I love you too," Brooke murmured. She opened her eyes and caught just a split-second of Amber's bare feet as she padded quietly to someone a few mats away. She paused to carefully adjust their hips.

"Do you teach any other classes during the week?" Another yogi asked. "I *love* this Wednesday night beginner's class. I'd really like to add another to my schedule."

Amber smiled, clearly pleasantly surprised by the question. "This *is* my only class," she confirmed. "I also work full-time during the day at the Chamber of Commerce, so one class per week is my limit." She stole another glance at Brooke. "Besides, I have a lovely partner with whom spending quality time with is also incredibly important to me."

A few of the attendees near Brooke threw knowing smiles at her amongst the chorus of *aww* that went up.

"I'm a lucky girl," Amber continued. "But that's the thing, we're all lucky in some way, aren't we? We're here. We're devoting a wonderful evening to our practice. Now, I want you to ease into child's pose. Just...take a few moments here. Take some deep breaths. Close your eyes and imagine each of those things that make *you* lucky, that make you thankful to be here. Give yourself a few moments to feel gratitude for each of those things and thank the Universe for bringing you those things or those people...Whatever or whomever they may be..."

Brooke didn't have to let her mind wander far. She closed her eyes after settling back into child's pose as Amber's soft voice continued to float over the room. Their parents' wedding was next weekend and she and Amber would be flying with Dave and Sandra to Mexico for an intimate destination ceremony on the Riviera Maya. After all the excitement of the wedding and vacation concluded, Brooke felt a shiver of anticipation at the thought that it would soon be their turn. Her mind wandered over the rose-gold diamond ring she had purchased two weekends before, with the help of Sandra. If Amber had thought it strange that, just one week after moving into the duplex, Brooke had hurried out of the house that Sunday under pretenses of helping Sandra list her condo, she didn't show it.

Brooke hadn't decided when or how she would ask for Amber's hand in marriage. Truthfully, marriage wasn't something either of them were in a rush to do. She didn't mind a long engagement, so long as she was able to put that gorgeous ring on Amber's finger – The ring that, as soon as Sandra and Brooke spotted it behind thick glass, had made them say "that's the one" in unison.

The sound of shuffling feet caused her to glance up. Brooke realized with a start that the class had been dismissed. Blushing, she quickly got to her knees and began rolling up her mat.

Amber cleared her throat and Brooke glanced up at her with a smile. "Sorry, I was…"

Amber's eyes crinkled at the corners. "Brooke Adriani, didn't I tell you a long time ago that those dimples wouldn't *always* get you out of trouble?" She teased. "You must have had a lot to thank the Universe for."

Brooke raised an eyebrow and stood. "Maybe I did," she replied as she hoisted her mat sling over her shoulder.

"Care to stay after class?" Amber asked. She crossed her arms and leaned casually against the wall. "I can show you a few…" she paused as her gaze slowly raked up and down Brooke's body. "…Adjustments to your downward dog."

Brooke had already taken two steps across the room. Only milliseconds later, she crushed her lips against Amber's and tangled her fingers in her hair. A rush of deep emotion coursed through her as Amber willingly opened her mouth to her kisses.

Yoga will always be one of my favorite times of the week Brooke thought mischievously.

"Come on," she whispered breathlessly. She forced herself to take a step backward and reached her hand out to Amber. "Let's go home."

Amber nodded, taking her hand, and they quietly left the studio and walked out into their future together.

THE END

ABOUT THE AUTHOR

Ashley Quinn is an avid writer, voracious reader and lover of all things art. A Chicago girl at heart, Ashley relocated to Dallas, Texas in 2014 and quickly discovered that she loves Tex-Mex, is terrified of Texas drivers and doesn't miss the blizzards. She also finds herself on the constant hunt for good deep dish pizza in the South – Suggestions for which are never ignored!

With a B.A. in Marketing Communications from Columbia College Chicago and several years of professional copywriting and content strategy experience across a diverse range of industries, Ashley's first love remains creative writing. She enjoys writing fiction and lesbian romance featuring developed, relatable characters and unique situations. Her first novel, All That Glitters, was released in 2012 and her second novel, Texas Blues, was released in 2016.

She lives in the Dallas-Fort Worth area with her partner and their two spoiled dogs. They are always looking forward to their next adventure while Ashley continues to plan future books. You can contact her through her website at www.ThisIsAshleyQuinn.com or on Facebook at Facebook.com/AshleyQuinnWrites.

Contact Ashley:

www.ThisIsAshleyQuinn.com

www.ingramcontent.com/pod-product-compliance
Lightning Source LLC
Chambersburg PA
CBHW071246170626
46809CB00001B/82

9780692890981